SHADOWS BENEATH
THE WRITING EXCUSES ANTHOLOGY

SHADOWS BENEATH
THE WRITING EXCUSES ANTHOLOGY

Brandon Sanderson
Mary Robinette Kowal
Dan Wells ◆ Howard Tayler

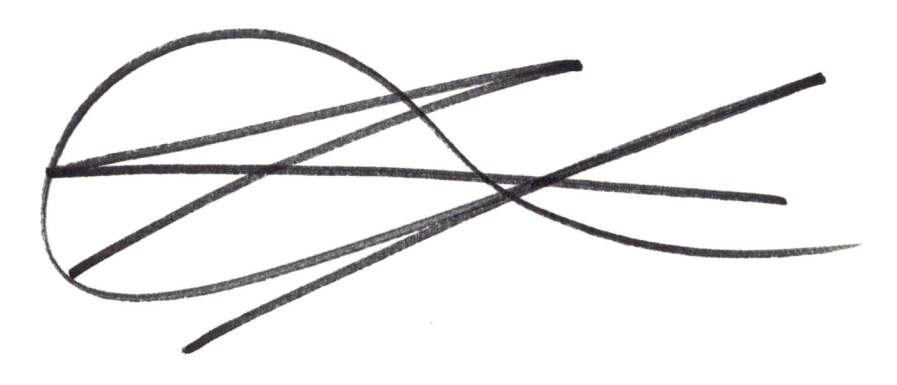

DRAGONSTEEL ENTERTAINMENT

This is a work of fiction. All of the characters, organizations, and events portrayed in these stories are either products of the authors' imaginations or are used fictitiously.

SHADOWS BENEATH: THE WRITING EXCUSES ANTHOLOGY

"A Fire in the Heavens" copyright © 2014 by Mary Robinette Kowal
"I.E.Demon" copyright © 2014 by Fearful Symmetry LLC
"An Honest Death" copyright © 2014 by The Tayler Corporation
"Sixth of the Dusk" copyright © 2014 by Dragonsteel Entertainment, LLC

All Rights Reserved.

Jacket Art copyright © 2014 by Julie Dillon
Page 10 Illustration by Rhiannon Rasmussen-Silverstein
Page 48 Illustration by Kathryn Layno
Page 60 Illustration by Ben McSweeney
Page 80 Illustration by Kekai Kotaki
Page 267 Illustration copyright © 2014 by Howard Tayler

Edited by Peter Ahlstrom
Designed by Isaac Stewart

A Dragonsteel Entertainment Book
Published by Dragonsteel Entertainment, LLC
American Fork, UT

WritingExcuses.com
BrandonSanderson.com
MaryRobinetteKowal.com
TheDanWells.com
SchlockMercenary.com

ISBN 978-1-938570-03-2

First Edition: July 2014

Printed in the United States of America
by Worzalla Publishing Company

0 9 8 7 6 5 4 3 2 1

CONTENTS

INTRODUCTION 7

A FIRE IN THE HEAVENS
MARY ROBINETTE KOWAL
10

I.E. DEMON
DAN WELLS
49

AN HONEST DEATH
HOWARD TAYLER
61

SIXTH OF THE DUSK
BRANDON SANDERSON
81

THE MAKING OF A FIRE IN THE HEAVENS 125
THE MAKING OF I.E. DEMON 189
THE MAKING OF AN HONEST DEATH 221
THE MAKING OF SIXTH OF THE DUSK 269

WELCOME TO THE
WRITING EXCUSES ANTHOLOGY

BRANDON SANDERSON

You hold in your hands one of Brandon Sanderson's patented Crazy Ideas™.

It started about two years ago. For those who don't know, Writing Excuses is an internet radio program that I cohost with the other wonderful people whose names you can find on the cover of this very volume. We offer writing advice from professionals.

I'm always searching for ways to make Writing Excuses more relevant and interesting. I want to try things we haven't tried before—and, if it can be done, things that nobody has ever tried before. This was one of those ideas. I wanted to brainstorm a story on one episode, write that story, then provide it for everyone to read afterward.

The idea took hold, and I pitched it to the team, suggesting that we each brainstorm a story together, then write it. We could workshop each story on another episode, then release an anthology with both the first drafts and the final drafts, giving readers and unprecedented look at the process of creating a story.

Now, I fully understand that many of you aren't writers yourselves and may not be interested in all of this. If that's you, feel free to skip the rest of this introduction and dive right into the stories! They're right up front, in their polished and final revisions, gloriously illustrated by talented artists we commissioned for each story. (And while we're on the subject of the art, have another look at that awesome cover by Julie Dillon. She's up for a Hugo Award this year in the Best Professional Artist category, and she heartily deserves your consideration.)

I recommend each story to you, particularly those by my cohosts. They're some of the finest pieces I've read this year, and I think their quality will speak for themselves. Go forth and enjoy!

For those of you who are interested in the writing process, whether you be an aspiring writer yourself or just someone who likes pulling back the curtain and looking at the guts of something, I have a real treat for you. After the polished stories (which I still suggest you read first) you'll find a wealth of bonus material, presented in a separate section for each individual story. These sections include the following for each story.

Original brainstorms: We have transcribed here for you the original brainstorming session, as we recorded it on-air, cleaned up a bit and streamlined so you can read over the conversation that inspired the story in the first place.

First drafts: We have included each original draft, which in some cases is wildly different from the final story.

Edits documents: Perhaps the most interesting, we've taken each story and merged the first and final drafts, putting a strikethrough on each word cut and an underline on each word added. This will look a little messy at first, but as you adjust to the notations, you can see exactly what was removed and what was added, allowing you to compare the drafts in a cool way.

However, if all that weren't enough, the anthology also contains the following items for some of the stories.

Essays on Writing: Dan, Howard, and I wrote up essays about the writing process—with our own story specifically in mind. (Mary was in the middle of a rigorous book tour when we decided to write these.)

Workshopping sessions: Transcripts for the workshopping sessions for my story, Mary's story, and Howard's story (Dan's story wasn't done yet at the time we recorded the episodes) have been included, just like the original brainstorming sessions.

Bonus goodies: I included my writing group's comments for my story. (I workshopped it there after doing so with the Writing Excuses team, as I still couldn't figure out my ending.) Howard did us an awesome cartoon. Dan and Howard not only gave us first and last, but an interim draft of their stories, for an extra look at the process.

Overall, this anthology is stuffed full of extra material, hopefully achieving my goal of giving you a look at the process of story generation from start to finish.

I'm extremely proud of what we've done here. I don't think there's anything quite like it on the market. However, the real bonus is how well each story turned out. Thanks so much for reading, listening, and supporting us.

Anyway, you're out of excuses.

Now go read.

Brandon Sanderson

SHADOWS BENEATH
THE WRITING EXCUSES ANTHOLOGY

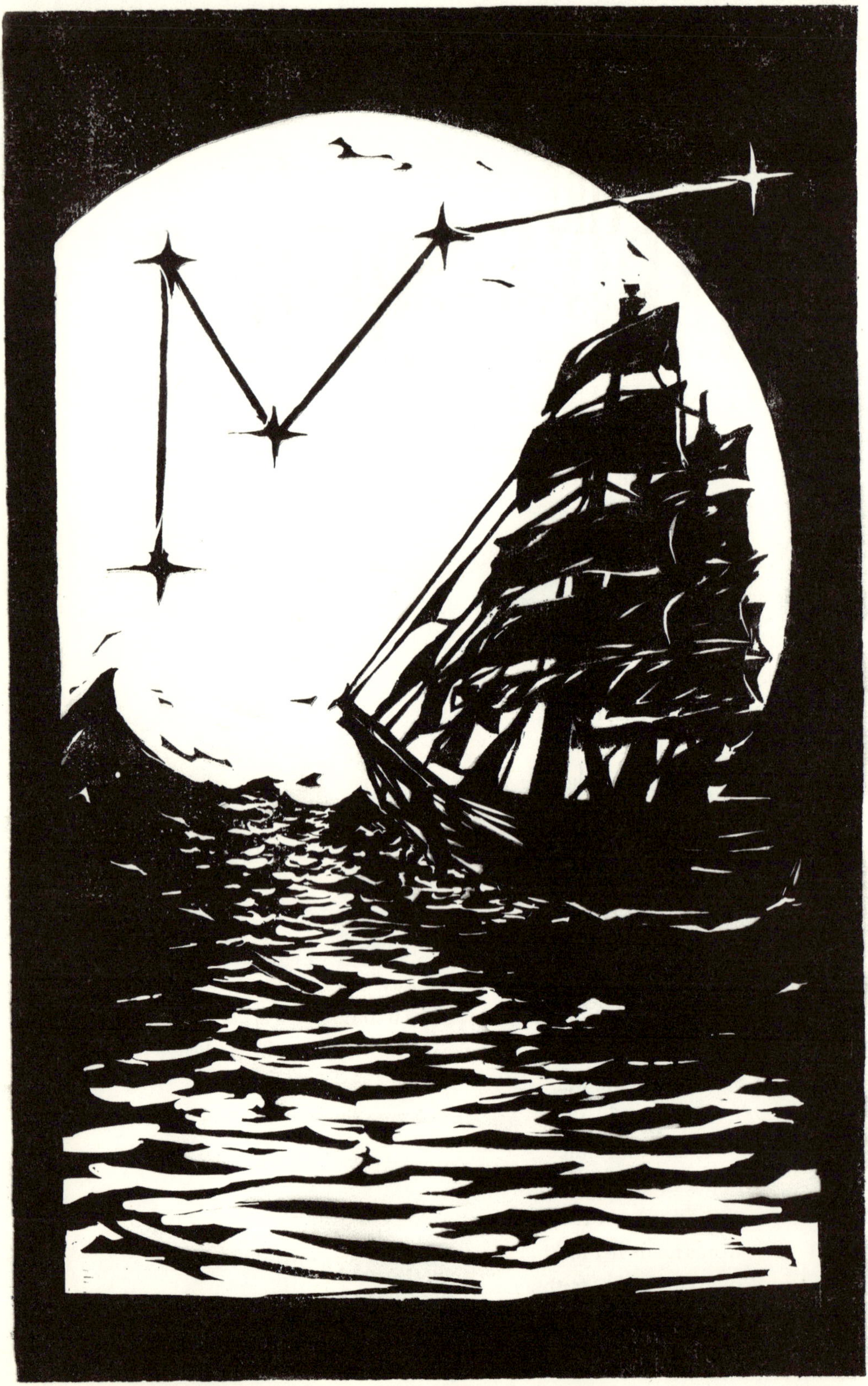

A Fire in the Heavens

Mary Robinette Kowal

A mutiny would not begin with a knock. At the simple rap upon her cabin door, Katin sent a prayer to the Five Sisters to grant her calm. Closing the *Principium*, she tucked the small book of scripture into the sash at her waist.

"Enter." She swung her legs over the side of her hammock and set her bare feet on the smooth wood floor of her cabin. She had removed her leg wraps to sleep, letting the loose fabric of her leggings puddle on the bridges of her feet.

In the deep night, the light of the sailor's glowdisc cast swaying shadows in the tiny space. Lesid ducked his head into the cabin. "Pardon, but the captain says we are in sight of land."

"Praise the Sisters." Months at sea, and even she had begun to think there was no other shore. She slipped the chain of her own glowdisc over her neck, with the cover flipped back to expose the phosphorescent surface. Ashore, a disc would fade to darkness as its dust settled during the course of a night, but the constant motion of the ship agitated the powder trapped within and kept discs always glowing at least dimly. She shook hers to brighten it further. With its light, she took a moment to bind her scarf of office around her neck before following Lesid above decks. The heavy beaded ends swung about her waist as she walked.

Katin looked up for the cluster of stars that the Five Sisters inhabited in the heavens and murmured praise to them for guiding the search this far.

The captain glanced over his shoulder as she approached. Stylian's tall form swayed easily with the rocking of the ship. "Well. You were right."

His words made her feel more alone among the Markuth sailors than ever. She had no one of her faith aboard the ship to share her joy.

Stylian had mocked her goals, but how was that different from the mockery that the followers of the Five Sisters faced daily? He had taken the church's commission. She was only grateful that he had been willing to sail on a course other captains had considered foolhardy, following the trail of ancient stories about a land far to the west. *And the storm chased the Five Sisters from Selen, across the dark sea.*

A glow lay on the horizon, marking the division of the ocean from the sky. In the darkness, she could just make out the rounded shadow of land. Katin closed her glowdisc so it would not interfere with her night vision. She frowned, slowly understanding what the light meant. She must be seeing a mountain with a city at its base. "I don't know why I expected the land to be uninhabited."

Captain Stylian grunted in agreement. "I'm of two minds about this. One part of me is relieved, because this means we can definitely restock. The other is apprehensive, because big cities have more regulations than others."

"Why are you expecting a big city?"

He nodded toward the horizon as if his statement were obvious. "The only time we see that much light before we arrive is when we cross the Narrow Sea to Arland and sail into the harbor at Porvath."

Katin looked back to the light and had to struggle to catch her breath. So many people . . . so many people who shared a heritage with her.

Her people had suffered persecution for their beliefs in every country. In Marth alone, the followers of the Sisters had been barred from holding office unless they renounced their beliefs. Even then, the visible differences of those who were ethnically of the Sisterhood still marked them. Hair twisted into pincurls at night to mask its coarse straight lines. Dye to cover the early gray—in some of the older families, hair grayed at puberty. Nut stains to darken the skin from the ruddy hue of a Sister, and still people could tell.

It was hard to comprehend that they had found Selen, the homeland.

She raised her gaze to the sky. She was not alone as long as the Sisters watched overhead. "The Five Sisters have prepared a way for us."

"To be honest, I wasn't sure how long I would be able to keep the crew sailing west. Thought we were going to go right off the edge, they did." He laughed and bent his head back to look at the sky. "Perhaps we'll see the 'moon,' too."

Katin snorted. "That's exaggerated superstition."

"And tales of a land aren't?"

"Modern scholars feel that our holy texts are guides for ways to live a better life. They are allegories, and yet . . ." She tucked her hands inside her sleeves, crossing her arms over her chest as though she were lecturing at the seminary. "There is always some basis for the tales. A land, even if it is not a new continent, must be at minimum an island. This moon? We believe that it is a corruption of the word 'musa,' which means 'city' or 'town' in Old Fretian. So we think that it refers to the city the Five Sisters came from. 'And the light of Musa lay behind them, casting silver across the sea.' This refers to the wealth and knowledge of the homeland, as does the passage which refers to Musa as the 'Brightest light in the darkness, it consumes all who enter.'"

He grunted again. "I've been to one of your Harvest Feast pageants. That whole glowing disc behind a sheet thing?"

"Illustrates a metaphor."

"Not much point in arguing with you about your own religion."

"It does seem unprofitable."

To her surprise, he gave her a crooked smile. They watched the distant glow brighten, while the wind played around her, lifting her scarf and tickling her with the ends. No one seemed inclined to go to bed as they raced across the ocean toward landfall.

The light from the city was like nothing she had seen before. It was cool and silvery as though a glowdisc were reflecting in a polished metal mirror. It grew brighter by the minute. She heard a startled cry from overhead.

In the crow's nest, a sailor pointed to the horizon. His words were snatched away. When she looked back to where he pointed, Katin's heart seized.

A low mound of light had emerged above the horizon. It was not city lights, but a single broad arc that glowed with an unearthly light. She tried to make sense of the size but could not grasp the distances. "How big is that?"

"I . . . I am not certain." Captain Stylian's voice had a hesitation she was unused to in the man. "Pardon." With a half bow, he made his way to the foot of the mainmast.

He called up to the sailor in the crow's nest, asking him for some numbers. The wind blew them away from her, but the answer caused the captain to spin abruptly and stare at the horizon.

She crossed the deck to where the captain stood. "What is the matter?"

"It's . . . The measurements . . . they cannot be correct."

"Surely you can't tell from so far—"

"But we can. When we see another ship upon the horizon, or land, we need to be able to calculate how large it is and how far away. This . . ." He waved toward it as though the words had been stripped from his mouth. "This is vast."

The glowing edge of the light pulled her gaze once more. Enough of it was visible now to draw shadows from the rails. Long crisp shadows as though a dimmer sun were rising. The light lay before them and cast silver across the sea. It was like seeing scripture come to life.

Katin's breath left her body in a rush. Dear Sisters . . . If the moon was real, what else was?

A sailor spat on the deck, and touched his fingers from his mouth to his forehead in a warding gesture. Scraps of conversation began, getting tossed on the wind toward her.

". . . no land after all . . ." "unnatural," "turn back," and then the epithet "nightlover."

"No." Not now. She would not let them stop this voyage when they were so close. "You may not believe in the Five Sisters, but you must acknowledge that our stories speak of this. Of the moon."

Stylian tugged an end of his mustache. "I thought you said it was a metaphor."

Looking at the—at the moon rising higher above the horizon, Katin swallowed. "We hired you to sail west. Thus far, all of the indications prove that our texts are correct. The land of Selen is ahead of us."

"Has it occurred to you that your Sisters may have sailed to this point from somewhere else and then turned back?"

Her gaze slipped to the light rising in the sky. She had been taught about the metaphors and had written papers on what they meant. Her work was, in part, what had led to this expedition. But what else could this be? Katin met the captain's gaze as though he were a congregation of one. "Old Fretian is not related to any other language. Where did it come from if not the West?"

A muscle twitched in his jaw. "You paid us to sail for four fifnights, and so we shall. You have until the eighth of Reed, but not a day past that."

Katin forced her voice to be calm. "There will be land."

The moon rose higher as they sailed farther west. Katin chewed her lower lip, watching the pale object. It was impossible to grasp the size of it. A dinner plate held out at arm's length would just cover it, but a dinner plate would not be visible past the curve of the world.

Its shape varied through the course of the day. From a bowlike crescent, it swelled to a shining disc, then gradually diminished again to just an arc of light. The cycle repeated with slow regularity, but the moon never vanished entirely. It was clear now that it hung in the heavens, stationary as the sun and the stars spun their course behind it. She had studied enough astronomy in seminary to understand that the stars were actually far-flung bodies, not the spirits of the dead. This object—this *moon* was closer, so of course stars would pass behind it.

It only appeared to rise higher because they sailed around the world. If they kept going, it would eventually hang directly overhead. But why did it not move?

At noon, the sun skirted the edges, and daylight dimmed as though a storm cloud covered the sky. Each day, the moon seemed to eat a little more of the sun as it passed. Again, she understood intellectually that the changing face of the moon was a shadow. She understood that the sun was not truly being consumed, and yet the line from scripture kept running through her head. *Brightest light in the darkness, it consumes all who enter.* . . .

The moon had risen high enough over the past week that it came close to the Five Sisters' path across the heavens. With the hour approaching midnight, it was now swollen to nearly a full disc.

Water splashed on Katin's skin as she went through the five postures of night meditation in the bow of the ship. Meditation did not come easily. As she balanced on one foot, in Dorot's stance, she watched the sky. Katin pulled at her scarf of office, which seemed too snug. She had trouble breathing as she watched the sky. It was one thing to believe, and quite another to see the proof of one's convictions floating in the sky.

"Ship ahead!" The call came from the topsail.

Katin lowered her foot and scanned the horizon for what the lookout had seen.

On the sea, backlit by the light of the moon, floated the unmistakable silhouette of a sailing ship like in a Harvest Feast pageant. And a ship sailing toward them could only mean that there was land ahead.

The captain called for the ship to turn abreast of the wind, and gradually they slowed in the water.

She hurried across the deck to him. "What is the matter?"

"They're running dark." He nodded toward the ship. "No lights. Either it's a pirate ship or everyone is dead. Either way, we wait until daylight to approach."

Once the dawn came, it took several hours for them to meet the other ship. Its rigging was strange, even to Katin's untrained eye. It rode very low in the water and had a beaked bow that curved in the air like a swan's neck.

By the light of day it was clear that the ship was inhabited, but they made no hostile moves. Fishing nets hung over the side, and bandy-legged men worked to haul catches aboard.

When it came close enough to really see the individuals, a weight lifted from Katin's heart. Gray hair. Ruddy skin. They must be from her homeland.

How glorious to see a ship filled with people who looked like her.

Captain Stylian stood at the rail and cupped his hands to shout to the other ship. "Where do you hail from?"

A man in tight blue trousers and a long tunic of embroidered silk shouted back. Katin frowned and cocked her head. The wind had garbled what he said. It was almost understandable, but slid so that she could barely distinguish the breaks between words.

The captain switched to Paku and asked again, but the other man just held up his hands in a shrug. Shaking his head, Captain Stylian said, "It was too much to hope that they spoke Markuth or Paku."

"I think that's a variant of Old Fretian."

He cocked his head at that. "Worth a try."

She only ever used Old Fretian to read scripture in its original form and hardly ever spoke it. Katin took a moment to gather her thoughts, trying to martial them into a semblance of order. The declension for this would be masculine interrogative case, which meant that she would have to append the appropriate suffix to the word "land."

Wrapping her mind around Fretian, Katin spoke in that tongue. "What land-the you from?"

"The Center Kingdom. You?" His next words eluded her. Then came a phrase almost straight from scripture, ". . . Sailing beyond the Moon?"

"We from Marth."

The captain leaned down. "You can understand him?"

It was a relief to switch back to Markuth. "Some. But we haven't said anything complicated yet." Beyond the Moon . . . did they never sail past here?

"Ask how far behind them the land is."

Katin nodded and painfully stitched the question together in her mind. "Land-the, how far?"

"Five days."

Katin reported this back to the captain. "May I hope that we are continuing on?"

"That's what you are paying us for." He stroked his chin, staring at the sailing ship. "Ask if they have any charts they're willing to trade."

The captain called Katin to his cabin. When she entered, he shut the door behind her and showed her to the map table. There, he had unrolled the chart they had traded for. "Look. We would have missed it with the course we were sailing."

A narrow spit of land jutted out from a landmass that filled the map. Islands dotted the coastline up and down it, but this one piece reached out into the ocean as though it were a finger pointing to the east. "How large is it?"

"I'm only guessing, but their captain says it's five days. If we're here, which he indicated we are, then that length of land alone is longer than the distance from Marth through Arland and into Gavri."

The scale staggered her and she put a hand on the table to steady herself. If the scale was correct, then this land—her people's homeland—was three times larger than all of the known countries assembled. The map was mostly concerned with the coasts, but even so, the towns that were shown were so numerous that she could not count them all. One city dominated, clearly, from the way it was drawn upon the map. A great river came through the continent to emerge at the base of the peninsula, and a city occupied both banks, spilling onto the narrow spit.

The script on the map was strange, with letters more simply shaped than what she was used to, all ornamentation stripped from them. Still she recognized the Old Fretian word "remek," which meant "center."

Scripture rose to her mind, *"The Sisters said, 'The center has held us together. Without it, we must create our own center and from this comes a new way of life.'"*

She had always taken it—the way she had been taught in seminary was that the center was a place of meditation within each of them, but looking at the map, the words revolved. *The capital has held us together. Without it, we must create our own place of government and with this comes a new way of life.* Katin touched the crescent drawn in the midst of the city, vaguely surprised that her fingers were not shaking. The Center Kingdom must revolve around the city Remek but . . . she saw no borders of the kingdom or other countries. The map was labeled as one vast empire. "This is the capital."

"Mm." Captain Stylian shook his head and tapped the map, finger coming to rest on a natural harbor farther down the mainland's coast, with a small town drawn around it. "What's this one called?"

"Iolokiv. It means Bardstown. Roughly."

"Good name. We'll head for here."

"Why not the capital?" The harbor he indicated was . . . well, if they were five days from the capital, it was a full day's sailing from Remek. *The center has held us together . . .*

"Because capital cities always have the tightest regulations. I would rather go into a smaller town to find out what harbor fees are like, if there are any shipping prohibitions, and so on . . . If we dock at too small a town, they won't know how to deal with foreign ships. So, we look for a mid-sized town." He flashed her a grin. "Plus, their officials tend to be easier to bribe."

Iolokiv seemed to sparkle in the sunlight. Glass filled windows in the walls and even in the roofs of buildings. In some places the walls seemed to be nothing more than thin pieces of metal existing solely to hold glass upright. The wealth on display staggered Katin, but the people in the port paid no heed to it. They walked along as if they passed nothing more exciting than simple stucco.

Their ship, on the other hand, attracted notice. As the crew worked to tie it up, they used a mixture of sign language and grunts to communicate with the dockworkers. Even the ships here had glass set into the cabins. Their own ship, *The Maiden's Leap*, seemed dark and squat next to the ships of Iolokiv.

The captain climbed onto the forecastle. "Listen up! You know the drill for a new port. Once we get the lay of the land, then and only then will I consider requests for leave. Expect to be aboard overnight at least. Until then, I want us to be ready to cast off at the first sign of trouble."

A sailor snorted. "That's a certainty with a harbor full of nightlovers."

He grinned and leaned over the man. "You knew this was a possibility when we accepted the commission."

"Ha! I thought we'd sail in circles and then come home."

The other sailors hooted with laughter and the captain let them.

Katin stood by the rail and felt her skin burn even redder with anger. If she could bring her people here, then any amount of abuse would be worth it.

Footsteps crossed the deck to stand behind her. Captain Stylian cleared his throat. "Is it a festival day?"

Not a word of apology. She turned from studying the dock to face him. "Festival?"

"The banners. Every ship is flying a red banner, sometimes two or three." He nodded toward the crowds. "And see. People with armbands in the same red. What does it mean?"

"I . . . I don't know." She had been so distracted by the variety of costume that she had not noticed the armbands. Despite the sailors' comments, the harbor was not full of "nightlovers," though they were certainly the dominant type. There were nutbrown men, women with flaming curls, and people whose pale skin had an almost green hue.

Now that the captain had pointed it out, the scraps of red were obvious, fluttering behind people as they walked. She pointed to a man with a blue armband who walked behind two burly men that appeared to be bodyguards, clearing a path. "There. Not everyone has red bands."

"I thought this was supposed to be your homeland. So you ought to know, even by the calendar, if this is a festival day."

Katin shook her head. "We've been gone so long . . . Perhaps they added festivals?"

"You sound uncertain."

"And how am I supposed to be certain? I have not set foot upon the land."

He held up his hands in a placating gesture. "Fair enough. Shall we remedy that now?"

Katin took a breath to steady herself and nodded. The captain led the way to the gangplank that stretched from their boat to the pier. The man with blue ribbons met them at the gangplank. His straight gray hair had been tied in a queue down his back, and his cheeks were so pink they looked rouged. He held a flat plank of wood with paper affixed to it by means of flat springs on the sides.

Katin wanted to retreat up the gangplank before the captain could look to her. She did not speak the language, for all that he thought she did. And yet, likely she *was* the best chance for understanding what the blue gentleman wanted.

He spoke very rapidly, with that same sliding inflection as the ship's captain they had met on the sea. Katin had spent the intervening three days reading scripture aloud in Old Fretian, trying to make herself more comfortable with the language. Still the torrent of words undid her.

She held up her hands in supplication and spoke one of the sentences she'd prepared. "Please slow down. I speak very badly, but am the only translator the ship has."

The official snorted, but did slow down. Still, she only caught scattered words and phrases: "Where from," then "none crew-yours," and he finished with "official language?"

She could answer only the beginning. "Across sea-the."

"Ah. South Islander . . ." His voice carried amused contempt. "What happened husband-your?"

"Sorry?"

He slowed even further, pausing after each phrase until she nodded. "Husband your. Husband ship's. Examinations. Must pass. Or he would not. Command. Be given. If no one aboard speaks Setish. Then something happened. Husband ship's your."

Katin stared at him while she tried to parse the separate phrases into a sentence. The meaning of the word "husband" must have shifted over the centuries. It was paired with "ship," so maybe it meant "captain"?

"What is he saying?" Captain Stylian's voice was low and easy, as if this were perfectly natural. He flashed the official a smile.

"I think . . . I think ship captains are required to know the language, which I think is called Setish, so he believes something has happened to ours. Also, I think he thinks we're from islands to the south."

"That's a lot of 'I thinks.'"

"Well, I don't actually speak the language. I'm making a lot of guesses."

"You sound fluent."

"I'm mostly saying, 'please slow down.'"

He grunted a little and offered the official another smile. "South Islands? Don't contradict him. Just make apologies for our stupidity and ask if we can offer him some hospitality for his trouble." His tone as he said this was so deeply apologetic that she almost thought he *was* apologizing. He bowed his head, as if abashed. "Don't look so surprised."

Katin bent her head in supplication and pulled some of the words of atonement from scripture. "Oh noble master, forgive us our trespasses." It got harder from there, and Katin could feel the language breaking under her tongue. "New husband-ours offer apology-the you. Would you hospitality-ours accept?"

At her side, Captain Stylian produced a flask and passed it to the official with a deep bow. That language seemed clearer than any Katin could produce. The official made a pleased noise. As the captain straightened, he flashed her a brief wink.

Katin would not be exploring the city just yet.

The negotiations with the official had not taken long. The celebrations with him, however, had eaten the better part of the morning. Still, they had permission to dock and with that accomplished, the captain had been content to let Katin go ashore—with protection.

The sailor Lesid trailed after her through the market, one hand on the knife at his belt. She was not entirely sure if he was there to keep her safe, or because the captain wanted to make certain that his translator returned to the ship. Stalls lined the sides of a large cobbled square, set between low stone walls. Canvas awnings in blues and pinks stretched between the walls to provide a little shade to the merchants. Tables sat under the canopies, spread with unfamiliar fruits, fish, great heaping bouquets of pink flowers, and bolts of cloth. In the center of the square, a fountain burbled merrily. Around its edges, people had spread blankets on the dusty cobbles and squatted displaying cheap handiwork.

Gazes followed them as she and Lesid walked through the market. Most of the people had ruddier skin than his. Their hair tended toward gray. There were a few with darker skin like Lesid and some with golden curls, but none with both. On the ship, he looked like any other sailor. Here he looked . . . exotic. Katin slowed and glanced back at the sailor. "Walk with me?"

"I am."

"You're walking behind me."

"Oh." He frowned and took two steps to close the gap between them. "Better?"

"Yes." Katin resumed her stroll, feeling a little less exposed with someone beside her. She shouldn't feel so much like a foreigner, if this were really their homeland. If. What else would it be? The land was in the right place, and they spoke a version of the sacred language. But the people here kept staring at them and . . . nothing was familiar. Katin rolled the beads of her shawl beneath her fingers. Gefen grant patience.

"What's that?" Lesid pointed to a stall that had pink egg-shaped fruit that seemed to be covered in green-tipped scales. At least, she thought it was fruit.

"I don't know."

Lesid furrowed his brow. "I thought this was—"

"My homeland, yes. I know. Everyone thinks I should know all about it." Including her. "My people have been gone from here for hundreds of years. . . . This is as new to me as it is to you."

"I— I hadn't thought about that. Sorry."

Katin shifted her hand to her belt where her coin purse was tucked. The official had given them some copper coins in exchange for a bottle of the captain's whiskey. She was certain they'd gotten the worse end of the deal, but the captain had seemed pleased. "Shall we buy a fruit and see what it's like?"

The sailor's eyes lit up at the suggestion. "Seems half a year since I had something that wasn't salted or preserved."

Katin grinned and steered them toward the stall. "I don't see how in the heavens you can stand to eat that all the time."

"Well, it's not always. Usually we aren't at sea for more than a week, maybe two. You can carry enough rindfruit to last that long." He rubbed the back of his neck. "Then, you know, you pull into port at someplace like Nil-Mazzer and they've got barkberries or, oh . . . in the late summer we get in sometimes in redmelon season and you can buy big slices sprinkled with spice and a tall glass of chilled juice. There's this one place off the south canal that has a chef that grills it, right there while you wait, but he does it so fast the inside is still cool and the outside is warm. Just lights your tongue up, it does."

She blinked at him in surprise. "Seaman Lesid, you are quite the gourmand."

He laughed, shaking his head. "I'm not fancy. I just like food is all."

Katin stepped up to the booth and pointed at the fruit. She wrapped her head around Old Fretian, which was as close as she was going to come to speaking the local Setish. "How much? Two?"

The old woman behind the fruit had her hair wrapped up in a yellow scarf, which let a puff of white hair escape out the back. "Two *musan* each. Four total."

Katin assumed that a *musan* was a coin and fished four of the smallest coins out of the wallet and handed them over. The woman took them without surprise or fuss, and Katin let out her breath.

She said something very fast and Katin had to shake her head. "I speak bad Setish. Slowly?"

The woman grunted and picked up a wicked machete, flecked with bits of pink rind, and gestured to the fruit. "Cut?"

"Um . . . Yes?"

The woman nodded and pulled two of the fruits off the pile. She paused before bringing the machete down, and peered at the sky. Speaking very slowly, she said, "Almost noon death. Wait? So *naro-a* dries not before birth-the."

Katin made a guess that the fruit was called *naro-a*. She wasn't entirely certain what noon death had to do with the fruit drying though, or even if she'd heard the question correctly. "Thank you."

The woman set the machete down below the table. When she stood, she had a small roll of heavy blue cloth. Woven into it were yellow quatrefoils of thread that suggested stars at night. She shuffled around the table, unrolling the cloth as she stepped out of the booth.

Lesid eyed her and then the fruit. "She just took our money and didn't give you anything?"

Katin shook her head, realizing that he had not understood any of the exchange. "She will. After the . . . Well, it translates as 'noon death,' but I think I have it wrong." Noon death . . . death . . . Maybe the point when the sun went behind the moon? That could be a death, couldn't it? But why did she think the fruit would dry because of that?

The market had stilled. Other people were pulling bundles of cloth out of bags, or from straps slung across their back. She drew her head back in surprise. It wasn't just a few people. *Everyone* in the market was doing the same thing. To be sure, some were continuing to shop with the cloth held loosely in one hand, but they all had a cloth. Some of them were threadbare, and others were so fine they had tiny mirrors sewn upon them.

The fruit vendor laid her cloth on the ground and unwrapped the scarf from her hair. Those with their hair covered were removing their hats or scarves. All of them had their heads turned down, watching the ground. What in the world were they looking for?

Then twilight swept across the market. Bells rang, seemingly from every corner of the city. As one, the people in the marketplace dropped to their knees and placed their foreheads on the cloth they had unrolled. A caged bird clucked in the sudden stillness, its chirruping cry bouncing across the stone walls of the market.

No one in the entire market, or down the nearby streets, had remained standing. It appeared that the entire city knelt.

Katin grabbed Lesid's arm and yanked him down. To his credit, he didn't fight her or ask what she was doing. He just mimicked the posture of the woman closest to them.

She could only hope it didn't make a difference that they had no cloth to kneel upon. With her face pressed to the hard cobbles and the dust caked between them, her nose twitched. She wrinkled it, trying to stifle the sneeze. Pulling her attention away, she tried to distract herself by playing a guessing game with what was happening.

"Noon death" clearly meant when the sun went behind the moon. That was happening now. The light continued to dim, further than it had aboard the ship it seemed, or perhaps that was her imagination. If the birth was when the sun emerged, then it would explain why the fruit vendor had been concerned about the *naro-a* drying. That was near to seven minutes.

The bells sounded again, while the dark still gripped the market. Cloth rustled around them and Katin pushed herself to her knees. She froze before rising any farther. The people were not moving to stand. They had rolled onto their backs. Lesid turned to look at her, brow turned up in confusion.

She had no idea what they were doing, but given that *everyone* was lying down, it didn't feel like they had a choice. She could think of nothing back home that would induce a crowd of people to act as one like this.

Swallowing, not knowing what else to do, Katin lay down on her back. Lesid followed a moment later.

She stared up at the sky and for a moment lost her worry about understanding what the people were doing. The sky . . . On the ship, the sun had passed almost behind the thin crescent of the moon, but an edge of it had been visible. Here though, they had evidently traveled far enough that the entire sphere had vanished.

What remained was a dark disc with a fiery halo surrounding it. It undulated in a glory of yellow and red against a backdrop of deep blue. The sky was dark enough that stars shone. She searched the sky for the Sisters, but—
But none of the stars were familiar. Katin shook her head, trying to slow her breathing. Of course they weren't. These were the daytime constellations only visible when the sun died. *Noon death.*

She took in a painful breath, understanding. *Brightest light in the darkness, it consumes all who enter* . . . Not when the sun died, but when the moon killed the sun and then gave birth to it. Had the Sisters worshiped in this manner? What had their lives been like to lose this display of magic in the sky?

Above her, it was as if the moon wore a fiery crown. Or a skirt. Dorot's bloody hands, but she wanted to find out how their scripture accounted for this. The myths and legends here must be as gorgeous as the streamers of fire that danced around the edges of the dark sphere.

For a third time, the bells in the city chimed. Again the sound of cloth rustled around them. Before moving, Katin glanced to the side to see that everyone was rolling back over to their stomachs, kneeling upon the ground with their heads bent. Lesid had already followed suit, tucking his knees under his body. Katin rolled over and pressed her face against the cobbles.

Had the entire city done this? Based on what she saw, everyone in the market had. She would have expected there to be nonbelievers at the least, and most definitely thieves who would take advantage of the time when everyone's faces were pressed to the ground. No one here seemed to have that worry. Katin couldn't imagine that happening in Marth, except in very small towns.

The ground lightened around her, shadows coming back to etch the edges of the cobbles. Around them, the bells pealed again.

She had expected a simultaneous movement, but the people in the market moved as if released from a spell that had momentarily bound them together. The fruit vendor bobbed to her knees, then pushed herself to her feet with a groan. She bent down to pick up her cloth, shaking the dust from it. The man on the ground to Katin's right stayed with his head down for a few seconds longer, before sitting back on his heels. Another woman knelt and rolled her cloth up before standing.

Lesid turned to Katin, eyes wide. Despite the fact that he spoke Markuth, he lowered his voice. "What by the blessed gods was that?"

"I think it was a group prayer service."

He glanced up at the sun. Overhead, the sky had returned to its usual daytime blue. No stars were visible. The sun, blazingly bright, rode in the sky where it had just been released from the crescent of the moon. Did they see the shape as a bow?

Lesid shook his head and lowered his eyes, blinking away tears from having stared too long at the sun. "Praying that the sun will come back?"

"I don't know. I'm sorry, I keep saying that a lot." Katin turned to the fruit vendor, who had hobbled behind her booth again. She had wrapped her hair back up in its yellow scarf. Katin switched back to Old Fretian to address her. "Pardon. University? Is there?"

The woman stared at her, mouth screwed up in a frown. "Oh— A university. Yes." She rattled something else off and then stopped at Katin's look of confusion. "Bardstown College. Water Street." She lifted the machete and swung it at the pink fruit. It split open to reveal a creamy interior, ringed with a thick circle of vivid pink. "South Islands, right?"

Remembering what the captain had said, Katin did not disagree with her. "Library-a there?"

"Aye." She swung the machete again, halving the other *naro-a*. With a little nod, she handed the *naro-a* to them, along with an odd wedge of some thick reed.

After a moment, Lesid grinned. "Oh! It's a spoon."

He stuck the end of the reed into the pale center of the fruit and dug out a scoop of the soft flesh. Passing it under his nose, he inhaled slowly, filling his lungs. Katin watched him slide the piece of fruit into his mouth and close his eyes in concentration.

"Well?"

He held up the hand with the reed-spoon, shushing her as he chewed. After a moment he gave a grin and opened his eyes. "Subtle. Almost creamy, but a little acidic. Not enough to make your mouth pucker like rindfruit. Maybe like a rindfruit ice . . . Anyway. There are also little seeds that crack when you bite. It's nice."

"Nice." Katin shook her head and scooped out a spoonful of her own. "You describe food the way other people describe wine." Anything else she was going to say was forgotten as she tasted the *naro-a*. The texture was the first thing that stopped her. It was soft, somewhere between a ripe melon and a pudding, while the little seeds in it burst in tiny pops. The flavor was a little like cream, but the thing Lesid had said about rindfruit was right. It made her mouth feel clean with each bite. "Wow."

"I know. We should find out how long they store, in case we can take them back to Marth."

Katin drew in a breath, somehow shocked by the reminder that they would be returning to Marth. It had always been the plan, of course. Find the homeland, then come back for her people. She just had not expected . . . this. Civilization. Or unfamiliar culture or— She wasn't sure what she had thought they would find, but not this city with its people praying to the moon. Did they do that in Center too? Did the entire city fall to its knees at noon?

Lesid cleared his throat. "Why do you want to find the university?"

"I'm hoping someone speaks Old Fretian."

"Isn't that what everyone here speaks?"

"No . . . It's related. Probably a descendant from a common tongue, but I'm fighting to understand anything." And maybe the university would have information about the Five Sisters. Surely they must have left some historical trace.

A knot in her stomach formed around the *naro-a*. Unless the Five Sisters were unknown here.

They found the university easily enough by simply repeating the words "Bardstown College?" as a question until someone pointed them on their way. The campus grounds had a broad expanse of fragrant ground cover with tiny leaves and even tinier purple flowers, spread between gravel lanes. Young men and women that Katin took to be students walked along the paths with yellow and blue ribbons tied to their left arms. The thin pieces of fabric fluttered behind them in a miniature festival.

She repeated her trick and said, "Library?" to the first student she met. Eventually, she and Lesid found themselves in front of a broad glass-fronted building. *Brightest light in the darkness, it consumes all who enter.*

Wide marble steps led up to glass doors set into brass facings. Did they use glass for everything here?

Inside, ranks of shelves stepped back through a well-lit great hall. At home it would have been filled with glowdiscs, while here the light came from a cunning arrangement of skylights and mirrors, but the sense of being a temple to books was still the same. Desks stood at intervals between the shelves, with students bent in study over stacks of books. At the center of the library a series of counters formed a square. In the hollow of the square, a pair of older faculty members sat at matching desks. A heavy book rested on the counter facing the front of the library, open to a page filled with names and dates. A registry, perhaps, of the people using the library.

As she approached the desk, Lesid dropped back slightly to stand behind her shoulder. Katin wet her lips and tried to think of how to phrase the questions she wanted to ask, but all of the sentences were too complicated for her meager grasp of the language. One of the librarians, an older man with thinning brown hair, looked up and smiled.

"May I help you?" He stood and approached the counter where Katin stood.

The relief that she had understood all of the words, even in such a simple sentence, made her sigh with thanks. "Please."

"What do you seek?" He waited, and still she had nothing easy to ask.

Did he have books about the Five Sisters or about a voyage beyond the moon, or ancient histories, or— Katin's head came up as she thought she saw a way out of her dilemma. "I speak not Setish."

She paused as his eyes widened with surprise, and she filed the surprise away to consider. Like the marketplace of people kneeling, what were the chances that a university, even in a middle-sized town, would not have foreigners passing through?

Katin put the questions it raised aside, and offered an apologetic smile as she constructed the next sentence in her head. "Is any person who speaks . . ." What was that phrase from scripture . . . ? "The ancient tongues?"

The librarian drew his head back, and turned to his colleague, a woman of middle years with blonde hair that had silvered at the temples. "Can you . . ." and then Katin lost the train of the rest of his question. Whatever it was caused the woman to raise her eyebrows and stand. She came to the counter, blue and yellow ribbons fluttering from her arm as she walked.

She tilted her head and studied Katin. "What language?"

"I call it Old Fretian."

There was no answering sign of recognition in the woman's eyes at the word "Fretian."

Gnawing her lower lip, Katin reached into her sash and pulled out her copy of the *Principium*. It was not a translation into Markuth, but had the original Old Fretian scriptural text. She opened it to the first page and slid it across the counter. "This?"

The woman pulled it closer and bent over the page with a frown. The man leaned over her shoulder, chewing on his lower lip. "Can you read it?"

"Not well." The woman traced a finger along the opening of the first chapter. With an accent strangely formed and stumbling, she read aloud from the *Principium*.

"We give all praise and thanks to the Five Sisters for our Safe Deliverance.
Straight the Course and True the Path of the righteous.
Dorot, Gefen, Nofar, Yorira, and Abriel have kept us safe from the Ravages of the Deep.
We left behind Woe and Hardship in the Path of the Moon."

After a moment, she simply traced her finger over the text, lips moving occasionally as she sounded out a word. The woman riffled forward to a later chapter and placed her finger on the text again, mouthing words.

Behind Katin, Lesid shifted his weight and nudged her in the back. She glanced over her shoulder at him.

His brow was furrowed and he jerked his chin at the librarians. "What's going on?"

"I'm hoping they can help us find a better translator than me," she answered in a low voice.

The sound of flipping pages pulled her attention back to the librarians. The woman had turned to the back of the book and frowned over it. "Where are the printer's marks?"

"Sorry?"

"The printer's marks." The woman tapped the back endpapers of the book.

Katin spread her hands and shook her head. "I understand not. I mean— I hear words, but I do not know meaning-the. Printer's marks. We come from beyond the Moon."

The woman laughed and scooped the book up, slapping it against the chest of the man. "A prank. You should—" The rest of her words slid past Katin's understanding.

He caught the book as she released it, striding back to her desk. As he looked down, a flush of red highlighted his cheeks. "But so much trouble . . . ?"

"One year, they . . ." Katin lost the words, but thought she was talking about a forged play. Or ox-tails. Or maybe a manuscript. The woman waved her hand in scorn at the book. ". . . not trying . . ." and "language" were all Katin caught.

"What language?" Katin held her hands out. "Please. What language is it?"

"Ancient Setish." The man answered reflexively.

"Anyone who speaks? A . . . ancient-an Setish speaker?" If Katin could talk to someone without having to struggle so much to understand modern Setish, then perhaps figuring out what had happened back in the days when the Five Sisters had left would be easier.

Again, she just barely grasped what they were saying, clawing meaning out of the words.

"Center University? Department of ancient languages?" She repeated to make certain she had understood it.

The woman's expression had gone from amused to annoyed. "Stop this farce."

Katin held up her hands in apology. "Sorry. And thank you."

"It is nothing." The man turned back to his desk, still holding her book.

"Excuse me?"

He paused, with his brow raised. "Yes?"

"My book."

Sighing, he looked down at the book in his hands. "You think not it return would I."

"But it is mine."

With exaggerated care, he said, "No printer's marks. Illegal."

Katin gaped at him for a moment. "I told you that we aren't from here."

"You are fortunate I do not call the Factors." The woman gestured to the man and took the book from him. With a glare, she dropped it into a waste bin. "Good day."

Lesid stepped forward and looked from Katin to the woman. In Markuth, he said, "Did they just throw your book away?"

"Yes— No!" She grabbed Lesid's arm as he put his hand on the hilt of his knife. By the Sisters, if he went after one of the librarians there was no telling what havoc it would bring down on them. "Lesid . . . We should go."

"But that's your holy book."

"I know." Her stomach twisted at the sight of the scripture lying in the waste bin. "We'll go back to the captain and see if he can ask the official to help us get it back, all right? But right now they think we're college students pulling some sort of prank." At least she thought that was what they had said. Maybe there was a fine she could pay.

"This isn't right." He glared at the librarians.

It wasn't, but for the moment, she had to accept it. "Let's go."

He lowered his hand with obvious reluctance and let her turn him back toward the doors of the library. She had taken no more than four steps when Lesid turned. "It's not right."

He ran back to the counter and vaulted over it. The librarians started up with shouts. The man hurried forward, but Lesid shoved him back with one hand to the chest.

Reaching the wastebasket, he grabbed the book and spun back. Tucking it under his arm, he ducked away from the woman librarian as she snatched for his arm.

She shouted and Katin understood the word all too clearly. "Alarm!"

Lesid put one hand down on the counter and sprang over it, running toward Katin. "Go! Go!"

His words released her from her shocked hold, and Katin spun to run for the doors. Students staggered up from their tables, hurrying to see what the commotion was about. Lesid caught Katin before they reached the door and passed her, pushing the heavy glass open on its springs. They ran through. She bounded down the steps two at a time, sprinting beside Lesid as they ran across the lawn. Behind them, the woman librarian had followed, still shouting, but her words were mercifully unintelligible.

When they reached the street, Lesid glanced behind them and slowed to a walk. "I don't see them, so I think we're all right. Best not to grab attention."

Katin laughed, the patter of excitement still urging her steps forward. "You sound like you've done this before."

"Let's just say, I had a strong reason to go to sea." He handed the book to her, with a wink. "We'll walk for a bit. See if we can find a shop to duck into, maybe."

"Thank you." Katin tried to slow her breathing to something that involved less panting. "Do you think they'll come after us?"

"Dunno." He shrugged. "I couldn't understand anything they were saying. Might be that I need you to teach me this language."

"If I actually knew it, I would."

From behind them came a shout that needed no translation. "Stop them!"

Katin whirled, her prayer scarf flying wide. On the university grounds behind them, the woman librarian stood on the walk, pointing with a straight arm. Running toward them were two burly men with blue streamers flapping from their arms. These must be the Factors. They each carried a short sword with a strange grip in a small sheath at the waist. Across their chests, little mirrors had been sewn into the dark blue silk and flashed light with each step.

With an intake of breath, Lesid grabbed Katin's arm and pulled her back around. Running in earnest now, they sprinted for the nearest side street. Lesid kept the pace rapid, dodging through the crowds of shoppers. He slipped between men in long tunics, women with bared midriffs, and everywhere the little ribbons streaming from their arms.

They wound through the unfamiliar streets, not slowing to look at textiles and brass vases or anything else that caught their eyes. Glass windows granted crazed views behind them, where their pursuers bobbed in and out of sight through the thick crowds. Lesid rounded another corner, narrowly missing a baker's cart.

Katin grabbed his arm and yanked him into the shop. He looked over his shoulder and pushed her farther into the shop, until a set of shelves filled with pastries hid them from the street. Standing in the shop with sweat-slick skin, Katin tried to master her breathing and look less suspicious. She inhaled deeply and stopped with her ribs expanded as a tantalizing fragrance caught her attention.

A stupid reason to think this shop was safe, but it was the first familiar thing she'd encountered here. It smelled sweet and spicy, and of dough that had been dipped in fat to fry until it was golden. She could almost taste the crust of sugar that would cling to the top.

"What?" Lesid whispered, still glancing back to the street.

"It smells like rolada. A pastry we make for the Harvest Feast in autumn." She inhaled again, savoring the comforting scent of home.

On the street, the blue-clad Factors ran past, pushing through the pedestrians without a glance into their refuge. Katin let out a breath and thanked the Sisters for guiding her here.

From behind the counter, a slender young woman was watching them with furrowed brows. She fiddled with a bell on the counter, as if on the verge of ringing it. Maybe it just brought someone from the rear of the shop, or maybe it called the Factors back. Either way it was best if she didn't ring it.

Katin smiled and stepped to the counter, looking for the crescent-shaped rolada. Hoping that the word wouldn't have changed much since they left the homeland, Katin cleared her throat. "Forgive me my trespasses."

"Excuse?" The young woman let go of the bell and cocked her head.

Katin made note of the short form of the apology and ducked her head to look at the pastries. Pale gold dough filled with some red jelly stood in rows next to a flatbread sprinkled with nuts. Heavy dark loaves glistened in the light from the ever-present windows. She did not see any crescent-shaped confections. "Are there rolada here?"

The baker stared at her. "What?"

"Rolada. A . . ." She winced, trying to think. What was the word for pastry in Old Fretian? "Bread? Hot oil . . . cooked in?"

The woman's brows came together in concentration and she repeated the words back to Katin. "Bread? Cooked in hot oil? What'd you call it?"

"Rolada?"

"Rolada." She said the word again, as if she were chewing it. Then her eyes widened. "Oh! Rolada!"

Katin blinked at her. What had she said, if not that? "Yes. Do you have them?"

"Aye." Hopping off her stool, the woman bent down to a lower shelf and pulled a tray out. Upon it were a dozen flat crescents of pastries, crusted with caramelized sugar. Peeks of color from the dried berries embedded in the dough made Katin's mouth water. "Just came out of the oil. How many?"

"Two, please."

The pastry cost less than the fruit, which said something about how the fruit was valued here. In a few moments, Katin had a handful of small coins in change for her single *musan*. The woman wrapped a sheet of waxed paper around the pastries and handed them to Lesid, who inhaled with a slow smile as he took them.

Katin almost snatched hers from him. The paper was already warm from the pastry within. She broke one horn off and the crust made a soft *crack* as the sugar broke. A sweet and spicy steam curled out of the flaky interior. She sent up a silent prayer that it would taste right, then felt silly for asking the Sisters to intervene in something so trivial. It either would or it wouldn't.

The crust dissolved against the roof of her mouth, carrying rich butter and the tang of spice. It was almost right, but in the way that pastries are different when someone else's grandmother makes them. The overall sensation was of comfort and home. Memories of being a little girl on her mother's lap, eating a pastry as the shadow play showed the Sisters' flight before the storm. A glowdisc behind a sheet had stood in for the light of Musa, but it had given her no preparation for the reality.

Katin's eyes watered with longing. Home. When had she started thinking of Marth as home? To be certain, she had been born there, but always, always she had been taught that it was not home. That their true home was across the ocean and that Marth was only a resting place until they could find their way back. There had to be more comfort here than a pastry. She just had to find it.

"Gods. That's good." Lesid sighed beside her. "Can we get some more to take back to the ship?"

Katin nodded and wiped her eyes. "Yes. That's a good idea."

They meandered back to the ship, following a circuitous route that took them far from the university, just to be safe. The baker had wrapped up a bundle of the rolada in heavy brown paper. It had cooled as they walked, but Lesid said the sailors would just be happy to have something that wasn't salted fish.

His pace slowed as they walked down the dock to the ship, so Katin pulled ahead of him a bit. Lesid shifted the pastries to his left arm. "Hold on."

At the foot of the ramp of *The Maiden's Leap*, the captain was speaking heatedly to a man who blocked his path. The man wore a blue armband like the official who had let them dock.

More troubling though were the two enormous bodyguards with him. They were the Factors who had chased them from the university grounds. Katin backed up. They would return later, after the men had gone.

"Katin!" The captain's voice boomed down the dock. "Thank the gods you're back. I can't make a seabound dog of anything the fellow is saying."

Sisters take them. Katin gestured Lesid to leave before she stepped toward the captain. Maybe Lesid could slip away in the crowd. With a smile, she faced the ship again. "I'm happy to help."

One of the guards nudged the other. At the same time, Katin felt Lesid's presence at her elbow. Curse him for being a stubborn gallant. The captain beckoned her, so Katin slipped past the guards and onto the gangplank. Remaining on the pier, Lesid watched her with the bundle of pastries still under his arm.

Clearing her throat, Katin marshaled the Old Fretian in her mind. "I give you greetings."

The official stared at her and said something very rapid. She could not even tell where one word ended and the next began. His voice slipped like oil upon the water.

"Speak slowly please." She slowed her own speech to demonstrate. "I do not understand."

His lip curled and he spoke slowly, mockingly, as though she were a damaged person. Still she caught only a few words, making her aware of how kind the other people had been to use simple words. "Name" and "travelers" and then "oxtail."

"Did you say ox-tail?"

"Yes. Show me your oxtail." Then his speech exploded into a confusion of words. "Oxtail" again and then "center" or perhaps "middle."

"I am sorry. I do not understand."

The man threw his hands up into the air in an obvious sign of aggravation. He turned to one of the bodyguards and gestured toward the ship imperiously. "Take it."

The bodyguard to his left stepped toward the ship and unsheathed his sword— Except it was not a sword. It was a hollow tube, which he pointed at the captain.

"Move." The bodyguard gestured roughly, making his meaning clear.

The captain put his hand on Katin's shoulder. "What is happening?"

"I—" She did not know. This was not what she had studied for. Katin turned to look over her shoulder at him. "They want something. He keeps asking for an ox-tail. Maybe it's an offering of some sort? And now, I think— but I don't really understand. It sounds like they want the ship. But I might be wrong."

Lesid shouted, "Hey, there! None of that."

Katin grabbed for the rough rope rail as the gangplank shuddered. She turned back in time to see Lesid grab a bodyguard by the arm and pull him back from the ramp. The huge man looked astonished and angry. He pointed the tube at Lesid and then—

There was a flash and a clap of thunder. Smoke billowed from the end of the tube. On the docks, people screamed and ran from the sound.

Lesid took a step backward and then sat heavily. Red stained the front of his jacket. He toppled to the side and fell into the water.

"Lesid." The captain pushed past her and stared at the spot where the sailor floated facedown. Blood curled around him in the water. "I need a lifeline!"

No. No! What had happened?

The blue man on the dock said something and it took Katin a moment to realize that he was speaking to her. "I do not understand."

"No one move."

"He's dying!"

"Dead. Already. Stay still. Tell them." He spoke with exaggerated care.

Swallowing, she said, "Captain. He wants everyone to stay still."

"No. I have a man down." He bellowed back to the ship, without taking his eyes off Lesid. "Where's that rope?"

A sailor ran to the edge and wrapped a coil around the rail. His fingers tightened a knot.

The blue man spoke again, in that strange sliding Fretian. "I said, no one move."

"A man drowns!" Katin pointed at Lesid. The water was so red.

He snorted and turned to the bodyguard. "Make it two."

The weapon flashed and thundered again. Katin covered her ears, shrieking at the noise. Below her, the captain jerked and stumbled. He grabbed the rope railing with both hands.

"No!"

His feet went out from under him and he dropped to his knees, still clutching the railing. As the acrid smoke curled around her, Katin found herself behind him, pulling him back before he could fall into the water.

She wrapped her arms around him, feeling the blood soak into her tunic. Her scarf of office fell across his chest. "Stop. We do what you say."

"Good." The blue man's teeth glinted in the sun. "Good."

The bundle of pastries sat on the pier beside him, still perfectly wrapped.

Katin sat by Captain Stylian's cot and dipped a cloth in the dish of water she had begged from the guards. "The guards tell me that we will have *titam* and *kalcoist* this afternoon for lunch."

He grunted and shifted on the cot. "Dare I ask what that means?"

"*Titam* are potatoes and I think that *kalcoist* is lamb. At any rate, it seems to share a root with *kalca*, which is the word for sheep. *Ist* should be a diminutive, so . . . lamb. I think."

A man came every day to give them language lessons. Proctor Veleh was patient to the point of seeming a machine, but she was the only one of the crew that made any effort. The others all muttered about escape, as though getting past the guards and their hollow tubes were a possibility.

"Any luck finding out what our crime is?"

She shook her head. In the fifnight since they had been taken, her grasp of Setish had improved enough to *almost* understand. Almost. Or rather, she understood the words "shy of an ox-tail," but the meaning eluded her. "When I ask what an ox-tail is, Proctor Veleh says that it is the tail of an ox."

"Next time I'll have one pickled." He shifted again on the cot and hissed. Stylian closed his eyes, breath held between tight-pressed lips. He let it out slowly. "So . . . lamb tonight, eh?"

"Yes." She dipped her cloth in the water again and looked across the dormitory. The first mate stood in a tight cluster with three other crewmen.

She kept imagining Lesid in the corner of her eye, jacket stained red. Katin swallowed and focused on the living crewmen. One of them seemed to be blatantly counting the number of times the guard walked past the door. "Proctor Veleh says that they would normally provide a translator for the trial, but no one knows Markuth. Or Old Fretian really for that matter."

One of the sailors broke away from the group and crossed to the captain's cot. "I can take over, if you like." It was not an offer.

The captain raised his eyebrows at the man's tone. Katin bit her lips and put the cloth back in the basin. "Of course."

She stood and strolled away, trying to linger long enough to hear what they were going to talk about, but the captain said only, "Katin tells me that we're having lamb tonight."

Scowling, she squatted by one of the walls and smoothed her scarf of office. With her arms crossed, she took the ends of the scarf between her hands, symbolizing the path the Five Sisters took through the heavens, and began rolling the beads between her fingers. Each Sister had a separate role in guiding a person's behavior through life. Katin appealed to Nofar, the middle Sister, to grant the captain resiliency. He must get well and do nothing foolish. She sent a plea to Abriel to guard Lesid's soul. Though, if the Sisters cared for an unbeliever, they should have granted him favor for rescuing her book.

Briefly rescuing. The guards had taken it from her and presumably back to the library to be destroyed.

"What are you doing?"

The man's voice called her back to herself. She opened her eyes, ready to scowl at the crewman who had disturbed her before realizing that the question had been in Setish. Proctor Veleh stood in front of her. It was not his day to teach.

"I am praying."

He frowned. Lines creased his face more deeply than they should have in one so young. "No, you are not."

"What—? I— Yes. Yes, I *am* praying." She held up her scarf. "This is how we pray where I come from." Or rather, it was how the followers of the Five Sisters prayed.

"I have studied all six of our provinces, and no one prays to the moon squatting."

"It's not the position, it's the—" Katin bit her explanation off. If she drew attention to her scarf of office, they might take it from her. "I have told you. We are not from one of the provinces. We are from the other side of the sea."

He lifted his chin. "Stand. The Apex Councilor has decided to hear what you have to say."

The Apex Councilor sat in a squat room, not at all grand, with a broad table in front of him. Yet even here, in the most utilitarian of chambers, great windows stood behind the councilor and cast light across his table. Stacks of paper crowded the surface in front of his aides, piled in neat right angles, every corner squared to the edge of the table.

On either side of the door stood guards with tall spears. Tassels hung from the shafts, making the weapons look almost ornamental, but the light that gleamed from the edges made it clear that these were honed and sharp. Their breastplates were painted with a lacquered rendition of the full moon, with silver rays blending into the metal of the armor. The velvet of their livery was a blue so deep as to be almost black. Tied around their upper arms were blue armbands, which appeared light only in contrast.

As Katin was brought into the room, the councilor shifted a pile of paper closer to himself. "You have been accused of being shy of an oxtail. How do you respond?"

"I do not know what an ox-tail is."

Silhouetted by the window, his face was not visible, but the sharp jerk of his head was unmistakable. "Do not toy with me."

"I am not! I have no understanding what you are speak of."

"Every citizen must have an oxtail to travel outside their city of birth."

"Perhaps that is the problem. I am not citizen. We are from Marth, across the sea."

The councilor broke into laughter at this. "Even if there were land across the sea, there is no way to navigate outside the light of the eternal moon. The fine for being without your oxtail is not so egregious that you must make up fairy stories."

"I am not! We have been trying explain since we got here that we are explorers from the other side of world. Where I come from, an ox-tail belongs firmly on an ox."

He cocked his head. "Are you saying 'ox-tail'?"

"Yes." Katin slowed down and tried to adjust her speech so it was more accurate. "That is what the man at the ship asked us for." Before he shot Lesid.

He uttered a noise that sounded as though he cursed. "You were supposed to have had language lessons."

"I did."

"From a historian. Your province speaks a particularly backward form of Setian." He rubbed his forehead. "Still, that might explain some of the confusion. You are saying 'ox-tail' but what I mean is 'oxtail.'"

Aside from a slight change in emphasis, Katin could hear no distinction. "What is the difference?"

"One is the tail of an ox. The other is a license to travel."

She gaped at him. Lesid had been shot . . . "One of my shipmates was killed because we couldn't understand what the man at the dock was saying."

"All provinces have the same requirements. You should have undertaken this before leaving your home."

Katin lost her temper and felt the touch of Dorot on her soul. "I told you. We are from across the ocean. We could not possibly have gotten an oxtail before leaving because we didn't know that there was such a thing. If you tell us where to go to get a license, I'm sure we'll all happily pay the fee."

One of the aides scribbled something on a piece of paper and passed it to the councilor. "I understand that you first disturbed the library with a prank." He studied it for a moment. "Why do you keep insisting on this fiction? Navigation is not possible out of the sight of the blessed moon."

"We navigate by the stars. Really, have you had no one else visit your shores?"

"Castaways from one of the lower islands." The councilor stroked his chin. "The stars move. How do you propose that one navigate by them?"

Katin faltered. She knew nothing of the subject beyond seeing the captain do it. "I . . . I am not certain."

"Because it cannot be done."

"No. Because I am not a navigator. If you were to ask our ship's husband, I am certain he could explain. I am here solely because I have some ability with your language."

"And to what do you attribute that?"

"It is related to our holy language. I am a priest and required to be versed in it."

With her words, something in the room changed. The councilor became very still. By the door, one of the guards shifted his hands on his spear.

The councilor leaned back in his chair slowly. "I will grant that you and your crew are not native speakers of Setish. That much of your story appears to be true. So it is possible that you mean something else by the word 'priest.'"

Katin reviewed what she had said and worried the inside of her lip. She had taken the word from Old Fretian, so perhaps the meaning had shifted. "I mean a holy woman, or man, dedicated to the service of the Five Sisters."

"Who?"

"The . . . the Five Sisters." She raised a hand to her scarf of office and held the beaded ends out to him. "Our holy book says that they came from across the ocean and we—"

"Are you saying that this is a *religion*?"

The sweat on Katin's hands clung to the scarf, adding to the dirt from the fifnight in the prison. She lowered it and wiped her palms on her leggings. "By my understanding of the word, yes, but the language may have changed."

"Do you worship these Five Sisters?"

"Yes."

"So brazen." The councilor barked a laugh. "Ironic that the most damning piece of evidence against you is the one that convinces me your story is true."

"I don't understand."

"Every year, the Council of Purity finds someone misled by one old cult or another and takes steps to correct the poor soul. These fools have turned their back on proper worship of the eternal moon and, knowing that it is wrong, they try to hide their depravity. Yet here you stand claiming allegiance to goddesses that no one has ever heard of as though there would be no consequences."

"They are not goddesses."

"So you deny it now?"

"No." Katin's voice was louder than she intended. "I merely wish to be clear. Goddesses are born that way, if one believes in such things. The Five Sisters came from here and shared their wisdom with the early Markuth people. It is said that they were elevated to the stars to continue to watch over us and guide us."

He waved his hand to dismiss her words. "You do not deny, though, that it is a religion."

"I do not." Katin licked her lips. "You spoke of consequences. What are those?"

"The moon is eternal and so we live by her light. Either accept that, or accept the absence of her light."

Laughter rose unbidden to Katin's lips. "Given that until a fifnight ago I had never seen the moon, I can easily accept the absence of her light."

Looking down, he made a mark upon the paper in front of him. "Place her in a cave. Then blind her."

"No!"

The councilor waved her away. "You are not to be trusted now. Of course you will profess to love the eternal moon, but you have already shown that you do not." As they led her from the room, the councilor spoke behind her. "Wait. Do not blind her yet. If she is the only one who speaks their language . . . It occurs to me that we should speak to this ship's husband. If they do come from out of the sight of the moon, then we should find this land and bring them into the light."

A torch flamed in an iron wall socket, lighting the crude underground passage. One of the guards held Katin's arms behind her as the other ran his hands over her body, searching for weapons. He focused his attention at her waist and sides, but when he found nothing tucked into her belt, he stepped back with a grunt. Neither man seemed to care about her scarf or notice the pockets sewn into her sleeves. She had a moment to realize that she'd seen no heavy sleeves here, before the guard thrust her into the cell. Katin stumbled over the threshold and nearly fell on the rough stone floor.

The guard smirked, face crazed in the dancing light. "Enjoy the dark."

The door slammed shut, dropping the cell into twilight. Katin waited for the darkness to descend.

Light trickled under the door and from a crack in the wall. It was not bright, but enough to make out the shape of the room. A small table with a chair stood by the wall. A cot stood opposite it. Her final piece of furnishing was a bucket to hold her waste.

The cave was nothing more than a windowless room.

Katin sank onto the bed and pulled the glowdisc out of her sleeve pocket. She turned the disc over in her hands without opening it. There was nothing she needed to see, but having the smooth surface under her hands helped her think.

Their ships ran dark. Windows everywhere. Crude torches . . . Had she seen a single artificial light besides the torch? No. With the light of the moon, they did not need anything except on cloudy nights.

And perhaps . . . perhaps they thought this *was* a dark room.

Regardless of what they thought, she needed to get out of here before they blinded her. Katin shuddered. The scriptures were full of stories of people being blinded, and she was suddenly certain she knew their origin.

On the small table, Katin had placed her glowdisc facing the door. The bedsheet hung from the rafters, to create a loose partition in the room. She held the bottom corner of the bedsheet in one hand, waiting until she heard the footsteps of her guard close to the room. Shaking the disc until the light reached its brightest, she tried to keep her breath steady.

Her glowdisc's silver-blue light slipped under the door into the hall. The guard's footsteps stopped outside.

"What in heaven's name?" His keys rattled.

Katin let the sheet fall in front of the glowdisc, to diffuse the light and make the source seem larger than it was, as if it were the Harvest Feast pageant. She leapt across the small room and grabbed the waste bucket by the door.

The keys scraped in the lock, and the door swung open. The guard gawked at the glowing sheet and took a step into the cell. His torch guttered as he crossed the threshold. Katin upended her bucket of waste on the torch, covering the smoking end with the metal. The guard cursed as the excrement and urine ran down his arm.

Katin swung the bucket hard, catching him across the side of his head. The guard stumbled forward and his feet tangled in the ties for her leggings. He staggered and fell into the cell. Katin dashed the bucket against his head again, and he lay still. Shuddering, she dropped the bucket. Moving as quickly as she could, Katin began to strip the guard of his clothes, wrinkling her nose at the stench of the waste bucket. As she rolled him over, her hand brushed the sheath by his side. He wore one of the hollow tubes.

Hesitating for only a moment, Katin unbuckled the belt that held the tube at his waist. It would surely be more useful than his uniform, if she could figure out how to work the weapon.

Katin kept her shoulders back and marched with as much authority as she could muster. She had needed to roll the cuffs of the guard uniform up, but it hid the worst of the staining, and in the shadows of the reflected moonlight she hoped it would pass. Though for all she knew, they had height restrictions on who could be a guard.

With her lower lip clenched in her teeth, she slipped into the building where her shipmates were held. The captain was not in good condition, but they needed to leave and this was likely their only chance. Katin approached the guard slouching by the window. It cast a beam of light across the corridor. Anyone approaching would be well visible.

The guard straightened upon seeing her and made a movement with his hand over his heart. A salute? A greeting?

Guessing, she hastily copied his movement, hoping it was even remotely appropriate.

"What can I do for you?"

Praying to Yorira for aid in the deception, Katin lowered her voice. "The foreigners." She had been rehearsing this phrase the entire way here, so it would roll off her tongue as if she were a native Setish speaker. "The Apex Councilor says they aren't worthy to see the light. Supposed to take them to the caves."

"Now? The eternal moon will be full in less than half an hour. You won't get them there before prayer time."

She shrugged, as if she didn't care. "Orders."

His frown deepened. "And by yourself? For twenty men?"

Before the guard could finish enumerating the reasons that this made no sense, Katin had the end of the tube pressed against his forehead. He choked off his words, going cross-eyed looking at the weapon. His swallow was audible in the stillness of the night.

"Is this clearer? Take me to the foreigners."

He held very still, which was fortunate, as she had no idea what to do with the weapon. Only the fact that one end was obviously a handle gave her even a hint of how to hold it. Reaching forward, she pulled his weapon from the sheath and tucked it into her belt.

His voice was steadier than hers would have been. "I could yell."

"I could kill you."

"The gunshot would call the other guards."

"So the outcome for me is the same either way, but very different for you." She pressed the tube against his head more firmly. "Stand. If you want a chance to live."

The guard wet his lips and let out a slow breath. He slowly rose and led her down the hall to where the crewmembers of the ship—no—to where her fellow countrymen were being held. Katin followed behind, with the weapon trained upon his back.

When they reached the cell, she rested the tip on his spine. "Unlock the door."

The guard reached for his keys. They unclipped from his belt and fell to the ground with a clatter. Katin scowled at him. That was clever. He had followed her instructions, but in such a way as it would force her to take the gun off his back to pick up the keys.

And this was where the Five Sisters' meditation exercises came in handy. Katin kept the weapon against his back as she reached forward with one foot. Sliding the keys toward her, she was able to scoop them off the floor with the toe of her boot as if she were practicing Dorot's stance. With her free hand, Katin gave them back. "Unlock the door."

The guard grimaced but did so, without attempting anything else.

When the door swung open, Katin gave him a shove forward. In the cell, the crew of her ship sat up, blinking in their beds. Tempting as it was to look to the captain, Katin kept her gaze on the guard. She spoke in her native tongue. "Someone secure him. Quietly."

One sailor stared at her in open disbelief for a moment, before yanking a rope made of torn sheets out of his cot's mattress. Where had the rope come from? In a matter of minutes, the guard was stripped of his uniform and trussed in the makeshift rope with a wad of cloth shoved in his mouth for a gag. The other crewmen scrambled into their clothes, pulling on boots and shirts in disciplined silence.

Now, Katin could take the time to look to Captain Stylian.

He stood by his bed, pulling on the guard's uniform. That morning he could barely sit and now, aside from a wince as he slipped the shirt on, it was as if his health had never been in question.

They had been planning an escape and had not told her. A knot of nausea twisted in her stomach. They had not trusted her because her people were from here. Clenching her jaw, Katin turned away from him and headed to the door.

A moment later, Stylian was by her side. He leaned down to breathe in her ear. "I give thanks to the Sisters that you are safe."

Katin shook her head. "You've been pretending to be sicker than you are."

"I kept hoping that they would take me out of the cell to a doctor, or bring a doctor here that we could use as a hostage."

"You didn't tell me."

"It seemed safer to pretend to everyone than to chance our captors guessing."

She snorted, just letting the air huff out of her nose softly. "You were ready to leave without me."

"We were ready to come find you." He laid two fingers on her wrist. "I wouldn't leave one of my crew behind."

At his words, her nausea eased. They were all fellow countrymen in this place. Katin handed the captain one of the weapons. "Thank you."

By the door, a sailor waved his hand, signaling that the hall was empty. They headed out into the moon's cold light.

With each turn, Katin expected them to be caught, but the shadows served them well. As the moon swelled to full, the cold silver light flooded the streets and houses. They were exposed when crossing the streets, but tucked under the eaves, in the shadows, they were nearly invisible.

The wind carried hints of salt air, and the captain straightened his head. Even without a nautical background, Katin's own stride quickened at the scent. The sea would carry her home.

The captain held up his hand, signaling a stop. He eyed the end of the street, where the harbor lay. He chewed his lip and straightened the guard's uniform. "I'm going to scout ahead in case they are waiting for us."

Katin whispered, "I can go."

"I can tell the state of the ship, and you won't know what to look for."

It was sensible, though she still wished he would not go. "Both of us? As if we are patrolling?"

He shifted his weight, looking again to the end of the street. "Agreed. It will look more natural with a pair, I think."

As they strode down the street toward the harbor, the captain rested his hand upon the hilt of the tube weapon. "Do you know how to work this?"

"No idea."

Ahead of them lay their ship, tied to the same dock they had first arrived at. Only a single guard waited at the foot of the gangplank.

The captain's breath eased out in relief. "Thank the Sisters. No one has noticed our absence yet."

Better than that, the guard lay on his back on a mat, with his face tilted up to face the moon in an attitude of prayer. Their arrival had coincided with the midnight moon reaching its full brightness. Though Katin and Stylian were exposed walking down the street, the guard would be night-blind from staring at the bright orb overhead.

Stylian turned briefly to wave the crew forward.

They responded instantly and hurried as one down the street to their ship. Katin quickened her own pace. When they hit the wood of the docks, their footsteps echoed against the houses behind them. The guard looked down from the moon.

He blinked, staggering to his feet. "Alarm!"

As his voice rose into the night, Katin recognized him—not a guard at all, but Proctor Veleh. Behind them, metal clattered as a half dozen soldiers appeared on the dock, cutting off their retreat.

Katin sprang forward and shoved the tube against the Proctor's chest. Her bluff had worked once; perhaps it would again. In Setish, she shouted, "Stop! Or the Proctor dies."

The soldiers slowed at the end of the pier, their weapons raised to point at the sailors. There were far more sailors than soldiers, but every single guard had one of these cursed tubes.

The proctor looked past her to the sailors and appeared to be counting their number. "I confess surprise. I had not thought to check the prison after your escape from the caves."

"Tell your soldiers to leave."

"No. You may shoot me if you like, but you shall not escape judgment under the blessed light of the eternal moon." Proctor Veleh looked down his nose at Katin.

"As long as we escape here, I'm fine taking my chance on judgment."

"Even if I stepped aside and let you aboard, what then? You are advocating a heresy, and the Apex Council will find you no matter where you go."

"We're from across the sea." The image of the moon sinking below the horizon gave her an idea. "If your ship follows us, our Five Sisters will drown the moon."

The Proctor laughed. "You think we do not know that our world is round? The moon does not drown if one goes too far east. She remains over the capital to provide her blessings upon our people."

Katin looked to the captain and switched back to her native language. "Ideas on what to do?"

"This?" Stylian pointed his weapon at the guards.

A tremendous flash and clap rang out in the night. The guards scattered, ducking behind barrels and poles, but none of them fell. The sound unleashed the sailors to fall upon the guards. More claps resounded through the night.

Yells, cries of pain, and a brimstone stench crowded against each other. Katin pushed the Proctor hard in the chest, and he stumbled back. His heel went out past the edge of the dock and he tumbled over.

"Move! Move!" Stylian bellowed, and like wharf rats, the sailors swarmed aboard the ship.

Scrambling and cursing, Katin hauled a wounded sailor up, throwing his arm over her shoulders. The others followed, leaving behind the bodies of the guards, but not their fellow shipmates.

As soon as the last one was aboard, Captain Stylian gave the order to cast off. Katin helped with the wounded, attempting to serve some purpose as they pulled away from the dock.

She glanced back once.

Proctor Veleh splashed in the water at the base of the dock. The blessed light of the moon shone upon him.

They sailed due east under full sail for hours. Katin stood with her hands tucked beneath her arms. Between her fingers she rolled the barrel of the weapon as if it were a prayer bead, begging each of the Sisters for aid in their escape.

The prayer was automatic, but the comfort did not follow. There was no safe place for her people. Not at home, not here.

The captain came to join her at the rail, still in his borrowed uniform. He sank down on a coil of rope with a groan.

Katin tore her gaze away from the waning moon. "Are you all right?"

"I may have lied a little about faking my illness."

She snorted and went back to watching the path behind them.

"Thinking about your Sisters' birthplace?"

She rolled the barrel another turn. "The Apex Councilor said that they would send ships after us."

"You mean the fellow at the dock? Even if they got a crew up and running as soon as he was out of the water, we've got a significant head start on them."

"No. His boss. And I don't mean just *us*, I mean Marth. I think they're going to invade. The map of the Center Kingdom had no borders. Remember? They've conquered the entire continent. Bringing everyone under the light of the eternal moon."

He pointed at the weapon in her hand. "With those . . . Maybe the Five Sisters led us here to give us warning."

Katin stared at him. "That's the third time you've spoken of the Sisters tonight. You don't have to act like you believe in them."

"To my surprise . . . I'm not. Not pretending, I mean." The captain pointed at the cluster of stars in the sky. "You told me that every story has some truth behind it. Finding the truth here . . . ? Makes me trust the parts I haven't seen the truth of yet. Feel like they must have been watching over us, you know?"

Katin followed his gaze up, to where the Sisters traveled their path across the heavens. The trail of stars behind them might even hold Lesid. Maybe the truth was that the Five Sisters had fled their homeland, or maybe they had been blown off course, or maybe they were guardians who looked over her people. *And the light of Musa lay behind them, casting silver across the sea.*

Brightest light in the darkness, it consumes all who enter. . . . Not all. She had passed through the light of the moon and returned.

The moon threw its silver light in a band across the sea, chasing her home.

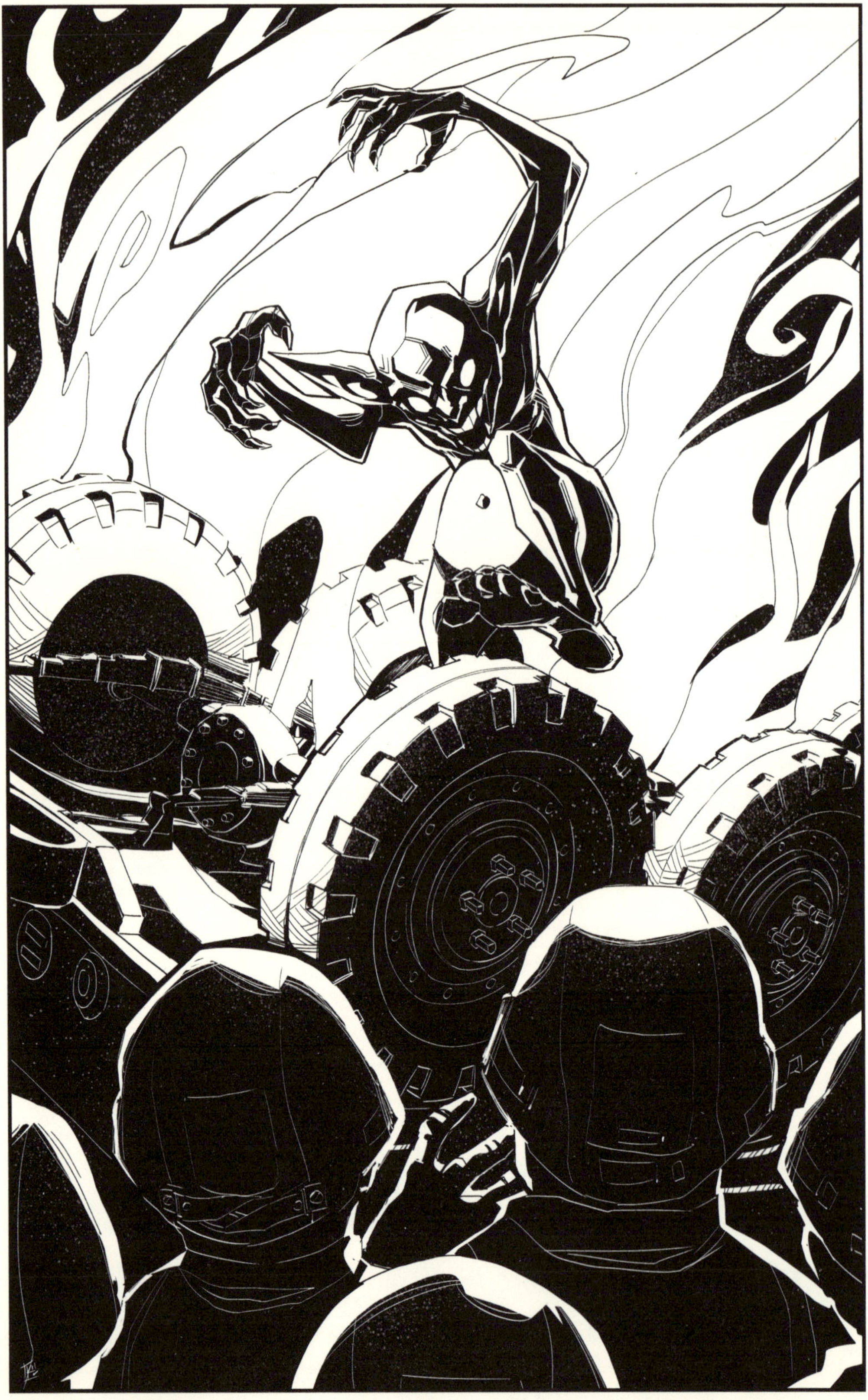

I. E. DEMON

DAN WELLS

They called it the BSE-7, but they didn't tell us what it stood for. We were just the EOD team, after all, and they were the engineers: they created the technology, and we had to test it. And that was fine; that was the way it had been since I'd been stationed in Afghanistan six months earlier, and that was the way it had been for years—for centuries—before that.

"What kind of test do you want?"

"The BSE-7 is an explosives nullification device," said the engineer. "We've installed it in a JERRV, and we need you to drive it through hostile territory and see if it works."

"'See if it works'?"

"If nothing blows up, it works," said the engineer. "We'll follow you with the best detection equipment we have, to see if we can find anything the BSE-7 nullifies."

"And how exactly does it 'nullify' IEDs?"

"I'm afraid you're not cleared for that information," said the engineer, so I kept a civil expression, got in the JERRV, and headed out into the desert with my driver and my gunner. We weren't cleared to know what we were driving, but we were cleared to drive it through Taliban Central hoping somebody tried to blow us up. The glamorous life of a soldier.

We were stationed in a firebase in what we called the Brambles: not only some of the worst terrain in Afghanistan, but famous for having the most IEDs per square mile of any region in the field of operations. I figured I'd be proud of that fact someday, if I lived long enough to brag about it in a bar, but for now it was a dubious accolade at best. Especially when it attracted the attentions of contractors trying to field-test their latest brain fart. It was far too dangerous to go outside the wire alone, so we joined a convoy; well, "joined." Seven MRAPs loaded for bear were heading north on a recon mission, and we were following on a nearby road, shorter but more likely to have IEDs. My team drove the modified JERRV, and the engineers followed behind in an MRAP of their own. If we got into any serious trouble, the convoy could reach us—theoretically—in just a few minutes. I hate relying on "theoretically."

The first IED turned up about an hour north of our firebase; we didn't notice anything, but the minesweeper behind us called an all-stop because their detectors had turned up a broken one—not so much broken, once we looked at it, as it was just built wrong from the beginning. Most IEDs are simple: two planks of wood separated by foam, with contact plates made of scrap metal, and an old lamp cord leading to a big yellow bucket of explosive. This one was one of the most poorly put together I'd ever seen; it looked like a broken clock in a Bugs Bunny cartoon, with wires and bits hanging off it in all directions. I told the two engineers I was sorry we hadn't found a real IED to test their device on, but they seemed just as excited with the broken one as you could possibly imagine, like it was the most thrilling damn thing dug out of the desert since King Tut. I rolled my eyes and got back in the JERRV, and my crew drove on through the Brambles for about twenty more minutes before the engineers called another all-stop. I got out to look at the new find.

"Useless," I told them, examining the new IED we'd driven over. "Better than the last one, but still hopelessly broken. The cord isn't even connected to anything."

"This is wonderful!" said the lead engineer.

"Two IEDs inside half an hour," I said gravely. "There's active insurgents in the area, no question."

"Grossly incompetent insurgents," said my driver.

"They only have to get lucky once," I said, but the engineers insisted we keep going, and my orders were to follow their orders, so I did. The third IED was only fifteen minutes down the road, and when I got out to examine it I didn't like what I saw.

"This one was live," I said, showing them the disassembled pieces. "We drove right over it, and it could have gone off, and as far as I can tell it should have gone off, but it didn't. I can't explain it."

"The insurgents' bomb guy is getting better," said my driver.

"Or our bomb-nullifier is getting worse," I said, looking at the engineers. "The BSE-7 is what's doing this, right? Whatever your little device is, it breaks the IEDs before they go off?"

"Correct," said the lead engineer.

"But it's not necessarily getting weaker," said the second engineer.

"He might be calibrating his power output to a sustainable level," said the lead engineer. "He doesn't need to destroy them like he did with the first two, just stop them like he did with this one."

I narrowed my eyes. "He?"

"It," said the first engineer. "I misspoke." He smiled, and the other engineer smiled, and I looked at my driver and I could tell he felt just as nervous as I did. I glanced at my gunner, perched in the turret and looking for trouble, and he gave me a thumbs-up. No Taliban in sight. I looked back at the engineers.

"So what happens on the next one?" I asked. "Is it calibrating its energy, or running out of it?"

"We won't know until we get more data."

"Another IED," I said.

"Correct."

"Which will either break, like these did, or blow up my JERRV."

"Correct," he said again. "But it's up-armored, so you should be fine. None of these bombs we've examined has been big enough to kill you."

I had a lot less faith in the armor than they did, and a lot more faith in the armor than in the BSE-7, but orders were orders, and when I radioed back to the firebase they agreed with the engineers. This test, and this device, were too crucial to give up halfway. I hung up the radio, shrugged my shoulders, and shook my driver's hand. "Alpha Mike Foxtrot," I said. "It's been nice to know you."

The fourth IED exploded.

It wasn't a big explosion—it didn't tear the JERRV in half, so the armor did its job—but it flipped us upside down off the side of the road. My gunner managed to duck down into the turret before the roll crushed him, and we were rattled and bruised but alive, and thanks to endless days of crash drills we managed to get all three of us out of the vehicle in just a few seconds. We came up just in time to see a wrinkly green three-year-old beating the living hell out of the engineers' truck, and I want to be as clear as possible about this so there's no misunderstanding: when I say the living hell, I mean the living, breathing, ever-loving hell. He was remarkably spry, that three-year-old, naked as can be and jumping around that truck like he was on springs, and everywhere he touched it the truck fell apart—not just fell apart, *burst* apart. Two quick leaps took him from the ground to the fender to the top of the grill, and the fender fell off before his toes even touched down on the hood. He reached out with one hand and grabbed the headlight, and somehow both headlights exploded—not just the one he touched, but both of them simultaneously, like New Year's Eve firecrackers packed with chrome and broken glass. The latch on the hood failed suddenly, spectacularly, launching the little green something in the air while below him the now-exposed engine erupted in a modern dance exhibition of bursting caps and hoses, each cylinder and compartment blowing off more steam than they could possibly have been holding, *pop pop pop* one after another like gunshots. The windshield cracked as the green thing sailed over it, and all I could see inside were the two engineers digging through their packs like madmen, their faces white with fear.

My crew and I ran toward them, racing to help, and as I ran I raised my rifle to fire at the little green thing dancing madly on the roof. The trigger fell off in my hand, and then the stock, and then the entire gun seemed to field strip itself in a cascade of oily gunmetal. The bullets spat and jumped on the ground like popcorn, their charges exploding impossibly in the dry dirt of the Brambles. My driver reached the truck's door and yanked on the handle; I expected the handle to come off, but was surprised to see the entire door come flying off, knocking my driver flat on his back as the sudden shift in weight unbalanced him. My gunner tried the lead engineer's seatbelt, but it was jammed too tight to move. The little green man was dancing on the roof now, metal cracking and warping and rusting with each wrinkly footstep. I tried to open the other door and pull the engineers to safety (the door didn't come off, just peeled away in long, corroded strips), but as scared as they were they refused to leave without their bags.

"Just get out!" I said. Springs were bursting out of the seats like twisted daggers, sending puffs of upholstery wafting through the chaos like fat foam snowflakes.

"We need MREs!"

"What?" Somehow, despite the crazy green weirdo destroying the truck—or maybe because of it—this was the last thing I'd ever expected them to say.

"We need the MREs," they continued, scouring madly through their bags. "It's the only way to stop it!"

"To stop the . . . green guy?" He was chewing on the ceiling now, literally tearing into it with his teeth and ripping out chunks of metal, cackling like a madman.

"Just help us!"

"You can look for them outside," I said, and hauled the engineers out by anything I could reach, shoulders and necks and arms, throwing the men in the dirt and tossing their heavy packs on the ground beside them. My belt came apart as I worked, the buckle bending nearly in half like someone was crushing it with invisible pliers, and the vehicle bucked wildly as the tires exploded in a string of deafening bursts. I went for my sidearm, drawing on the wrinkly green man at close range, but the rack slid off like it wasn't even attached, and the bullets sprayed up out of the magazine like a bubbling metal fountain.

"This one caught shrapnel in his neck during that last burst," my driver shouted, looking at the second engineer, but the lead engineer drowned him out with cries of "MREs! Find the MREs, as many as you can!" He was already tearing open a plastic bag, dumping the interior pouches in the dirt and fumbling for one in particular. I turned to the wounded engineer and found a twisted chunk of truck frame lodged in his neck. He was already dead.

"We need to get out of here!" I shouted.

"I found one!" cried the lead engineer, and he tore open the smallest pouch from the MRE, the salt, and threw a pinch of the stuff at the wrinkly green thing still tearing the truck to pieces. When the salt hit him the green man screamed, leaped off the truck, and scampered behind a boulder.

I stared in surprise, my eyes wide. I still didn't know what was going on, but I didn't need another demonstration to convince me. "We need more salt," I said, and turned to the group with a shout. "Find more MREs!" Soon all of us were tearing open pouches of food, searching for the little packets of salt, and the engineer led us back to the flipped JERRV and directed us to dump the salt in a circle around it. We had barely enough to complete a thin, scattered border before the wrinkly green thing charged us in a rage, howling and brandishing a jagged tailpipe. When he came within a few feet of the salt circle his howl turned to a scream of fear, and he retreated again to the demolished truck, smashing it with wicked glee.

My breath came in gasps. "What," I asked, "in the bright blue hell, is that thing?"

"It's a BSE," said the engineer, collapsing to the ground and leaning back against the JERRV. "Though it isn't really bound anymore, so it's just an SE. A supernatural entity: lambda-class demon, minor manifestation."

"Minor?"

"It's a gremlin," he said. "They destroy technology. Made them a bitch to study in the lab."

I had no idea what to think, and my mouth seemed incapable of forming any words beyond the first aborted syllables of sentences: "To— I—" I shook my head. "What?"

"That creature is the power source for the BSE-7," said the engineer. "A Bound Supernatural Entity. The 7 refers to a gremlin, maliciously eager to destroy anything technological it comes across."

"And you strapped it to my truck?"

"It was bound," he said quickly. "Its energies were directed, like a . . . like a shaped explosive. All the tech-breaking power is pointed out and down, so anything you drive over, like a landmine or an IED, gets broken before it can do anything to hurt you. It can't do anything to your own vehicle—unless, obviously, the binding breaks and it gets loose." He gestured feebly at the truck, which the gremlin was now gleefully disemboweling.

"That thing came after us," said the driver. "Unless one of you's a robot and didn't tell me, I don't think it limits its destruction to technological devices."

"Case in point," said the gunner, "your dead friend over there."

"Now you understand why we needed to find the salt as quickly as possible," said the engineer. "The salt will hold it, though, as long as nothing breaks the circle."

"So we're safe here until the next stiff breeze," I said, "or until we starve to death, whichever comes first."

"We've got plenty of MREs," said the driver.

"I think I'd prefer to starve," said the gunner.

"There's got to be a way to kill it," I said. "Our guns fell apart, but the knife didn't—maybe that's too simple a machine to be affected?"

"You can't kill a demon," said the engineer. "Trust us on this one. You can only bind it."

"Exactly what kind of engineer are you?" I asked.

He didn't answer.

"And we can't forget the Taliban," said my driver. "This is the fourth IED we've run across in the last hour. There's a group here, and they're active, and they're doing something they don't want anyone to see. And after all the noise our gremlin's been making, they're going to know we're here."

I turned to the engineer. "Can we use the radio with that thing's . . . anti-technology field ruining everything?"

"Anything inside the salt circle should work fine."

"Get it working," I told my driver. "Tell the convoy where we are, and that we've been hit with an IED. Leave the . . . weirder details vague." He saluted and climbed in through the window of the overturned vehicle. I looked at the engineer. "Now: tell me everything you know about this gremlin."

"It would probably be easier to just read the manual."

"You have a manual for a gremlin?"

"The BSE-7 is intended for field use," he said. "We have a Dash-10 operator's manual already printed, though it's obviously just a prototype." He pulled a slim paper booklet from his backpack and handed it to me.

"'BSE-7 Vehicle-Mounted Anti-Explosive Device,'" I read. "'The BSE-7 is powered by a lambda-class demon, commonly called a gremlin. It is designed to be mounted under . . .'" I skipped ahead, leafing past the usage sections to the fifth chapter: Maintenance. "'If the device fails and the supernatural entity becomes unbound, it can be held at bay with salt.' Which we've done. 'Salt can be found in every MRE, and should be easy to come by, even in the field. Your first action should be to contain the demon in a circle of salt, as an unbound gremlin inside a base or camp can be surprisingly destructive.'" I threw the manual down. "It says our first action should be to contain the demon, you idiot, not us."

"The manual makes that sound a lot easier than it is."

"They always do." I picked up the booklet, found the same page again, and continued reading. "'With the demon neutralized in a salt circle, report the malfunction immediately to your assigned demonologist.' We have an assigned demonologist?"

"They're still in training," said the engineer, "with plans to deploy just before the BSEs go into general use. We'd never send a demon into the field without a trained demonologist to wrangle it."

"Which means you wouldn't test it without one, either," I said, and looked at the corpse of the dead engineer. "Is that him?"

The living engineer shrugged helplessly. "There's a chapter on troubleshooting," he said meekly.

I looked up at the gremlin, still loudly tearing the truck to pieces. "If it causes trouble, we shoot it?"

"I don't recommend it."

"We have an RPG-7 in the JERRV," said the gunner. "Took it off some Taliban last week."

"I really don't recommend it," the engineer insisted. "Any weapon you use against it will fail as soon as it leaves the salt circle, and I don't think I have to tell you what happens when a rocket-propelled grenade fails."

"It was just a suggestion," said the gunner.

"'Chapter 6,'" I read, "'Troubleshooting. If you have no access to a demonologist, your first priority is to reinforce the salt circle containing the demon and requisition a new demonologist immediately.' Thanks, that's very helpful. 'If you absolutely must attempt to control the demon without a trained expert, there are some tricks that may be useful. One: gremlins love sugar.' Seriously?"

"Absolutely love it," said the engineer.

"Huh. 'Two: the binding agent on the BSE-7, unless completely destroyed, can be used again, with the understanding that damaged binding agents are prone to unexpected catastrophic failure.'"

"Take a picture of him eating the truck," said the driver, crawling back out of the JERRV. "You can put the photo in the manual as a demonstration of 'unexpected catastrophic failure.'"

"Did the radio work?" I asked him.

"Well enough. The good news is, the insurgents in this area won't be coming after us, because they're engaged in a firefight with our convoy."

"And the bad news," I said, "is that our convoy can't come get us because they're engaged in a firefight with insurgents."

"Exactamundo. And so far they're losing, so they might not come get us at all. It's a very big group of insurgents."

I stood up and looked at the JERRV's blackened undercarriage. "So we're on our own, in enemy territory, under direct assault by a demon, and the only thing we can use to stop it is that thing." I pointed at the shattered BSE-7, a charred lump that looked like a pie plate. It had been torn open, and the inside was full of something dark and sticky.

"Smells sweet," said the gunner.

"They like sugar," said the engineer with a shrug.

"So it *is* a pie plate." I leaned in and smelled it. "Smells like . . . strawberry jam."

"That gremlin's almost three feet tall," said the gunner. "If he was crammed inside that tiny thing, it's no wonder he's pissed."

"That goop—which, yes, probably contains strawberry jam—is an arcane demon-binding agent," said the lead engineer. "Once he's bound into it, the physical space doesn't really matter; you could bind him into a teaspoon, and that's all the space you'd need. The majority of the BSE-7 is made up of the shaping agents that direct the gremlin's power away from the vehicle."

"How do we get it back in?"

"The manual explains it in detail," said the engineer, "but the basic gist is fire and blood."

"That's horrible."

"It's a demon," he said. "What did you expect?"

I sat down again, a plan slowly forming in my head. "What kind of grenades do we have for the captured RPG?"

"PG-2s," said the gunner. "Old Soviet stuff."

"You really don't want to shoot him," said the lead engineer.

"Sure I do," I told him, skimming through the section on demon binding. It was far more gruesome than expected. "Just not in the way you think." I turned to the gunner. "Get me a grenade; take off the casing." I told the driver to get a fire going, and last I pointed at the engineer. "One of those MREs we dumped out looking for salt was spaghetti, which means that somewhere out there is a pouch full of cherry cobbler. Go get it."

"Outside of the circle?"

"Unless you brought it with you, yeah."

"But . . . there's a gremlin out there."

"There's *your* gremlin out there," I said, "so anything it does to you, you probably deserve. Don't be scared, though, I'm coming with you—I'll get the body, you get the cobbler."

"Why do you need the body?"

"Have you read the demon binding manual?"

His face went pale. "Cobbler. Check."

I took a pinch of salt from the edge of the circle, careful not to break it completely, and on three we ran, me for the dead man and the engineer for the pile of scattered MRE pouches. The gremlin ignored us at first, too busy trashing the truck, but as I dragged the body back toward the JERRV he finally noticed us and leaped toward the engineer with a cry of malicious joy. I threw the dead body into the circle and ran back toward the engineer, still scrambling on his hands and knees for the cherry cobbler. I threw the salt at the gremlin, buying us a few precious seconds, and together we found the pouch of cobbler and ran back to the JERRV. The engineer's shirt pocket was stained dark blue, and his pants and belt were singed.

"All my pens broke," he said sadly, gesturing at the stains.

"And the burn marks?"

"My phone caught fire."

I tore open the cobbler pack, reached out past the salt, and placed it on the ground. The gremlin snarled at us, furious that we'd gotten away a second time, but soon he paused, sniffed the air, and crept closer. He looked at the cobbler, then at the salt, then at us. He sniffed again and took another step. A few moments later he was sitting by the open dessert pouch, his hands and face smeared with thick red syrup as he munched happily on the cherries.

"That's the weirdest damn thing I've ever seen," said the gunner.

"You got my grenade?"

"Here." He handed me a PG-2, basically a metal tube with a short, stubby metal cone on the end. He'd removed the tapered endpiece, exposing a cone of explosives inside, and I set that part down far away from the fire. The empty endpiece I filled with binding agent from the BSE-7, scooping it out with the flat of my knife, and then I sat back, looking at the others.

"This is going to get gross."

They nodded, eyes grim. I took a deep breath, propped open the demon's Dash-10 manual with a rock, and proceeded to perform unspeakably horrible acts on the body of the dead engineer. The lead engineer fainted twice before the ritual was done, and I admit that I was pretty woozy as well—from disgust rather than blood loss, since I only needed a couple of drops of my own. With the bloody symbols drawn on the sides of the grenade, and the endpiece thoroughly smeared with newly reinforced binding goop, I took a deep breath, said a quick prayer (apologizing, as I did, for dabbling in demonology), and tossed the endpiece out past the salt and into the gremlin's half-finished cobbler. The Dash-10 included a handy pronunciation guide for the incantation, and as I recited the words the gremlin was sucked into the binding agent like a genie going into a bottle.

"I take it back," said the gunner. "*That* is the weirdest damn thing I've ever seen."

"Reassemble the grenade," I said, and handed him the gently smoking endpiece. He looked at it, then at the exposed explosives of the grenade, and shook his head.

"You want me to attach a 'make things break' demon to a high-explosive warhead? I'm not convinced that this is the smartest thing either of us has ever done."

"Just fit it on," I said. "This fresh, it'll hold for a couple of hours without any trouble."

The engineer was awake again. "What now?" he asked.

"Now we shoot him."

He frowned, confused, and I smiled.

"Now we shoot him *at the insurgents.*"

The Taliban were still attacking our convoy, and we were only about five klicks away; with the gremlin no longer wreaking havoc on the truck we could hear the occasional burst of gunfire. The gunner finished reassembling the grenade, and we packed as much gear as we could before running back through the desert. The Afghanistan hills were steep and rocky under any circumstances, and even more so here in the Brambles; our travel was slow, but the engineer kept up more admirably than I expected. We made it to a low ridge after barely twenty minutes of running. We didn't have a perfect view of the battle, but we could tell the insurgents were winning—they had mortars, snipers, good cover, and higher ground than our guys, who were essentially pinned down behind the smoking wreckage of their vehicles. It was the biggest group of insurgents I'd ever seen, and there was no backup in sight; well, none but us. I loaded the Rocket-Propelled Gremlin in the launch tube and handed it to the gunner.

"Don't worry about a target," I said, "just land the little bastard in the middle of their gun line and let him go to work."

The gunner judged the distance carefully, tested the wind, aimed high for extra range. "Alpha Mike Foxtrot," he whispered, and pulled the trigger.

The grenade sailed over the valley, trailing smoke in a fierce, straight line, and exploded in a giant ball of fire against the back of a Taliban jeep. One by one we watched as the distant insurgents stopped firing forward and turned to look at their own battle line, at the clouds of dust and oil that flew up first in one place and then another. We were too far away to see the gremlin himself, but we could track his progress easily, watching as a truck fell to pieces, as a mounted machine gun sloughed parts like a crumbling cookie, as a mortar misfired and exploded on the ground. A few of the Taliban tried to fight it, but others simply ran in terror, some toward us and some toward our convoy. No longer pinned down by fire, our friendly forces caught them easily. We zip-tied their thumbs, frisked them for weapons, and started the slow walk around the frenzied gremlin toward our convoy.

"There's enough machinery in that insurgent battle line to keep him busy for a week," I said. "You'd better get another demonologist in by then, because if I have to do another binding ritual I'm using you for parts."

"I'll put in a call the instant we get back to base."

"Good," I said. "Now tell me something else: this gremlin was the BSE-7?"

"Correct."

"So there are at least six other Bound Supernatural Entities being developed for field use?"

"Eleven, actually." The engineer smiled. "How would you like to perform another test next week?"

○REC

An Honest Death

HOWARD TAYLER

The chirp in my earbud means that Sinclair Wollreich has pushed the panic button in his office. I slide my sidearm clear of its shoulder holster and point it at the floor in front of me in less than a second. Barry and Mohammed have theirs out and down as well, and the three of us run for the office door. I nod at Barry, who grabs the handle and pulls the door open, stepping back as Mo and I sweep straight into the room.

In and to the left. My side is clear.

"Clear," says Mo, and I reply, "Clear!"

Barry swings in behind us, a third set of eyes on a room that is empty except for our boss.

Mr. Wollreich looks pale, like he's seen a ghost, or maybe just jumped back onto the curb after being missed by a bus. Other than that he looks fine—middle-aged, and a little soft, but dressed to the nines in a suit that costs more than my car.

"What is it, sir?" I ask.

"It's . . ." He glances around, still wearing that I-dodged-a-bullet-but-maybe-there's-another-one-coming look. Then he turns and looks me in the eye, and for only the third time in the eighteen months I've worked for him, he lies to me. "It's nothing, Cole. Just a drill."

Mo mouths the word "inconceivable," quoting *The Princess Bride* in order to stifle a stream of blasphemy.

"Yes, sir," I say. "Let's finish like it's the real thing, then. Mo, take the corners. Barry, window. I'll check the desk."

"Cole," Wollreich addresses me again, "It's okay. I just wanted to see how quickly you guys could get here. I think you took four seconds."

Liar. Also, that was seven seconds at least. I don't know what he's hiding, but my brain is already spinning scenarios. Something scared him, something he thought we could protect him from, but by the time we arrived it was gone. Or maybe it had never been here. Maybe Sinclair Wollreich hallucinated something frightening, and is now covering up for that hallucination. That . . . that makes a lot of sense. He doesn't strike me as the hallucinating type, but he is the head of a pharmaceutical company, so maybe he's on something.

Regardless, he pushed the panic button, and that means I don't get to stand down until I'm sure he's safe. He lied to me, very uncharacteristically, and that worries me.

"Sorry, sir. You're feigning duress pretty effectively. We have to finish the sweep, and put our eyes on everything."

Barry looks at me from behind Wollreich, and I nod. *Eyes on everything* is his cue for some impromptu misdirection. He holsters his weapon, pulls a chair over to the window, and steps onto it as if to check the upper frame. He balances poorly—deliberately poorly—and begins to fall.

"Oops, watch out!" he says as he corrects and jumps clear of the tipping chair.

Wollreich turns, and also steps clear.

Mo, in the far corner of the room, reaches up and sticks a cam-dot on the spot where the molding joins the ceiling, a position where it can see the entire room while remaining almost invisible.

By design, Wollreich's office has no cameras in it. I objected to this on general principles a year and a half ago, but backed down. Now it does have a camera in it. Just because I backed down doesn't mean I didn't plan for contingencies.

"First day in the new shoes, Barry?" asks Mo.

"Actually it's the fourth day, but I'm trying new inserts today and I don't think I like them."

"Secure the chatter, guys," I say. Part of the act.

"It's okay, it's okay," says Wollreich. His face has returned to normal. "The way you came through that door, you startled me even though I knew you were coming. You guys looked like you were straight out of an action movie—one of the good ones where they get everything right."

"They never get everything right, sir," I say. "But thank you."

"No, thank you, Cole. It's apparent that I'm not paying you or your team enough. I think a fifteen percent raise is in order. I'll send word to HR."

That wasn't a lie. That was him committing to the earlier lie with a bribe, which means, if I'm reading him correctly, that he knows I know he lied, and he wants to talk to me in private about why he really pushed the button.

"Thank you, sir," I say.

"Very generous, sir. Sorry about the chair thing," says Barry.

"I'll make sure Barry spends his bonus on better inserts," says Mo.

"We'll leave you to your business, sir." And we do.

Out in the anteroom, which does have cameras, I screen Mo as he sits down at the edge of the camera's field of vision and reaches around and under the chair. The receiver he plants against the wall looks exactly like a wall plate.

I check my phone's Bluetooth list, and "GENERIC HEADSET" appears. I select it and punch in my phone number, and it vanishes from the list. Just like it's supposed to.

That afternoon, Wollreich calls me into his office.

"Sir?" I ask.

"Take a seat, Cole," Wollreich says.

I sit, and wait for Wollreich to speak.

"You know that wasn't just a drill earlier?"

"Yes, sir. Something scared you. What was it?"

"Probably a hallucination. There was somebody in my office. I looked up, sensing movement I guess, and then hit the panic button when I didn't recognize the intruder. I think he was about to speak, but as soon as I hit the panic button he vanished."

"Vanished how, sir?"

"Like a screen wipe." Wollreich is describing a PowerPoint transition. I know exactly what that looks like, having been a captive audience for more than a few of them. "Except," he continues after a moment, "there was some dissolve to it as well. As if, from top to bottom, the intruder evaporated. Only faster than that."

He's not lying.

I'm not sure exactly how I know he's not lying, but I think it's kind of like how some people always know where there's a speed trap. There are cues out there to be read, but I'm reading them unconsciously. It's not a hundred percent accurate at first, but once I've spent enough time with somebody I'm never wrong.

"I believe you, sir."

"You believe it happened, or you believe that I saw what I'm telling you I saw?"

"I believe your account of the event, sir. You're not making this up.

I suspect you're also concerned. Concerned for your own sanity, and for your position here with the company."

He blows out the breath he'd been half holding.

"There's more to it than that, Cole. I'm concerned that this may be a side effect. How much have you been told about our upcoming product lines?"

"We're approaching the approval phase of a 'vaccination' against Alzheimer's, we're in late-stage testing on a telomerase regulator that promises to prevent a large percentage of cancers, and we've just gotten approval for an HIV treatment."

"Very succinct."

"That's a summary of what I've been told, sir. I can tell there's something else going on, and that I'm not supposed to be in on the secret."

He sits back in his chair, steeples his fingers, and purses his lips. "So, what have you figured out?"

"Nothing, sir. And if you're about to let me in on the secret, please keep in mind that if the information is valuable enough, a competitor may be willing to kill to get it. You're paying me and my team quite well, but if you're sitting on a billion dollars' worth of information, my threat assessment will change, we'll have to hire more people, and everybody will get paid more."

"So be it. Cole, the drug interaction between these three products is going to extend human lifespan, maybe by a full order of magnitude. Old-age deterioration is going to go away. You and I will live to see the twenty-second century, and I'm not betting against seeing the thirtieth."

I think about that for a moment. If this is true . . .

"Sir, are you sure this works?"

"Quite sure. We've got a lab full of eight-year-old white mice, and we're three years into some secret trials on in-house volunteers. Including me. I've never felt better, and my eyesight has improved as the lenses in my eyes regained their youthful flexibility."

"Obviously this secret is worth way more than just a billion dollars."

"There's more. We've got a brain trust positioning the company for the long game. We already know what the short-term future looks like. When the news breaks that this three-drug interaction extends the human lifespan, the entire product line will be nationalized by overwhelming popular demand, probably in a special legislative session. But before the United States does that, half a dozen other countries will already have deployed it within their national health care systems. We won't own any of it."

I nod. As predictions go, this makes perfect sense. There might be some small variations, but the end result sounds spot on.

"So," he continues, "the only way for us to make money is for us to be pre-positioned in other fields. That team is preparing us to capitalize on the disruptions introduced by an order-of-magnitude increase in human longevity."

"Oh, I get it. You're not planning to get rich selling immortality. You're going to get rich helping the human race make the transition to immortality."

"How valuable do you think this secret is?"

"In numbers? I can't count that high. You don't need to be protected from competitors. You need to secure yourself against governments. They'll break all their own laws and empty their treasuries to control this, if they think they can."

"Exactly."

I shake my head sadly. "Sir, my team is good, but if a sovereign state decides to pull a hostile takeover, the only thing we can do for you is shoot you before they have a chance to begin interrogating, and they'll probably just take us down before we see them coming. You need an army, and a bunker."

"Those aren't realistic options."

"Oh, I know that. I'm already contemplating expanded perimeters, plainclothes agents, dead-man-switch alarms. And of course I'm even more concerned about why you pushed the panic button."

"Yes . . . about that. The intruder . . . I never described him to you."

"I figured you'd get around to it."

"It was Death."

I went into the Marines when I was eighteen, bright-eyed, broad-shouldered, and ready to save the world. Most of that idealism got sanded flat in Afghanistan, but in the intervening twenty years I've determined that I don't need to save the world. I just need to save good people. I started my own firm so I could be picky about my clients, and Sinclair Wollreich is the best man I've ever worked for.

Which is why I'm aching inside. The bug in Wollreich's office is a betrayal of trust, and I know that. He came clean with me, and I didn't come clean with him. I could have told him about the bug, but I didn't.

I did, however, get him to agree to a physical the next day.

I don't know how you go about testing to see if someone is prone to hallucinating, or if something's going wrong with their brain, but Tuesday morning's checkup runs into Wednesday with no breaks. We've had eyes on Wollreich ever since he briefed me, and that's meant double shifts. Triple for me. It's proving to be a bit of a strain.

It's six A.M. on Wednesday. Barry has just checked in to let me know Wollreich is sleeping in today. Sleeping in sounds nice, but personal security for our CEO now means securing where he's going to be, not just where he is.

Mo and I are in the second-floor lobby having coffee with two other team members, Failalo and Jace. We've got a nice view of the buildings that stand between us and the sunrise. We're not really securing anything right now, to be honest. We're hoping the sunlight will perk us up a bit.

"How long are we going to keep doing this, Cole?" asks Failalo. She's soft-spoken, but nobody shortens her name to "Fail" more than once.

"The extra shifts? Until HR and I can clear some more team members."

Mo sips at his coffee. "What's the holdup?"

"Well, if the event in Wollreich's office was enemy action, probative or otherwise, then we're up against somebody connected and equipped."

I've told my team that our boss saw an intruder, all in black, who then vanished. Mo's theory is that it was a hologram made with lasers, but none of us have the background to research that. I didn't tell them about the immortality drugs, or that our boss thinks he saw Death. And only Mo and Barry know about the camera we planted.

"Oh, I get it," says Failalo. "You think we're being played. Somebody's planted their own people among our candidates. They shoot some lasers through the window to spook us, we beef up, and now they've got peeps on the inside."

"That's one scenario. They might also have our hiring pool bugged, tapped, and flagged on their end, so they can watch our background check process and find the holes in it. So yes, I'm concerned that somebody yanked our chain, and now we're reacting instead of acting."

"Don't go *Princess Bride* paranoid, boss," says Mo. "Both cups might be poisoned." He tosses back his coffee, swallows, then smiles broadly at me. "And there aren't enough of us for a land war in Asia."

I've always loved that scene. I used to imagine how I would have handled things if I'd been in Vizzini's shoes, and it was fun until I finally figured out that he'd been outplayed from the start. If Westley didn't kill him, Humperdinck certainly would have.

My phone chirps. It's a text message from the phony wall plate, an alert to let me know the feed is active. The camera has seen something. The message looks innocent enough: SUP YO. GO 4 EATZ?

Mo's smile flattens. "Somebody miss breakfast?" He knows the codes.

"Upstairs, now. Mo, you're with me in the service elevator. Failalo, Jace, take a lobby elevator to thirty-one, then take the west stairs to forty." I drop a ten on our table to take care of the barista who usually doesn't have to clean up after us.

On our way to the elevator, Mo places a call. "Hey, Sal. Mohammed here. Check electrical and find out if the lights just went on in Wollreich's office."

Good thinking. Building security may not have cameras in Wollreich's office, but there is a motion detector on his light switch, and the company monitors usage for conservation purposes.

"Got it. Thanks." He turns to me as we reach the elevator. "Lights just went on. They're still out in the anteroom and the west hallway. Whoever turned on the office lights didn't walk in the usual way. Also, the cameras on the rest of the floor haven't seen anybody since Wollreich left with Barry at three A.M."

I key the elevator for a nonstop ride. The illuminated numbers count up quickly. Mo and I are silent, but we're both listening.

At forty the elevator doors slide open. That motion sets off the detectors, and the hallway lights come up.

Mo moves to step out, but I stop him. Somebody got onto this floor and into Wollreich's office, and we know nothing about them. They got here first, and might be expecting us. Maybe they spoofed the cameras and the motion detectors, but we can't. Anywhere we go the lights will come up, so we can't be stealthy.

Then again, whoever spooked Wollreich the first time vanished pretty quickly, perhaps because they were afraid of us. If we're slow we'll miss them, and if they're afraid of us, that might mean we've got them outgunned.

Or maybe both cups are poisoned. Ah, Vizzini, how I hate being you. Just once I want to be the guy with the iocaine immunity and the winning plan.

"We go fast. Straight to the office, then standard entry."

Mo nods, and we both draw and begin to run, weapons held low in two-handed grips. We run through two hallway intersections without clearing them properly, and each time I worry that I'm being a reckless idiot. But nobody shoots at us, and those intersections light up to the north and south, so nobody else came that way recently.

We reach the office. Through the frosted glass the anteroom is dark. Not full dark, thanks to west-facing windows, but it's oh six fifteen. I hear a soft *tick* as the lock pad reads my badge and unlocks the anteroom door.

I'm in first, pushing the door open and sweeping with it to the left as the lights come up.

"Clear," says Mo.

"Clear."

"*Ting*," says my phone. Bluetooth connection, with data streaming in. We can look at that later.

I key in my code for the door to Wollreich's office. No frosted glass here, and the door is soundproof. No way to know what's on the other side.

Tick. I grab the handle and push the door open, sweeping left while Mo goes to the right in the brightly lit office.

"Clear," says Mo.

"And empty," I say. Not that I expected to find anybody here, not really.

Mo steps to the corner of the room where our cam dot should be. "It's still there."

"I'm pretty sure there's no point sweeping the rest of the floor." I holster my weapon. "Let's see if the camera saw anything."

I pull out my phone. Swipe, code, and then a tap on the spy app, whose icon looks like the one for a pizza place. I respond to the ZIP CODE prompt with an eleven-digit passcode, and up comes the video file. PLAY.

The video begins with the room lit only by the brightening sky through the windows. Then a human-size shadow dissolve-wipes into existence in the middle of the room, backlit by those windows so I can't make out any details the moment it appears, but the lights come up very quickly.

"Holy shit," says Mo.

Hooded and all in black, the stereotypical, iconic representation of Death, complete with a scythe, stands in the middle of the office and turns to face the camera.

We've got my phone casting video to the wall screen by the time Mr. Wollreich arrives in his office with Barry on his heels. Wollreich is flushed, there are bags under his eyes, and he's angry. Barry has all the expression of a granite bust, which means Wollreich has been chewing him out on the way over here.

"Cole, how long have you been spying on me?"

"Since Monday morning, sir. I'm sorry, but it seemed prudent."

"Prudent? After the lecture you gave me about the value of secrets? Spying on me is a lot of things, but prudent is not one of them."

"With all due respect, sir, you called us in a panic, then lied to us. I made a snap decision in order to ensure that my team and I could keep you safe."

"How come you didn't tell me about it later?"

"Guilty conscience, sir. But I think you should watch this before we continue to discuss the matter."

"Fine."

I push PLAY, and Death appears onscreen.

Wollreich gasps. "That's him. Hot damn, Cole, you got him!"

I push PAUSE.

"We did, sir, but he's about to start talking, and he talks fast. You really need to listen to this."

Wollreich nods, and I push PLAY.

Death is facing the camera, and begins to speak.

"Sinclair Wollreich and . . . friends," he begins. The voice is deep, so it sounds masculine, but it's almost musically artificial, like somebody autotuned Christopher Lee. "You must immediately cancel your organization's life extension plans. Further, you must destroy the information related to it. Otherwise human beings will lose all access to the eternal realms."

Mo and I have already watched the whole thing. I had to explain to Mo that yes, the company was going to be extending human life. I watched it a second time while Mo called Barry and told him to get the boss in here. Right now I'm watching Wollreich, who is sneering and eyerolling, giving the screen his this-is-bullshit face.

"The human spirit, or soul, is a turbulent waveform. At death, this turbulence allows the waveform to imprint across the boundary wave, transducing the wave to an eternal state with minimal degradation. As humans grow older, however, the turbulence is reduced. Some very old humans fail to imprint. Their original waveforms cease. In your terms, this means they die forever. Should human lives be extended to more than a century, very few humans will imprint successfully, and eternal life will be denied to your race."

Wollreich's this-is-bullshit face gives way to deep concern.

"You have the ability, Sinclair Wollreich, to end this project and save humans eternally. Act swiftly."

Death vanishes. A moment later, the video shows Mo and me bursting through the office door. Mo reaches up to check the camera, and the image freezes because I've pushed STOP.

Wollreich is leaning against his desk, arms folded, head down.

"Cole, could this have been faked?"

"Probably. I'm not a video expert. But the second time I watched it I looked out the window. There's a cloud that remained unchanged between the Death part and the part where Mo and I arrived. We could probably match that to other cameras in the building."

Wollreich straightens up.

"Is that the only copy of the video?" he asks as he points at my phone.

"There's a copy in the transmitter too."

"And one in the cache on the wallscreen," says Mo. "That one's in dynamic allocation, though. Might already be gone."

"Bring me the transmitter, and then we're all waiting in here for the brain trust."

Wollreich's office is big. Even with nine of us in here it doesn't really feel crowded. Tense, yes, but not crowded. Three members of the genius team have arrived, and one of them has video tools in hand. Two senior members of R&D are here as well, and they're both scientist types, complete with the lab coats. Wollreich, Mo, Barry, and I are the only ones in suits.

We've all watched the video.

"This is spaghetti-monster stuff," says Kurtzman, one of the labcoat guys. "It's non-falsifiable. We can't test any of what he told us. Sure, it sounds convincing because he used words like waveform and transducing, but there's no science in here for us to check."

"Sure there is," says Michel. He opens his case of video tools. "I need to see the camera, though."

Mo pulls it down from the corner of the room and passes it to Michel. It's about the size of a pencil eraser.

Michel turns it over in his hands and squints at it.

"Yup! We have science. This camera sees in broad-spectrum. The transmitted video is standard HD, but the raw file has some goodies in it." He takes the transmitter from the table, jacks a cable into it, and bends over his equipment. "This'll take a few minutes."

Wollreich turns to Kurtzman.

"The statements Death made are non-falsifiable, yes. We have no way to prove or disprove any of what we were told. Due diligence suggests that we at least consider the information, and that's why you're here."

"Can we call him something besides Death, please?" says Kurtzman. "That costume he was wearing was part of the message, and if we accept it at face value, we're undermining our ability to evaluate any of this. Oh, and for the record, I think it's a crank, and what we should be doing is grilling the hired guns."

When the boss is in a meeting I only speak when spoken to. My job is to be invisible. Under the current circumstances, that's not going to work well.

"Grill away, Mr. Kurtzman," I say.

"*Doctor* Kurtzman."

"My apologies, doctor. But please, grill us. Ask us anything. From your perspective, my team and I are your prime suspects. From our perspective, we need to get cleared as quickly as possible so that we're free to continue doing our jobs."

"I've already got an independent agency running deep checks on you, Cole," says Wollreich. "Your whole team, in fact. They've been doing it since Monday, when I brought you into the fold."

"Outstanding, sir."

Kurtzman looks stymied.

"And Dr. Kurtzman," Wollreich continues, "you're absolutely right. We don't call our intruder 'Death' anymore. He is the Intruder."

"I'm not quite sure how this video plays into any corporate espionage scenario," says Lee, a stout woman in khakis and a Hawaiian print shirt. "I haven't plugged any of this into our X-form, but I shouldn't have to. The payoffs and strategies, the incentive matrix . . . those don't change. This event, this monologue, it should align itself with existing player strategies, and it does not."

"Dr. Lee is a game theorist," says Wollreich. "Without the jargon now, doctor?"

"The X-form assumes rational and informed agents in the access tier. An irrational, uninformed agent might adopt the dress-like-death tactic in hopes of a payoff, but . . ."

"I said without the jargon."

"She means," says Michel, "that we're either dealing with an irrational, uninformed person with a stupid agenda, but who has access to our plans, or there are payoffs missing from the matrix."

"There aren't any payoffs missing," says Lee.

"Let's come back to that," says Michel. "I have more video for you to watch."

He gestures at the screen. "This is the original image, with an overlay of neon-green representing UV frequencies all the way to the edge of the camera's range."

On the wall-screen the video begins again, muted. It looks exactly the same as before, except a green shimmer appears in the middle of the room. It brightens, and then flashes as the Intruder appears. It then fades to a low shimmer again, surrounding his form as he speaks. The flash occurs again when he vanishes.

"Michel, what does that mean?"

"It means that the Intruder's appearance and disappearance were accompanied by UV emissions."

"Michel," says Lee, "those speakers in your office, the ones that build the audible cone out of interference patterns? Could somebody make a hologram by doing that with light? Like, ultraviolet lasers bouncing off each other just right to make a picture?"

The hologram thing. That was Mo's theory. I look at Mo, and he smirks.

"Maybe," says Michel, "but did you notice how there wasn't any green in the sky outside the window, or in the sunrise reflections on the buildings across the street? These windows filter UV. Any laser that tried to beam UV through them would have to cut the glass to do so."

"Then how did the UV get into the room?"

"Obviously it came with the Intruder," Michel answers. "But what you really want to see is the infrared. Watch this. No UV this time. I'm only going to play the infrared channel."

The picture returns, and now it's a monochromatic green.

Several of us gasp when the intruder appears. Including me.

I've seen infrared video of people before, and most folks have at least seen it simulated in movies. This is not that.

The form under the cloak is clearly outlined, and asymmetrical. The torso is short, and high. The legs are too long, and appear to bend the wrong way. If there's a left arm, it's not showing up. The right arm reaches all the way to the floor, then up to head-height, where it ends in the scythe blade.

But the cloak itself is the freakiest part. Lacy networks of veins are visible throughout it, and they all connect to the torso, the scythe limb, and the legs. It's not clothing. It's a layer of skin, like a bat wing, wrapped around the Intruder and hooding his face.

His? I see no male genitalia, but this thing is alien enough that I'm not ready to suggest that means it's female either.

Kurtzman speaks first. "Michel, how hard would it be to fake that?"

"Not very hard. If the whole thing was computer animated and hacked into the camera feed, the infrared and ultraviolet elements would simply be another part of the model. It's the work of a real artist, though."

"Okay, good," says Kurtzman, blowing out a sigh of relief. "I'm going to choose to believe that this is a brilliant computer animation modeled by someone with an outstanding attention to anatomical detail."

"What would motivate that?" Lee asks. "Where is the payoff?"

"I'm going to let you figure that out, because I refuse to believe that an alien teleported into this office."

The brain trust begins yammering in jargon again.

It's esoteric jargon, but the gist of things is that somebody is looking at a different set of payoffs than we are, and without more information we have no way to deduce motivations. Lee has graphs that prove this. But even without this information nobody is seriously considering taking the Intruder's message about the afterlife at face value, and nobody seems willing to believe that the Intruder is an alien, or an angel, or anything other than a very complicated hoax.

Somebody needs to take the not-a-hoax angle. It's hard to think with all the noise, and technically I'm being paid to pay attention, not close my eyes and concentrate, but I close my eyes anyway.

If I were responsible for shepherding human souls into the afterlife, and I could teleport anywhere in the world, I'd go talk to the pope, or maybe the president. I'd offer evidence, and be as helpful as I could. Of course, appearing in those halls of power would be like begging to get shot. So I'd do what heads of state do, and find a way to make an appointment.

The Intruder is definitely not acting like I would. Maybe it can't teleport just anywhere. Maybe teleporting is difficult, dangerous, or expensive. Maybe the Intruder's brain is so different from mine that I can't figure out how it thinks. Except that line of thought is the same as giving up, so I'll throw that out, and keep assuming that if I knew more I could understand its motives.

I can spot a lie from somebody I know, but the Intruder is, frankly, alien. I can't tell if it's lying. Or at least I can't trust myself to spot the lie the easy way. But if I think this through, if I assume that the Intruder is a rational creature, then the way it delivered its message just reeks of subterfuge.

So if I assume that it's rational, I'm now assuming it's dishonest. If it's dishonest, what is it hiding? What does the lying accomplish?

If we believe the Intruder, then it will cost our company a lot of money, and it'll keep human lifespans from getting longer. From that perspective it's a lot like killing people. The Intruder is asking us to kill people. That's something I've got some experience with. Every day I remind myself that I might need to kill people who are trying to kill *my* people.

When I roll out of bed tomorrow morning and remind myself that I might have to kill someone, I should also consider where to aim if a one-armed, scythe-handed alien teleported into the room and tried to kill my boss.

That's actually something I can work on.

"Hey, Michel," I say, snapping out of my chair. "May I review the infrared again?"

"I'm busy trying to reverse-engineer the auto-tune effect on the voice, Mr. Cole."

"I'll do it," says Wollreich. "The play button is this one, right?"

Michel sighs in exasperation and fiddles with his kit. "There."

I look up at the screen, and there is the infrared image of the Intruder, the eerie vein pattern wrapped around it, with other green patches showing the limbs and the head. The intensity varies, steadily pulsing in some places, gradually shifting around in others. Human forms do the same thing in infrared, only without the vein-riddled cloak.

Like a human, the Intruder's head stays fairly bright. The distribution of heat is a little different, but it still looks like a head.

Then, just before the Intruder vanishes, a bulbous shape near its second elbow brightens and then fades quickly to black.

"That spot there!" I say, pointing. "What was that?"

Michel rewinds and pauses. "The cold patch?"

"Yeah. It was hot a few frames back."

Michel rewinds further. "Oh. So it is."

"I've never seen that happen before in infrared. Usually when something cools off you can see the heat migrating to surrounding tissues."

"Obviously," says Kurtzman, "the heat went into hyperspace where we can't see it. Now can you please go stand guard in your corner? Or maybe outside. You're making me nervous."

"Mo, I've got this," I say, stepping back into my corner. "Go put some coffee into Barry."

Mo nods, and he and Barry slip out.

Despite his sarcasm Kurtzman made a good point. The elbow hot spot dumped heat someplace, and then the Intruder disappeared. "Hyperspace" is as good an answer as any. More importantly, I have the answer I was looking for. The Intruder's head emits steadily the same way a human head does. If I shoot the way I've practiced, a double-tap to the center of mass, and then a single shot to the head, that should work.

Michel has begun lecturing Kurtzman and Lee on what can and cannot be hacked in the camera and the transmitter, and what kind of supporting hardware would be required in the various scenarios. It's interesting, and I can actually follow most of it, but what I should be doing is a threat assessment regarding a teleporting alien. Just in case.

Not that anyone else in here is likely to think that's a good use of my time. The brain trust still thinks this is a hoax of some sort, and I suspect I've only got a few minutes before they come back around to grilling—

"Mr. Cole," says Michel. "Where did you acquire your spy gear?"

Okay, then. Less time than I thought.

"Handbrains & Hi-Def, it's an electronics boutique uptown. Mostly they sell smartphones and surround-sound systems, but the owner is ex-CIA, and he's a friend of mine. He sells custom equipment like this out of his apartment upstairs."

"And you just happened to have this equipment on you on Monday?"

"No. I bought it thirteen months ago when I started feeling uneasy about the fact that this office was unmonitored. Then I felt guilty for buying it, so I told Mo to carry it. Then Mr. Wollreich lied to us about why he pushed the panic button, and I had Barry distract Mr. Wollreich while Mo planted the camera in the corner."

"Thirteen months? You've been planning to bug my office for over a year?" Wollreich is turning red.

Oh. If I had that bug for a year I can see how the hacking story would start to look good.

This is difficult to explain, but it's not the first time I've had this kind of conversation.

It's never pleasant.

"I plan a lot of things, sir. Every morning I get out of bed and I plan to shoot someone. I don't know who that someone is, but in my mind's eye they're trying to assault you, or perhaps shove you into a van. My life revolves around planning to do things I would really rather not have to do, but which I will do, without hesitation, to keep you safe. I carry a loaded weapon, as does every member of my team. I'm fifteen pounds lighter than I look because some of my upper-body bulk is a twelve-hundred-dollar undershirt that will allow me to intercept a bullet on your behalf and still come in to work the following week. So yes, I planned to bug your office, but I didn't plant the bug until it seemed important."

Wollreich stares at me, and I stare back.

Lee speaks first, and she sounds shaken. "You have a gun in here? In this office?"

I don't look away from Wollreich when I answer her. "I do, Dr. Lee. I'm sorry if that makes you uncomfortable."

And then it occurs to me that as a game theorist, she's been doing a threat assessment, same as me, only with math, and the numbers are telling her that the biggest threat in the room right now is me.

I look away from Wollreich, losing that staring contest on purpose. I slump my shoulders just a little bit, a trick a bouncer friend showed me for those times when you want to look less dangerous than you really are. I pull a chair away from the wall and sit down. Everybody is looking at me nervously.

"Yes, you can explain the video by pinning it on me and Mo, but there's no good reason for us to have done that, and that still doesn't account for what your CEO saw." I look up at Wollreich.

He's still red-faced. Angry about the bug, and probably angry at his colleagues for not believing he saw what he said he saw. He might have started doubting it himself.

"Cole," he says. "Humor them and wait outside, please."

I nod, and slip through the door. Wollreich clears his throat, a sure sign that he's about to start in on somebody, but the soundproof door shuts and I miss the show.

Wollreich knows my team and I didn't do this, doesn't he? I'm not out here because he doesn't trust me, though that trust did take a beating when I bugged the office. No, I'm out here because I look dangerous, even slouching, and Wollreich needs his geniuses to relax.

I understand. Armed people make everybody nervous. Hell, even the Intruder was careful not to be there when Mo and I arrived. It timed the whole speech perfectly. Smart.

How smart, though? Can it predict our behavior? Has it been observing us, and learning about us? If so, it must know that Wollreich's team won't just shut the project down. It might even know that they'd blame me and my team, and shoo us out of the office to the far side of the soundproof doors. . . .

Both cups are poisoned.

I draw my pistol and turn for the office door.

"Everybody, my position."

It doesn't matter what the brain trust decides. What matters is that they gather where they can be separated from their security. And if I'm wrong? I hope I am wrong, really.

I fumble the number on the keypad and get an angry beep. That's something I should have practiced more.

"Roger. All call to forty. Hang in there, boss." Right in my ear.

I fumble the number again, adding a forty right in the middle. I definitely should have practiced this more.

On my third attempt the door unlocks with a *click*. Weapon up, I throw the door open to the sound of screaming.

There is a shadow in the middle of the room, a shadow swinging a scythe.

The Intruder is ready for me, lunging. That scythe is swinging my way, and I have no doubts at all regarding its lethality. But unlike that damned keypad this is something I've trained myself to do. I focus on the center of mass, and squeeze off my first shot.

The Intruder staggers at the impact, lunge interrupted. My pistol returns to position, the recoil compensated for by rehearsed reflex.

I squeeze off the second shot just as the scythe swings into view, missing my face by inches. The round strikes the elbow joint, which explodes in light and sound, like a flash-bang grenade, but made out of purple and bells.

It's not blinding or deafening, but as I squeeze off my third shot, the headshot, I realize that my target is not where it was supposed to be. The Intruder has tucked and crumpled into a dark heap, and my third shot spalls into the bulletproof glass of the window.

I step into the room, sweeping for threats. Wollreich is crouched behind the end of his desk, the opposite end from where the panic button is concealed. Michel is under a chair in the corner. Kurtzman, Lee, and the two biologist types are all sprawled unmoving and bloody on the floor.

"Cole! What—"

Wollreich is cut off by a burst of static noise, and by more screaming as the room starts to fill with shadows.

I dive toward Wollreich and feel a tug at the collar of my suit. The shadows resolve into two more Intruders, scythes swinging.

My Glock 30 has a ten-round magazine. Seven of those rounds remain. I double-tap the nearest Intruder, and then put a third round through its pale face. It drops. I hip-check Wollreich to the ground as I spin toward the second, only to find a third much closer, the one whose scythe must have grazed my suit collar.

Double-tap, and one to the face. That one's down too.

Taking nothing but headshots is a trick for video game junkies. That's not what I've trained for, but the last Intruder's pale, dinner-plate-size face is an easier target than its shadow-shrouded center of mass, and I only have one round left.

I focus on that face as the Intruder rushes me, and then I fire. Its head rocks back, those weird arm and leg joints splay out almost spiderlike, and then it drops motionless.

I eject the empty magazine and reload. Reflex. I step around the table. Wollreich and Michel are fine, but the other four are slashed up and lie completely still. They look cold, like they've been dead for hours under the fresh blood. Those scythes must do more than just cut.

"My God, Cole . . . How did you know?"

"Strong hunch, but I didn't know anything. I was ready for you to fire me for barging in."

There is another burst of static. It's coming from the shuddering lump of darkness that is the original Intruder. That's right, I missed its head. But I did hit something important, because it hasn't teleported out of here.

I step over to it and put my foot on the scythe blade.

"Who are you and what do you want?"

There's more static, and then it clears and we're back to an auto-tuned Christopher Lee.

"We are the Angels of Death. We shepherd you to—"

"Oh, shut *up!*" says Wollreich. "You're no shepherd! You murdered four people!"

I still don't have a read on this thing, but I'm pretty sure it's lying.

"Talk," I say, gesturing with my pistol.

It hisses with static, and then speaks.

"We number in the millions. Your deaths sustain us. Our population has grown with yours, alongside yours. If you stop dying, we starve. If we cannot pick up fallen fruit, we will have to shake the tree."

It's telling the truth. I'm sure of it. Maybe there's more to my gift than the ability to read facial cues.

"You're done shaking trees. We know you're out there," Wollreich says.

"You know nothing. We can strike anywhere, at any time. We can see you, from our side. There will be a brief, bloody war, and then we will shepherd the rest of you more carefully. This will not be the first time we have culled in order to feed."

"Except this time you tried to negotiate," I say. "There are a lot of us, and we're smarter and tougher than we've ever been. You tried diplomacy and subterfuge because war is expensive."

I should know. I was in Afghanistan, fighting an actual land war in Asia. I smile.

Failalo shouts into my headset. "Cole! Intruders in the data center! They look like Death, sir."

I can hear gunshots in the background. Gunshots and screaming. "Grab your stuff and stay with me, gentlemen," I say to Wollreich and Michel. "We're not done."

This war is going to be more expensive than the one in Asia, but I think this time I may actually get to save the world.

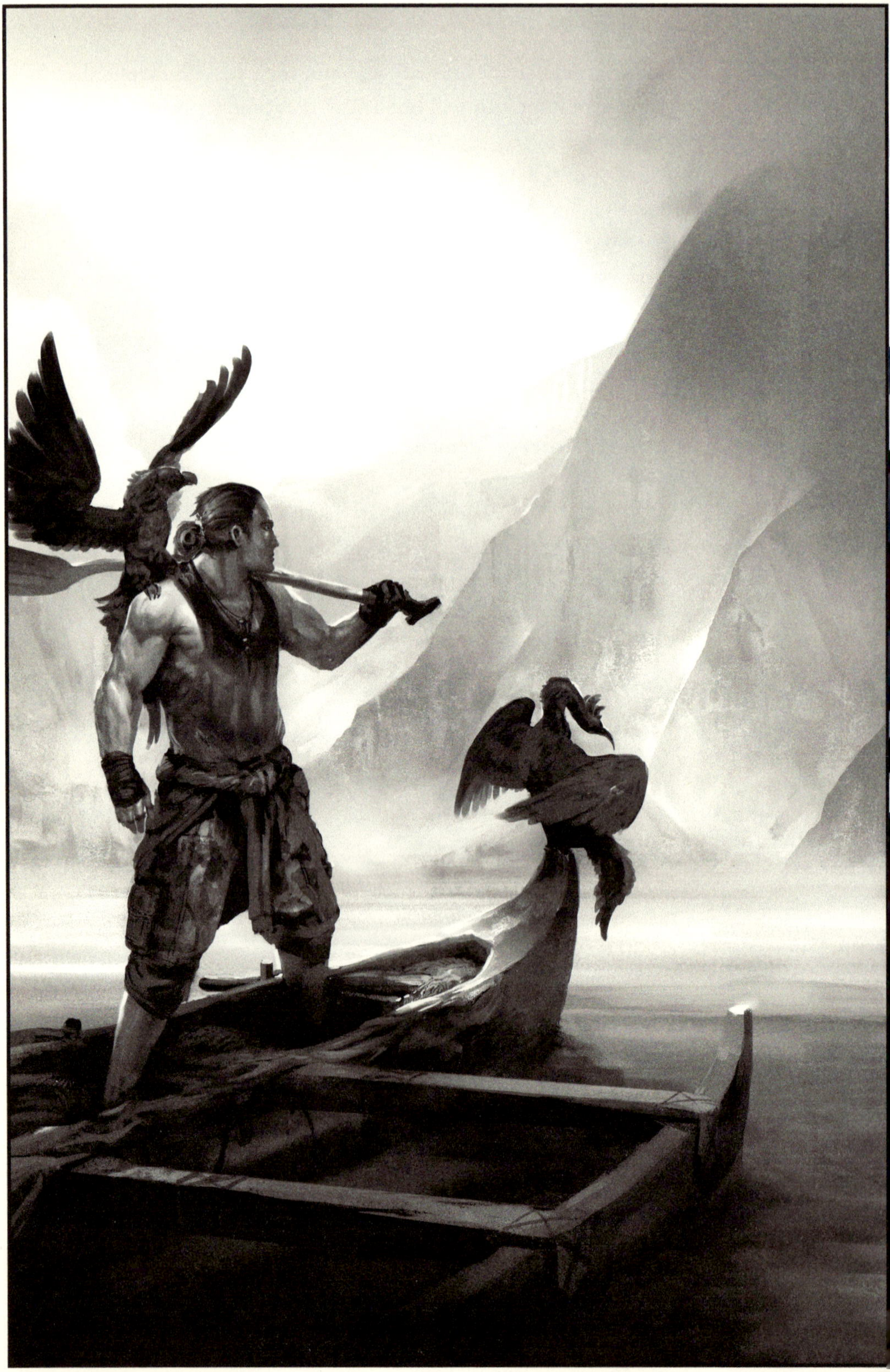

Sixth of the Dusk

BRANDON SANDERSON

Death hunted beneath the waves. Dusk saw it approach, an enormous blackness within the deep blue, a shadowed form as wide as six narrowboats tied together. Dusk's hands tensed on his paddle, his heartbeat racing as he immediately sought out Kokerlii.

Fortunately, the colorful bird sat in his customary place on the prow of the boat, idly biting at one clawed foot raised to his beak. Kokerlii lowered his foot and puffed out his feathers, as if completely unmindful of the danger beneath.

Dusk held his breath. He always did, when unfortunate enough to run across one of these things in the open ocean. He did not know what they looked like beneath those waves. He hoped to never find out.

The shadow drew closer, almost to the boat now. A school of slimfish passing nearby jumped into the air in a silvery wave, spooked by the shadow's approach. The terrified fish showered back to the water with a sound like rain. The shadow did not deviate. The slimfish were too small a meal to interest it.

A boat's occupants, however . . .

It passed directly underneath. Sak chirped quietly from Dusk's shoulder; the second bird seemed to have some sense of the danger. Creatures like the shadow did not hunt by smell or sight, but by sensing the minds of prey. Dusk glanced at Kokerlii again, his only protection against a danger that could swallow his ship whole. He had never clipped Kokerlii's wings, but at times like this he understood why many sailors preferred Aviar that could not fly away.

The boat rocked softly; the jumping slimfish stilled. Waves lapped against the sides of the vessel. Had the shadow stopped? Hesitated? Did it sense them? Kokerlii's protective aura had always been enough before, but . . .

The shadow slowly vanished. It had turned to swim downward, Dusk realized. In moments, he could make out nothing through the waters. He hesitated, then forced himself to get out his new mask. It was a modern device he had acquired only two supply trips back: a glass faceplate with leather at the sides. He placed it on the water's surface and leaned down, looking into the depths. They became as clear to him as an undisturbed lagoon.

Nothing. Just that endless deep. *Fool man,* he thought, tucking away the mask and getting out his paddle. *Didn't you just think to yourself that you never wanted to see one of those?*

Still, as he started paddling again, he knew that he'd spend the rest of this trip feeling as if the shadow were down there, following him. That was the nature of the waters. You never knew what lurked below.

He continued on his journey, paddling his outrigger canoe and reading the lapping of the waves to judge his position. Those waves were as good as a compass for him—once, they would have been good enough for any of the Eelakin, his people. These days, just the trappers learned the old arts. Admittedly, though, even *he* carried one of the newest compasses, wrapped up in his pack with a set of the new sea charts—maps given as gifts by the Ones Above during their visit earlier in the year. They were said to be more accurate than even the latest surveys, so he'd purchased a set just in case. You could not stop times from changing, his mother said, no more than you could stop the surf from rolling.

It was not long, after the accounting of tides, before he caught sight of the first island. Sori was a small island in the Pantheon, and the most commonly visited. Her name meant child; Dusk vividly remembered training on her shores with his uncle.

It had been long since he'd burned an offering to Sori, despite how well she had treated him during his youth. Perhaps a small offering would not be out of line. Patji would not grow jealous. One could not be jealous of Sori, the least of the islands. Just as every trapper was welcome on Sori, every other island in the Pantheon was said to be affectionate of her.

Be that as it may, Sori did not contain much valuable game. Dusk continued rowing, moving down one leg of the archipelago his people knew as the Pantheon. From a distance, this archipelago was not so different from the homeisles of the Eelakin, now a three-week trip behind him.

From a distance. Up close, they were very, very different. Over the next five hours, Dusk rowed past Sori, then her three cousins. He had never set foot on any of those three. In fact, he had not landed on many of the forty-some islands in the Pantheon. At the end of his apprenticeship, a trapper chose one island and worked there all his life. He had chosen Patji—an event some ten years past now. Seemed like far less.

Dusk saw no other shadows beneath the waves, but he kept watch. Not that he could do much to protect himself. Kokerlii did all of that work as he roosted happily at the prow of the ship, eyes half-closed. Dusk had fed him seed; Kokerlii did like it so much more than dried fruit.

Nobody knew why beasts like the shadows only lived here, in the waters near the Pantheon. Why not travel across the seas to the Eelakin Islands or the mainland, where food would be plentiful and Aviar like Kokerlii were far more rare? Once, these questions had not been asked. The seas were what they were. Now, however, men poked and prodded into everything. They asked, "Why?" They said, "We should explain it."

Dusk shook his head, dipping his paddle into the water. That sound—wood on water—had been his companion for most of his days. He understood it far better than he did the speech of men.

Even if sometimes their questions got inside of him and refused to go free.

After the cousins, most trappers would have turned north or south, moving along branches of the archipelago until reaching their chosen island. Dusk continued forward, into the heart of the islands, until a shape loomed before him. Patji, largest island of the Pantheon. It towered like a wedge rising from the sea. A place of inhospitable peaks, sharp cliffs, and deep jungle.

Hello, old destroyer, he thought. *Hello, Father.*

Dusk raised his paddle and placed it in the boat. He sat for a time, chewing on fish from last night's catch, feeding scraps to Sak. The black-plumed bird ate them with an air of solemnity. Kokerlii continued to sit on the prow, chirping occasionally. He would be eager to land. Sak seemed never to grow eager about anything.

Approaching Patji was not a simple task, even for one who trapped his shores. The boat continued its dance with the waves as Dusk considered which landing to make. Eventually, he put the fish away, then dipped his paddle back into the waters. Those waters remained deep and blue, despite the proximity to the island. Some members of the Pantheon had sheltered bays and gradual beaches. Patji had no patience for such foolishness. His beaches were rocky and had steep drop-offs.

You were never safe on his shores. In fact, the beaches were the most dangerous part—upon them, not only could the horrors of the land get to you, but you were still within reach of the deep's monsters. Dusk's uncle had cautioned him about this time and time again. Only a fool slept on Patji's shores.

The tide was with him, and he avoided being caught in any of the swells that would crush him against those stern rock faces. Dusk approached a partially sheltered expanse of stone crags and outcroppings, Patji's version of a beach. Kokerlii fluttered off, chirping and calling as he flew toward the trees.

Dusk immediately glanced at the waters. No shadows. Still, he felt naked as he hopped out of the canoe and pulled it up onto the rocks, warm water washing against his legs. Sak remained in her place on Dusk's shoulder.

Nearby in the surf, Dusk saw a corpse bobbing in the water.

Beginning your visions early, my friend? he thought, glancing at Sak. The Aviar usually waited until they'd fully landed before bestowing her blessing.

The black-feathered bird just watched the waves.

Dusk continued his work. The body he saw in the surf was his own. It told him to avoid that section of water. Perhaps there was a spiny anemone that would have pricked him, or perhaps a deceptive undercurrent lay in wait. Sak's visions did not show such detail; they gave only warning.

Dusk got the boat out of the water, then detached the floats, tying them more securely onto the main part of the canoe. Following that, he worked the vessel carefully up the shore, mindful not to scrape the hull on sharp rocks. He would need to hide the canoe in the jungle. If another trapper discovered it, Dusk would be stranded on the island for several extra weeks preparing his spare. That would—

He stopped as his heel struck something soft as he backed up the shore. He glanced down, expecting a pile of seaweed. Instead he found a damp piece of cloth. A shirt? Dusk held it up, then noticed other, more subtle signs across the shore. Broken lengths of sanded wood. Bits of paper floating in an eddy.

Those fools, he thought.

He returned to moving his canoe. Rushing was never a good idea on a Pantheon island. He did step more quickly, however.

As he reached the tree line, he caught sight of his corpse hanging from a tree nearby. Those were cutaway vines lurking in the fernlike treetop. Sak squawked softly on his shoulder as Dusk hefted a large stone from the beach, then tossed it at the tree. It thumped against the wood, and sure enough, the vines dropped like a net, full of stinging barbs.

They would take a few hours to retract. Dusk pulled his canoe over and hid it in the underbrush near the tree. Hopefully, other trappers would be smart enough to stay away from the cutaway vines—and therefore wouldn't stumble over his boat.

Before placing the final camouflaging fronds, Dusk pulled out his pack. Though the centuries had changed a trapper's duties very little, the modern world did offer its benefits. Instead of a simple wrap that left his legs and chest exposed, he put on thick trousers with pockets on the legs and a buttoning shirt to protect his skin against sharp branches and leaves. Instead of sandals, Dusk tied on sturdy boots. And instead of a tooth-lined club, he bore a machete of the finest steel. His pack contained luxuries like a steel-hooked rope, a lantern, and a firestarter that created sparks simply by pressing the two handles together.

He looked very little like the trappers in the paintings back home. He didn't mind. He'd rather stay alive.

Dusk left the canoe, shouldering his pack, machete sheathed at his side. Sak moved to his other shoulder. Before leaving the beach, Dusk paused, looking at the image of his translucent corpse, still hanging from unseen vines by the tree.

Could he really have ever been foolish enough to be caught by cutaway vines? Near as he could tell, Sak only showed him plausible deaths. He liked to think that most were fairly unlikely—a vision of what could have happened if he'd been careless, or if his uncle's training hadn't been so extensive.

Once, Dusk had stayed away from any place where he saw his corpse. It wasn't bravery that drove him to do the opposite now. He just . . . needed to confront the possibilities. He needed to be able to walk away from this beach knowing that he could still deal with cutaway vines. If he avoided danger, he would soon lose his skills. He could not rely on Sak too much.

For Patji would try on every possible occasion to kill him.

Dusk turned and trudged across the rocks along the coast. Doing so went against his instincts—he normally wanted to get inland as soon as possible. Unfortunately, he could not leave without investigating the origin of the debris he had seen earlier. He had a strong suspicion of where he would find their source.

He gave a whistle, and Kokerlii trilled above, flapping out of a tree nearby and winging over the beach. The protection he offered would not be as strong as it would be if he were close, but the beasts that hunted minds on the island were not as large or as strong of psyche as the shadows of the ocean. Dusk and Sak would be invisible to them.

About a half hour up the coast, Dusk found the remnants of a large camp. Broken boxes, fraying ropes lying half submerged in tidal pools, ripped canvas, shattered pieces of wood that might once have been walls. Kokerlii landed on a broken pole.

There were no signs of his corpse nearby. That could mean that the area wasn't immediately dangerous. It could also mean that whatever might kill him here would swallow the corpse whole.

Dusk trod lightly on wet stones at the edge of the broken campsite. No. Larger than a campsite. Dusk ran his fingers over a broken chunk of wood, stenciled with the words *Northern Interests Trading Company*. A powerful mercantile force from his homeland.

He had told them. He had *told* them. Do not come to Patji. Fools. And they had camped here on the beach itself! Was nobody in that company capable of listening? He stopped beside a group of gouges in the rocks, as wide as his upper arm, running some ten paces long. They led toward the ocean.

Shadow, he thought. *One of the deep beasts*. His uncle had spoken of seeing one once. An enormous . . . *something* that had exploded up from the depths. It had killed a dozen krell that had been chewing on oceanside weeds before retreating into the waters with its feast.

Dusk shivered, imagining this camp on the rocks, bustling with men unpacking boxes, preparing to build the fort they had described to him. But where was their ship? The great steam-powered vessel with an iron hull they claimed could rebuff the attacks of even the deepest of shadows? Did it now defend the ocean bottom, a home for slimfish and octopus?

There were no survivors—nor even any corpses—that Dusk could see. The shadow must have consumed them. He pulled back to the slightly safer locale of the jungle's edge, then scanned the foliage, looking for signs that people had passed this way. The attack was recent, within the last day or so.

He absently gave Sak a seed from his pocket as he located a series of broken fronds leading into the jungle. So there were survivors. Maybe as many as a half dozen. They had each chosen to go in different directions, in a hurry. Running from the attack.

Running through the jungle was a good way to get dead. These company types thought themselves rugged and prepared. They were wrong. He'd spoken to a number of them, trying to persuade as many of their "trappers" as possible to abandon the voyage.

It had done no good. He wanted to blame the visits of the Ones Above for causing this foolish striving for progress, but the truth was the companies had been talking of outposts on the Pantheon for years. Dusk sighed. Well, these survivors were likely dead now. He should leave them to their fates.

Except . . . The thought of it, outsiders on Patji, it made him shiver with something that mixed disgust and anxiety. They were *here*. It was wrong. These islands were sacred, the trappers their priests.

The plants rustled nearby. Dusk whipped his machete about, leveling it, reaching into his pocket for his sling. It was not a refugee who left the bushes, or even a predator. A group of small, mouselike creatures crawled out, sniffing the air. Sak squawked. She had never liked meekers.

Food? the three meekers sent to Dusk. *Food?*

It was the most rudimentary of thoughts, projected directly into his mind. Though he did not want the distraction, he did not pass up the opportunity to fish out some dried meat for the meekers. As they huddled around it, sending him gratitude, he saw their sharp teeth and the single pointed fang at the tips of their mouths. His uncle had told him that once, meekers had been dangerous to men. One bite was enough to kill. Over the centuries, the little creatures had grown accustomed to trappers. They had minds beyond those of dull animals. Almost he found them as intelligent as the Aviar.

You remember? he sent them through thoughts. *You remember your task?*

Others, they sent back gleefully. *Bite others!*

Trappers ignored these little beasts; Dusk figured that maybe with some training, the meekers could provide an unexpected surprise for one of his rivals. He fished in his pocket, fingers brushing an old stiff piece of feather. Then, not wanting to pass up the opportunity, he got a few long, bright green and red feathers from his pack. They were mating plumes, which he'd taken from Kokerlii during the Aviar's most recent molting.

He moved into the jungle, meekers following with excitement. Once he neared their den, he stuck the mating plumes into some branches, as if they had fallen there naturally. A passing trapper might see the plumes and assume that Aviar had a nest nearby, fresh with eggs for the plunder. That would draw them.

Bite others, Dusk instructed again.

Bite others! they replied.

He hesitated, thoughtful. Had they perhaps seen something from the company wreck? Point him in the right direction. *Have you seen any others?* Dusk sent them. *Recently? In the jungle?*

Bite others! came the reply.

They were intelligent . . . but not *that* intelligent. Dusk bade the animals farewell and turned toward the forest. After a moment's deliberation, he found himself striking inland, crossing—then following—one of the refugee trails. He chose the one that looked as if it would pass uncomfortably close to one of his own safecamps, deep within the jungle.

It was hotter here beneath the jungle's canopy, despite the shade. Comfortably sweltering. Kokerlii joined him, winging up ahead to a branch where a few lesser Aviar sat chirping. Kokerlii towered over them, but sang at them with enthusiasm. An Aviar raised around humans never quite fit back in among their own kind. The same could be said of a man raised around Aviar.

Dusk followed the trail left by the refugee, expecting to stumble over the man's corpse at any moment. He did not, though his own dead body did occasionally appear along the path. He saw it lying half-eaten in the mud or tucked away in a fallen log with only the foot showing. He could never grow too complacent, with Sak on his shoulder. It did not matter if Sak's visions were truth or fiction; he needed the constant reminder of how Patji treated the unwary.

He fell into the familiar, but not comfortable, lope of a Pantheon trapper. Alert, wary, careful not to brush leaves that could carry biting insects. Cutting with the machete only when necessary, lest he leave a trail another could follow. Listening, aware of his Aviar at all times, never outstripping Kokerlii or letting him drift too far ahead.

The refugee did not fall to the common dangers of the island—he cut across game trails, rather than following them. The surest way to encounter predators was to fall in with their food. The refugee did not know how to mask his trail, but neither did he blunder into the nest of firesnap lizards, or brush the deathweed bark, or step into the patch of hungry mud.

Was this another trapper, perhaps? A youthful one, not fully trained? That seemed something the company would try. Experienced trappers were beyond recruitment; none would be foolish enough to guide a group of clerks and merchants around the islands. But a youth, who had not yet chosen his island? A youth who, perhaps, resented being required to practice only on Sori until his mentor determined his apprenticeship complete? Dusk had felt that way ten years ago.

So the company had hired itself a trapper at last. That would explain why they had grown so bold as to finally organize their expedition. *But Patji himself?* he thought, kneeling beside the bank of a small stream. It had no name, but it was familiar to him. *Why would they come here?*

The answer was simple. They were merchants. The biggest, to them, would be the best. Why waste time on lesser islands? Why not come for the Father himself?

Above, Kokerlii landed on a branch and began pecking at a fruit. The refugee had stopped by this river. Dusk had gained time on the youth. Judging by the depth the boy's footprints had sunk in the mud, Dusk could imagine his weight and height. Sixteen? Maybe younger? Trappers apprenticed at ten, but Dusk could not imagine even the company trying to recruit one so ill trained.

Two hours gone, Dusk thought, turning a broken stem and smelling the sap. The boy's path continued on toward Dusk's safecamp. How? Dusk had never spoken of it to anyone. Perhaps this youth was apprenticing under one of the other trappers who visited Patji. One of them could have found his safecamp and mentioned it.

Dusk frowned, considering. In ten years on Patji, he had seen another trapper in person only a handful of times. On each occasion, they had both turned and gone a different direction without saying a word. It was the way of such things. They would try to kill one another, but they didn't do it in person. Better to let Patji claim rivals than to directly stain one's hands. At least, so his uncle had taught him.

Sometimes, Dusk found himself frustrated by that. Patji would get them all eventually. Why help the Father out? Still, it was the way of things, so he went through the motions. Regardless, this refugee was making directly for Dusk's safecamp. The youth might not know the proper way of things. Perhaps he had come seeking help, afraid to go to one of his master's safecamps for fear of punishment. Or . . .

No, best to avoid pondering it. Dusk already had a mind full of spurious conjectures. He would find what he would find. He had to focus on the jungle and its dangers. He started away from the stream, and as he did so, he saw his corpse appear suddenly before him.

He hopped forward, then spun backward, hearing a faint hiss. The distinctive sound was made by air escaping from a small break in the ground, followed by a flood of tiny yellow insects, each as small as a pinhead. A new deathant pod? If he'd stood there a little longer, disturbing their hidden nest, they would have flooded up around his boot. One bite, and he'd be dead.

He stared at that pool of scrambling insects longer than he should have. They pulled back into their nest, finding no prey. Sometimes a small bulge announced their location, but today he had seen nothing. Only Sak's vision had saved him.

Such was life on Patji. Even the most careful trapper could make a mistake—and even if they didn't, death could still find them. Patji was a domineering, vengeful parent who sought the blood of all who landed on his shores.

Sak chirped on his shoulder. Dusk rubbed her neck in thanks, though her chirp sounded apologetic. The warning had come almost too late. Without her, Patji would have claimed him this day. Dusk shoved down those itching questions he should not be thinking, and continued on his way.

He finally approached his safecamp as evening settled upon the island.

Two of his tripwires had been cut, disarming them. That was not surprising; those were meant to be obvious. Dusk crept past another deathant nest in the ground—this larger one had a permanent crack as an opening they could flood out of, but the rift had been stoppered with a smoldering twig. Beyond it, the nightwind fungi that Dusk had spent years cultivating here had been smothered in water to keep the spores from escaping. The next two tripwires—the ones not intended to be obvious—had *also* been cut.

Nice work, kid, Dusk thought. He hadn't just avoided the traps, but disarmed them, in case he needed to flee quickly back this direction. However, someone really needed to teach the boy how to move without being trackable. Of course, those tracks could be a trap unto themselves—an attempt to make Dusk himself careless. And so, he was extra careful as he edged forward. Yes, here the youth had left more footprints, broken stems, and other signs....

Something moved up above in the canopy. Dusk hesitated, squinting. A *woman* hung from the tree branches above, trapped in a net made of jellywire vines—they left someone numb, unable to move. So, one of his traps had finally worked.

"Um, hello?" she said.

A woman, Dusk thought, suddenly feeling stupid. *The smaller footprint, lighter step* ...

"I want to make it perfectly clear," the woman said. "I have no intention of stealing your birds or infringing upon your territory."

Dusk stepped closer in the dimming light. He recognized this woman. She was one of the clerks who had been at his meetings with the company. "You cut my tripwires," Dusk said. Words felt odd in his mouth, and they came out ragged, as if he'd swallowed handfuls of dust. The result of weeks without speaking.

"Er, yes, I did. I assumed you could replace them." She hesitated. "Sorry?"

Dusk settled back. The woman rotated slowly in her net, and he noticed an Aviar clinging to the outside—like his own birds, it was about as tall as three fists atop one another, though this one had subdued white and green plumage. A streamer, which was a breed that did not live on Patji. He did not know much about them, other than that like Kokerlii, they protected the mind from predators.

The setting sun cast shadows, the sky darkening. Soon, he would need to hunker down for the night, for darkness brought out the island's most dangerous of predators.

"I promise," the woman said from within her bindings. What was her name? He believed it had been told to him, but he did not recall. Something untraditional. "I really don't want to steal from you. You remember me, don't you? We met back in the company halls?"

He gave no reply.

"Please," she said. "I'd really rather not be hung by my ankles from a tree, slathered with blood to attract predators. If it's all the same to you."

"You are not a trapper."

"Well, no," she said. "You may have noticed my gender."

"There have been female trappers."

"One. One female trapper, Yaalani the Brave. I've heard her story a hundred times. You may find it curious to know that almost every society has its myth of the female role reversal. She goes to war dressed as a man, or leads her father's armies into battle, or traps on an island. I'm convinced that such stories exist so that parents can tell their daughters, 'You are not Yaalani.'"

This woman spoke. A lot. People did that back on the Eelakin Islands. Her skin was dark, like his, and she had the sound of his people. The slight accent to her voice . . . he had heard it more and more when visiting the homeisles. It was the accent of one who was educated.

"Can I get down?" she asked, voice bearing a faint tremor. "I cannot feel my hands. It is . . . unsettling."

"What is your name?" Dusk asked. "I have forgotten it." This was too much speaking. It hurt his ears. This place was supposed to be soft.

"Vathi."

That's right. It was an improper name. Not a reference to her birth order and day of birth, but a name like the mainlanders used. That was not uncommon among his people now.

He walked over and took the rope from the nearby tree, then lowered the net. The woman's Aviar flapped down, screeching in annoyance, favoring one wing, obviously wounded. Vathi hit the ground, a bundle of dark curls and green linen skirts. She stumbled to her feet, but fell back down again. Her skin would be numb for some fifteen minutes from the touch of the vines.

She sat there and wagged her hands, as if to shake out the numbness. "So . . . uh, no ankles and blood?" she asked, hopeful.

"That is a story parents tell to children," Dusk said. "It is not something we actually do."

"Oh."

"If you had been another trapper, I would have killed you directly, rather than leaving you to avenge yourself upon me." He walked over to her Aviar, which opened its beak in a hissing posture, raising both wings as if to be bigger than it was. Sak chirped from his shoulder, but the bird didn't seem to care.

Yes, one wing was bloody. Vathi knew enough to care for the bird, however, which was pleasing. Some homeislers were completely ignorant of their Aviar's needs, treating them like accessories rather than intelligent creatures.

Vathi had pulled out the feathers near the wound, including a blood feather. She'd wrapped the wound with gauze. That wing didn't look good, however. Might be a fracture involved. He'd want to wrap both wings, prevent the creature from flying.

"Oh, Mirris," Vathi said, finally finding her feet. "I tried to help her. We fell, you see, when the monster—"

"Pick her up," Dusk said, checking the sky. "Follow. Step where I step."

Vathi nodded, not complaining, though her numbness would not have passed yet. She collected a small pack from the vines and straightened her skirts. She wore a tight vest above them, and the pack had some kind of metal tube sticking out of it. A map case? She fetched her Aviar, who huddled happily on her shoulder.

As Dusk led the way, she followed, and she did not attempt to attack him when his back was turned. Good. Darkness was coming upon them, but his safecamp was just ahead, and he knew by heart the steps to approach along this path. As they walked, Kokerlii fluttered down and landed on the woman's other shoulder, then began chirping in an amiable way.

Dusk stopped, turning. The woman's own Aviar moved down her dress away from Kokerlii to cling near her bodice. The bird hissed softly, but Kokerlii—oblivious, as usual—continued to chirp happily. It was fortunate his breed was so mind-invisible, even deathants would consider him no more edible than a piece of bark.

"Is this . . ." Vathi said, looking to Dusk. "Yours? But of course. The one on your shoulder is not Aviar."

Sak settled back, puffing up her feathers. No, her species was not Aviar. Dusk continued to lead the way.

"I have never seen a trapper carry a bird who was not from the islands," Vathi said from behind.

It was not a question. Dusk, therefore, felt no need to reply.

This safecamp—he had three total on the island—lay atop a short hill following a twisting trail. Here, a stout gurratree held aloft a single-room structure. Trees were one of the safer places to sleep on Patji. The treetops were the domain of the Aviar, and most of the large predators walked.

Dusk lit his lantern, then held it aloft, letting the orange light bathe his home. "Up," he said to the woman.

She glanced over her shoulder into the darkening jungle. By the lantern-light, he saw that the whites of her eyes were red from lack of sleep, despite the unconcerned smile she gave him before climbing up the stakes he'd planted in the tree. Her numbness should have worn off by now.

"How did you know?" he asked.

Vathi hesitated, near to the trapdoor leading into his home. "Know what?"

"Where my safecamp was. Who told you?"

"I followed the sound of water," she said, nodding toward the small spring that bubbled out of the mountainside here. "When I found traps, I knew I was coming the right way."

Dusk frowned. One could not hear this water, as the stream vanished only a few hundred yards away, resurfacing in an unexpected location. Following it here . . . that would be virtually impossible.

So was she lying, or was she just lucky?

"You wanted to find me," he said.

"I wanted to find *someone*," she said, pushing open the trapdoor, voice growing muffled as she climbed up into the building. "I figured that a trapper would be my only chance for survival." Above, she stepped up to one of the netted windows, Kokerlii still on her shoulder. "This is nice. Very roomy for a shack on a mountainside in the middle of a deadly jungle on an isolated island surrounded by monsters."

Dusk climbed up, holding the lantern in his teeth. The room at the top was perhaps four paces square, tall enough to stand in, but only barely. "Shake out those blankets," he said, nodding toward the stack and setting down the lantern. "Then lift every cup and bowl on the shelf and check inside of them."

Her eyes widened. "What am I looking for?"

"Deathants, scorpions, spiders, bloodscratches . . ." He shrugged, putting Sak on her perch by the window. "The room is built to be tight, but this is Patji. The Father likes surprises."

As she hesitantly set aside her pack and got to work, Dusk continued up another ladder to check the roof. There, a group of bird-size boxes, with nests inside and holes to allow the birds to come and go freely, lay arranged in a double row. The animals would not stray far, except on special occasions, now that they had been raised with him handling them.

Kokerlii landed on top of one of the homes, trilling—but softly, now that night had fallen. More coos and chirps came from the other boxes.

Dusk climbed out to check each bird for hurt wings or feet. These Aviar pairs were his life's work; the chicks each one hatched became his primary stock in trade. Yes, he would trap on the island, trying to find nests and wild chicks—but that was never as efficient as raising nests.

"Your name was Sixth, wasn't it?" Vathi said from below, voice accompanied by the sound of a blanket being shaken.

"It is."

"Large family," Vathi noted.

An ordinary family. Or, so it had once been. His father had been a twelfth and his mother an eleventh.

"Sixth of what?" Vathi prompted below.

"Of the Dusk."

"So you were born in the evening," Vathi said. "I've always found the traditional names so . . . uh . . . *descriptive*."

What a meaningless comment, Dusk thought. *Why do homeislers feel the need to speak when there is nothing to say?*

He moved on to the next nest, checking the two drowsy birds inside, then inspecting their droppings. They responded to his presence with happiness. An Aviar raised around humans—particularly one that had lent its talent to a person at an early age—would always see people as part of their flock. These birds were not his companions, like Sak and Kokerlii, but they were still special to him.

"No insects in the blankets," Vathi said, sticking her head up out of the trapdoor behind him, her own Aviar on her shoulder.

"The cups?"

"I'll get to those in a moment. So these are your breeding pairs, are they?"

Obviously they were, so he didn't need to reply.

She watched him check them. He felt her eyes on him. Finally, he spoke. "Why did your company ignore the advice we gave you? Coming here was a disaster."

"Yes."

He turned to her.

"Yes," she continued, "this whole expedition will likely be a disaster—a disaster that takes us a step closer to our goal."

He checked Sisisru next, working by the light of the now-rising moon. "Foolish."

Vathi folded her arms before her on the roof of the building, torso still disappearing into the lit square of the trapdoor below. "Do you think that our ancestors learned to wayfind on the oceans without experiencing a few disasters along the way? Or what of the first trappers? You have knowledge passed down for generations, knowledge earned through trial and error. If the first trappers had considered it too 'foolish' to explore, where would you be?"

"They were single men, well-trained, not a ship full of clerks and dockworkers."

"The world is changing, Sixth of the Dusk," she said softly. "The people of the mainland grow hungry for Aviar companions; things once restricted to the very wealthy are within the reach of ordinary people. We've learned so much, yet the Aviar are still an enigma. Why don't chicks raised on the homeisles bestow talents? Why—"

"Foolish arguments," Dusk said, putting Sisisru back into her nest. "I do not wish to hear them again."

"And the Ones Above?" she asked. "What of their technology, the wonders they produce?"

He hesitated, then he took out a pair of thick gloves and gestured toward her Aviar. Vathi looked at the white and green Aviar, then made a comforting clicking sound and took her in two hands. The bird suffered it with a few annoyed half bites at Vathi's fingers.

Dusk carefully took the bird in his gloved hands—for him, those bites would not be as timid—and undid Vathi's bandage. Then he cleaned the wound—much to the bird's protests—and carefully placed a new bandage. From there, he wrapped the bird's wings around its body with another bandage, not too tight, lest the creature be unable to breathe.

She didn't like it, obviously. But flying would hurt that wing more, with the fracture. She'd eventually be able to bite off the bandage, but for now, she'd get a chance to heal. Once done, he placed her with his other Aviar, who made quiet, friendly chirps, calming the flustered bird.

Vathi seemed content to let her bird remain there for the time, though she watched the entire process with interest.

"You may sleep in my safecamp tonight," Dusk said, turning back to her.

"And then what?" she asked. "You turn me out into the jungle to die?"

"You did well on your way here," he said, grudgingly. She was not a trapper. A scholar should not have been able to do what she did. "You will probably survive."

"I got lucky. I'd never make it across the entire island."

Dusk paused. "Across the island?"

"To the main company camp."

"There are *more* of you?"

"I . . . Of course. You didn't think . . ."

"What happened?" *Now who is the fool?* he thought to himself. *You should have asked this first.* Talking. He had never been good with it.

She shied away from him, eyes widening. Did he look dangerous? Perhaps he had barked that last question forcefully. No matter. She spoke, so he got what he needed.

"We set up camp on the far beach," she said. "We have two ironhulls armed with cannons watching the waters. Those can take on even a deepwalker, if they have to. Two hundred soldiers, half that number in scientists and merchants. We're determined to find out, once and for all, why the Aviar must be born on one of the Pantheon Islands to be able to bestow talents.

"One team came down this direction to scout sites to place another fortress. The company is determined to hold Patji against other interests. I thought the smaller expedition a bad idea, but had my own reasons for wanting to circle the island. So I went along. And then, the deepwalker . . ." She looked sick.

Dusk had almost stopped listening. Two *hundred* soldiers? Crawling across Patji like ants on a fallen piece of fruit. Unbearable! He thought of the quiet jungle broken by the sounds of their racketous voices. The sound of humans yelling at each other, clanging on metal, stomping about. Like a city.

A flurry of dark feathers announced Sak coming up from below and landing on the lip of the trapdoor beside Vathi. The black-plumed bird limped across the roof toward Dusk, stretching her wings, showing off the scars on her left. Flying even a dozen feet was a chore for her.

Dusk reached down to scratch her neck. It was happening. An invasion. He had to find a way to stop it. Somehow . . .

"I'm sorry, Dusk," Vathi said. "The trappers are fascinating to me; I've read of your ways, and I respect them. But this was *going* to happen someday; it's inevitable. The islands *will* be tamed. The Aviar are too valuable to leave in the hands of a couple hundred eccentric woodsmen."

"The chiefs . . ."

"All twenty chiefs in council agreed to this plan," Vathi said. "I was there. If the Eelakin do not secure these islands and the Aviar, someone else will."

Dusk stared out into the night. "Go and make certain there are no insects in the cups below."

"But—"

"*Go*," he said, "and make *certain* there are no insects in the cups below!"

The woman sighed softly, but retreated into the room, leaving him with his Aviar. He continued to scratch Sak on the neck, seeking comfort in the familiar motion and in her presence. Dared he hope that the shadows would prove too deadly for the company and its iron-hulled ships? Vathi seemed confident.

She did not tell me why she joined the scouting group. She had seen a shadow, witnessed it destroying her team, but had still managed the presence of mind to find his camp. She was a strong woman. He would need to remember that.

She was also a company type, as removed from his experience as a person could get. Soldiers, craftsmen, even chiefs he could understand. But these soft-spoken scribes who had quietly conquered the world with a sword of commerce, they baffled him.

"Father," he whispered. "What do I do?"

Patji gave no reply beyond the normal sounds of night. Creatures moving, hunting, rustling. At night, the Aviar slept, and that gave opportunity to the most dangerous of the island's predators. In the distance a nightmaw called, its horrid screech echoing through the trees.

Sak spread her wings, leaning down, head darting back and forth. The sound always made her tremble. It did the same to Dusk.

He sighed and rose, placing Sak on his shoulder. He turned, and almost stumbled as he saw his corpse at his feet. He came alert immediately. What was it? Vines in the tree branches? A spider, dropping quietly from above? There wasn't supposed to be anything in his safecamp that could kill him.

Sak screeched as if in pain.

Nearby, his other Aviar cried out as well, a cacophony of squawks, screeches, chirps. No, it wasn't just them! All around . . . echoing in the distance, from both near and far, wild Aviar squawked. They rustled in their branches, a sound like a powerful wind blowing through the trees.

Dusk spun about, holding his hands to his ears, eyes wide as corpses appeared around him. They piled high, one atop another, some bloated, some bloody, some skeletal. Haunting him. Dozens upon *dozens*.

He dropped to his knees, yelling. That put him eye-to-eye with one of his corpses. Only this one . . . this one was not quite dead. Blood dripped from its lips as it tried to speak, mouthing words that Dusk did not understand.

It vanished.

They all did, every last one. He spun about, wild, but saw no bodies. The sounds of the Aviar quieted, and his flock settled back into their nests. Dusk breathed in and out deeply, heart racing. He felt tense, as if at any moment a shadow would explode from the blackness around his camp and consume him. He anticipated it, felt it coming. He wanted to run, run *somewhere*.

What had that been? In all of his years with Sak, he had never seen anything like it. What could have upset all of the Aviar at once? Was it the nightmaw he had heard?

Don't be foolish, he thought. *This was different, different from anything you've seen. Different from anything that has been seen on Patji.* But what? What had changed . . .

Sak had not settled down like the others. She stared northward, toward where Vathi had said the main camp of invaders was setting up.

Dusk stood, then clambered down into the room below, Sak on his shoulder. "What are your people doing?"

Vathi spun at his harsh tone. She had been looking out of the window, northward. "I don't—"

He took her by the front of her vest, pulling her toward him in a two-fisted grip, meeting her eyes from only a few inches away. *"What are your people doing?"*

Her eyes widened, and he could feel her tremble in his grip, though she set her jaw and held his gaze. Scribes were not supposed to have grit like this. He had seen them scribbling away in their windowless rooms. Dusk tightened his grip on her vest, pulling the fabric so it dug into her skin, and found himself growling softly.

"Release me," she said, "and we will speak."

"Bah," he said, letting go. She dropped a few inches, hitting the floor with a thump. He hadn't realized he'd lifted her off the ground.

She backed away, putting as much space between them as the room would allow. He stalked to the window, looking through the mesh screen at the night. His corpse dropped from the roof above, hitting the ground below. He jumped back, worried that it was happening again.

It didn't, not the same way as before. However, when he turned back into the room, his corpse lay in the corner, bloody lips parted, eyes staring sightlessly. The danger, whatever it was, had not passed.

Vathi had sat down on the floor, holding her head, trembling. Had he frightened her that soundly? She did look tired, exhausted. She wrapped her arms around herself, and when she looked at him, there was a cast to her eyes that hadn't been there before—as if she were regarding a wild animal let off its chain.

That seemed fitting.

"What do you know of the Ones Above?" she asked him.

"They live in the stars," Dusk said.

"We at the company have been meeting with them. We don't understand their ways. They look like us; at times they talk like us. But they have . . . rules, laws that they won't explain. They refuse to sell us their marvels, but in like manner, they seem forbidden from taking things from us, even in trade. They promise it, someday when we are more advanced. It's like they think we are children."

"Why should we care?" Dusk said. "If they leave us alone, we will be better for it."

"You haven't seen the things they can do," she said softly, getting a distant look in her eyes. "We have barely worked out how to create ships that can sail on their own, against the wind. But the Ones Above . . . they can sail the skies, sail the *stars themselves*. They know so much, and they won't *tell* us any of it."

She shook her head, reaching into the pocket of her skirt. "They are after something, Dusk. What interest do we hold for them? From what I've heard them say, there are many other worlds like ours, with cultures that cannot sail the stars. We are not unique, yet the Ones Above come back here time and time again. They *do* want something. You can see it in their eyes. . . ."

"What is that?" Dusk asked, nodding to the thing she took from her pocket. It rested in her palm like the shell of a clam, but had a mirrorlike face on the top.

"It is a machine," she said. "Like a clock, only it never needs to be wound, and it . . . shows things."

"What things?"

"Well, it translates languages. Ours into that of the Ones Above. It also . . . shows the locations of Aviar."

"*What?*"

"It's like a map," she said. "It points the way to Aviar."

"That's how you found my camp," Dusk said, stepping toward her.

"Yes." She rubbed her thumb across the machine's surface. "We aren't supposed to have this. It was the possession of an emissary sent to work with us. He choked while eating a few months back. They *can* die, it appears, even of mundane causes. That . . . changed how I view them.

"His kind have asked after his machines, and we will have to return them soon. But this one tells us what they are after: the Aviar. The Ones Above are always fascinated with them. I think they want to find a way to trade for the birds, a way their laws will allow. They hint that we might not be safe, that not everyone Above follows their laws."

"But why did the Aviar react like they did, just now?" Dusk said, turning back to the window. "Why did . . ." *Why did I see what I saw? What I'm still seeing, to an extent?* His corpse was there, wherever he looked. Slumped by a tree outside, in the corner of the room, hanging out of the trapdoor in the roof. Sloppy. He should have closed that.

Sak had pulled into his hair like she did when a predator was near.

"There . . . is a second machine," Vathi said.

"Where?" he demanded.

"On our ship."

The direction the Aviar had looked.

"The second machine is much larger," Vathi said. "This one in my hand has limited range. The larger one can create an enormous map, one of an entire island, then *write* out a paper with a copy of that map. That map will include a dot marking every Aviar."

"And?"

"And we were going to engage the machine tonight," she said. "It takes hours to prepare—like an oven, growing hot—before it's ready. The schedule was to turn it on tonight just after sunset so we could use it in the morning."

"The others," Dusk demanded, "they'd use it without you?"

She grimaced. "Happily. Captain Eusto probably did a dance when I didn't return from scouting. He's been worried I would take control of this expedition. But the machine isn't harmful; it merely locates Aviar."

"Did it do *that* before?" he demanded, waving toward the night. "When you last used it, did it draw the attention of all the Aviar? Discomfort them?"

"Well, no," she said. "But the moment of discomfort has passed, hasn't it? I'm sure it's nothing."

Nothing. Sak quivered on his shoulder. Dusk saw death all around him. The moment they had engaged that machine, the corpses had piled up. If they used it again, the results would be horrible. Dusk knew it. He could *feel* it.

"We're going to stop them," he said.

"What?" Vathi asked. "*Tonight?*"

"Yes," Dusk said, walking to a small hidden cabinet in the wall. He pulled it open and began to pick through the supplies inside. A second lantern. Extra oil.

"That's insane," Vathi said. "Nobody travels the islands at night."

"I've done it once before. With my uncle."

His uncle had died on that trip.

"You can't be serious, Dusk. The nightmaws are out. I've heard them."

"Nightmaws track minds," Dusk said, stuffing supplies into his pack. "They are almost completely deaf, and close to blind. If we move quickly and cut across the center of the island, we can be to your camp by morning. We can stop them from using the machine again."

"But why would we *want* to?"

He shouldered the pack. "Because if we don't, it will destroy the island."

She frowned at him, cocking her head. "You can't know that. Why do you think you know that?"

"Your Aviar will have to remain here, with that wound," he said, ignoring the question. "She would not be able to fly away if something happened to us." The same argument could be made for Sak, but he would not be without the bird. "I will return her to you after we have stopped the machine. Come." He walked to the floor hatch and pulled it open.

Vathi rose, but pressed back against the wall. "I'm staying here."

"The people of your company won't believe me," he said. "You will have to tell them to stop. You are coming."

Vathi licked her lips in what seemed to be a nervous habit. She glanced to the sides, looking for escape, then back at him. Right then, Dusk noticed his corpse hanging from the pegs in the tree beneath him. He jumped.

"What was that?" she demanded.

"Nothing."

"You keep glancing to the sides," Vathi said. "What do you think you see, Dusk?"

"We're going. Now."

"You've been alone on the island for a long time," she said, obviously trying to make her voice soothing. "You're upset about our arrival. You aren't thinking clearly. I understand."

Dusk drew in a deep breath. "Sak, show her."

The bird launched from his shoulder, flapping across the room, landing on Vathi. She turned to the bird, frowning.

Then she gasped, falling to her knees. Vathi huddled back against the wall, eyes darting from side to side, mouth working but no words coming out. Dusk left her to it for a short time, then raised his arm. Sak returned to him on black wings, dropping a single dark feather to the floor. She settled in again on his shoulder. That much flying was difficult for her.

"What was *that*?" Vathi demanded.

"Come," Dusk said, taking his pack and climbing down out of the room.

Vathi scrambled to the open hatch. "No. Tell me. What *was* that?"

"You saw your corpse."

"All about me. Everywhere I looked."

"Sak grants that talent."

"There is no such talent."

Dusk looked up at her, halfway down the pegs. "You have seen your death. That is what will happen if your friends use their machine. Death. All of us. The Aviar, everyone living here. I do not know why, but I know that it *will* come."

"You've discovered a new Aviar," Vathi said. "How . . . When . . . ?"

"Hand me the lantern," Dusk said.

Looking numb, she obeyed, handing it down. He put it into his teeth and descended the pegs to the ground. Then he raised the lantern high, looking down the slope.

The inky jungle at night. Like the depths of the ocean.

He shivered, then whistled. Kokerlii fluttered down from above, landing on his other shoulder. He would hide their minds, and with that, they had a chance. It would still not be easy. The things of the jungle relied upon mind sense, but many could still hunt by scent or other senses.

Vathi scrambled down the pegs behind him, her pack over her shoulder, the strange tube peeking out. "You have two Aviar," she said. "You use them both at once?"

"My uncle had three."

"How is that even possible?"

"They like trappers." So many questions. Could she not think about what the answers might be before asking?

"We're actually going to do this," she said, whispering, as if to herself. "The jungle at night. I should stay. I should refuse . . ."

"You've seen your death if you do."

"I've seen what you claim is my death. A new Aviar . . . It has been centuries." Though her voice still sounded reluctant, she walked after him as he strode down the slope and passed his traps, entering the jungle again.

His corpse sat at the base of a tree. That made him immediately look for what could kill him here, but Sak's senses seemed to be off. The island's impending death was so overpowering, it seemed to be smothering smaller dangers. He might not be able to rely upon her visions until the machine was destroyed.

The thick jungle canopy swallowed them, hot, even at night; the ocean breezes didn't reach this far inland. That left the air feeling stagnant, and it dripped with the scents of the jungle. Fungus, rotting leaves, the perfumes of flowers. The accompaniment to those scents was the sounds of an island coming alive. A constant crinkling in the underbrush, like the sound of maggots writhing in a pile of dry leaves. The lantern's light did not seem to extend as far as it should.

Vathi pulled up close behind him. "Why did you do this before?" she whispered. "The other time you went out at night?"

More questions. But sounds, fortunately, were not too dangerous.

"I was wounded," Dusk whispered. "We had to get from one safecamp to the other to recover my uncle's store of antivenom." Because Dusk, hands trembling, had dropped the other flask.

"You survived it? Well, obviously you did, I mean. I'm surprised, is all."

She seemed to be talking to fill the air.

"They could be watching us," she said, looking into the darkness. "Nightmaws."

"They are not."

"How can you know?" she asked, voice hushed. "Anything could be out there, in that darkness."

"If the nightmaws had seen us, we'd be dead. That is how I know." He shook his head, sliding out his machete and cutting away a few branches before them. Any could hold deathants skittering across their leaves. In the dark, it would be difficult to spot them, and so brushing against foliage seemed a poor decision.

We won't be able to avoid it, he thought, leading the way down through a gully thick with mud. He had to step on stones to keep from sinking in. Vathi followed with remarkable dexterity. *We have to go quickly. I can't cut down every branch in our way.*

He hopped off a stone and onto the bank of the gully, and there passed his corpse sinking into the mud. Nearby, he spotted a second corpse, so translucent it was nearly invisible. He raised his lantern, hoping it wasn't happening again.

Others did not appear. Just these two. And the very faint image . . . yes, that was a sinkhole there. Sak chirped softly, and he fished in his pocket for a seed to give her. She had figured out how to send him help. The fainter images were immediate dangers—he would have to watch for those.

"Thank you," he whispered to her.

"That bird of yours," Vathi said, speaking softly in the gloom of night, "are there others?"

They climbed out of the gully, continuing on, crossing a krell trail in the night. He stopped them just before they wandered into a patch of deathants. Vathi looked at the trail of tiny yellow insects, moving in a straight line.

"Dusk?" she asked as they rounded the ants. "Are there others? Why haven't you brought any chicks to market?"

"I do not have any chicks."

"So you found only the one?" she asked.

Questions, questions. Buzzing around him like flies.

Don't be foolish, he told himself, shoving down his annoyance. *You would ask the same, if you saw someone with a new Aviar.* He had tried to keep Sak a secret; for years, he hadn't even brought her with him when he left the island. But with her hurt wing, he hadn't wanted to abandon her.

Deep down, he'd known he couldn't keep his secret forever. "There are many like her," he said. "But only she has a talent to bestow."

Vathi stopped in place as he continued to cut them a path. He turned back, looking at her alone on the new trail. He had given her the lantern to hold.

"That's a mainlander bird," she said. She held up the light. "I knew it was when I first saw it, and I assumed it wasn't an Aviar, because mainlander birds can't bestow talents."

Dusk turned back and continued cutting.

"You brought a mainlander chick to the Pantheon," Vathi whispered behind. "And it *gained a talent*."

With a hack he brought down a branch, then continued on. Again, she had not asked a question, so he needed not answer.

Vathi hurried to keep up, the glow of the lantern tossing his shadow before him as she stepped up behind. "Surely someone else has tried it before. Surely . . ."

He did not know.

"But why would they?" she continued, quietly, as if to herself. "The Aviar are special. Everyone knows the separate breeds and what they do. Why assume that a fish would learn to breathe air, if raised on land? Why assume a non-Aviar would become one if raised on Patji. . . ."

They continued through the night. Dusk led them around many dangers, though he found that he needed to rely greatly upon Sak's help. *Do not follow that stream, which has your corpse bobbing in its waters. Do not touch that tree; the bark is poisonous with rot. Turn from that path. Your corpse shows a deathant bite.*

Sak did not speak to him, but each message was clear. When he stopped to let Vathi drink from her canteen, he held Sak and found her trembling. She did not peck at him as was usual when he enclosed her in his hands.

They stood in a small clearing, pure dark all around them, the sky shrouded in clouds. He heard distant rainfall on the trees. Not uncommon, here.

Nightmaws screeched, one then another. They only did that when they had made a kill or when they were seeking to frighten prey. Often, krell herds slept near Aviar roosts. Frighten away the birds, and you could sense the krell.

Vathi had taken out her tube. Not a scroll case—and not something scholarly at all, considering the way she held it as she poured something into its end. Once done, she raised it like one would a weapon. Beneath her feet, Dusk's body lay mangled.

He did not ask after Vathi's weapon, not even as she took some kind of short, slender spear and fitted it into the top end. No weapon could penetrate the thick skin of a nightmaw. You either avoided them or you died.

Kokerlii fluttered down to his shoulder, chirping away. He seemed confused by the darkness. Why were they out like this, at night, when birds normally made no noise?

"We must keep moving," Dusk said, placing Sak on his other shoulder and taking out his machete.

"You realize that your bird changes everything," Vathi said quietly, joining him, shouldering her pack and carrying her tube in the other hand.

"There will be a new kind of Aviar," Dusk whispered, stepping over his corpse.

"That's the *least* of it. Dusk, we assumed that chicks raised away from these islands did not develop their abilities because they were not around others to train them. We assumed that their abilities were innate, like our ability to speak—it's inborn, but we require help from others to develop it."

"That can still be true," Dusk said. "Other species, such as Sak, can merely be trained to speak."

"And your bird? Was it trained by others?"

"Perhaps." He did not say what he really thought. It was a thing of trappers. He noted a corpse on the ground before them.

It was not his.

He held up a hand immediately, stilling Vathi as she continued on to ask another question. What was *this*? The meat had been picked off much of the skeleton, and the clothing lay strewn about, ripped open by animals that feasted. Small, funguslike plants had sprouted around the ground near it, tiny red tendrils reaching up to enclose parts of the skeleton.

He looked up at the great tree, at the foot of which rested the corpse. The flowers were not in bloom. Dusk released his breath.

"What is it?" Vathi whispered. "Deathants?"

"No. Patji's Finger."

She frowned. "Is that . . . some kind of curse?"

"It is a name," Dusk said, stepping forward carefully to inspect the corpse. Machete. Boots. Rugged gear. One of his colleagues had fallen. He *thought* he recognized the man from the clothing. An older trapper named First of the Sky.

"The name of a person?" Vathi asked, peeking over his shoulder.

"The name of a tree," Dusk said, poking at the corpse's clothing, careful of insects that might be lurking inside. "Raise the lamp."

"I've never heard of that tree," she said skeptically.

"They are only on Patji."

"I have read a lot about the flora on these islands. . . ."

"Here you are a child. Light."

She sighed, raising it for him. He used a stick to prod at pockets on the ripped clothing. This man had been killed by a tuskrun pack, larger predators—almost as large as a man—that prowled mostly by day. Their movement patterns were predictable unless one happened across one of Patji's Fingers in bloom.

There. He found a small book in the man's pocket. Dusk raised it, then backed away. Vathi peered over his shoulder. Homeislers stood so *close* to each other. Did she need to stand right by his elbow?

He checked the first pages, finding a list of dates. Yes, judging by the last date written down, this man was only a few days dead. The pages after that detailed the locations of Sky's safecamps, along with explanations of the traps guarding each one. The last page contained the farewell.

I am First of the Sky, taken by Patji at last. I have a brother on Suluko. Care for them, rival.

Few words. Few words were good. Dusk carried a book like this himself, and he had said even less on his last page.

"He wants you to care for his family?" Vathi asked.

"Don't be stupid," Dusk said, tucking the book away. "His birds."

"That's sweet," Vathi said. "I had always heard that trappers were incredibly territorial."

"We are," he said, noting how she said it. Again, her tone made it seem as if she considered trappers to be like animals. "But our birds might die without care—they are accustomed to humans. Better to give them to a rival than to let them die."

"Even if that rival is the one who killed you?" Vathi asked. "The traps you set, the ways you try to interfere with one another . . ."

"It is our way."

"That is an awful excuse," she said, looking up at the tree.

She was right.

The tree was massive, with drooping fronds. At the end of each one was a large closed blossom, as long as two hands put together. "You don't seem worried," she noted, "though the plant seems to have killed that man."

"These are only dangerous when they bloom."

"Spores?" she asked.

"No." He picked up the fallen machete, but left the rest of Sky's things alone. Let Patji claim him. Father did so like to murder his children. Dusk continued onward, leading Vathi, ignoring his corpse draped across a log.

"Dusk?" Vathi asked, raising the lantern and hurrying to him. "If not spores, then how does the tree kill?"

"So many questions."

"My life is about questions," she replied. "And about answers. If my people are going to work on this island . . ."

He hacked at some plants with the machete.

"It *is* going to happen," she said, more softly. "I'm sorry, Dusk. You can't stop the world from changing. Perhaps my expedition will be defeated, but others will come."

"Because of the Ones Above," he snapped.

"They may spur it," Vathi said. "Truly, when we finally convince them we are developed enough to be traded with, we will sail the stars as they do. But change will happen even without them. The world is progressing. One man cannot slow it, no matter how determined he is."

He stopped in the path.

You cannot stop the tides from changing, Dusk. No matter how determined you are. His mother's words. Some of the last he remembered from her.

Dusk continued on his way. Vathi followed. He would need her, though a treacherous piece of him whispered that she would be easy to end. With her would go her questions, and more importantly her answers. The ones he suspected she was very close to discovering.

You cannot change it. . . .

He could not. He hated that it was so. He wanted so badly to protect this island, as his kind had done for centuries. He worked this jungle, he loved its birds, was fond of its scents and sounds—despite all else. How he wished he could prove to Patji that he and the others were worthy of these shores.

Perhaps. Perhaps then . . .

Bah. Well, killing this woman would not provide any real protection for the island. Besides, had he sunk so low that he would murder a helpless scribe in cold blood? He would not even do that to another trapper, unless they approached his camp and did not retreat.

"The blossoms can think," he found himself saying as he turned them away from a mound that showed the tuskrun pack had been rooting here. "The Fingers of Patji. The trees themselves are not dangerous, even when blooming—but they attract predators, imitating the thoughts of a wounded animal that is full of pain and worry."

Vathi gasped. "A *plant*," she said, "that broadcasts a mental signature? Are you certain?"

"Yes."

"I need one of those blossoms." The light shook as she turned to go back.

Dusk spun and caught her by the arm. "We must keep moving."

"But—"

"You will have another chance." He took a deep breath. "Your people will soon infest this island like maggots on carrion. You will see other trees. Tonight, we must *go*. Dawn approaches."

He let go of her and turned back to his work. He had judged her wise, for a homeisler. Perhaps she would listen.

She did. She followed behind.

Patji's Fingers. First of the Sky, the dead trapper, should not have died in that place. Truly, the trees were not that dangerous. They lived by opening many blossoms and attracting predators to come feast. The predators would then fight one another, and the tree would feed off the corpses. Sky must have stumbled across a tree as it was beginning to flower, and got caught in what came.

His Aviar had not been enough to shield so many open blossoms. Who would have expected a death like that? After years on the island, surviving much more terrible dangers, to be caught by those simple flowers. It almost seemed a mockery, on Patji's part, of the poor man.

Dusk and Vathi's path continued, and soon grew steeper. They'd need to go uphill for a while before crossing to the downward slope that would lead to the other side of the island. Their trail, fortunately, would avoid Patji's main peak—the point of the wedge that jutted up the easternmost side of the island. His camp had been near the south, and Vathi's would be to the northeast, letting them skirt around the base of the wedge before arriving on the other beach.

They fell into a rhythm, and she was quiet for a time. Eventually, atop a particularly steep incline, he nodded for a break and squatted down to drink from his canteen. On Patji one did not simply sit, without care, upon a stump or log to rest.

Consumed by worry, and not a little frustration, he didn't notice what Vathi was doing until it was too late. She'd found something tucked into a branch—a long colorful feather. A mating plume.

Dusk leaped to his feet.

Vathi reached up toward the lower branches of the tree.

A set of spikes on ropes dropped from a nearby tree as Vathi pulled the branch. They swung down as Dusk reached her, one arm thrown in the way. A spike hit, the long, thin nail ripping into his skin and jutting out the other side, bloodied, and stopping a hair from Vathi's cheek.

She screamed.

Many predators on Patji were hard of hearing, but still that wasn't wise. Dusk didn't care. He yanked the spike from his skin, unconcerned with the bleeding for now, and checked the other spikes on the drop-rope trap.

No poison. Blessedly, they had not been poisoned.

"Your arm!" Vathi said.

He grunted. It didn't hurt. Yet. She began fishing in her pack for a bandage, and he accepted her ministrations without complaint or groan, even as the pain came upon him.

"I'm so sorry!" Vathi sputtered. "I found a mating plume! That meant an Aviar nest, so I thought to look in the tree. Have we stumbled across another trapper's safecamp?"

She was babbling out words as she worked. Seemed appropriate. When he grew nervous, he grew even more quiet. She would do the opposite.

She was good with a bandage, again surprising him. The wound had not hit any major arteries. He would be fine, though using his left hand would not be easy. This would be an annoyance. When she was done, looking sheepish and guilty, he reached down and picked up the mating plume she had dropped.

"This," he said with a harsh whisper, holding it up before her, "is the symbol of your ignorance. On the Pantheon Islands, nothing is easy, nothing is simple. That plume was placed by another trapper to catch someone who does not deserve to be here, someone who thought to find an easy prize. You cannot be that person. Never move without asking yourself, is this too easy?"

She paled. Then she took the feather in her fingers.

"Come."

He turned and walked on their way. That was the speech for an apprentice, he realized. Upon their first major mistake. A ritual among trappers. What had possessed him to give it to her?

She followed behind, head bowed, appropriately shamed. She didn't realize the honor he had just paid her, if unconsciously. They walked onward, an hour or more passing.

By the time she spoke, for some reason, he almost welcomed the words breaking upon the sounds of the jungle. "I'm sorry."

"You need not be sorry," he said. "Only careful."

"I understand." She took a deep breath, following behind him on the path. "And I *am* sorry. Not just about your arm. About this island. About what is coming. I think it inevitable, but I do wish that it did not mean the end of such a grand tradition."

"I . . ."

Words. He hated trying to find words.

"It . . . was not dusk when I was born," he finally said, then hacked down a swampvine and held his breath against the noxious fumes that it released toward him. They were only dangerous for a few moments.

"Excuse me?" Vathi asked, keeping her distance from the swampvine. "You were born . . ."

"My mother did not name me for the time of day. I was named because my mother saw the dusk of our people. The sun will soon set on us, she often told me." He looked back to Vathi, letting her pass him and enter a small clearing.

Oddly, she smiled at him. Why had he found those words to speak? He followed into the clearing, concerned at himself. He had not given those words to his uncle; only his parents knew the source of his name.

He was not certain why he'd told this scribe from an evil company. But . . . it did feel good to have said them.

A nightmaw broke through between two trees behind Vathi.

The enormous beast would have been as tall as a tree if it had stood upright. Instead it leaned forward in a prowling posture, powerful legs behind bearing most of its weight, its two clawed forelegs ripping up the ground. It reached forward its long neck, beak open, razor-sharp and deadly. It looked like a bird—in the same way that a wolf looked like a lapdog.

He threw his machete. An instinctive reaction, for he did not have time for thought. He did not have time for fear. That snapping beak—as tall as a door—would have the two of them dead in moments.

His machete glanced off the beak and actually cut the creature on the side of the head. That drew its attention, making it hesitate for just a moment. Dusk leaped for Vathi. She stepped back from him, setting the butt of her tube against the ground. He needed to pull her away, to—

The explosion deafened him.

Smoke bloomed around Vathi, who stood—wide eyed—having dropped the lantern, oil spilling. The sudden sound stunned Dusk, and he almost collided with her as the nightmaw lurched and fell, skidding, the ground *thumping* from the impact.

Dusk found himself on the ground. He scrambled to his feet, backing away from the twitching nightmaw mere inches from him. Lit by flickering lanternlight, it was all leathery skin that was bumpy like that of a bird who had lost her feathers.

It was dead. Vathi had killed it.

She said something.

Vathi had *killed* a nightmaw.

"Dusk!" Her voice seemed distant.

He raised a hand to his forehead, which had belatedly begun to prickle with sweat. His wounded arm throbbed, but he was otherwise tense. He felt as if he should be running. He had never wanted to be so close to one of these. *Never.*

She'd actually killed it.

He turned toward her, his eyes wide. Vathi was trembling, but she covered it well. "So, that worked," she said. "We weren't certain it would, even though we'd prepared these specifically for the nightmaws."

"It's like a cannon," Dusk said. "Like from one of the ships, only in your *hands.*"

"Yes."

He turned back toward the beast. Actually, it *wasn't* dead, not completely. It twitched, and let out a plaintive screech that shocked him, even with his hearing muffled. The weapon had fired that spear right into the beast's chest.

The nightmaw quaked and thrashed a weak leg.

"We could kill them all," Dusk said. He turned, then rushed over to Vathi, taking her with his right hand, the arm that wasn't wounded. "With those weapons, we could kill them *all*. Every nightmaw. Maybe the shadows too!"

"Well, yes, it has been discussed. However, they are important parts of the ecosystem on these islands. Removing the apex predators could have undesirable results."

"Undesirable results?" Dusk ran his left hand through his hair. "They'd be gone. All of them! I don't care what other problems you think it would cause. They would all be *dead*."

Vathi snorted, picking up the lantern and stamping out the fires it had started. "I thought trappers were connected to nature."

"We are. That's how I know we would all be better off without any of these things."

"You are disabusing me of many romantic notions about your kind, Dusk," she said, circling the dying beast.

Dusk whistled, holding up his arm. Kokerlii fluttered down from high branches; in the chaos and explosion, Dusk had not seen the bird fly away. Sak still clung to his shoulder with a death grip, her claws digging into his skin through the cloth. He hadn't noticed. Kokerlii landed on his arm and gave an apologetic chirp.

"It wasn't your fault," Dusk said soothingly. "They prowl the night. Even when they cannot sense our minds, they can smell us." Their sense of smell was said to be incredible. This one had come up the trail behind them; it must have crossed their path and followed it.

Dangerous. His uncle always claimed the nightmaws were growing smarter, that they knew they could not hunt men only by their minds. *I should have taken us across more streams,* Dusk thought, reaching up and rubbing Sak's neck to soothe her. *There just isn't time. . . .*

His corpse lay wherever he looked. Draped across a rock, hanging from the vines of trees, slumped beneath the dying nightmaw's claw . . .

The beast trembled once more, then amazingly it lifted its gruesome head and let out a last screech. Not as loud as those that normally sounded in the night, but bone-chilling and horrid. Dusk stepped back despite himself, and Sak chirped nervously.

Other nightmaw screeches rose in the night, distant. That sound . . . he had been trained to recognize that sound as the sound of death.

"We're going," he said, stalking across the ground and pulling Vathi away from the dying beast, which had lowered its head and fallen silent.

"Dusk?" She did not resist as he pulled her away.

One of the other nightmaws sounded again in the night. Was it closer? *Oh, Patji, please,* Dusk thought. *No. Not this.*

He pulled her faster, reaching for his machete at his side, but it was not there. He had thrown it. He took out the one he had gathered from his fallen rival, then dragged her out of the clearing, back into the jungle, moving quickly. He could no longer worry about brushing against deathants.

A greater danger was coming.

The calls of death came again.

"Are those getting *closer?*" Vathi asked.

Dusk did not answer. It was a question, but he did not know the answer. At least his hearing was recovering. He released her hand, moving more quickly, almost at a trot—faster than he ever wanted to go through the jungle, day or night.

"Dusk!" Vathi hissed. "Will they come? To the call of the dying one? Is that something they do?"

"How should I know? I have never known one of them to be killed before." He saw the tube, again carried over her shoulder, lit by the light of the lantern she carried.

That gave him pause, though his instincts screamed at him to keep moving and he felt a fool. "Your weapon," he said. "You can use it again?"

"Yes," she said. "Once more."

"*Once* more?"

A half dozen screeches sounded in the night.

"Yes," she replied. "I only brought three spears and enough powder for three shots. I tried firing one at the shadow. It didn't do much."

He spoke no further, ignoring his wounded arm—the bandage was in need of changing—and towing her through the jungle. The calls came again and again. Agitated. How did one escape nightmaws? His Aviar clung to him, a bird on each shoulder. He had to leap over his corpse as they traversed a gulch and came up the other side.

How do you escape them? he thought, remembering his uncle's training. *You don't draw their attention in the first place!*

They were fast. Kokerlii would hide his mind, but if they picked up his trail at the dead one . . .

Water. He stopped in the night, turning right, then left. Where would he find a stream? Patji was an island. Fresh water came from rainfall, mostly. The largest lake . . . the only one . . . was up the wedge. Toward the peak. Along the eastern side, the island rose to some heights with cliffs on all sides. Rainfall collected there, in Patji's Eye. The river was his tears.

It was a dangerous place to go with Vathi in tow. Their path had skirted the slope up the heights, heading across the island toward the northern beach. They were close. . . .

Those screeches behind spurred him on. Patji would just have to forgive him for what came next. Dusk seized Vathi's hand and towed her in a more eastern direction. She did not complain, though she did keep looking over her shoulder.

The screeches grew closer.

He ran. He ran as he had never expected to do on Patji, wild and reckless. Leaping over troughs, around fallen logs coated in moss. Through the dark underbrush, scaring away meekers and startling Aviar slumbering in the branches above. It was foolish. It was crazy. But did it matter? Somehow, he knew those other things would not claim him. The kings of Patji hunted him; lesser dangers would not dare steal from their betters.

Vathi followed with difficulty. Those skirts were trouble, but she caught up to him each time Dusk had to occasionally stop and cut their way through underbrush. Urgent, frantic. He expected her to keep up, and she did. A piece of him—buried deep beneath the terror—was impressed. This woman would have made a fantastic trapper. Instead she would probably destroy all trappers.

He froze as screeches sounded behind, so close. Vathi gasped, and Dusk turned back to his work. Not far to go. He hacked through a dense patch of undergrowth and ran on, sweat streaming down the sides of his face. Jostling light came from Vathi's lantern behind; the scene before him was one of horrific shadows dancing on the jungle's boughs, leaves, ferns, and rocks.

This is your fault, Patji, he thought with an unexpected fury. The screeches seemed almost on top of him. Was that breaking brush he could hear behind? *We are your priests, and yet you hate us! You hate all.*

Dusk broke from the jungle and out onto the banks of the river. Small by mainland standards, but it would do. He led Vathi right into it, splashing into the cold waters.

He turned upstream. What else could he do? Downstream would lead closer to those sounds, the calls of death.

Of the Dusk, he thought. *Of the Dusk.*

The waters came only to their calves, bitter cold. The coldest water on the island, though he did not know why. They slipped and scrambled as they ran, best they could, upriver. They passed through some narrows, with lichen-covered rock walls on either side twice as tall as a man, then burst out into the basin.

A place men did not go. A place he had visited only once. A cool emerald lake rested here, sequestered.

Dusk towed Vathi to the side, out of the river, toward some brush. Perhaps she would not see. He huddled down with her, raising a finger to his lips, then turned down the light of the lantern she still held. Nightmaws could not see well, but perhaps the dim light would help. In more ways than one.

They waited there, on the shore of the small lake, hoping that the water had washed away their scent—hoping the nightmaws would grow confused or distracted. For one thing about this place was that the basin had steep walls, and there was no way out other than the river. If the nightmaws came up it, Dusk and Vathi would be trapped.

Screeches sounded. The creatures had reached the river. Dusk waited in near darkness, and so squeezed his eyes shut. He prayed to Patji, whom he loved, whom he hated.

Vathi gasped softly. "What . . . ?"

So she had seen. Of course she had. She was a seeker, a learner. A questioner.

Why must men ask so many questions?

"Dusk! There are Aviar here, in these branches! Hundreds of them." She spoke in a hushed, frightened tone. Even as they awaited death itself, she saw and could not help speaking. "Have you seen them? What is this place?" She hesitated. "So many juveniles. Barely able to fly . . ."

"They come here," he whispered. "Every bird from every island. In their youth, they must come here."

He opened his eyes, looking up. He had turned down the lantern, but it was still bright enough to see them roosting there. Some stirred at the light and the sound. They stirred more as the nightmaws screeched below.

Sak chirped on his shoulder, terrified. Kokerlii, for once, had nothing to say.

"Every bird from every island . . ." Vathi said, putting it together. "They all come here, to this place. Are you certain?"

"Yes." It was a thing that trappers knew. You could not capture a bird before it had visited Patji.

Otherwise it would be able to bestow no talent.

"They come here," she said. "We knew they migrated between islands. . . . Why do they come here?"

Was there any point in holding back now? She would figure it out. Still, he did not speak. Let her do so.

"They gain their talents here, don't they?" she asked. "How? Is it where they are trained? Is this how you made a bird who was not an Aviar into one? You brought a hatchling here, and then . . ." She frowned, raising her lantern. "I recognize those trees. They are the ones you called Patji's Fingers."

A dozen of them grew here, the largest concentration on the island. And beneath them, their fruit littered the ground. Much of it eaten, some of it only halfway so, bites taken out by birds of all stripes.

Vathi saw him looking, and frowned. "The fruit?" she asked.

"Worms," he whispered in reply.

A light seemed to go on in her eyes. "It's not the birds. It never has been . . . it's a parasite. They carry a parasite that bestows talents! That's why those raised away from the islands cannot gain the abilities, and why a mainland bird you brought here could."

"Yes."

"This changes everything, Dusk. Everything."

"Yes."

Of the Dusk. Born during that dusk, or bringer of it? What had he done?

Downriver, the nightmaw screeches drew closer. They had decided to search upriver. They were clever, more clever than men off the islands thought them to be. Vathi gasped, turning toward the small river canyon.

"Isn't this dangerous?" she whispered. "The trees are blooming. The nightmaws will come! But no. So many Aviar. They can hide those blossoms, like they do a man's mind?"

"No," he said. "All minds in this place are invisible, always, regardless of Aviar."

"But . . . how? Why? The worms?"

Dusk didn't know, and for now didn't care. *I am trying to protect you, Patji!* Dusk looked toward Patji's Fingers. *I need to stop the men and their device. I know it! Why? Why do you hunt me?*

Perhaps it was because he knew so much. Too much. More than any man had known. For he had asked questions.

Men. And their questions.

"They're coming up the river, aren't they?" she asked.

The answer seemed obvious. He did not reply.

"No," she said, standing. "I won't die with this knowledge, Dusk. I *won't*. There must be a way."

"There is," he said, standing beside her. He took a deep breath. *So I finally pay for it.* He took Sak carefully in his hand, and placed her on Vathi's shoulder. He pried Kokerlii free too.

"What are you doing?" Vathi asked.

"I will go as far as I can," Dusk said, handing Kokerlii toward her. The bird bit with annoyance at his hands, although never strong enough to draw blood. "You will need to hold him. He will try to follow me."

"No, wait. We can hide in the lake, they—"

"They will find us!" Dusk said. "It isn't deep enough by far to hide us."

"But you can't—"

"They are nearly here, woman!" he said, forcing Kokerlii into her hands. "The men of the company will not listen to me if I tell them to turn off the device. You are smart, you can make them stop. You can reach them. With Kokerlii you can reach them. Be ready to go."

She looked at him, stunned, but she seemed to realize that there was no other way. She stood, holding Kokerlii in two hands as he pulled out the journal of First of the Sky, then his own book that listed where his Aviar were, and tucked them into her pack. Finally, he stepped back into the river. He could hear a rushing sound downstream. He would have to go quickly to reach the end of the canyon before they arrived. If he could draw them out into the jungle even a short ways to the south, Vathi could slip away.

As he entered the stream, his visions of death finally vanished. No more corpses bobbing in the water, lying on the banks. Sak had realized what was happening.

She gave a final chirp.

He started to run.

One of Patji's Fingers, growing right next to the mouth of the canyon, was blooming.

"Wait!"

He should not have stopped as Vathi yelled at him. He should have continued on, for time was so slim. However, the sight of that flower—along with her yell—made him hesitate.

The flower . . .

It struck him as it must have struck Vathi. An idea. Vathi ran for her pack, letting go of Kokerlii, who immediately flew to his shoulder and started chirping at him in annoyed chastisement. Dusk didn't listen. He yanked the flower off—it was as large as a man's head, with a large bulging part at the center.

It was invisible in this basin, like they all were.

"A flower that can think," Vathi said, breathing quickly, fishing in her pack. "A flower that can draw the attention of predators."

Dusk pulled out his rope as she brought out her weapon and prepared it. He lashed the flower to the end of the spear sticking out slightly from the tube.

Nightmaw screeches echoed up the canyon. He could see their shadows, hear them splashing.

He stumbled back from Vathi as she crouched down, set the weapon's butt against the ground, and pulled a lever at the base.

The explosion, once again, nearly deafened him.

Aviar all around the rim of the basin screeched and called in fright, taking wing. A storm of feathers and flapping ensued, and through the middle of it, Vathi's spear shot into the air, flower on the end. It arced out over the canyon into the night.

Dusk grabbed her by the shoulder and pulled her back along the river, into the lake itself. They slipped into the shallow water, Kokerlii on his shoulder, Sak on hers. They left the lantern burning, giving a quiet light to the suddenly empty basin.

The lake was not deep. Two or three feet. Even crouching, it didn't cover them completely.

The nightmaws stopped in the canyon. His lanternlight showed a couple of them in the shadows, large as huts, turning and watching the sky. They were smart, but like the meekers, not as smart as men.

Patji, Dusk thought. *Patji, please . . .*

The nightmaws turned back down the canyon, following the mental signature broadcast by the flowering plant. And, as Dusk watched, his corpse bobbing in the water nearby grew increasingly translucent.

Then faded away entirely.

Dusk counted to a hundred, then slipped from the waters. Vathi, sodden in her skirts, did not speak as she grabbed the lantern. They left the weapon, its shots expended.

The calls from the nightmaws grew farther and farther away as Dusk led the way out of the canyon, then directly north, slightly downslope. He kept expecting the screeches to turn and follow.

They did not.

The company fortress was a horridly impressive sight. A work of logs and cannons right at the edge of the water, guarded by an enormous iron-hulled ship. Smoke rose from it, the burning of morning cook fires. A short distance away, what must have been a dead shadow rotted in the sun, its mountainous carcass draped half in the water, half out.

He didn't see his own corpse anywhere, though on the final leg of their trip to the fortress he had seen it several times. Always in a place of immediate danger. Sak's visions had returned to normal.

Dusk turned back to the fortress, which he did not enter. He preferred to remain on the rocky, familiar shore—perhaps twenty feet from the entrance—his wounded arm aching as the company people rushed out through the gate to meet Vathi. Their scouts on the upper walls kept careful watch on Dusk. A trapper was not to be trusted.

Even standing here, some twenty feet from the wide wooden gates into the fort, he could smell how wrong the place was. It was stuffed with the scents of men—sweaty bodies, the smell of oil, and other, newer scents that he recognized from his recent trips to the homeisles. Scents that made him feel like an outsider among his own people.

The company men wore sturdy clothing, trousers like Dusk's but far better tailored, shirts and rugged jackets. Jackets? In Patji's heat? These people bowed to Vathi, showing her more deference than Dusk would have expected. They drew hands from shoulder to shoulder as they started speaking—a symbol of respect. Foolishness. Anyone could make a gesture like that; it didn't mean anything. True respect included far more than a hand waved in the air.

But they did treat her like more than a simple scribe. She was better placed in the company than he'd assumed. Not his problem anymore, regardless.

Vathi looked at him, then back at her people. "We must hurry to the machine," she said to them. "The one from Above. We must turn it off."

Good. She would do her part. Dusk turned to walk away. Should he give words at parting? He'd never felt the need before. But today, it felt . . . wrong not to say something.

He started walking. Words. He had never been good with words.

"Turn it off?" one of the men said from behind. "What do you mean, Lady Vathi?"

"You don't need to feign innocence, Winds," Vathi said. "I know you turned it on in my absence."

"But we didn't."

Dusk paused. What? The man sounded sincere. But then, Dusk was no expert on human emotions. From what he'd seen of people from the homeisles, they could fake emotion as easily as they faked a gesture of respect.

"What *did* you do, then?" Vathi asked them.

"We . . . opened it."

Oh no . . .

"Why would you do that?" Vathi asked.

Dusk turned to regard them, but he didn't need to hear the answer. The answer was before him, in the vision of a dead island he'd misinterpreted.

"We figured," the man said, "that we should see if we could puzzle out how the machine worked. Vathi, the insides . . . they're complex beyond what we could have imagined. But there are seeds there. Things we could—"

"No!" Dusk said, rushing toward them.

One of the sentries above planted an arrow at his feet. He lurched to a stop, looking wildly from Vathi up toward the walls. Couldn't they see? The bulge in mud that announced a deathant den. The game trail. The distinctive curl of a cutaway vine. Wasn't it *obvious*?

"It will destroy us," Dusk said. "Don't seek . . . Don't you see . . . ?"

For a moment, they all just stared at him. He had a chance. Words. He needed *words*.

"That machine is deathants!" he said. "A den, a . . . Bah!" How could he explain?

He couldn't. In his anxiety, words fled him, like Aviar fluttering away into the night.

The others finally started moving, pulling Vathi toward the safety of their treasonous fortress.

"You said the corpses are gone," Vathi said as she was ushered through the gates. "We've succeeded. I will see that the machine is not engaged on this trip! I promise you this, Dusk!"

"But," he cried back, "it was never *meant* to be engaged!"

The enormous wooden gates of the fortress creaked closed, and he lost sight of her. Dusk cursed. Why hadn't he been able to explain?

Because he didn't know how to talk. For once in his life, that seemed to matter.

Furious, frustrated, he stalked away from that place and its awful smells. Halfway to the tree line, however, he stopped, then turned. Sak fluttered down, landing on his shoulder and cooing softly.

Questions. Those questions wanted into his brain.

Instead he yelled at the guards. He demanded they return Vathi to him. He even pled.

Nothing happened. They wouldn't speak to him. Finally, he started to feel foolish. He turned back toward the trees, and continued on his way. His assumptions were probably wrong. After all, the corpses *were* gone. Everything could go back to normal.

. . . Normal. Could anything *ever* be normal with that fortress looming behind him? He shook his head, entering the canopy. The dense humidity of Patji's jungle should have calmed him.

Instead it annoyed him. As he started the trek toward another of his safecamps, he was so distracted that he could have been a youth, his first time on Sori. He almost stumbled straight onto a gaping deathant den; he didn't even notice the vision Sak sent. This time, dumb luck saved him as he stubbed his toe on something, looked down, and only then spotted both corpse and crack crawling with motes of yellow.

He growled, then sneered. "Still you try to kill me?" he shouted, looking up at the canopy. "Patji!"

Silence.

"The ones who protect you are the ones you try hardest to kill," Dusk shouted. "Why!"

The words were lost in the jungle. It consumed them.

"You deserve this, Patji," he said. "What is coming to you. You *deserve to be destroyed!*"

He breathed out in gasps, sweating, satisfied at having finally said those things. Perhaps there was a purpose for words. Part of him, as traitorous as Vathi and her company, was *glad* that Patji would fall to their machines.

Of course, then the company itself would fall. To the Ones Above. His entire people. The world itself.

He bowed his head in the shadows of the canopy, sweat dripping down the sides of his face. Then he fell to his knees, heedless of the nest just three strides away.

Sak nuzzled into his hair. Above, in the branches, Kokerlii chirped uncertainly.

"It's a trap, you see," he whispered. "The Ones Above have rules. They can't trade with us until we're advanced enough. Just like a man can't, in good conscience, bargain with a child until they are grown. And so, they have left their machines for us to discover, to prod at and poke. The dead man was a ruse. Vathi was *meant* to have those machines.

"There will be explanations, left as if carelessly, for us to dig into and learn. And at some point in the near future, we will build something like one of their machines. We will have grown more quickly than we should have. We will be childlike still, ignorant, but the laws from Above will let these visitors trade with us. And then, they will take this land for themselves."

That was what he should have said. Protecting Patji was impossible. Protecting the Aviar was impossible. Protecting their entire *world* was impossible. Why hadn't he explained it?

Perhaps because it wouldn't have done any good. As Vathi had said . . . progress would come. If you wanted to call it that.

Dusk had arrived.

Sak left his shoulder, winging away. Dusk looked after her, then cursed. She did not land nearby. Though flying was difficult for her, she fluttered on, disappearing from his sight.

"Sak?" he asked, rising and stumbling after the Aviar. He fought back the way he had come, following Sak's squawks. A few moments later, he lurched out of the jungle.

Vathi stood on the rocks before her fortress.

Dusk hesitated at the brim of the jungle. Vathi was alone, and even the sentries had retreated. Had they cast her out? No. He could see that the gate was cracked, and some people watched from inside.

Sak had landed on Vathi's shoulder down below. Dusk frowned, reaching his hand to the side and letting Kokerlii land on his arm. Then he strode forward, calmly making his way down the rocky shore, until he was standing just before Vathi.

She'd changed into a new dress, though there were still snarls in her hair. She smelled of flowers.

And her eyes were terrified.

He'd traveled the darkness with her. Had faced nightmaws. Had seen her near to death, and she had not looked this worried.

"What?" he asked, finding his voice hoarse.

"We found instructions in the machine," Vathi whispered. "A manual on its workings, left there as if accidentally by someone who worked on it before. The manual is in their language, but the smaller machine I have . . ."

"It translates."

"The manual details how the machine was constructed," Vathi said. "It's so complex I can barely comprehend it, but it seems to explain concepts and ideas, not just give the workings of the machine."

"And are you not happy?" he asked. "You will have your flying machines soon, Vathi. Sooner than anyone could have imagined."

Wordless, she held something up. A single feather—a mating plume. She had kept it.

"Never move without asking yourself, is this too easy?" she whispered. "You said it was a trap as I was pulled away. When we found the manual, I . . . Oh, Dusk. They are planning to do to us what . . . what we are doing to Patji, aren't they?"

Dusk nodded.

"We'll lose it all. We can't fight them. They'll find an excuse, they'll *seize* the Aviar. It makes perfect sense. The Aviar use the worms. We use the Aviar. The Ones Above use us. It's inevitable, isn't it?"

Yes, he thought. He opened his mouth to say it, and Sak chirped. He frowned and turned back toward the island. Jutting from the ocean, arrogant. Destructive.

Patji. Father.

And finally, at long last, Dusk understood.

"No," he whispered.

"But—"

He undid his pants pocket, then reached deeply into it, digging around. Finally, he pulled something out. The remnants of a feather, just the shaft now. A mating plume that his uncle had given him, so many years ago, when he'd first fallen into a trap on Sori. He held it up, remembering the speech he'd been given. Like every trapper.

This is the symbol of your ignorance. Nothing is easy, nothing is simple.

Vathi held hers. Old and new.

"No, they will not have us," Dusk said. "We will see through their traps, and we will not fall for their tricks. For we have been trained by the Father himself for this very day."

She stared at his feather, then up at him.

"Do you really think that?" she asked. "They are cunning."

"They may be cunning," he said. "But they have not lived on Patji. We will gather the other trappers. We will not let ourselves be taken in."

She nodded hesitantly, and some of the fear seemed to leave her. She turned and waved for those behind her to open the gates to the building. Again, the scents of mankind washed over him.

Vathi looked back, then held out her hand to him. "You will help, then?"

His corpse appeared at her feet, and Sak chirped warningly. Danger. Yes, the path ahead would include much danger.

Dusk took Vathi's hand and stepped into the fortress anyway.

THE MAKING OF A FIRE IN THE HEAVENS

WRITING EXCUSES 7.51

BRAINSTORMING WITH MARY

Brandon: We thought it was a blast when we did this with Dan, so we're going to do it with Mary. She's actually going to pitch at us—three stories I believe?

Mary: Yes, the way I normally work is that I do a whole bunch of what I call thumbnail sketches where I just jot down a couple of different ideas of different stories, usually wildly different, and I see which one grabs me. I'm going to read them—these are little one-paragraph things—and we'll see which one grabs the guys, and then we're going to brainstorm that. Just as an aside, this is also the way I work with my agent; I will send her one-paragraph synopses of the novels I'm interested in, and she'll tell me which ones she thinks she can sell.

Mary: Idea one: In a tidally locked world or a world with a tidally locked moon, an explorer sails over the curved world and sees the moon for the first time. The coastal city he visits is of course completely different culturally and, because their nights are not dark, more advanced technologically.

Mary: Idea two: a reality show for wizards. First-person, as though he's talking to the confession box. "What happens when you strand a whole group of wizards on an island and film them trying to perform increasingly complex magic to stay in the game?" The main character thinks that one of the wizards is exerting mind-control, but isn't sure if he's been influenced yet or not. Or, as an alternate plot, he's eventually asked to cross an ethical line and raise the dead. How much does he really want to win?

Mary: Idea three: Werewolves are real and the condition is passed on by a virus. Though there is a cure, most werewolves choose not to be cured, claiming it as a subculture like the hearing impaired. A sommelier uses his superior olfactory sense in his job in the wine industry, but wants to keep his condition a secret because of a social stigma. Then he falls in love with one of the winemakers at an event. She invites him to come to the winery for harvest, but he has to turn it down because it's over his time of the month. He's only contagious when he's in wolf form, but at what point does he confess to her that he's a werewolf?

Brandon: Okay. I'm voting wizards.

Dan: I'm actually temped by the tidally locked one, because—

Howard: Tidally locked is more interesting to me, but I'm willing to be outvoted.

Brandon: Here's the thing. With the tidally locked one you don't have as much there, so it may be more fun for us to explore.

Dan: That's what I was going to say. There's no story, there's just a setting.

Mary: This is one that I've been wanting to do for a long time.

Brandon: Let's do that one.

Mary: I've been stumped because I can come

up with this world and setting, but I have yet to come up with a story to go with it.

Brandon: The one I want to read most is the wizard one, but there you already have the whole plot. Even the perspective and everything. So I'd say let's go tidally locked. On a tidally locked world this means that the moon stays in one place with the planet at all times. Your character sails over. Is he the first person who has ever done this?

Mary: Yes.

Brandon: So, he's like Columbus. There might be people who have done it before, but—

Mary: Yeah, and my idea roughly is that it's more like Marco Polo. China was significantly more advanced than Europe at that point, and so he goes to this place and he says, "Everything is different." But aside from "my worldview is shaken," I have no conflict yet.

Brandon: Throw it at us. You want us to start talking conflict?

Mary: Yeah!

Brandon: What is the conflict, guys? And what is our ending? That's another big one.

Dan: One potential conflict here is that they have developed better seafaring technology than the first side, and so they're gearing up for an invasion. They're ready to mount one, and he knows that his country's navy has no prayer of defending.

Brandon: Now, I would really like it if they didn't know anything was over the ocean until he arrived. Then it puts the invasion on him. There is the potential of—they thought that the world came to a stop. They now realize it didn't. They've already conquered everything over here. But now there's proof from the other side, which some will see as a religious sign. There's been talk of sending exploration that way, and when someone comes, they say, "The gods—the moon or whatever—has sent this person to show us there are riches to be had."

Mary: I think that the reason that the people from that side of the planet have never gone to the other side is because they would have to sail beyond the moon, and the idea of being in complete darkness—they've always turned around and gone back.

Howard: At risk of turning it on its head, the side that has more light at night, the reason for them to be more technologically advanced is that they can get more done without the need for light at night? You could flip that on its head and say that the dark side is more technologically advanced because necessity is the mother of invention.

Mary: Oh, interesting.

Howard: They had to come up with lighting, and so if we have an explorer who literally sails into the dark—

Mary: Or sails out of the darkness.

Howard: He would be from the light side.

Mary: Oh, I'm not as interested in that. The thing that really interests me about this is the idea of seeing the moon for the first time.

Brandon: I think you could make an argument for either side being more technological. I think the side that has darkness, but not complete darkness, is going to have the advantage.

Mary: Yeah, but I think you're right that the argument could be made either way. One thing that I'm also particularly interested in exploring with this is the idea of the cultural differences. That there would be, particularly, religious differences, and whether or not—

Brandon: Well I love the idea, religiously, of "We can't sail to where the moon can't see us."

Howard: You sail the sun, the sun rises and sets and is temporary and gives us a warming influence during the day, but the moon is constant.

Brandon: That's actually pretty cool, because it gives us a reverse of the way most earth cultures developed. If there's a sun god, the sun god is among the highest and most important of the gods, and there you could say, "The sun god is the evil one, because it's transient, and the moon is always there and soft."

Howard: Let me think about this for a moment. The moon is tidally locked to the world they live on, but the body is still rotating in its orbit.

Mary: Right. Which means that side of the planet would get more solar eclipses.

Howard: Yes, and the only tides they would get would be solar tides.

Brandon: Which are not that strong.

Howard: They're not, but they are measurable.

Brandon: Here's a question for you. We're doing a lot of worldbuilding—I think we should go to culture after this—but what about the concept that this is a very bright sun for whatever reason? (We'd have to ask the science people; I'm the fantasy guy.) So, during the day there's a period of such heat and light that it's hard to get anything done, but you can be productive all night, because that very bright sun translates into a modestly bright moon, which means that's a great time to get stuff done.

Mary: I have thought about saying that the moon is a moon around the size of ours, but that the characters are on the tidally locked moon that is orbiting something like Saturn. So the planetary body that is in the sky is massive. It puts out an enormous amount of light.

Howard: Mary, I love the idea of the orbiting Saturn thing, because when you're orbiting a gas giant that big, or world that big, you can start talking about the external magnetic field as an additional influence, which could be doing fun things with ocean life.

Brandon: Can it be doing fun things with navigation too?

Howard: Yeah, and that could be one of the reasons why nobody's left the dark side via an ocean voyage in a long time, because there are things happening in the water. It occurred to me that—you mentioned Marco Polo; a possible conflict is that this guy has staked the family fortune on building a trade route and he gets to the other side and realizes: one, I have nothing to offer, and two, I have just led the conquistadors back to my house.

Mary: Oh. That's interesting.

Brandon: Just before we move off that, should we see if there are any other conflicts we can throw out, because that's the part you're having troubles with?

Mary: Yes.

Brandon: Worldbuilding doesn't seem to be as much of a problem. What other potential conflicts could there be for this story?

Howard: You put other people on the boat, and you can build all kinds of character conflicts.

Brandon: He could be escaping something.

Mary: He could be escaping something....

Brandon: It could be the opposite of the Columbus thing, and they decided to sail to the other side of the ocean because they wanted to get away.

Mary: It could also be that he was leaving his country to escape religious persecution. Then he arrives at a place that is not only colonized completely, but—

Brandon: It could even be a ship full of religious refugees saying, "We're going to escape, but there is a Promised Land in our records that we know about where they don't have to deal with the tyranny of the sun every day or at night." There's this beautiful thing that they go searching for, and they get there and it's this horribly, horribly worse culture for religious tolerance reasons.

Mary: Or we could say that the ship that he is on is one that is from the side of the world with the moon and he is returning with them as—

Brandon: They show up just all of a sudden?

Mary: Yeah, and that he says, "The moon? What are you guys talking about, the moon, the moon, the moon?"

Brandon: I'd really like it if he discovers it though—or she, it does not have to be a him. I love the idea.

Howard: One of the things I love about seeing the moon for the first time is that, if it is a gas giant, you are going to have a significant chunk of the horizon that lights up at once, and mythologies about sailing far enough to see the great crescent, sailing far enough—

Brandon: To see the seas start on fire.

Howard: Yeah. In fact if you do things with the atmosphere—I don't know if you're familiar with effects like the green flash. You play games with the spectrum and the atmosphere, and you can have all kinds of mystical stuff about what that planet looks like.

Brandon: We keep coming back to worldbuilding! That's not where we want to be.

Dan: Howard, you mentioned something about how that kind of proximity to a massive planet could do things with the electrical fields and the magnetic fields. Maybe the conflict is that his compass doesn't work anymore and he can't get home. Or maybe the conflict is that he somehow becomes ill; there is something on the other side, either magnetically or just pure plant life, that is killing him.

Howard: Oh my gosh, they're divergent species; they have been apart for long enough that they have adapted differently to the magnetic properties, the magnetic sunshine and magnetic shadow.

Mary: The other thing I'm thinking is that if I go back to the MICE quotient [milieu, idea, character, event], if the story starts with him sailing toward this land, then structurally speaking it should end with him either deciding to stay there or returning. If I just go with the easy one which is the return, then one of my conflicts can be things on that side that are keeping him from departing.

Brandon: I've latched completely onto the idea of "I have just informed the conquistadors of where we live," and so the conflict can be "Do I go back and warn my people? How do I get back and warn my people?" That could be one. Or it could be "I've got to find a way to convince them not to follow." Trick them in some way into thinking that—using their religion—

Mary: If his side of the world is the side that has had to invent artificial lighting—much more effective artificial lighting than the side with the moon—then that is one of the tricks that he can use. "Look, I've got the moon in a box."

Brandon: I'm liking this. Warfare-wise, they are amazing compared to his people. He has to come up with a way to trick them that if they follow them they will all die. It would be really cool if he were seeking religious freedom, but then on this side he has to reinforce their horrible religious intolerances in order to escape and warn his people.

Howard: Another thing to bear in mind, if we play the mild speciation card, is that after crossing the horizon, crossing that magnetic threshold, he may start getting sick.

Mary: Yeah, I'm not sure if I want to do magnetic threshold just because I think that's going to be really hard to get across in a fantasy. In a short story; in novel form—

Howard: True. You're doing short.

Brandon: We have a plot here. We have a great plot. We don't have time to really dig into it, but I love plots of "I've got to trick the whole species into thinking that they will die if they follow me." It's very much a reversal—

Mary: "If you follow me I will drown the moon, because he knows what happens if you go."

Brandon: Something like that, exactly! "I have to go be a sacrifice," and tricks them into letting him go using their own religion in a very clever and interesting way. We keep saying "he" again—I actually feel like female works better for this story, for whatever reason. But I don't know, it could be male. We have the whole "the moon is female" thing on our side, so a guy discovering the moon is more thematically—

Howard: If you want to lift a piece of the hero's journey for this, the return with the elixir, if on the way back it's not just the knowledge of having seen the moon, but there is some piece of technology that he is bringing back or she is bringing back to her people with—

Brandon: With a warning: This isn't going to hold them off forever. "I've convinced the emperor that if he follows we will drown the moon, but there is a huge contingent that when he dies—we have ten years to modernize and I've got this piece of technology. I've stolen fire from the Gods; we have got to figure out how this works or we are all doomed." That is a great ending.

Howard: I've stolen the steel from Damascus.

Mary: Probably gunpowder.

Brandon: Yeah, I've stolen gunpowder, and we have ten years to jump from 1200 A.D. to 1700 A.D.

Mary: Okay, cool. Thanks, guys.

First Draft: A Fire in the Heavens

Mary Robinette Kowal

Katin was awake before the sailor knocked on the door to her cabin. She had slept poorly since they had left Marth and tonight the sway of her hammock mixed with uneasy dreams. Her heart sped. Had the crew finally decided to mutiny? No. A mutiny would not begin with a knock. She sent a prayer to the Seven Sisters to grant her calm.

"Enter." Katin swung her legs over the side of her hammock and set her bare feet on the smooth wood floor. She had removed her leg wraps to sleep, letting the loose fabric of her leggings puddle on the bridges of her feet.

In the deep night, the light of the sailor's glowdisc cast swaying shadows against the tiny space. "Pardon, Mother, but the captain says we are in sight of land."

"Praise the Sisters." Months at sea, and they finally had land in sight. She picked up her own glowdisc and flipped the cover back to expose the phosphorescent surface. Ashore, a disc would fade to darkness during the course of a night, but the constant motion of the ship agitated the powder trapped within and kept them always glowing at least dimly. She shook hers to brighten it further. With its light, she took a moment to bind her scarf of office around her neck before following the sailor above decks. The heavy beaded ends swung about her waist as she walked.

Katin looked up for the cluster of stars that the Seven Sisters inhabited in the heavens and murmured praise to them for guiding the search this far.

The captain turned as she approached. Stylian's tall form swayed easily with the rocking of the ship. "Well. You were right."

Katin did not take the triumph that he offered her, tempting though it was. Stylian had mocked her goals, but taken the church's commission nonetheless. His acknowledgment that she had been right could be counted a victory, but it did not belong to her. The triumph lay with the Sisters. She was too grateful that he had been willing to sail on a course other captains considered foolhardy, following the trail of ancient stories about a land far to the West. She looked past him to the horizon.

A glow lay on the horizon, marking the division of the world from the sky with its light. The sea retained its dark mystery while the sky brightened as though dawn were approaching, but the sun would rise behind them. Katin closed her glowdisc, tucking it into the pocket inside her left sleeve so that it did not interfere with her night vision. She frowned, slowly understanding what the glow meant. "I don't know why I expected the land to be uninhabited."

Captain Stylian grunted in agreement. "It must have a massive city ahead, to cast so much light."

"The Sisters have prepared a way for us." Her people had suffered enough persecution for their beliefs back in Marth. Old stories told that the Seven Sisters had been blown away by a storm from Selen, a homeland far to the West. They now lived in the heavens to watch over their children. Passed down from mother to daughter, the beliefs had eroded over the centuries spent in Marth among the worship of the Sun. The corruption and greed in Marth had finally led the Sisters' Sayer to fund this expedition to find the way back to Selen.

"To be honest, I wasn't sure how long I would be able to keep the crew sailing west. Thought we were going to go right off the edge, they did." He laughed and bent his head back to look at the sky. "Perhaps we'll see 'the moon,' too."

Katin snorted. "That's exaggerated superstition."

"And tales of a land aren't?"

"Modern scholars feel that our holy texts are guides for ways to live a better life. They are allegories and yet . . ." She tucked her hands inside her sleeves, crossing her arms over her chest as though she were lecturing at the seminary. "There is always some basis for the tales. A land, even if it is not a new continent, must be at minimum an island. This moon? We believe that it is a corruption of the word "Monde" which means 'City' or 'Town' in Old Fretian. So we think that it refers to the city the Seven Sisters came from. 'And the light of Monde lay behind them, casting silver across the sea.' This refers to the wealth and knowledge of the homeland, as does the passage which refers to Monde as the 'Brightest light in the darkness.'"

He grunted again. "Not much point in arguing with you about your own religion."

"It does seem unprofitable."

To her surprise, he gave her a crooked smile. They said nothing else, but watched the distant glow grow nearer. All the while the wind played around her, lifting her seven braids and tickling her with the ends. No one seemed inclined to go to bed as they raced across the ocean toward landfall.

The light from the city was like nothing she had seen before. It was cool and silvery as though a glowdisc were reflecting in a polished metal mirror. It grew brighter by the minute. She heard a startled cry from overhead.

In the crow's nest, a sailor pointed to the horizon. His words were snatched away. When she looked back to where he pointed, Katin's heart seized.

A low mound of light had emerged above the horizon. It was not the glow of city lights, but a single broad arc that glowed with an unearthly light. She tried to make sense of the size but could not grasp the distances. "How big is that?"

"I . . . I am not certain." Captain Stylian's voice had a hesitation she was unused to in the man. "Pardon." With a half bow, he made his way to the foot of the main mast. He called up to the sailor in the crow's nest asking him for some numbers. The wind blew them away from her, but the answer caused the captain to turn abruptly and stare at the horizon.

He pressed his hand to his mouth and his eyes were wide with something that, on another man, Katin would name terror. She crossed the deck to where the captain stood. "What is the matter?"

He lowered his hand and swallowed. "It's . . . The measurements . . . they cannot be correct."

"Surely you can't tell from so far—"

"But we can. When we see another ship upon the horizon, or land, we need to be able to calculate how large it is and how far away. This . . ." He waved toward it as though the words had been stripped from his mouth. "This is vast."

The glowing edge of the disc pulled her gaze once more. Enough of it was visible now to draw shadows from the rails. Long crisp shadows as though a dimmer sun were rising. The light lay before them and cast silver across the sea.

#

Water splashed on Katin's skin as she went through the seven postures of the morning meditation in the bow of the ship. Meditation did not come easily today. As she balanced on one foot, in Dorot's stance, she watched the sky. The sun had risen as it always did. On the horizon, the mound grew larger but seemed no closer. It was fainter during the day, but just as visible. She had not gone to bed, nor had most of the crew. Those not on duty watched, as she did, seemingly transfixed by the way the light had grown to a half sphere. When more if it had become visible over the horizon, it became clear that it was not land, but some vast disc.

It was impossible to grasp the size of it. A dinner plate held out at arm's length would just cover it, but a dinner plate would not be visible past the curve of the world. Perhaps it was a beacon or a source to light their land at night.

The base of it should be visible soon. Katin leaned out as though that would help her see the support sooner. It too must be impossibly large.

The disc cleared the horizon. Katin squinted against the haze and set her foot down, breaking the sequence. She could not see a base.

She stepped to the rail as the ship skipped over the waves in front of a brisk wind. Her braids beat against her cheeks as she waited. The orb seemed to rise higher but nothing held it.

A sailor spat on the deck, and touched his fingers from his mouth to his forehead in a warding gesture. Scraps of conversation began, getting tossed on the wind toward her.

". . . no land after all . . ." "It's unnatural." "We should turn back."

"No." Katin pushed herself back from the rail. She shaded her eyes against the sun and looked for the captain. He stood on the [nautical term] speaking with the navigator and the first mate. Their heads were close together in tight conversation. Katin tucked her hands into her sleeves and hurried across the deck.

The navigator lifted her head and scowled openly. "Don't you go spouting some hocum about this being a sign." Porit jabbed her finger at the orb. "That thing is unnatural."

"But not unexpected." Katin straightened her back. "You may not believe in the Seven Sisters, but you must acknowledge that the stories speak of this."

"Occult nonsense. The fact that someone sailed this far and saw that thing does not mean that land is in front of us." Porit crossed her arms under her breasts and glared at the captain and first mate.

Katin turned from the navigator to face Captain Stylian. "We hired you to sail West. Thus far, all of the indications prove that our texts are correct. The land of Selen is ahead of us. Is there a reason, beyond your navigator's fear, to turn back?"

Porit scowled. "It's common sense, not fear."

"Peace." The captain held up his hand between them and turned to Katin. "Your religious texts are allegories, you said. Has it occurred to you that your Sisters may have sailed to this point from somewhere else and then turned back?"

Her gaze slipped to the orb hanging in the sky. What else could this be, but the moon? Katin met the captain's gaze as though he were a congregation of one. "Old Fretian is not related to any other language. Where did it come from if not the West?"

A muscle twitched in his jaw. "You paid us to sail for four fifnights and so we shall. You have until the eighth of Reed, but not a day past that."

Katin forced her voice to be calm. "There will be land."

#

The moon rose higher as they sailed farther west. Katin chewed her lower lip, watching the pale object. Its shape varied through the course of the day from a bowlike crescent it swelled to a shining disc, then gradually diminished again to just an arc of light. The cycle repeated with slow regularity, but the moon never vanished entirely. It had risen high enough over the past week that it came close to the Seven Sister's path across the heavens. With the hour approaching midnight, it was now swollen to nearly a full disc. Other stars had dimmed and disappeared behind it, then reappeared upon the other side.

Would the Sisters yield their place as well? Katin tugged at her scarf of office, which seemed too tightly tied tonight. She had trouble breathing as she watched the sky.

The Sisters' stately progress carried them to the moon. They dimmed as they approached it.

They vanished.

Katin sank to her knees. She had guessed they would. And yet . . . And yet, it was the night sky without the Sisters to watch over them. They had to come back out on the other side. Footsteps approached and the captain crouched beside her. "Are you all right?"

"I— yes. Thank you. I was just watching that." She could not voice the disappearance of the sisters to him.

"Perhaps you should not." He cast a glance over his shoulder. "I think it may drive men mad to contemplate it. We are not prepared for something so vast."

"But at some point, my people did know it." She pressed her fingers to her temples trying to soothe the pressure building there.

He grimaced. "But it is one thing to believe. Or to disbelieve. It is quite another to see the proof of one's convictions floating in the sky."

She lifted her head. Was he speaking of her or himself?

"Ship ahead!" The call came from the topsail.

The captain scrambled to his feet and dashed to the [nautical term], Katin completely forgotten. She climbed to her feet, scanning the horizon for what the lookout had seen.

On the sea, backlit by the light of the orb, floated the unmistakable silhouette of a sailing ship. And a ship sailing toward them could only mean that there was land ahead.

The captain called for the sails to be lowered and gradually the ship slowed in the water.

"What is the matter?"

"They're running dark." He nodded toward the ship. "No lights. Either it's a pirate ship or every one is dead. Either way, we wait until daylight to approach."

#

Once the dawn came, it took several hours for them to meet the other ship. Its rigging was strange, even to Katin's untrained eye. It rode very low in the water and had a beaked bow which curved in the air like a swan's neck. It was clear, by the light of day, that the ship was inhabited but they made no hostile moves. Fishing nets hung over the side and bandy-legged men worked to haul catches aboard.

Captain Stylian stood at the rail and cupped his hands to shout to the other ship. "Where do you hail from?"

A man in tight blue trousers and a long tunic of embroidered silk shouted back. Katin frowned and cocked her head. The wind had garbled what he said. It was almost understandable but slid so that she could barely distinguish the breaks between words.

Shaking his head, Captain Stylian said, "It was too much to hope that they spoke Marth."

"I think that's a variant of Old Fretian."

"Worth a try."

She only ever used Old Fretian to read scripture in its original form and hardly ever spoke it. Katin took a moment to gather her thoughts trying to martial them into a semblance of order. The declension for this would be masculine interrogative case, which mean that she would have to use the appropriate suffix to the word "land."

Wrapping her mind around Fretian, Katin spoke in that tongue. "What land-the you from?"

"The Center Kingdom. And you?" His next words eluded her. Then came a phrase almost straight from scripture. "sailing beyond the Moon?"

"We from Marth."

The captain leaned down. "You can understand him?"

It was a relief to switch back to Marskuth. "Some. But we haven't said anything complicated yet." Beyond the Moon . . . did they never sail past here?

"Ask how far behind them the land is."

Katin nodded and painfully stitched the question together in her mind. "Land-the, how far?"

"Five days."

Katin reported this back to the captain. She looked past him to the part of their boat that the navigator inhabited. "May I hope that we are going to continue on?"

"That's what you are paying us for." He stroked his chin, staring at the sailing ship. "Ask them if they have any charts they want to trade."

"What will we offer in exchange?"

The captain studied the ship. "Show him a glowdisc."

#

The city seemed to sparkle in the sunlight. Glass filled windows in the walls and even in the roofs of buildings. In some places the walls seeemed to be nothing more than thin pieces of metal existing solely to hold glass upright. The wealth on display staggered Katin, but the people in the port paid no heed to it. They walked past the docks on their business paying no more attention than if they had passed simple stucco at home.

Their ship, on the other hand, attracted notice. As the crew worked to tie it up, they used a mixture of sign language and grunts to communicate with the dockworkers. Even the ships here had glass set into the cabins. Their own ship, the Maiden's Leap, seemed dark and squat next to the ships of Monde.

The captain stood by her shoulder. "Is it a festival day?"

"Sorry?" She turned from studying the dock to face him. His frown had grown deeper the closer they had gotten to Monde, the city that the Seven Sisters must have departed.

"The banners. Every ship is flying a red banner, sometimes two or three." He nodded toward the crowds. "And see. People with arm bands in the same red. What does it mean?"

"I . . . I don't know." Now that he had pointed it out, the scraps of red were obvious, fluttering behind people as they walked. She had been so distracted by the variety of costume that she had not noticed that common thread. She pointed to a man with a blue armband who walked behind two burly men who appeared to be bodyguards, clearing a path. "Not everyone has the red bands."

"Hm. I thought this was supposed to be your homeland. Weren't you keen to come back so you could practice your religion freely? So you ought to know, even by the calendar, if this is a festival day."

Katin shook her head. "It's not. But we've been gone so long . . . Perhaps they added festivals?"

"You sound uncertain."

"And how am I supposed to be certain? I have not set foot upon the land."

He held up his hands in a placating gesture. "Fair enough. Shall we remedy that now?"

Katin took a breath to steady herself and nodded. The captain led the way to the gangplank which stretched from their boat to the pier. At the foot of the ramp, the first mate was speaking heatedly to a man who blocked his path. The man wore a blue armband and, like the one they had seen before, had two enormous bodyguards. They each carried a short sword with a strange grip in a small sheath at the waist. Even the men obviously engaged to be fighters wore dark blue silk. Across their chests, little mirrors had been sew into the fabric and flashed light with each breath.

Tucking his hands behind his back, the captain stopped behind his mate. "What is the problem here?"

"Blamed if I know, sir. They won't let us off the ship, that's clear enough, but I can't make a seabound dog of anything the fellow is saying."

Katin wanted to retreat up the gangplank before the captain could turn to look at her. She did not speak the language, for all that he thought she did. She took a step backwards and stopped herself. It would do no good to hide and likely she was the best chance for understanding what they blue gentleman wanted. "Perhaps I can help?"

"I would be grateful if you would try." He turned sideways so she could slip past him on the gangplank.

Clearing her throat, Katin marshaled the Old Fretian in her mind. "I give you greetings."

The man stared at her and said something very rapid. She could not even tell where one word ended and the next began. His voice slipped like oil upon the water.

"Speak slowly please." She slowed her own speech to demonstrate. "I do not understand."

His lip curled and he spoke slowly, mockingly, as though she were a damaged person. Still she caught only a few words. "Name" and "travelers" and then "ox-tail."

"Did you say ox-tail?"

"Yes. Show me your ox-tail." Then his speech exploded into a confusion of words. "Ox-tail" again and then "Center" or perhaps "Middle."

"I am sorry. I do not understand."

The man threw his hands up into the air in an obvious sign of aggravation. He turned to one of the bodyguards and gestured toward the ship imperiously. He spoke only two words, and the meaning would have been clear even if Katin hadn't, finally, been able to understand him. "Take it."

The bodyguard to his left stepped forward, unsheathing his sword— Except it was not a sword. It was a hollow tube, which he pointed at the first mate, who still stood at the bottom of the gangplank.

"Move" The bodyguard gestured roughly, making his meaning clear.

The captain put a hand on Katin's shoulder. "What is happening?"

"I—" She did not know. This was not what she had studied for. Katin turned to look over her shoulder at him. "They want something. He keeps asking for an ox-tail. Maybe it's an offering of some sort? And now, I think— but I don't really understand. It sounds like they want the ship. But I might be wrong."

The gangplank shifted as new weight stepped upon it.

Behind her, the first mate shouted, "I said you aren't coming aboard my ship."

Katin grabbed for the rough rope rail as the gangplank shuddered. She turned back in time to see the first mate shove the bodyguard back. The huge man looked astonished and angry. He pointed the tube at the first mate and then—

There was a flash and a clap of thunder. Smoke billowed of the end of the tube. On the docks, people screamed and pushed away from the sound.

The first mate took a step backwards and then sat heavily. The back of his jacket was staining red. He toppled to the side and fell into the water.

"Gnistin" The captain stared at the spot where his first mate floated face down in the water. Blood curled around him in the water. "I need a lifeline!"

As a crewman ran to get rope, the captain pushed past Katin, never taking his eyes off the first mate. What had happened? She did not understand what had happened.

The blue man on the dock said something and it took Katin a moment realize that he was speaking to her. "I do not understand."

"No one move. Tell them." He spoke with exaggerated care.

Swallowing, she said, "Captain. He wants everyone to stay still."

"No. I have a man down." He turned and bellowed back to the ship. "Where's that rope?"

A crewman ran to the edge and wrapped a coil around the rail. His fingers tightened a knot.

The blue man spoke again, in that strange sliding Fretian. "I said, no one move."

"A man drowns!" Katin pointed at the first mate. The water was so red.

"Dead. Already." He snorted and turned to the bodyguard. "Make it two."

The weapon flashed and thundered again. Katin covered her ears, shrieking at the noise. Below her, the captain jerked and stumbled. He grabbed the rope railing with both hands.

"No!"

His feet went out from under him and he dropped to his knees, still clutching the banister. Katin found herself behind him, pulling him back from the water as the acrid smoke curled around him.

She wrapped her arms around him, feeling the blood soak into her tunic. Her scarf of office fell across his chest. "Stop. We do what you say."

"Good." The blue man's teeth glinted in the sun. "Good."

#

The square of sunlight in the prison wall sent a harsh beam across the wood floor. Katin could not think of it as anything other than a prison, for all that it had large windows overlooking a center courtyard. The guards made their status clear. The ship's crew was held in a dormitory, quarantined from the other prisoners.

Katin sat by Captain Stylian's cot and dipped a cloth in the dish of water she had begged from Proctor Veleh. "The guards tell me that we will have *titam* and *kalcoist* this afternoon for lunch."

He grunted and shifted on the cot. "Dare I ask what that means?"

"*Titam* are potatoes and I think that *kalcoist* is lamb. At any rate, it seems to share a root with *kalca* which is the word for sheep. *Ist* should be a diminutive, so . . . lamb. I think."

A man came every day to give them language lessons. Proctor Veleh was patient to the point of seeming a machine, but she was the only one of the crew that made any effort. The others all muttered about escape, as though getting past the guards and their hollow tubes was a possibility.

"Any luck finding out what our crime is?"

She shook her head. In the fifnight since they had been taken, her grasp of Setish had improved enough to *almost* understand why the others were being held. Almost. It was so clearly descended from the same roots as Old Fretian that learning it had been easier for her than for shipmates.

Still, she only *almost* understood. Or rather, she understood the words, "shy of an ox-tail," but the meaning eluded her. "When I ask what an ox-tail is, Proctor Veleh says that it is the tail of an ox."

"Next time I'll have one pickled." He shifted again on the bed and hissed. Stylian closed his eyes, breathing held between tight-pressed lips. He let it out slowly. "So . . . lamb tonight, eh?"

"Yes." She dipped her cloth in the water again and looked across the dormitory. Porit, the navigator, stood in a tight cluster with three other crewmen. One of them seemed to be blatantly counting the number of times the guard walked past the door. "Proctor Veleh says that they would normally provide a translator so we could answer for our crimes, but no one knows Marskuth. Or Old Fretian for that matter."

Porit broke away from the group and crossed to the captain's cot. "I can take over, if you like." It was not an offer.

The captain raised his eyebrows at her tone. Katin bit her lips and put the cloth back in the basin. "Of course."

She stood and strolled away, trying to linger long enough to hear what they were going to talk about but the captain said only, "Katin tells me that we're having lamb tonight."

Scowling, she squatted by one of the walls and smoothed her scarf of office. With her arms crossed, she took the ends of the scarf between her hands, symbolizing the path the Seven Sisters took through the heavens, and began rolling the beads between her fingers. Each sister had a separate role in guiding a person's behavior through life. Katin appealed to Zo, the middle sister, to grant the Captain resiliency. He must get well and do nothing foolish.

"What are you doing?"

The man's voice called her back to herself. She opened her eyes, ready to frown at the crewman who had disturbed her before realizing that the question had been in Setish. Proctor Veleh stood in front of her. It was not his day to teach.

"I am praying."

He frowned. Lines creased his face more deeply than they should have in one so young. "No, you are not."

"What—? I— Yes. Yes, I *am* praying." She held up her scarf. "This is how we pray where I come from." Or rather, it was how the followers of the Seven Sisters prayed.

"I have studied all six of our provinces, and no one prays to the moon squatting."

"It's not the position, it's the—" Katin bit her explanation off. If she drew attention to her scarf of office, they might take it from her. "I have told you. We are not from one of the provinces. We are from the other side of the sea."

He lifted his chin. "Stand. The Apex Councillor has decided to hear what you have to say."

#

The council sat in a squat room, not at all grand, with a broad table in front of them. Yet even here, in the most utilitarian of chambers, great windows stood behind the councilor and cast light across his table. Stacks of paper crowded the surface in front of his aides, piled in neat right angles, every corner squared to the edge of the table.

On either side of the door, stood guards with tall spears. Tassels hung from the shafts, making the weapons look almost ornamental, but the light that gleamed from the edges made it clear that these were honed and sharp. Their breastplates were painted with a lacquered rendition of the moon, with silver rays blending into the metal of the armor. The velvet of their livery was a blue so deep as to be almost black. Tied around their upper arms were blue armbands which appeared light only in contrast

As Katin was brought into the room, the councilor shifted a pile of paper closer to himself. "You have been accused of being shy of an oxtail. How do you respond?"

"I do not know what an ox-tail is"

Silhouetted by the window, his face was not visible, but the sharp jerk of his head was unmistakable. "Do not toy with me."

"I am not! I have no understanding what you are speak of."

"Every citizen must have an oxtail to travel outside their city of birth."

"Perhaps that is the problem. I am not a citizen. We are from Marth, across the sea."

The councilor broke into laughter at this. "Even if there were something across the sea, there is no way to navigate outside the light of the eternal moon. The fine for being without your ox-tail is not so egregious that you must make-up fairy stories."

"I am not! We have been trying to explain since we got here that we are explorers from the other side of the world. Where I come from, an ox-tail belongs firmly on an ox."

He cocked his head. "Are you saying 'ox-tail?'"

"Yes." Katin slowed down and tried to adjust her speech so it was more accurate. "That is what the man at the ship asked us for."

He uttered a noise that sounded as though he cursed. "You were supposed to have had language lessons."

"I did."

"From a historian. Your province speaks a particularly backward form of Setian." He rubbed his forehead. "Still, that might explain some of the confusion. You are saying 'ox-tail' but what I mean is 'oxtail.'"

Aside from a slight change in emphasis, Katin could hear no distinction. "What is the difference?"

"One is the tail of an ox. The other is a license to travel."

She gaped at him. The first mate who had been shot . . . "One of my shipmates was killed because we couldn't understand what the man at the dock was saying."

"All provinces have the same requirements. You should have undertaken this before leaving your home. "

Katin lost her temper and felt the touch of Fahra on her soul. "I told you. We are from across the ocean. We could not possibly have gotten an oxtail before leaving because we didn't know that there was such a thing. If you tell use where to go to get a license, I'm sure we'll all happily pay the fee."

One of the aides scribbled something on a piece of paper and passed it to the councilor. He studied it for a moment. "Why she do you keep insisting on this fiction? Navigation is not possible out of the sight of the blessed moon."

"We navigate by the stars. Really, have you had no one else visit your shores?"

"Castaways from one of the darker islands." The councilor stroked his chin. "The stars move, how do you propose that one navigate by them?"

Katin faltered. She knew nothing of the subject beyond seeing Porit do it. "I . . . I am not certain."

"Because it cannot be done."

"No. Because I am not a navigator. If you were to ask her, I am certain she could explain. I am here solely because I have some ability with your language."

"And to what do you attribute that?"

"It is related to our holy language. I am a priest and required to be versed in it."

With her words, something in the room changed. The councilor became very still. By the door, one of the guards shifted his hands on his spear.

The councilor leaned back in his chair slowly. "I will grant that you are not a native speaker of Setish. That much of your story appears to be true. So it is possible that you mean something else by the word 'priest.'"

Katin reviewed what she had said and worried the inside of her lip. She had taken the word from Old Fretian, and it was possible that the meaning had shifted. "I mean a holy woman, or man, dedicated to the service of the Seven Sisters."

"Who?"

"The . . . the Seven Sisters." She raised a hand to her scarf of office and held the beaded ends out to him. "Our holy book says that they came from across the ocean and we—"

"Are you saying that this is *a religion*?"

The sweat on Katin's hands clung to the scarf, adding to the dirt from fifnight in the prison. She lowered it and wiped her palms on her leggings. "By my understanding of the word, yes. It is possible that the language has shifted."

"Do you worship these Seven Sisters?"

"Yes."

"So brazen." The councilor barked a laugh. "Ironic that the most damning piece of evidence against you is the one that convinces me your story is true."

"I don't understand."

"Every year, the Council of Purity finds someone misled by one old cult or another and takes steps to correct the poor soul. These misled fools have turned their back on the eternal moon and, knowing that it is wrong, they try to hide their depravity. Yet here you stand claiming allegiance to goddesses that no one has ever heard of as though there would be no consequences."

"They are not goddesses." The words were out of her mouth before she realized that she should have asked what he meant by consequences.

"So you deny it now?"

"No." Katin's voice was louder than she intended. "I merely wish to be clear. Goddesses are born that way, if one believes in such things. The Seven Sisters came from here and shared their wisdom with the early Fretian people. It is said that they were elevated to the stars to continue to watch over us and guide us."

He waved his hand to dismiss her words. "You do not deny, though, that it is a religion."

"I do not." Katin licked her lips. "You spoke of consequences. What are those?"

"The moon is eternal and so we live by her light. Either accept that, or accept the absence of her light."

Laughter rose unbidden to Katin's lips. "Given that until a fifnight ago, I had never seen the moon, I can easily accept the absence of her light."

Looking down, he made a mark upon the paper in front of him. "Place her in a cave."

A protest formed on her lips, but Katin bit it back. What could she say? She did not accept the eternal moon, not when she had good reason to know that it was not eternal. She kept her chin high as the guards came to flank her.

As they lead her from the room, the councilor spoke behind her. "It occurs to me that we should speak to this navigator. If they do come from out of the sight of the moon, then we should find this land and bring them into the light."

#

Katin stumbled over the threshold as the guard thrust her into the cell. A torch flamed in his partner's hand, lighting the crude underground passage.

He smirked, face crazed in the dancing light. "Enjoy the dark."

The door slammed shut, dropping the cell into twilight. Katin waited for the darkness to descend.

Light trickled under the door and from a crack in the wall. It was not bright, but enough to make out the shape of the room. A small table with a chair stood by the wall. A cot stood opposite it. Her final piece of furnishing was a bucket to hold her waste.

The cave was nothing more than a windowless room.

Katin sank onto the bed and pulled the glowdisc out of her sleeve pocket. She turned the disc over in her hands without opening it. There was nothing she needed to see, but having the smooth surface under her hands helped her think.

Their ships ran dark. Windows everywhere. Crude torches... Had she seen a single artificial light besides the torch? No. With the light of the moon, they did not need anything except on cloudy nights.

And perhaps... perhaps they thought this *was* a dark room.

#

On the small table, Katin had placed her glowdisc facing the door. She held the bed sheet in one hand, waiting until she heard the footsteps of her guard with her daily meal. Shaking the disc until the light reached its brightest, she tried to keep her breath steady.

The guard's footsteps stopped outside her door. A moment later, the small slot in the base opened so he could pass her tray through.

"Behold the moon! The eternal moon has come to visit."

Her glowdisc could not overpower the torch, but its silver-blue light beat it back some.

The guard cursed and scrabbled to his feet. His keys rattled.

Katin let the sheet fall in front of the glowdisc, to difuse the light and make the source seem larger than it was. She leapt across the small room, and grabbed the waste bucket by the door.

The keys scraped in the lock, and the door swung open. The guard gawked at the glowing sheet and took a step into the cell. His torch guttered as he crossed the threshold. Katin upended her bucket of waste on the torch, covering the smoking end with the metal. The guard cursed as the excrement and urine ran down his arm.

Katin swung the bucket hard, catching him across the side of his head. The guard stumbled forward and his feet tangled in the ties for her leggings. He staggered and fell into the cell. Katin dashed the bucket against his head again, and he lay still. Shuddering, she dropped the bucket and moving as quickly as she could, Katin began to strip the guard of his clothes. As she rolled him over, her hand brushed the sheath by his side. He wore one of the hollow tubes.

Hesitating for only a moment, Katin unbuckled the belt that held the tube at his waist. It would surely be more useful than his uniform, if she could figure out how to work the weapon.

#

Katin kept her shoulders back and marched with as much authority as she could muster. She had needed to role the cuffs of the guard uniform up, but in the shadows of the reflected moonlight, she hoped it would pass. Though, for all she knew, they had height restrictions on who could be a guard. With her lower lip clenched in her teeth, she slipped into the building where her fellow shipmates were held.

The captain was not in good condition, but they needed to leave and this was likely their only chance. Katin approached the guard slouching by the window. A window in the wall cast a beam of light across the corridor. Anyone approaching would be well visible then.

The guard straightened upon seeing her and made a movement with his hand over his heart. A salute?

Guessing, she hastily copied his movement, hoping he would buy it as a salute back.

"What can I do for you?"

Praying to Pasha for aid in the deception, Katin lowered her voice. "The foreigners." She had been thinking of this phrase the entire way here, so it would roll off her tongue as if she were a native Setish speaker. "The Apex Councilor says they aren't worthy to see the light. Supposed to take them to the caves."

"Now? The moon will be full in less than half an hour. You won't get them there before prayer time."

She shrugged, as if she didn't care. "Orders."

His frown deepened. "And by yourself? For twenty men?"

Before the guard could finish enumerating the reasons that this made no senese, Katin had the end of the tube pressed against his forehead. He choked off his words, going cross-eyed looking at the weapon. His swallow was audible in the stillness of the night.

"Is this clearer? Take me to the foreigners."

He held very still, which was fortunate, as she had no idea what to do with the weapon she held. Only the fact that one end was obviously a handle gave her even a hint of how to hold it. Reaching forward, she pulled his weapon from the sheath on his belt and tucked it into her own belt.

His voice was steadier than hers would have been. "I could yell."

"I could kill you."

"The gunshot would call the other guards."

"So the outcome for me is the same either way." She pressed the tube against his head more firmly. "Stand."

The guard wet his lips and let out a slow breath. He slowly rose and led her down the hall to where the members of her ship—no, to where her fellow countrymen were being held. Katin followed behind, with the weapon trained upon his back.

When they reached the cell, she rested the tip on his spine. "Unlock the door."

The guard reached for his keys. They unclipped from his belt, and fell to the ground with a clatter. Katin scowled at him. That was clever. He had followed her instructions, but in such a way as it would force her to take the gun off his back to pick up the keys.

And this was where the Seven Sisters meditation exercises came in handy. Katin kept the weapon against his back as she reached forward with one foot. Sliding the keys toward her, she was able to scoop them off the floor with the toe of her boot as if she were practicing Dorot's stance. With her free hand, Katin

The guard grimaced and pulled the weapon out, without attempting anything else.

He opened the door and Katin gave him a shove forward. In the cell, the crew of her ship sat up, blinking in their beds. Tempting as it was to look to the captain, Katin kept her gaze on the guard. She spoke in her native tongue. "Someone secure him. Quietly."

Porit stared at her in open disbelief for a moment, before yanking a rope made of torn sheets out of her cot's mattress. Where had the rope come from? In a matter of minutes, the guard was stripped of his uniform and trussed in makeshift rope with a wad of cloth shoved in his mouth for a gag. The other crewmen scrambled into their clothes, pulling on boots and shirts in disciplined silence.

Now, Katin could take the time to look to Captain Stylian.

He stood by his bed, pulling on the guard's uniform. That morning he could barely sit and now aside from a wince as he slipped the shirt on, it was as if his health had never been in question.

They had been planning an escape and had not told her. A knot of nausea twisted in her stomach. They had not trusted her because her people were from here. Clenching her jaw, Katin turned away from him and headed to the door.

A moment later, Stylian was by her side. He leaned down to breathe in her ear. "I give thanks to the sisters that you are safe."

Katin shook her head. "You've been pretending to be sicker than you are."

"I kept hoping that they would take me out of the cell to a doctor, or bring a doctor here we could use as a hostage."

"You didn't tell me."

"It seemed safer to pretend to everyone than to chance our captors guessing."

She snorted, just letting the air huff out of her nose softly. "You were ready to leave without me."

"We were ready to come find you." He lay two fingers on her wrist. "I wouldn't leave one of my crew behind."

Her nausea eased at his words. They were all fellow countrymen in this place. Katin handed the captain one of the weapons. "Thank you."

By the door, the navigator waved her hand, signaling that the hall was empty and they headed out into the moon's cold light.

#

With each turn, Katin expected them to be caught but the shadows served them well. As the moon rose to its full height, the cold silver light flooded the streets and houses. They were exposed when crossing the streets, but tucked under the eaves, in the shadows, they were nearly invisible.

The wind carried hints of salt air, and the captain straightened his head. Even without a nautical background, Katin's own stride quickened at the scent. The sea would carry her home. All this time, seeking her people's homeland and she was fleeing it in the night.

In front of them, Porit held up her hand, signaling a stop. She beckoned Stylian and Katin closer. In a low murmer, the navigator said, "We should send one ahead. In case they are waiting for us."

"Likely they are." The captain chewed the inside of his lip and straightened the guard's uniform. "I'll go."

"Don't be silly," Katin whispered. "You need to be aboard to get us home."

"Mostly you need Porit for that." Captain Stylian eyed the end of the street, where the harbor was just visible. "Besides I can tell the state of the ship and you won't know what to look for."

It was sensible, though she still wished he would not go. "Both of us? As if we are patrolling?"

He shifted his weight, looking again to the end of the street. "Agreed. It will look more natural with a pair, I think."

Katin lead the way before Stylian could change his mind. He caught up with her a moment later and they strode down the street toward the harbor.

The captain rested his hand upon the hilt of the tube weapon. "Do you know how to work this?"

"No idea."

He inhaled sharply a moment later. "Thank the sisters. No one has noticed our absence yet."

Ahead of them lay their ship, tied to the same dock they had first arrived at. Only a single guard stood at the foot of the gangplank. Better than merely standing, he had his face tilted up to face the moon in an attitude of prayer. Their arrival coincided with the midnight moon reaching its fullest brightness. Though Katin and Stylian were exposed walking down the street, the guard would be night blind from staring at the bright orb overhead.

Stylian turned briefly to wave Porit forward.

The crew responded instantly and hurried as one down the street to their ship. Katin quickened her own pace. The sound of their footfalls changed when they hit the wood of the docks, and echoed back against the houses behind them. The guard looked down from the moon.

He blinked. "Alarm!"

As his voice rose into the night, Katin recognized him—not a guard at all, but Proctor Veleh. Behind them, metal clattered as a half dozen soldiers appeared on the dock, cutting off their retreat.

Katin sprang forward and shoved the tube against the Proctor's chest. Her bluff had worked once, perhaps it would again. In Setish, she shouted, "Stop! Or the Proctor is a dead man."

The soldiers slowed at the end of the pier, their weapons raised to point at the sailors. There were far more sailors than soldiers, but every single one of the guards had one of these cursed tubes.

The proctor looked past her to the sailors and appeared to be counting their number. "I confess surprise. I had not thought to check the prison after your escape from the caves."

"Tell your soldiers to leave."

"No. You may shoot me if you like, but you shall not escape judgment under the blessed light." Proctor Veleh looked down his nose at Katin.

"As long as we escape here, I'm fine taking my chance on judgment."

"Even if I stepped aside and let you aboard, what then? You are advocating a heresy and the Apex Council will find you no matter where in the kingdom you go."

"We're from across the sea." The image of the moon sinking below the horizon gave her an idea. "If your ship follows us, our Seven Sisters will drown the moon."

The Proctor laughed. "You think we do not know that our world is round? The moon does not drown if one goes too far west. She remains over the capital to provide her blessings upon our people. No life exists outside of her divine sight."

Katin did not bother giving him an answer. She looked to the captain and switched back to her native language. "Ideas on what to do?"

"This?" Stylian pointed his weapon at the guards.

A tremendous flash and clap rang out in the night. The guards scattered, ducking behind barrel and poles, but none of them fell. This unleashed the sailors to fall upon the guards. More claps resounded through the night.

Yells, cries of pain, and a brimstone stench crowded against each other. Katin pushed the Proctor hard in the chest, and he stumbled back. His heel went out past the edge of the dock and he tumbled over.

"Move! Move!" Stylian bellowed, and like wharf rats, the sailors obeyed their captain.

Scrambling and cursing, Porit was the first past Katin, hauling a wounded sailor over her shoulders. The others followed, leaving behind the bodies of the guards, but not their fellow shipmates.

As soon as the last one was aboard, Captan Stylian gave the order to cast off. Katin retreated to the rail, attempting to serve some purpose by watching for pursuit as they pulled away from the dock. Her last image of the city was of Proctor Veleh splashing in the water at the base of the dock. The blessed light of the moon shone upon him.

They sailed due east under full sails for hours. Porit told the captain to take the course that would put the most distance between them and the land and she would get them home from there. Katin stood with her hands tucked under her arms. Between her fingers she rolled barrell of the weapon as if it were a prayer bead, begging each of the sisters for aid in their escape.

The prayer was automatic, but the belief did not follow. Katin had been to her homeland and discovered that it was not the thing of legends. There was no safe place for her people, not here.

The captain came to join her at the rail, still in his borrowed uniform. He sank down on a coil of rope with a groan.

Katin tore her gaze way from the thinning moon. "Are you all right?"

"I may have lied a little about faking my illness."

She snorted and went back to watching the path behind them.

"Thinking about your sisters' birthplace?"

She rolled the barrel another turn. "The Apex Councillor said that they would send ships after us."

"You mean the fellow at the dock? Even if they got a crew up and running as soon as he was out of the water, we've got a significant headstart on them."

"I don't mean just *us*, I mean Marth. I think they're going to invade." She held up the gun. "I keep thinking that our country will need to work to catch up with their weapons."

He grunted and stared up at the sky. "I guess the seven sisters may have lead us here to give us warning."

Katin turned to stare at him. "That's the third time you've spoken of the sisters tonight. You don't have to act like you believe in them."

"To my surprise . . . I'm not. Not pretending, I mean." The captain pointed at the cluster of stars in the sky. "You told me that every story has some truth behind it. Finding the truth here . . . ? Makes me trust the parts I haven't seen the truth of yet."

Katin followed his gaze up, to where the sisters traveled their path across the heavens. Maybe the truth was that the Seven Sisters had fled their homeland, or maybe they had been blown off course, or perhaps they were guardians who looked over her people. *And the light of Monde lay behind them, casting silver across the sea.*

The moon threw its silver light in a band across the sea them, chasing her home.

WRITING EXCUSES 9.30

WORKSHOPPING A FIRE IN THE HEAVENS

Brandon: Mary, you get to steer this as you do your writing group. Tell us the process.

Mary: Brandon showed one method of critiquing. What we're about to now do is sometimes called the Milford method, which is that you go around the circle and people take turns. Usually you set a timer so that each person has X amount of time to talk. The person who wrote the story is not allowed to talk until the end, and then we can ask questions.

Howard: How long do you usually set the timer?

Mary: Usually we set it for two minutes. The idea is that you list the takeaway things that you really want the author to think about. Things that they've done wrong, or usually things that confused you, things that you did not believe, things that you didn't care about, and then also things that you thought were cool so the author does not accidentally fix them.

Howard: Okay, I'll go first. I really liked the story. It had a lot more polish on it than I expected, based on your email that said "raw, raw, raw." The things that I loved: The reveal of the moon coming up over the horizon. The culture clash. The treatment of languages. I did have a little bit of difficulty believing that the languages wouldn't have drifted further, but since you didn't give us a timeframe I can handwave that. The places where I had the most trouble were the blocking of the action scenes, and there was another thing that I've forgotten. I was trying to go in a hurry, and I'm only a minute in, so I've got a little more time. But I ran out of things to say. So Dan, go.

Dan: Okay. I also liked this story, but I had more problems with it than Howard did, apparently. One of the things that you knew—that I remember we'd discussed in the original brainstorm—that I don't think you solved, was the conflict in the idea that these two cultures have no idea that the other one exists. Neither side can even fathom anything on the other side of the world. And yet, they are so recently related, but they have no relationship at all. That felt very weird to me, especially the constant references between the captain and the main character going back and forth, "Well, these are your people," or "You come from here, so maybe you're more aligned with them than with us." Things like that seem to push them very close together. Then on the other hand, everyone had these very cool, yet very hard to believe, attitudes about how they refused to even acknowledge that someone could be from across the sea. I don't feel like that paradox was solved in this draft.

Dan: The other thing is that I loved the whole middle section. Howard mentioned the languages. That really was, for me, the strongest part of the entire story, as they are trying to learn to communicate and you're seeing that their customs, their religions, and languages are different. I like the constant harping on the oxtail, because that's exactly the kind of idiom that arises in a language, that doesn't make any sense to someone from outside that culture. But that took over the story for me and pulled all the focus away from the moon. The moon seemed like it was your excuse to write a story, and then you got really excited about the culture clash. The moon wasn't as important as I felt it would be. It doesn't *need* to be—just because that's the idea that started the story doesn't mean it needs to rule over it. But if you want that to be a focus, it totally took a back seat.

Howard: For Dan. It didn't for me. I thought it was awesome, especially the "cave." That was great.

Brandon: That whole concept was awesome. She thinks, "Oh, I'll just sit down in the dark. Okay. This is fine."

Dan: I just had trouble believing that their problems could be solved by the fact that they don't think it's very dark.

Brandon: Howard, I need to see that stopwatch. Let's do my two minutes. I really did like the idea that something so terrifying to them, the darkness, could be nothing for her. It was really fun for me to read. I liked how clever she was in getting out of it, and the move into proactiveness. I liked when she got back to the sailors and they say, "No. We weren't going to escape without you." But then they really weren't going to. That whole fear and panic on her part was really strong for me. I also really enjoyed the image of the moon. I was prepared for it, but it was just described really well, and it felt beautiful to me.

Brandon: My biggest problem with the story is that it felt like you were cramming so much into this that you had to jump from idea to idea to idea. I'm left at the end of the story saying, "But what was this about? What was I supposed to feel?" Is this an action-adventure story with "We're escaping from the enemy"? Is this a culture clash story where we come to understand them better? Is this about a dawning of awareness that "My religion is not unique"? I didn't understand at all what this story was about. That really bothered me through the whole story.

Brandon: With the time jumps between section breaks—and there were so many section breaks—it felt like you were trying to cram a 30,000-word story into 8,000 words. That's not because this needs to be longer. It's just that it felt like you're thinking, "Well, we'll do this idea and this idea and this idea." I wanted to know, coming out here, was this spiritually meaningful for her? That didn't seem to have that much to do with it. When they find out that there are people there, I wanted them to stop and say, "Whoa! What do we do? Do they have three eyes? Are they monsters?" What's going to be the reaction?

Brandon: I had a little bit of trouble with how they acted. If you were going to sail to a new country even on your own continent without any context, you would be frightened about the laws. You would want to know what the tariffs were. You would want to know all these things. They didn't even think about that. They just sailed up and said, "Hi. We're from the new world. You guys don't have three eyes. That's cool. Oh, wait. You're shooting us." That really bothered me at that point. They didn't have any plan. They didn't have any idea what they were doing. I'm out of my time though, so I will stop. All right, Mary. I assume this is the part where the writing group turns back to you and you start asking us questions?

Mary: Yes. First of all, thank you. This was very

helpful. I also felt like I had too many ideas crammed into this. One of the things that we had talked about when we were brainstorming was that this was a story where I had this idea of someone coming over the edge of the world and seeing the moon for the first time, and that was really all I had. I don't actually need to focus on the moon. I just wanted a story in which I could have that moment happen. Thank you for the note about asking for more details. I originally had a scene in which they bargained with the trader that they first met, and got a map and a little bit of an idea. Basically, they looked at the landmass on the map and thought, "Holy crap, this is not what we were expecting." Dan, you said that you had trouble believing that these two cultures would have no idea that the other one existed, and then were less freaked, but then everyone kept saying, "But you came from here." My intention was that there were legends that referred to where she came from. If I punched that up a little bit more and made it a more concrete thing—where her people absolutely believed that there was an island on the other side of the world, and that they were scoffed at by the rest of them—if I punched that up, would that solve that for you?

Dan: Well, the fact that those legends existed came across strongly, particularly through the religion of the sisters. Because I knew that that's where they came from. That religious connection was there.

Mary: I may not have understood what the problem was that you were citing.

Dan: Well, I suppose part of the problem was her assumption—and maybe this was just her insecurity and I misread it, but this came up a couple of different times—that the crew of the ship wouldn't trust her because she came from here. I think the captain even said something about, "Why are you so weirded out? This is where you come from." Or something like that. Which seemed to be at odds with the idea that nobody else believed it was even possible.

Mary: Oh, I see.

Dan: I hope you see. I don't know if I'm expressing this correctly. I suppose part of the idea is that once they finally get there, it is so alien and so hostile, that those suggestions that just because she believes that this place exists— It's like, if I believe in Atlantis, and then we get there and it's full of jerks who hate us and throw us in jail, no one is going to assume that I will side with them over any issue, just because I believe in Atlantis.

Brandon: I think you're overemphasizing that. Because I got that she was worried they thought that. But then he says, "No, we didn't. We wouldn't leave you behind. You're not one of them," that sort of thing.

Dan: That was just a part of the issue, though. The language was another one. Maybe that secretly is what my issue was about.

Howard: I don't know if this will address either of those, but I hit a speed bump early on, which was "I'm not sure exactly whether this is the story that we brainstormed, because we had these concepts in the brainstorming." And then I said, "You know what? I need to forget about what we were brainstorming, because I just need to pay attention to what's on the page." Once I cleared that in my head, I was able to enjoy what's on the page. I had the same problem when I was reading Brandon's, which is that—

Brandon: You brainstorm something and then if it becomes something different, you're going to talk about it.

Howard: Yeah, I had already told myself the story that you were going to write. And then you wrote a different story, and I need to address the story you wrote, not the one I told myself after we brainstormed. That's hard to do when the critique group has been through both phases.

Mary: Readers, I will say that this is one reason that I and other people often suggest that you not run a story through the same group twice. Because they are pre-prejudiced. They come with a set of baggage for your story. So do recognize that some of that is going on.

Brandon: Can I mention one other thing about the story that I have notes on, that I just noticed, scanning back through? This might get with my other point. But the context of their trip bothered me a little bit. I think it's that her whole order hired them to come out here, but there is only one of her on the ship. That bothers me. If you're going to rent out a ship, you don't send one person. You send her and her guards. Or her and a whole bunch of them. Part of me thought, "Shouldn't the sailors have more in this?" It would be wonderful if they had more skin in the game. This is getting prescriptive, but it's just that they've been hired. Part of the problem is that once they see a fully populated empire, I don't think any ship captain's going to say, "Okay, let's go sail there." He's going to say, "My job was to bring you this far. Now we have an empire. I don't know anything about them." Every seafaring empire out there will confiscate your ship if they can get away with it. Right? The reason they don't is because of hostile nations and things like that. I think sailing into an unfamiliar port with no treaties is something that very few ship captains would ever do just because they're hired. That context was bothering me, I think, and that has to do with my other issue. Maybe if there were more of a reason that he is going to try this thing, and she gets on board and says, "Well, take me along." I don't know. I'm trying to fix your story, and I shouldn't do that. But that thing bothered me a lot.

Mary: No, I see what you're talking about there. I have to think about how to fix that, because that introduces . . .

Dan: I was making the assumption—and this was admittedly not in your story—that the place where they came from had multiple nations. So it was normal for him to arrive in a strange seaport, and that the anomaly here is that they were this kind of fascist religious group that was extremely suspicious of outsiders. Therefore, he had a good reason to show up, and they took him by surprise.

Brandon: Okay. I could buy that. Maybe I just didn't add that to the story myself.

Mary: It was there, but not very heavily, and I can bump that up.

Brandon: If this captain said, "I can get myself into any port and trade. I've sailed the most exotic places on our side of the world. I've never had any trouble. Maybe we get chased off, but I always get away with the goods." If he's that type. But this doesn't seem very safe to me. Maybe you should actually talk to a primary source.

Howard: If you actually make that a flaw in the captain—

Mary: If I make him Han Solo?

Howard: Yeah, if you turn him into a little bit of a Han Solo type, I'll totally buy it. Because I was almost all the way there. I was enjoying the story. I was having a good time.

Mary: What if part of what's at stake, and I'm just—

Howard: Spitballing.

Mary: Yep. I was not going to use as polite a term. What if the deal is that he gets the rest of his money after they come back, and the only way he's going to get the rest of his money is if he actually finishes.

Brandon: That could be it. But once again, I need to know his personality, and why he's— Again, why there's only one of her. But also, it just seems so dangerous. Normally stories like this—and I'm glad you didn't go this way, because it's overdone—go with the whole Columbus thing. There are riches to be had. If you go you get to plunder the place and come back with the riches. Sailors seem a superstitious lot, in my expectation. The idea of "Go sail to this foreign port where you don't speak the language, and then sail back"? I don't know. That seems so dangerous to me, that I feel a lot of captains would say, "No. We're turning around. They've got a navy." But maybe I'm totally wrong, and this is just something I'm adding to the story. Dan and Howard didn't seem to have this reaction.

Mary: Yeah. I also have to look at some historical things. I think that this is an issue that is not an issue. But I think that bumping up the fact that there are multiple countries, that he's—

Brandon: I guess I'm getting at the core idea of, I thought the way they acted when they sailed up was so foolhardy. Maybe it wasn't. But I just felt like they were asking to get shot or something like that. That was my response. I thought, "Well, what do you expect? Unfamiliar port, you don't speak the language, you're not obeying their orders, you *can't* obey their orders." It seems like a really dangerous place to be. But maybe I've read so many stories that I know that that's a dangerous place to be in a story, because that's what happens. It happened all the time in our world, I guess.

Howard: The captain totally went into the basement all by himself in the dark.

Mary: I will go and look at other first contacts, historical first contacts.

Brandon: First contact between West and East might be a good one, because that was advanced cultures.

Mary: All right. Cool. Thanks, guys.

Edits: A Fire in the Heavens

Mary Robinette Kowal

~~Katin was awake before the sailor knocked on the door to her cabin. She had slept poorly since they had left Marth and tonight the sway of her hammock mixed with uneasy dreams. Her heart sped. Had the crew finally decided to mutiny? No.~~ A mutiny would not begin with a knock. ~~She~~<ins>At the simple rap upon her cabin door,</ins> Katin sent a prayer to the ~~Seven~~<ins>Five</ins> Sisters to grant her calm<ins>. Closing the *Principium,* she tucked the small book of scripture into the sash at her waist</ins>.

"Enter." ~~Katin~~<ins>She</ins> swung her legs over the side of her hammock and set her bare feet on the smooth wood floor<ins> of her cabin</ins>. She had removed her leg wraps to sleep, letting the loose fabric of her leggings puddle on the bridges of her feet.

In the deep night, the light of the sailor's glowdisc cast swaying shadows ~~against~~ <ins>in</ins> the tiny space. <ins>Lesid ducked his head into the cabin.</ins> "Pardon~~, Mother~~, but the captain says we are in sight of land."

"Praise the Sisters." Months at sea, and ~~they finally~~<ins>even she</ins> had ~~land in sight~~ <ins>begun to think there was no other shore</ins>. She ~~picked up~~<ins>slipped the chain of</ins> her own glowdisc ~~and flipped~~<ins>over her neck, with</ins> the cover <ins>flipped </ins>back to expose the phosphorescent surface. Ashore, a disc would fade to darkness<ins> as its dust settled</ins> during the course of a night, but the constant motion of the ship agitated the powder trapped within and kept ~~them~~<ins>discs</ins> always glowing at least dimly. She shook hers to brighten it further. With its light, she took a moment to bind her scarf of office around her neck before following ~~the sailor~~<ins>Lesid</ins> above decks. The heavy beaded ends swung about her waist as she walked.

Katin looked up for the cluster of stars that the ~~Seven~~<ins>Five</ins> Sisters inhabited in the heavens and murmured praise to them for guiding the search this far.

The captain ~~turn~~<ins>glanc</ins>ed<ins> over his shoulder</ins> as she approached. Stylian's tall form swayed easily with the rocking of the ship. "Well. You were right."

~~Katin did not take the triumph that he offered her, tempting though it was~~<ins>His words made her feel more alone among the Markuth sailors than ever. She had no one of her faith aboard the ship to share her joy.</ins>

<ins>   </ins>Stylian had mocked her goals, but <ins>how was that different from the mockery that the followers of the Five Sisters faced daily? He had </ins>taken the church's commission

~~nonetheless. His acknowledgment that she had been right could be counted a victory, but it did not belong to her. The triumph lay with the Sisters.~~ She was ~~too~~only grateful that he had been willing to sail on a course other captains had considered foolhardy, following the trail of ancient stories about a land far to the ~~W~~west. ~~She looked past him to the horizon~~*And the storm chased the Five Sisters from Selen, across the dark sea*.

A glow lay on the horizon, marking the division of the ~~world~~ocean from the sky ~~with its light. The sea retained its dark mystery while the sky brightened as though dawn were approaching, but the sun would rise behind them~~In the darkness, she could just make out the rounded shadow of land. Katin closed her glowdisc~~, tucking it into the pocket inside her left sleeve~~ so ~~that~~ it ~~did~~would not interfere with her night vision. She frowned, slowly understanding what the ~~glow~~light meant. She must be seeing a mountain with a city at its base. "I don't know why I expected the land to be uninhabited."

Captain Stylian grunted in agreement. "~~It must have a massive city ahead, to cast so much light~~I'm of two minds about this. One part of me is relieved, because this means we can definitely restock. The other is apprehensive, because big cities have more regulations than others."

"~~The Sisters have prepared a way for us.~~Why are you expecting a big city?"

He nodded toward the horizon as if his statement were obvious. "The only time we see that much light before we arrive is when we cross the Narrow Sea to Arland and sail into the harbor at Porvath."

Katin looked back to the light and had to struggle to catch her breath. So many people . . . so many people who shared a heritage with her.

Her people had suffered ~~enough~~ persecution for their beliefs ~~back in Marth~~every country. ~~Old stories told that the Seven Sisters had been blown away by a storm from Selen, a homeland far to the West. They now lived in the heavens to watch over their children. Passed down from mother to daughter, the beliefs had eroded over the centuries spent in Marth among the worship of the Sun. The corruption and greed in Marth had finally led the Sisters' Sayer to fund this expedition to find the way back to~~In Marth alone, the followers of the Sisters had been barred from holding office unless they renounced their beliefs. Even then, the visible differences of those who were ethnically of the Sisterhood still marked them. Hair twisted into pincurls at night to mask its coarse straight lines. Dye to cover the early gray—in some of the older families, hair grayed at puberty. Nut stains to darken the skin from the ruddy hue of a Sister, and still people could tell.

It was hard to comprehend that they had found Selen, the homeland.

She raised her gaze to the sky. She was not alone as long as the Sisters watched overhead. "The Five Sisters have prepared a way for us."

"To be honest, I wasn't sure how long I would be able to keep the crew sailing west. Thought we were going to go right off the edge, they did." He laughed and bent his head back to look at the sky. "Perhaps we'll see ~~'~~the '*moon*,' too."

Katin snorted. "That's exaggerated superstition."

"And tales of a land aren't?"

"Modern scholars feel that our holy texts are guides for ways to live a better life. They are allegories, and yet . . ." She tucked her hands inside her sleeves, crossing her arms over her chest as though she were lecturing at the seminary. "There is always some basis for the tales. A land, even if it is not a new continent, must be at minimum an island. This moon? We believe that it is a corruption of the word ~~"Monde"~~ 'musa,' which means '~~G~~city' or '~~T~~town' in Old Fretian. So we think that it refers to the city the ~~Seven~~Five Sisters came from. 'And the light of M~~onde~~usa lay behind them, casting silver across the sea.' This refers to the wealth and knowledge of the homeland, as does the passage which refers to M~~onde~~usa as the 'Brightest light in the darkness, it consumes all who enter.'"

He grunted again. "I've been to one of your Harvest Feast pageants. That whole glowing disc behind a sheet thing?"

"Illustrates a metaphor."

"Not much point in arguing with you about your own religion."

"It does seem unprofitable."

To her surprise, he gave her a crooked smile. They ~~said nothing else, but~~ watched the distant glow ~~grow nearer. All the~~brighten, while the wind played around her, lifting her ~~seven braids~~scarf and tickling her with the ends. No one seemed inclined to go to bed as they raced across the ocean toward landfall.

The light from the city was like nothing she had seen before. It was cool and silvery as though a glowdisc were reflecting in a polished metal mirror. It grew brighter by the minute. She heard a startled cry from overhead.

In the crow's nest, a sailor pointed to the horizon. His words were snatched away. When she looked back to where he pointed, Katin's heart seized.

A low mound of light had emerged above the horizon. It was not ~~the glow of~~ city lights, but a single broad arc that glowed with an unearthly light. She tried to make sense of the size but could not grasp the distances. "How big is that?"

"I . . . I am not certain." Captain Stylian's voice had a hesitation she was unused to in the man. "Pardon." With a half bow, he made his way to the foot of the main-mast.

He called up to the sailor in the crow's nest, asking him for some numbers. The wind blew them away from her, but the answer caused the captain to ~~turs~~spin abruptly and stare at the horizon.

~~He pressed his hand to his mouth and his eyes were wide with something that, on another man, Katin would name terror.~~ She crossed the deck to where the captain stood. "What is the matter?"

~~He lowered his hand and swallowed.~~ "It's . . . The measurements . . . they cannot be correct."

"Surely you can't tell from so far—"

"But we can. When we see another ship upon the horizon, or land, we need to be able to calculate how large it is and how far away. This . . ." He waved toward it as though the words had been stripped from his mouth. "This is vast."

The glowing edge of the ~~disc~~__light__ pulled her gaze once more. Enough of it was visible now to draw shadows from the rails. Long crisp shadows as though a dimmer sun were rising. The light lay before them and cast silver across the sea.__ It was like seeing scripture come to life.__

#

~~Water splashed on Katin's skin as she went through the seven postures of the morning meditation in the bow of the ship. Meditation did not come easily today. As she balanced on one foot, in Dorot's stance, she watched the sky. The sun had risen as it always did. On the horizon, the mound grew larger but seemed no closer. It was fainter during the day, but just as visible. She had not gone to bed, nor had most of the crew. Those not on duty watched, as she did, seemingly transfixed by the way the light had grown to a half sphere. When more if it had become visible over the horizon, it became clear that it was not land, but some vast disc.~~

~~It was impossible to grasp the size of it. A dinner plate held out at arm's length would just cover it, but a dinner plate would not be visible past the curve of the world. Perhaps it was a beacon or a source to light their land at night.~~

~~The base of it should be visible soon. Katin leaned out as though that would help her see the support sooner. It too must be impossibly large.~~

~~The disc cleared the horizon. Katin squinted against the haze and set her foot down, breaking the sequence. She could not see a base.~~

~~She stepped to the rail as the ship skipped over the waves in front of a brisk wind. Her braids beat against her cheeks as she waited. The orb seemed to rise higher but nothing held it.~~

__Katin's breath left her body in a rush. Dear Sisters . . . If the moon was real, what else was?__

A sailor spat on the deck, and touched his fingers from his mouth to his forehead in a warding gesture. Scraps of conversation began, getting tossed on the wind toward her.

". . . no land after all . . ." "~~It's~~ unnatural~~.~~" "~~We should~~," "turn back__,__" and then the epithet "nightlover."

"No." ~~Katin pushed herself back from the rail~~__Not now__. She ~~shaded her eyes against the sun and looked for the captain. He stood on the [nautical term] speaking with the navigator and the first mate. Their heads__would not let them stop this voyage when they__ were __so__ close ~~together in tight conversation. Katin tucked her hands into her sleeves and hurried across the deck.~~

~~The navigator lifted her head and scowled openly. "Don't you go spouting some hocum about this being a sign." Porit jabbed her finger at the orb. "That thing is unnatural."~~

~~"But not unexpected." Katin straightened her back.~~ "You may not believe in the ~~Seven__Five__ Sisters, but you must acknowledge that ~~the~~__our__ stories speak of this__. Of the moon__."

~~"Occult nonsense. The fact that someone sailed this far and saw that thing does not mean that land is in front of us." Porit crossed her arms under her breasts~~

~~and glared at the captain and first mate~~Stylian tugged an end of his mustache. "I thought you said it was a metaphor."

~~Katin turned from the navigator to face Captain Stylian~~Looking at the—at the moon rising higher above the horizon, Katin swallowed. "We hired you to sail ~~W~~west. Thus far, all of the indications prove that our texts are correct. The land of Selen is ahead of us. ~~Is there a reason, beyond your navigator's fear, to turn back?~~"

~~Porit scowled. "It's common sense, not fear."~~

~~"Peace." The captain held up his hand between them and turned to Katin.~~ "Your ~~religious texts are allegories, you said.~~ Has it occurred to you that your Sisters may have sailed to this point from somewhere else and then turned back?"

Her gaze slipped to the ~~orb hang~~light rising in the sky. She had been taught about the metaphors and had written papers on what they meant. Her work was, in part, what had led to this expedition. But ~~W~~what else could this be~~, but the moon~~? Katin met the captain's gaze as though he were a congregation of one. "Old Fretian is not related to any other language. Where did it come from if not the West?"

A muscle twitched in his jaw. "You paid us to sail for four fifnights, and so we shall. You have until the eighth of Reed, but not a day past that."

Katin forced her voice to be calm. "There will be land."

#

The moon rose higher as they sailed farther west. Katin chewed her lower lip, watching the pale object. It was impossible to grasp the size of it. A dinner plate held out at arm's length would just cover it, but a dinner plate would not be visible past the curve of the world.

Its shape varied through the course of the day. ~~f~~From a bowlike crescent, it swelled to a shining disc, then gradually diminished again to just an arc of light. The cycle repeated with slow regularity, but the moon never vanished entirely. It was clear now that it hung in the heavens, stationary as the sun and the stars spun their course behind it. She had studied enough astronomy in seminary to understand that the stars were actually far-flung bodies, not the spirits of the dead. This object—this *moon* was closer, so of course stars would pass behind it.

It only appeared to rise higher because they sailed around the world. If they kept going, it would eventually hang directly overhead. But why did it not move?

At noon, the sun skirted the edges, and daylight dimmed as though a storm cloud covered the sky. Each day, the moon seemed to eat a little more of the sun as it passed. Again, she understood intellectually that the changing face of the moon was a shadow. She understood that the sun was not truly being consumed, and yet the line from scripture kept running through her head. *Brightest light in the darkness, it consumes all who enter....*

The moon had risen high enough over the past week that it came close to the ~~Seven~~Five Sister~~'s~~s' path across the heavens. With the hour approaching midnight, it was now swollen to nearly a full disc. ~~Other stars had dimmed and disappeared behind it, then reappeared upon the other side.~~

~~Would the Sisters yield their place as well?~~Water splashed on Katin's skin as she went through the five postures of night meditation in the bow of the ship. Meditation did not come easily. As she balanced on one foot, in Dorot's stance, she watched the sky. Katin ~~tugg~~pulled at her scarf of office, which seemed too ~~tightly tied tonight~~ snug. She had trouble breathing as she watched the sky.

~~The Sisters' stately progress carried them to the moon. They dimmed as they approached it.~~

~~They vanished.~~

~~Katin sank to her knees. She had guessed they would. And yet . . . And yet, it was the night sky without the Sisters to watch over them. They had to come back out on the other side. Footsteps approached and the captain crouched beside her. "Are you all right?"~~

~~"I— yes. Thank you. I was just watching that." She could not voice the disappearance of the sisters to him.~~

~~"Perhaps you should not." He cast a glance over his shoulder. "I think it may drive men mad to contemplate it. We are not prepared for something so vast."~~

~~"But at some point, my people did know it." She pressed her fingers to her temples trying to soothe the pressure building there.~~

~~He grimaced. "But i~~I~~t~~ ~~i~~was one thing to believe~~. Or to disbelieve. It is~~, and quite another to see the proof of one's convictions floating in the sky~~."~~

~~She lifted her head. Was he speaking of her or himself?~~

"Ship ahead!" The call came from the topsail.

~~The captain scrambled to his feet and dashed to the [nautical term].~~ Katin ~~completely forgotten. She climbed to~~lowered her fee~~t~~oot, and scann~~ing~~ed the horizon for what the lookout had seen.

On the sea, backlit by the light of the ~~orb~~moon, floated the unmistakable silhouette of a sailing ship like in a Harvest Feast pageant. And a ship sailing toward them could only mean that there was land ahead.

The captain called for the ~~sails~~ship to ~~be lowered~~turn abreast of the wind, and gradually they ~~ship~~ slowed in the water.

She hurried across the deck to him. "What is the matter?"

"They're running dark." He nodded toward the ship. "No lights. Either it's a pirate ship or every~~-~~one is dead. Either way, we wait until daylight to approach."

#

Once the dawn came, it took several hours for them to meet the other ship. Its rigging was strange, even to Katin's untrained eye. It rode very low in the water and had a beaked bow ~~which~~that curved in the air like a swan's neck. ~~It was clear, b~~By the light of day~~,~~ it was clear that the ship was inhabited, but they made no hostile moves. Fishing nets hung over the side, and bandy-legged men worked to haul catches aboard.

When it came close enough to really see the individuals, a weight lifted from Katin's heart. Gray hair. Ruddy skin. They must be from her homeland.

How glorious to see a ship filled with people who looked like her.

Captain Stylian stood at the rail and cupped his hands to shout to the other ship. "Where do you hail from?"

A man in tight blue trousers and a long tunic of embroidered silk shouted back. Katin frowned and cocked her head. The wind had garbled what he said. It was almost understandable, but slid so that she could barely distinguish the breaks between words.

The captain switched to Paku and asked again, but the other man just held up his hands in a shrug. Shaking his head, Captain Stylian said, "It was too much to hope that they spoke Markuth or Paku."

"I think that's a variant of Old Fretian."

He cocked his head at that. "Worth a try."

She only ever used Old Fretian to read scripture in its original form and hardly ever spoke it. Katin took a moment to gather her thoughts, trying to martial them into a semblance of order. The declension for this would be masculine interrogative case, which meant that she would have to append the appropriate suffix to the word "land."

Wrapping her mind around Fretian, Katin spoke in that tongue. "What land-the you from?"

"The Center Kingdom. You?" His next words eluded her. Then came a phrase almost straight from scripture. "... Sailing beyond the Moon?"

"We from Marth."

The captain leaned down. "You can understand him?"

It was a relief to switch back to Marskuth. "Some. But we haven't said anything complicated yet." Beyond the Moon . . . did they never sail past here?

"Ask how far behind them the land is."

Katin nodded and painfully stitched the question together in her mind. "Land-the, how far?"

"Five days."

Katin reported this back to the captain. "May I hope that we are continuing on?"

"That's what you are paying us for." He stroked his chin, staring at the sailing ship. "Ask if they have any charts they're willing to trade."

#

The captain called Katin to his cabin. When she entered, he shut the door behind her and showed her to the map table. There, he had unrolled the chart they had traded for. "Look. We would have missed it with the course we were sailing."

A narrow spit of land jutted out from a landmass that filled the map. Islands dotted the coastline up and down it, but this one piece reached out into the ocean as though it were a finger pointing to the east. "How large is it?"

"I'm only guessing, but their captain says it's five days. If we're here, which he indicated we are, then that length of land alone is longer than the distance from Marth through Arland and into Gavri."

The scale staggered her and she put a hand on the table to steady herself. If the scale was correct, then this land—her people's homeland—was three times larger than all of the known countries assembled. The map was mostly concerned with the coasts, but even so, the towns that were shown were so numerous that she could not count them all. One city dominated, clearly, from the way it was drawn upon the map. A great river came through the continent to emerge at the base of the peninsula, and a city occupied both banks, spilling onto the narrow spit.

The script on the map was strange, with letters more simply shaped than what she was used to, all ornamentation stripped from them. Still she recognized the Old Fretian word "remek," which meant "center."

Scripture rose to her mind, "*The Sisters said, 'The center has held us together. Without it, we must create our own center and from this comes a new way of life.'*"

She had always taken it—the way she had been taught in seminary was that the center was a place of meditation within each of them, but looking at the map, the words revolved. *The capital has held us together. Without it, we must create our own place of government and with this comes a new way of life.* Katin touched the crescent drawn in the midst of the city, vaguely surprised that her fingers were not shaking. The Center Kingdom must revolve around the city Remek but . . . she saw no borders of the kingdom or other countries. The map was labeled as one vast empire. "This is the capital."

"Mm." Captain Stylian shook his head and tapped the map, finger coming to rest on a natural harbor farther down the mainland's coast, with a small town drawn around it. "What's this one called?"

"Iolokiv. It means Bardstown. Roughly."

"Good name. We'll head for here."

"Why not the capital?" The harbor he indicated was . . . well, if they were five days from the capital, it was a full day's sailing from Remek. *The center has held us together . . .*

"Because capital cities always have the tightest regulations. I would rather go into a smaller town to find out what harbor fees are like, if there are any shipping prohibitions, and so on . . . If we dock at too small a town, they won't know how to deal with foreign ships. So, we look for a mid-sized town." He flashed her a grin. "Plus, their officials tend to be easier to bribe."

#

~~The city~~Iolokiv seemed to sparkle in the sunlight. Glass filled windows in the walls and even in the roofs of buildings. In some places the walls seeemed to be nothing more than thin pieces of metal existing solely to hold glass upright. The wealth on display staggered Katin, but the people in the port paid no heed to it. They walked ~~past the docks on their business paying no more attention than~~along as if they ~~had~~ passed nothing more exciting than simple stucco ~~at home~~.

Their ship, on the other hand, attracted notice. As the crew worked to tie it up, they used a mixture of sign language and grunts to communicate with the dockworkers. Even the ships here had glass set into the cabins. Their own ship, ~~t~~*The Maiden's Leap,* seemed dark and squat next to the ships of ~~Mondel~~olokiv.

The captain ~~stood by her shoulder~~climbed onto the forecastle. "Listen up! You know the drill for a new port. Once we get the lay of the land, then and only then will I consider requests for leave. Expect to be aboard overnight at least. Until then, I want us to be ready to cast off at the first sign of trouble."

A sailor snorted. "That's a certainty with a harbor full of nightlovers."

He grinned and leaned over the man. "You knew this was a possibility when we accepted the commission."

"Ha! I thought we'd sail in circles and then come home."

The other sailors hooted with laughter and the captain let them.

Katin stood by the rail and felt her skin burn even redder with anger. If she could bring her people here, then any amount of abuse would be worth it.

Footsteps crossed the deck to stand behind her. Captain Stylian cleared his throat. "Is it a festival day?"

~~"Sorry?"~~Not a word of apology. She turned from studying the dock to face him. ~~His frown had grown deeper the closer they had gotten to Monde, the city that the Seven Sisters must have departed.~~"Festival?"

"The banners. Every ship is flying a red banner, sometimes two or three." He nodded toward the crowds. "And see. People with arm-bands in the same red. What does it mean?"

"I . . . I don't know." She had been so distracted by the variety of costume that she had not noticed the armbands. Despite the sailors' comments, the harbor was not full of "nightlovers," though they were certainly the dominant type. There were nutbrown men, women with flaming curls, and people whose pale skin had an almost green hue.

Now that ~~the~~ captain had pointed it out, the scraps of red were obvious, fluttering behind people as they walked. ~~She had been so distracted by the variety of costume that she had not noticed that common thread.~~ She pointed to a man with a blue armband who walked behind two burly men ~~who~~that appeared to be bodyguards, clearing a path. "There. Not everyone has ~~the~~ red bands."

"~~Hm.~~ I thought this was supposed to be your homeland. ~~Weren't you keen to come back so you could practice your religion freely?~~ So you ought to know, even by the calendar, if this is a festival day."

Katin shook her head. "~~It's not. But w~~We've been gone so long . . . Perhaps they added festivals?"

"You sound uncertain."

"And how am I supposed to be certain? I have not set foot upon the land."

He held up his hands in a placating gesture. "Fair enough. Shall we remedy that now?"

Katin took a breath to steady herself and nodded. The captain led the way to the gangplank ~~which~~that stretched from their boat to the pier. ~~At the foot of the ramp, the first mate was speaking heatedly to a man who blocked his path.~~ The man ~~wore a~~with blue ~~armband~~ribbons ~~and, like the one they had seen before, had two enormous bodyguards. They each carried a short sword with a strange grip in a small~~

~~sheath at the waist. Even the men obviously engaged to be fighters wore dark blue silk. Across their chests, little mirrors had been sew into the fabric and flashed light with each breath~~met them at the gangplank. His straight gray hair had been tied in a queue down his back, and his cheeks were so pink they looked rouged. He held a flat plank of wood with paper affixed to it by means of flat springs on the sides.

~~Tucking his hands behind his back, the captain stopped behind his mate. "What is the problem here?"~~

~~"Blamed if I know, sir. They won't let us off the ship, that's clear enough, but I can't make a seabound dog of anything the fellow is saying."~~

Katin wanted to retreat up the gangplank before the captain could ~~turn to~~ look at~~o~~ her. She did not speak the language, for all that he thought she did. ~~She took a step backwards and stopped herself. It would do no good to hide a~~And yet, likely she *was* the best chance for understanding what ~~they~~ blue gentleman wanted. ~~"Perhaps I can help?"~~

~~"I would be grateful if you would try."~~ He ~~turned sideways so she could slip past him on the gangplank~~spoke very rapidly, with that same sliding inflection as the ship's captain they had met on the sea. Katin had spent the intervening three days reading scripture aloud in Old Fretian, trying to make herself more comfortable with the language. Still the torrent of words undid her.

She held up her hands in supplication and spoke one of the sentences she'd prepared. "Please slow down. I speak very badly, but am the only translator the ship has."

The official snorted, but did slow down. Still, she only caught scattered words and phrases: "Where from," then "none crew-yours," and he finished with "official language?"

She could answer only the beginning. "Across sea-the."

"Ah. South Islander . . ." His voice carried amused contempt. "What happened husband-your?"

"Sorry?"

He slowed even further, pausing after each phrase until she nodded. "Husband your. Husband ship's. Examinations. Must pass. Or he would not. Command. Be given. If no one aboard speaks Setish. Then something happened. Husband ship's your."

Katin stared at him while she tried to parse the separate phrases into a sentence. The meaning of the word "husband" must have shifted over the centuries. It was paired with "ship," so maybe it meant "captain"?

"What is he saying?" Captain Stylian's voice was low and easy, as if this were perfectly natural. He flashed the official a smile.

"I think . . . I think ship captains are required to know the language, which I think is called Setish, so he believes something has happened to ours. Also, I think he thinks we're from islands to the south."

"That's a lot of 'I thinks.'"

"Well, I don't actually speak the language. I'm making a lot of guesses."

"You sound fluent."

"I'm mostly saying, 'please slow down.'"

He grunted a little and offered the official another smile. "South Islands? Don't contradict him. Just make apologies for our stupidity and ask if we can offer him some hospitality for his trouble." His tone as he said this was so deeply apologetic that she almost thought he *was* apologizing. He bowed his head, as if abashed. "Don't look so surprised."

Katin bent her head in supplication and pulled some of the words of atonement from scripture. "Oh noble master, forgive us our trespasses." It got harder from there, and Katin could feel the language breaking under her tongue. "New husband-ours offer apology-the you. Would you hospitality-ours accept?"

At her side, Captain Stylian produced a flask and passed it to the official with a deep bow. That language seemed clearer than any Katin could produce. The official made a pleased noise. As the captain straightened, he flashed her a brief wink.

Katin would not be exploring the city just yet.

#

The negotiations with the official had not taken long. The celebrations with him, however, had eaten the better part of the morning. Still, they had permission to dock and with that accomplished, the captain had been content to let Katin go ashore—with protection.

The sailor Lesid trailed after her through the market, one hand on the knife at his belt. She was not entirely sure if he was there to keep her safe, or because the captain wanted to make certain that his translator returned to the ship. Stalls lined the sides of a large cobbled square, set between low stone walls. Canvas awnings in blues and pinks stretched between the walls to provide a little shade to the merchants. Tables sat under the canopies, spread with unfamiliar fruits, fish, great heaping bouquets of pink flowers, and bolts of cloth. In the center of the square, a fountain burbled merrily. Around its edges, people had spread blankets on the dusty cobbles and squatted displaying cheap handiwork.

Gazes followed them as she and Lesid walked through the market. Most of the people had ruddier skin than his. Their hair tended toward gray. There were a few with darker skin like Lesid and some with golden curls, but none with both. On the ship, he looked like any other sailor. Here he looked . . . exotic. Katin slowed and glanced back at the sailor. "Walk with me?"

"I am."

"You're walking behind me."

"Oh." He frowned and took two steps to close the gap between them. "Better?"

"Yes." Katin resumed her stroll, feeling a little less exposed with someone beside her. She shouldn't feel so much like a foreigner, if this were really their homeland. If. What else would it be? The land was in the right place, and they spoke a version of the sacred language. But the people here kept staring at them and . . . nothing was familiar. Katin rolled the beads of her shawl beneath her fingers. Gefen grant patience.

"What's that?" Lesid pointed to a stall that had pink egg-shaped fruit that seemed to be covered in green-tipped scales. At least, she thought it was fruit.

"I don't know."

Lesid furrowed his brow. "I thought this was—"

"My homeland, yes. I know. Everyone thinks I should know all about it." Including her. "My people have been gone from here for hundreds of years. . . . This is as new to me as it is to you."

"I— I hadn't thought about that. Sorry."

Katin shifted her hand to her belt where her coin purse was tucked. The official had given them some copper coins in exchange for a bottle of the captain's whiskey. She was certain they'd gotten the worse end of the deal, but the captain had seemed pleased. "Shall we buy a fruit and see what it's like?"

The sailor's eyes lit up at the suggestion. "Seems half a year since I had something that wasn't salted or preserved."

Katin grinned and steered them toward the stall. "I don't see how in the heavens you can stand to eat that all the time."

"Well, it's not always. Usually we aren't at sea for more than a week, maybe two. You can carry enough rindfruit to last that long." He rubbed the back of his neck. "Then, you know, you pull into port at someplace like Nil-Mazzer and they've got barkberries or, oh . . . in the late summer we get in sometimes in redmelon season and you can buy big slices sprinkled with spice and a tall glass of chilled juice. There's this one place off the south canal that has a chef that grills it, right there while you wait, but he does it so fast the inside is still cool and the outside is warm. Just lights your tongue up, it does."

She blinked at him in surprise. "Seaman Lesid, you are quite the gourmand."

He laughed, shaking his head. "I'm not fancy. I just like food is all."

Katin stepped up to the booth and pointed at the fruit. She wrapped her head around Old Fretian, which was as close as she was going to come to speaking the local Setish. "How much? Two?"

The old woman behind the fruit had her hair wrapped up in a yellow scarf, which let a puff of white hair escape out the back. "Two *musan* each. Four total."

Katin assumed that a *musan* was a coin and fished four of the smallest coins out of the wallet and handed them over. The woman took them without surprise or fuss, and Katin let out her breath.

She said something very fast and Katin had to shake her head. "I speak bad Setish. Slowly?"

The woman grunted and picked up a wicked machete, flecked with bits of pink rind, and gestured to the fruit. "Cut?"

"Um . . . Yes?"

The woman nodded and pulled two of the fruits off the pile. She paused before bringing the machete down, and peered at the sky. Speaking very slowly, she said, "Almost noon death. Wait? So *naro-a* dries not before birth-the."

Katin made a guess that the fruit was called *naro-a*. She wasn't entirely certain what noon death had to do with the fruit drying though, or even if she'd heard the question correctly. "Thank you."

The woman set the machete down below the table. When she stood, she had a small roll of heavy blue cloth. Woven into it were yellow quatrefoils of thread that suggested stars at night. She shuffled around the table, unrolling the cloth as she stepped out of the booth.

Lesid eyed her and then the fruit. "She just took our money and didn't give you anything?"

Katin shook her head, realizing that he had not understood any of the exchange. "She will. After the ... Well, it translates as 'noon death,' but I think I have it wrong." Noon death ... death ... Maybe the point when the sun went behind the moon? That could be a death, couldn't it? But why did she think the fruit would dry because of that?

The market had stilled. Other people were pulling bundles of cloth out of bags, or from straps slung across their back. She drew her head back in surprise. It wasn't just a few people. *Everyone* in the market was doing the same thing. To be sure, some were continuing to shop with the cloth held loosely in one hand, but they all had a cloth. Some of them were threadbare, and others were so fine they had tiny mirrors sewn upon them.

The fruit vendor laid her cloth on the ground and unwrapped the scarf from her hair. Those with their hair covered were removing their hats or scarves. All of them had their heads turned down, watching the ground. What in the world were they looking for?

Then twilight swept across the market. Bells rang, seemingly from every corner of the city. As one, the people in the marketplace dropped to their knees and placed their foreheads on the cloth they had unrolled. A caged bird clucked in the sudden stillness, its chirruping cry bouncing across the stone walls of the market.

No one in the entire market, or down the nearby streets, had remained standing. It appeared that the entire city knelt.

Katin grabbed Lesid's arm and yanked him down. To his credit, he didn't fight her or ask what she was doing. He just mimicked the posture of the woman closest to them.

She could only hope it didn't make a difference that they had no cloth to kneel upon. With her face pressed to the hard cobbles and the dust caked between them, her nose twitched. She wrinkled it, trying to stifle the sneeze. Pulling her attention away, she tried to distract herself by playing a guessing game with what was happening.

"Noon death" clearly meant when the sun went behind the moon. That was happening now. The light continued to dim, further than it had aboard the ship it seemed, or perhaps that was her imagination. If the birth was when the sun emerged, then it would explain why the fruit vendor had been concerned about the *naro-a* drying. That was near to seven minutes.

The bells sounded again, while the dark still gripped the market. Cloth rustled around them and Katin pushed herself to her knees. She froze before rising any farther. The people were not moving to stand. They had rolled onto their backs. Lesid turned to look at her, brow turned up in confusion.

She had no idea what they were doing, but given that *everyone* was lying down, it didn't feel like they had a choice. She could think of nothing back home that would induce a crowd of people to act as one like this.

Swallowing, not knowing what else to do, Katin lay down on her back. Lesid followed a moment later.

She stared up at the sky and for a moment lost her worry about understanding what the people were doing. The sky ... On the ship, the sun had passed almost behind the thin crescent of the moon, but an edge of it had been visible. Here though, they had evidently traveled far enough that the entire sphere had vanished.

What remained was a dark disc with a fiery halo surrounding it. It undulated in a glory of yellow and red against a backdrop of deep blue. The sky was dark enough that stars shone. She searched the sky for the Sisters, but— But none of the stars were familiar. Katin shook her head, trying to slow her breathing. Of course they weren't. These were the daytime constellations only visible when the sun died. *Noon death*.

She took in a painful breath, understanding. *Brightest light in the darkness, it consumes all who enter . . .* Not when the sun died, but when the moon killed the sun and then gave birth to it. Had the Sisters worshiped in this manner? What had their lives been like to lose this display of magic in the sky?

Above her, it was as if the moon wore a fiery crown. Or a skirt. Dorot's bloody hands, but she wanted to find out how their scripture accounted for this. The myths and legends here must be as gorgeous as the streamers of fire that danced around the edges of the dark sphere.

For a third time, the bells in the city chimed. Again the sound of cloth rustled around them. Before moving, Katin glanced to the side to see that everyone was rolling back over to their stomachs, kneeling upon the ground with their heads bent. Lesid had already followed suit, tucking his knees under his body. Katin rolled over and pressed her face against the cobbles.

Had the entire city done this? Based on what she saw, everyone in the market had. She would have expected there to be nonbelievers at the least, and most definitely thieves who would take advantage of the time when everyone's faces were pressed to the ground. No one here seemed to have that worry. Katin couldn't imagine that happening in Marth, except in very small towns.

The ground lightened around her, shadows coming back to etch the edges of the cobbles. Around them, the bells pealed again.

She had expected a simultaneous movement, but the people in the market moved as if released from a spell that had momentarily bound them together. The fruit vendor bobbed to her knees, then pushed herself to her feet with a groan. She bent down to pick up her cloth, shaking the dust from it. The man on the ground to Katin's right stayed with his head down for a few seconds longer, before sitting back on his heels. Another woman knelt and rolled her cloth up before standing.

Lesid turned to Katin, eyes wide. Despite the fact that he spoke Markuth, he lowered his voice. "What by the blessed gods was that?"

"I think it was a group prayer service."

He glanced up at the sun. Overhead, the sky had returned to its usual daytime blue. No stars were visible. The sun, blazingly bright, rode in the sky where it had just been released from the crescent of the moon. Did they see the shape as a bow?

Lesid shook his head and lowered his eyes, blinking away tears from having stared too long at the sun. "Praying that the sun will come back?"

"I don't know. I'm sorry, I keep saying that a lot." Katin turned to the fruit vendor, who had hobbled behind her booth again. She had wrapped her hair back up in its yellow scarf. Katin switched back to Old Fretian to address her. "Pardon. University? Is there?"

The woman stared at her, mouth screwed up in a frown. "Oh— A university. Yes." She rattled something else off and then stopped at Katin's look of confusion. "Bardstown College. Water Street." She lifted the machete and swung it at the pink fruit. It split open to reveal a creamy interior, ringed with a thick circle of vivid pink. "South Islands, right?"

Remembering what the captain had said, Katin did not disagree with her. "Library-a there?"

"Aye." She swung the machete again, halving the other *naro-a*. With a little nod, she handed the *naro-a* to them, along with an odd wedge of some thick reed.

After a moment, Lesid grinned. "Oh! It's a spoon."

He stuck the end of the reed into the pale center of the fruit and dug out a scoop of the soft flesh. Passing it under his nose, he inhaled slowly, filling his lungs. Katin watched him slide the piece of fruit into his mouth and close his eyes in concentration.

"Well?"

He held up the hand with the reed-spoon, shushing her as he chewed. After a moment he gave a grin and opened his eyes. "Subtle. Almost creamy, but a little acidic. Not enough to make your mouth pucker like rindfruit. Maybe like a rindfruit ice... Anyway. There are also little seeds that crack when you bite. It's nice."

"Nice." Katin shook her head and scooped out a spoonful of her own. "You describe food the way other people describe wine." Anything else she was going to say was forgotten as she tasted the *naro-a*. The texture was the first thing that stopped her. It was soft, somewhere between a ripe melon and a pudding, while the little seeds in it burst in tiny pops. The flavor was a little like cream, but the thing Lesid had said about rindfruit was right. It made her mouth feel clean with each bite. "Wow."

"I know. We should find out how long they store, in case we can take them back to Marth."

Katin drew in a breath, somehow shocked by the reminder that they would be returning to Marth. It had always been the plan, of course. Find the homeland, then come back for her people. She just had not expected... this. Civilization. Or unfamiliar culture or— She wasn't sure what she had thought they would find, but not this city with its people praying to the moon. Did they do that in Center too? Did the entire city fall to its knees at noon?

Lesid cleared his throat. "Why do you want to find the university?"

"I'm hoping someone speaks Old Fretian."

"Isn't that what everyone here speaks?"

"No . . . It's related. Probably a descendant from a common tongue, but I'm fighting to understand anything." And maybe the university would have information about the Five Sisters. Surely they must have left some historical trace.

A knot in her stomach formed around the *naro-a*. Unless the Five Sisters were unknown here.

#

They found the university easily enough by simply repeating the words "Bardstown College?" as a question until someone pointed them on their way. The campus grounds had a broad expanse of fragrant ground cover with tiny leaves and even tinier purple flowers, spread between gravel lanes. Young men and women that Katin took to be students walked along the paths with yellow and blue ribbons tied to their left arms. The thin pieces of fabric fluttered behind them in a miniature festival.

She repeated her trick and said, "Library?" to the first student she met. Eventually, she and Lesid found themselves in front of a broad glass-fronted building. *Brightest light in the darkness, it consumes all who enter.*

Wide marble steps led up to glass doors set into brass facings. Did they use glass for everything here?

Inside, ranks of shelves stepped back through a well-lit great hall. At home it would have been filled with glowdiscs, while here the light came from a cunning arrangement of skylights and mirrors, but the sense of being a temple to books was still the same. Desks stood at intervals between the shelves, with students bent in study over stacks of books. At the center of the library a series of counters formed a square. In the hollow of the square, a pair of older faculty members sat at matching desks. A heavy book rested on the counter facing the front of the library, open to a page filled with names and dates. A registry, perhaps, of the people using the library.

As she approached the desk, Lesid dropped back slightly to stand behind her shoulder. Katin wet her lips and tried to think of how to phrase the questions she wanted to ask, but all of the sentences were too complicated for her meager grasp of the language. One of the librarians, an older man with thinning brown hair, looked up and smiled.

"May I help you?" He stood and approached the counter where Katin stood.

The relief that she had understood all of the words, even in such a simple sentence, made her sigh with thanks. "Please."

"What do you seek?" He waited, and still she had nothing easy to ask.

Did he have books about the Five Sisters or about a voyage beyond the moon, or ancient histories, or— Katin's head came up as she thought she saw a way out of her dilemma. "I speak not Setish."

She paused as his eyes widened with surprise, and she filed the surprise away to consider. Like the marketplace of people kneeling, what were the chances that a university, even in a middle-sized town, would not have foreigners passing through?

Katin put the questions it raised aside, and offered an apologetic smile as she constructed the next sentence in her head. "Is any person who speaks..." What was that phrase from scripture...? "The ancient tongues?"

The librarian drew his head back, and turned to his colleague, a woman of middle years with blonde hair that had silvered at the temples. "Can you..." and then Katin lost the train of the rest of his question. Whatever it was caused the woman to raise her eyebrows and stand. She came to the counter, blue and yellow ribbons fluttering from her arm as she walked.

She tilted her head and studied Katin. "What language?"

"I call it Old Fretian."

There was no answering sign of recognition in the woman's eyes at the word "Fretian."

Gnawing her lower lip, Katin reached into her sash and pulled out her copy of the *Principium*. It was not a translation into Markuth, but had the original Old Fretian scriptural text. She opened it to the first page and slid it across the counter. "This?"

The woman pulled it closer and bent over the page with a frown. The man leaned over her shoulder, chewing on his lower lip. "Can you read it?"

"Not well." The woman traced a finger along the opening of the first chapter. With an accent strangely formed and stumbling, she read aloud from the *Principium*.

"We give all praise and thanks to the Five Sisters for our Safe Deliverance.

Straight the Course and True the Path of the righteous.

Dorot, Gefen, Nofar, Yorira, and Abriel have kept us safe from the Ravages of the Deep.

We left behind Woe and Hardship in the Path of the Moon."

After a moment, she simply traced her finger over the text, lips moving occasionally as she sounded out a word. The woman riffled forward to a later chapter and placed her finger on the text again, mouthing words.

Behind Katin, Lesid shifted his weight and nudged her in the back. She glanced over her shoulder at him.

His brow was furrowed and he jerked his chin at the librarians. "What's going on?"

"I'm hoping they can help us find a better translator than me," she answered in a low voice.

The sound of flipping pages pulled her attention back to the librarians. The woman had turned to the back of the book and frowned over it. "Where are the printer's marks?"

"Sorry?"

"The printer's marks." The woman tapped the back endpapers of the book.

Katin spread her hands and shook her head. "I understand not. I mean— I hear words, but I do not know meaning-the. Printer's marks. We come from beyond the Moon."

The woman laughed and scooped the book up, slapping it against the chest of the man. "A prank. You should—" The rest of her words slid past Katin's understanding.

He caught the book as she released it, striding back to her desk. As he looked down, a flush of red highlighted his cheeks. "But so much trouble...?"

"One year, they..." Katin lost the words, but thought she was talking about a forged play. Or ox-tails. Or maybe a manuscript. The woman waved her hand in scorn at the book. "...not trying..." and "language" were all Katin caught.

"What language?" Katin held her hands out. "Please. What language is it?"

"Ancient Setish." The man answered reflexively.

"Anyone who speaks? A... ancient-an Setish speaker?" If Katin could talk to someone without having to struggle so much to understand modern Setish, then perhaps figuring out what had happened back in the days when the Five Sisters had left would be easier.

Again, she just barely grasped what they were saying, clawing meaning out of the words.

"Center University? Department of ancient languages?" She repeated to make certain she had understood it.

The woman's expression had gone from amused to annoyed. "Stop this farce."

Katin held up her hands in apology. "Sorry. And thank you."

"It is nothing." The man turned back to his desk, still holding her book.

"Excuse me?"

He paused, with his brow raised. "Yes?"

"My book."

Sighing, he looked down at the book in his hands. "You think not it return would I."

"But it is mine."

With exaggerated care, he said, "No printer's marks. Illegal."

Katin gaped at him for a moment. "I told you that we aren't from here."

"You are fortunate I do not call the Factors." The woman gestured to the man and took the book from him. With a glare, she dropped it into a waste bin. "Good day."

Lesid stepped forward and looked from Katin to the woman. In Markuth, he said, "Did they just throw your book away?"

"Yes— No!" She grabbed Lesid's arm as he put his hand on the hilt of his knife. By the Sisters, if he went after one of the librarians there was no telling what havoc it would bring down on them. "Lesid... We should go."

"But that's your holy book."

"I know." Her stomach twisted at the sight of the scripture lying in the waste bin. "We'll go back to the captain and see if he can ask the official to help us get it back, all right? But right now they think we're college students pulling some sort of prank." At least she thought that was what they had said. Maybe there was a fine she could pay.

"This isn't right." He glared at the librarians.

It wasn't, but for the moment, she had to accept it. "Let's go."

He lowered his hand with obvious reluctance and let her turn him back toward the doors of the library. She had taken no more than four steps when Lesid turned. "It's not right."

He ran back to the counter and vaulted over it. The librarians started up with shouts. The man hurried forward, but Lesid shoved him back with one hand to the chest.

Reaching the wastebasket, he grabbed the book and spun back. Tucking it under his arm, he ducked away from the woman librarian as she snatched for his arm.

She shouted and Katin understood the word all too clearly. "Alarm!"

Lesid put one hand down on the counter and sprang over it, running toward Katin. "Go! Go!"

His words released her from her shocked hold, and Katin spun to run for the doors. Students staggered up from their tables, hurrying to see what the commotion was about. Lesid caught Katin before they reached the door and passed her, pushing the heavy glass open on its springs. They ran through. She bounded down the steps two at a time, sprinting beside Lesid as they ran across the lawn. Behind them, the woman librarian had followed, still shouting, but her words were mercifully unintelligible.

When they reached the street, Lesid glanced behind them and slowed to a walk. "I don't see them, so I think we're all right. Best not to grab attention."

Katin laughed, the patter of excitement still urging her steps forward. "You sound like you've done this before."

"Let's just say, I had a strong reason to go to sea." He handed the book to her, with a wink. "We'll walk for a bit. See if we can find a shop to duck into, maybe."

"Thank you." Katin tried to slow her breathing to something that involved less panting. "Do you think they'll come after us?"

"Dunno." He shrugged. "I couldn't understand anything they were saying. Might be that I need you to teach me this language."

"If I actually knew it, I would."

From behind them came a shout that needed no translation. "Stop them!"

Katin whirled, her prayer scarf flying wide. On the university grounds behind them, the woman librarian stood on the walk, pointing with a straight arm. Running toward them were two burly men with blue streamers flapping from their arms. These must be the Factors. They each carried a short sword with a strange grip in a small sheath at the waist. Across their chests, little mirrors had been sewn into the dark blue silk and flashed light with each step.

With an intake of breath, Lesid grabbed Katin's arm and pulled her back around. Running in earnest now, they sprinted for the nearest side street. Lesid kept the pace rapid, dodging through the crowds of shoppers. He slipped between men in long tunics, women with bared midriffs, and everywhere the little ribbons streaming from their arms.

They wound through the unfamiliar streets, not slowing to look at textiles and brass vases or anything else that caught their eyes. Glass windows granted crazed views behind them, where their pursuers bobbed in and out of sight through the thick crowds. Lesid rounded another corner, narrowly missing a baker's cart.

Katin grabbed his arm and yanked him into the shop. He looked over his shoulder and pushed her farther into the shop, until a set of shelves filled with pastries hid them from the street. Standing in the shop with sweat-slick skin, Katin tried to master her breathing and look less suspicious. She inhaled deeply and stopped with her ribs expanded as a tantalizing fragrance caught her attention.

A stupid reason to think this shop was safe, but it was the first familiar thing she'd encountered here. It smelled sweet and spicy, and of dough that had been dipped in fat to fry until it was golden. She could almost taste the crust of sugar that would cling to the top.

"What?" Lesid whispered, still glancing back to the street.

"It smells like rolada. A pastry we make for the Harvest Feast in autumn." She inhaled again, savoring the comforting scent of home.

On the street, the blue-clad Factors ran past, pushing through the pedestrians without a glance into their refuge. Katin let out a breath and thanked the Sisters for guiding her here.

From behind the counter, a slender young woman was watching them with furrowed brows. She fiddled with a bell on the counter, as if on the verge of ringing it. Maybe it just brought someone from the rear of the shop, or maybe it called the Factors back. Either way it was best if she didn't ring it.

Katin smiled and stepped to the counter, looking for the crescent-shaped rolada. Hoping that the word wouldn't have changed much since they left the homeland, Katin cleared her throat. "Forgive me my trespasses."

"Excuse?" The young woman let go of the bell and cocked her head.

Katin made note of the short form of the apology and ducked her head to look at the pastries. Pale gold dough filled with some red jelly stood in rows next to a flatbread sprinkled with nuts. Heavy dark loaves glistened in the light from the ever-present windows. She did not see any crescent-shaped confections. "Are there rolada here?"

The baker stared at her. "What?"

"Rolada. A . . ." She winced, trying to think. What was the word for pastry in Old Fretian? "Bread? Hot oil . . . cooked in?"

The woman's brows came together in concentration and she repeated the words back to Katin. "Bread? Cooked in hot oil? What'd you call it?"

"Rolada?"

"Rolada." She said the word again, as if she were chewing it. Then her eyes widened. "Oh! Rolada!"

Katin blinked at her. What had she said, if not that? "Yes. Do you have them?"

"Aye." Hopping off her stool, the woman bent down to a lower shelf and pulled a tray out. Upon it were a dozen flat crescents of pastries, crusted with caramelized sugar. Peeks of color from the dried berries embedded in the dough made Katin's mouth water. "Just came out of the oil. How many?"

"Two, please."

The pastry cost less than the fruit, which said something about how the fruit was valued here. In a few moments, Katin had a handful of small coins in change for her single *musan*. The woman wrapped a sheet of waxed paper around the pastries and handed them to Lesid, who inhaled with a slow smile as he took them.

Katin almost snatched hers from him. The paper was already warm from the pastry within. She broke one horn off and the crust made a soft *crack* as the sugar broke. A sweet and spicy steam curled out of the flaky interior. She sent up a silent prayer that it would taste right, then felt silly for asking the Sisters to intervene in something so trivial. It either would or it wouldn't.

The crust dissolved against the roof of her mouth, carrying rich butter and the tang of spice. It was almost right, but in the way that pastries are different when someone else's grandmother makes them. The overall sensation was of comfort and home. Memories of being a little girl on her mother's lap, eating a pastry as the shadow play showed the Sisters' flight before the storm. A glowdisc behind a sheet had stood in for the light of Musa, but it had given her no preparation for the reality.

Katin's eyes watered with longing. Home. When had she started thinking of Marth as home? To be certain, she had been born there, but always, always she had been taught that it was not home. That their true home was across the ocean and that Marth was only a resting place until they could find their way back. There had to be more comfort here than a pastry. She just had to find it.

"Gods. That's good." Lesid sighed beside her. "Can we get some more to take back to the ship?"

Katin nodded and wiped her eyes. "Yes. That's a good idea."

#

They meandered back to the ship, following a circuitous route that took them far from the university, just to be safe. The baker had wrapped up a bundle of the rolada in heavy brown paper. It had cooled as they walked, but Lesid said the sailors would just be happy to have something that wasn't salted fish.

His pace slowed as they walked down the dock to the ship, so Katin pulled ahead of him a bit. Lesid shifted the pastries to his left arm. "Hold on."

At the foot of the ramp of *The Maiden's Leap*, the captain was speaking heatedly to a man who blocked his path. The man wore a blue armband like the official who had let them dock.

More troubling though were the two enormous bodyguards with him. They were the Factors who had chased them from the university grounds. Katin backed up. They would return later, after the men had gone.

"Katin!" The captain's voice boomed down the dock. "Thank the gods you're back. I can't make a seabound dog of anything the fellow is saying."

Sisters take them. Katin gestured Lesid to leave before she stepped toward the captain. Maybe Lesid could slip away in the crowd. With a smile, she faced the ship again. "I'm happy to help."

One of the guards nudged the other. At the same time, Katin felt Lesid's presence at her elbow. Curse him for being a stubborn gallant. The captain beckoned her, so Katin slipped past the guards and onto the gangplank. Remaining on the pier, Lesid watched her with the bundle of pastries still under his arm.

Clearing her throat, Katin marshaled the Old Fretian in her mind. "I give you greetings."

The ~~man~~official stared at her and said something very rapid. She could not even tell where one word ended and the next began. His voice slipped like oil upon the water.

"Speak slowly please." She slowed her own speech to demonstrate. "I do not understand."

His lip curled and he spoke slowly, mockingly, as though she were a damaged person. Still she caught only a few words, making her aware of how kind the other people had been to use simple words. "Name" and "travelers" and then "ox-tail."

"Did you say ox-tail?"

"Yes. Show me your ox-tail." Then his speech exploded into a confusion of words. "Ox-tail" again and then "~~C~~center" or perhaps "~~M~~middle."

"I am sorry. I do not understand."

The man threw his hands up into the air in an obvious sign of aggravation. He turned to one of the bodyguards and gestured toward the ship imperiously. ~~He spoke only two words, and the meaning would have been clear even if Katin hadn't, finally, been able to understand him.~~ "Take it."

The bodyguard to his left stepped f~~to~~orward~~,~~ the ship and unsheath~~ing~~ed his sword— Except it was not a sword. It was a hollow tube, which he pointed at the ~~first mate, who still stood at the bottom of the gangplank~~captain.

"Move~~.~~" The bodyguard gestured roughly, making his meaning clear.

The captain put ~~a~~his hand on Katin's shoulder. "What is happening?"

"I—" She did not know. This was not what she had studied for. Katin turned to look over her shoulder at him. "They want something. He keeps asking for an ox-tail. Maybe it's an offering of some sort? And now, I think—but I don't really understand. It sounds like they want the ship. But I might be wrong."

~~The gangplank shifted as new weight stepped upon it.~~

~~Behind her, the first mate~~Lesid shouted, "~~I said you aren't coming aboard my ship~~Hey, there! None of that."

Katin grabbed for the rough rope rail as the gangplank shuddered. She turned back in time to see ~~the first mate shove the~~Lesid grab a bodyguard by the arm and pull him back ~~from the ramp~~. The huge man looked astonished and angry. He pointed the tube at ~~the first mate~~Lesid and then—

There was a flash and a clap of thunder. Smoke billowed ~~of~~from the end of the tube. On the docks, people screamed and ~~pushed away~~ran from the sound.

~~The first mate~~Lesid took a step backward~~s~~ and then sat heavily. ~~The back~~Red stained the front of his jacket ~~was staining red~~. He toppled to the side and fell into the water.

"~~Gnistin~~Lesid." The captain pushed past her and stared at the spot where ~~his first mate~~the sailor floated face-down ~~in the water~~. Blood curled around him in the water. "I need a lifeline!"

~~As a crewman ran to get rope, the captain pushed past Katin, never taking his~~

~~eyes off the first mate~~No. No! What had happened? ~~She did not understand what had happened.~~

The blue man on the dock said something and it took Katin a moment to realize that he was speaking to her. "I do not understand."

"No one move."

"He's dying!"

"Dead. Already. Stay still. Tell them." He spoke with exaggerated care.

Swallowing, she said, "Captain. He wants everyone to stay still."

"No. I have a man down." He ~~turned and~~ bellowed back to the ship, without taking his eyes off Lesid. "Where's that rope?"

A ~~crewman~~sailor ran to the edge and wrapped a coil around the rail. His fingers tightened a knot.

The blue man spoke again, in that strange sliding Fretian. "I said, no one move."

"A man drowns!" Katin pointed at ~~the first mate~~Lesid. The water was so red.

~~"Dead. Already."~~ He snorted and turned to the bodyguard. "Make it two."

The weapon flashed and thundered again. Katin covered her ears, shrieking at the noise. Below her, the captain jerked and stumbled. He grabbed the rope railing with both hands.

"No!"

His feet went out from under him and he dropped to his knees, still clutching the ~~banister~~railing. As the acrid smoke curled around her, Katin found herself behind him, pulling him back ~~from~~before he could fall into the water ~~as the acrid smoke curled around him~~.

She wrapped her arms around him, feeling the blood soak into her tunic. Her scarf of office fell across his chest. "Stop. We do what you say."

"Good." The blue man's teeth glinted in the sun. "Good."

The bundle of pastries sat on the pier beside him, still perfectly wrapped.

#

~~The square of sunlight in the prison wall sent a harsh beam across the wood floor. Katin could not think of it as anything other than a prison, for all that it had large windows overlooking a center courtyard. The guards made their status clear. The ship's crew was held in a dormitory, quarantined from the other prisoners.~~

Katin sat by Captain Stylian's cot and dipped a cloth in the dish of water she had begged from ~~Proctor Veleh~~the guards. "The guards tell me that we will have *titam* and *kalcoist* this afternoon for lunch."

He grunted and shifted on the cot. "Dare I ask what that means?"

"*Titam* are potatoes and I think that *kalcoist* is lamb. At any rate, it seems to share a root with *kalca*, which is the word for sheep. *Ist* should be a diminutive, so ... lamb. I think."

A man came every day to give them language lessons. Proctor Veleh was patient to the point of seeming a machine, but she was the only one of the crew that made any effort. The others all muttered about escape, as though getting past the guards and their hollow tubes wa~~s~~ere a possibility.

"Any luck finding out what our crime is?"

She shook her head. In the fifnight since they had been taken, her grasp of Setish had improved enough to *almost* understand ~~why the others were being held~~. Almost. ~~It was so clearly descended from the same roots as Old Fretian that learning it had been easier for her than for shipmates.~~

~~Still, she only *almost* understood.~~ Or rather, she understood the words~~,~~ "shy of an ox-tail," but the meaning eluded her. "When I ask what an ox-tail is, Proctor Veleh says that it is the tail of an ox."

"Next time I'll have one pickled." He shifted again on the ~~bed~~cot and hissed. Stylian closed his eyes, breath~~ing~~ held between tight-pressed lips. He let it out slowly. "So . . . lamb tonight, eh?"

"Yes." She dipped her cloth in the water again and looked across the dormitory. ~~Porit, the navigator,~~ The first mate stood in a tight cluster with three other crewmen. She kept imagining Lesid in the corner of her eye, jacket stained red. Katin swallowed and focused on the living crewmen. One of them seemed to be blatantly counting the number of times the guard walked past the door. "Proctor Veleh says that they would normally provide a translator ~~so we could answer~~ for ~~our crimes~~the trial, but no one knows Marskuth. Or Old Fretian really for that matter."

~~Porit~~One of the sailors broke away from the group and crossed to the captain's cot. "I can take over, if you like." It was not an offer.

The captain raised his eyebrows at ~~her~~the man's tone. Katin bit her lips and put the cloth back in the basin. "Of course."

She stood and strolled away, trying to linger long enough to hear what they were going to talk about, but the captain said only, "Katin tells me that we're having lamb tonight."

Scowling, she squatted by one of the walls and smoothed her scarf of office. With her arms crossed, she took the ends of the scarf between her hands, symbolizing the path the ~~Seven~~Five Sisters took through the heavens, and began rolling the beads between her fingers. Each ~~s~~Sister had a separate role in guiding a person's behavior through life. Katin appealed to ~~Zo~~Nofar, the middle ~~s~~Sister, to grant the ~~C~~captain resiliency. He must get well and do nothing foolish. She sent a plea to Abriel to guard Lesid's soul. Though, if the Sisters cared for an unbeliever, they should have granted him favor for rescuing her book.

Briefly rescuing. The guards had taken it from her and presumably back to the library to be destroyed.

"What are you doing?"

The man's voice called her back to herself. She opened her eyes, ready to ~~frown~~ scowl at the crewman who had disturbed her before realizing that the question had been in Setish. Proctor Veleh stood in front of her. It was not his day to teach.

"I am praying."

He frowned. Lines creased his face more deeply than they should have in one so young. "No, you are not."

"What—? I— Yes. Yes, I *am* praying." She held up her scarf. "This is how we pray where I come from." Or rather, it was how the followers of the ~~Seven~~Five Sisters prayed.

"I have studied all six of our provinces, and no one prays to the moon squatting."

"It's not the position, it's the—" Katin bit her explanation off. If she drew attention to her scarf of office, they might take it from her. "I have told you. We are not from one of the provinces. We are from the other side of the sea."

He lifted his chin. "Stand. The Apex Councilor has decided to hear what you have to say."

#

The Apex Ceouncilor sat in a squat room, not at all grand, with a broad table in front of ~~the~~im. Yet even here, in the most utilitarian of chambers, great windows stood behind the councilor and cast light across his table. Stacks of paper crowded the surface in front of his aides, piled in neat right angles, every corner squared to the edge of the table.

On either side of the door, stood guards with tall spears. Tassels hung from the shafts, making the weapons look almost ornamental, but the light that gleamed from the edges made it clear that these were honed and sharp. Their breastplates were painted with a lacquered rendition of the full moon, with silver rays blending into the metal of the armor. The velvet of their livery was a blue so deep as to be almost black. Tied around their upper arms were blue armbands, which appeared light only in contrast.

As Katin was brought into the room, the councilor shifted a pile of paper closer to himself. "You have been accused of being shy of an oxtail. How do you respond?"

"I do not know what an ox-tail is."

Silhouetted by the window, his face was not visible, but the sharp jerk of his head was unmistakable. "Do not toy with me."

"I am not! I have no understanding what you are speak of."

"Every citizen must have an oxtail to travel outside their city of birth."

"Perhaps that is the problem. I am not ~~a~~ citizen. We are from Marth, across the sea."

The councilor broke into laughter at this. "Even if there were ~~something~~land across the sea, there is no way to navigate outside the light of the eternal moon. The fine for being without your ox-tail is not so egregious that you must make -up fairy stories."

"I am not! We have been trying ~~to~~ explain since we got here that we are explorers from the other side of ~~the~~ world. Where I come from, an ox-tail belongs firmly on an ox."

He cocked his head. "Are you saying 'ox-tail'?"

"Yes." Katin slowed down and tried to adjust her speech so it was more accurate. "That is what the man at the ship asked us for." Before he shot Lesid.

He uttered a noise that sounded as though he cursed. "You were supposed to have had language lessons."

"I did."

"From a historian. Your province speaks a particularly backward form of Setian." He rubbed his forehead. "Still, that might explain some of the confusion. You are saying 'ox-tail' but what I mean is 'oxtail.'"

Aside from a slight change in emphasis, Katin could hear no distinction. "What is the difference?"

"One is the tail of an ox. The other is a license to travel."

She gaped at him. ~~The first mate who~~Lesid had been shot ... "One of my shipmates was killed because we couldn't understand what the man at the dock was saying."

"All provinces have the same requirements. You should have undertaken this before leaving your home~~."~~."

Katin lost her temper and felt the touch of ~~Fahra~~Dorot on her soul. "I told you. We are from across the ocean. We could not possibly have gotten an oxtail before leaving because we didn't know that there was such a thing. If you tell use where to go to get a license, I'm sure we'll all happily pay the fee."

One of the aides scribbled something on a piece of paper and passed it to the councilor. <u>"I understand that you first disturbed the library with a prank."</u> He studied it for a moment. "Why ~~she~~ do you keep insisting on this fiction? Navigation is not possible out of the sight of the blessed moon."

"We navigate by the stars. Really, have you had no one else visit your shores?"

"Castaways from one of the ~~dark~~lower islands." The councilor stroked his chin. "The stars move~~,~~. ~~h~~How do you propose that one navigate by them?"

Katin faltered. She knew nothing of the subject beyond seeing ~~Porit~~the captain do it. "I ... I am not certain."

"Because it cannot be done."

"No. Because I am not a navigator. If you were to ask ~~her~~our ship's husband, I am certain ~~she~~ could explain. I am here solely because I have some ability with your language."

"And to what do you attribute that?"

"It is related to our holy language. I am a priest and required to be versed in it."

With her words, something in the room changed. The councilor became very still. By the door, one of the guards shifted his hands on his spear.

The councilor leaned back in his chair slowly. "I will grant that you <u>and your crew</u> are not ~~a~~ native speaker<u>s</u> of Setish. That much of your story appears to be true. So it is possible that you mean something else by the word 'priest~~.~~.'"

Katin reviewed what she had said and worried the inside of her lip. She had taken the word from Old Fretian, ~~and it was possible that~~<u>so perhaps</u> the meaning had shifted. "I mean a holy woman, or man, dedicated to the service of the ~~Seven~~Five Sisters."

"Who?"

"The ... the ~~Seven~~Five Sisters." She raised a hand to her scarf of office and held the beaded ends out to him. "Our holy book says that they came from across the ocean and we—"

"Are you saying that this is a *religion*?"

The sweat on Katin's hands clung to the scarf, adding to the dirt from the fifnight in the prison. She lowered it and wiped her palms on her leggings. "By my understanding of the word, yes. It is possible that, but the language has shiftedmay have changed."

"Do you worship these SevenFive Sisters?"

"Yes."

"So brazen." The councilor barked a laugh. "Ironic that the most damning piece of evidence against you is the one that convinces me your story is true."

"I don't understand."

"Every year, the Council of Purity finds someone misled by one old cult or another and takes steps to correct the poor soul. These misled fools have turned their back on proper worship of the eternal moon and, knowing that it is wrong, they try to hide their depravity. Yet here you stand claiming allegiance to goddesses that no one has ever heard of as though there would be no consequences."

"They are not goddesses." The words were out of her mouth before she realized that she should have asked what he meant by consequences.

"So you deny it now?"

"No." Katin's voice was louder than she intended. "I merely wish to be clear. Goddesses are born that way, if one believes in such things. The SevenFive Sisters came from here and shared their wisdom with the early FretianMarkuth people. It is said that they were elevated to the stars to continue to watch over us and guide us."

He waved his hand to dismiss her words. "You do not deny, though, that it is a religion."

"I do not." Katin licked her lips. "You spoke of consequences. What are those?"

"The moon is eternal and so we live by her light. Either accept that, or accept the absence of her light."

Laughter rose unbidden to Katin's lips. "Given that until a fifnight ago, I had never seen the moon, I can easily accept the absence of her light."

Looking down, he made a mark upon the paper in front of him. "Place her in a cave. Then blind her."

"No!"A protest formed on her lips, but Katin bit it back. What could she say? She did not accept

The councilor waved her away. "You are not to be trusted now. Of course you will profess to love the eternal moon, not when she had good reason to know that it was not eternal. She kept her chin high as the guards came to flank herbut you have already shown that you do not."

—As they lead her from the room, the councilor spoke behind her. "Wait. Do not blind her yet. If she is the only one who speaks their language . . . It occurs to me that we should speak to this navigatorship's husband. If they do come from out of the sight of the moon, then we should find this land and bring them into the light."

#

Katin stumbled over the threshold as the guard thrust her into the cell. A torch flamed in his partner's handan iron wall socket, lighting the crude underground passage. <ins>One of the guards held Katin's arms behind her as the other ran his hands over her body, searching for weapons. He focused his attention at her waist and sides, but when he found nothing tucked into her belt, he stepped back with a grunt. Neither man seemed to care about her scarf or notice the pockets sewn into her sleeves. She had a moment to realize that she'd seen no heavy sleeves here, before the guard thrust her into the cell. Katin stumbled over the threshold and nearly fell on the rough stone floor.</ins>

~~He~~<ins>The guard</ins> smirked, face crazed in the dancing light. "Enjoy the dark."

The door slammed shut, dropping the cell into twilight. Katin waited for the darkness to descend.

Light trickled under the door and from a crack in the wall. It was not bright, but enough to make out the shape of the room. A small table with a chair stood by the wall. A cot stood opposite it. Her final piece of furnishing was a bucket to hold her waste.

The cave was nothing more than a windowless room.

Katin sank onto the bed and pulled the glowdisc out of her sleeve pocket. She turned the disc over in her hands without opening it. There was nothing she needed to see, but having the smooth surface under her hands helped her think.

Their ships ran dark. Windows everywhere. Crude torches . . . Had she seen a single artificial light besides the torch? No. With the light of the moon, they did not need anything except on cloudy nights.

And perhaps . . . perhaps they thought this *was* a dark room.

<ins>Regardless of what they thought, she needed to get out of here before they blinded her. Katin shuddered. The scriptures were full of stories of people being blinded, and she was suddenly certain she knew their origin.</ins>

#

On the small table, Katin had placed her glowdisc facing the door. <ins>The bedsheet hung from the rafters, to create a loose partition in the room.</ins> She held the <ins>bottom corner of the</ins> bed-sheet in one hand, waiting until she heard the footsteps of her guard ~~with her daily meal~~<ins>close to the room</ins>. Shaking the disc until the light reached its brightest, she tried to keep her breath steady.

<ins>Her glowdisc's silver-blue light slipped under the door into the hall.</ins> The guard's footsteps stopped outside ~~her door. A moment later, the small slot in the base opened so he could pass her tray through.~~

~~"Behold the moon! The eternal moon has come to visit."~~

~~Her glowdisc could not overpower the torch, but its silver-blue light beat it back some.~~

~~The guard cursed and scrabbled to his feet.~~ <ins>"What in heaven's name?"</ins> His keys rattled.

Katin let the sheet fall in front of the glowdisc, to diffuse the light and make the source seem larger than it was<ins>, as if it were the Harvest Feast pageant</ins>. She leapt across the small room~~,~~ and grabbed the waste bucket by the door.

The keys scraped in the lock, and the door swung open. The guard gawked at the glowing sheet and took a step into the cell. His torch guttered as he crossed the threshold. Katin upended her bucket of waste on the torch, covering the smoking end with the metal. The guard cursed as the excrement and urine ran down his arm.

Katin swung the bucket hard, catching him across the side of his head. The guard stumbled forward and his feet tangled in the ties for her leggings. He staggered and fell into the cell. Katin dashed the bucket against his head again, and he lay still. Shuddering, she dropped the bucket. ~~and m~~Moving as quickly as she could, Katin began to strip the guard of his clothes, wrinkling her nose at the stench of the waste bucket. As she rolled him over, her hand brushed the sheath by his side. He wore one of the hollow tubes.

Hesitating for only a moment, Katin unbuckled the belt that held the tube at his waist. It would surely be more useful than his uniform, if she could figure out how to work the weapon.

#

Katin kept her shoulders back and marched with as much authority as she could muster. She had needed to rol~~e~~l the cuffs of the guard uniform up, but it hid the worst of the staining, and in the shadows of the reflected moonlight~~,~~ she hoped it would pass. Though~~,~~ for all she knew, they had height restrictions on who could be a guard.

With her lower lip clenched in her teeth, she slipped into the building where her ~~fellow~~ shipmates were held. The captain was not in good condition, but they needed to leave and this was likely their only chance. Katin approached the guard slouching by the window. ~~A window in the wall~~It cast a beam of light across the corridor. Anyone approaching would be well visible ~~then~~.

The guard straightened upon seeing her and made a movement with his hand over his heart. A salute? A greeting?

Guessing, she hastily copied his movement, hoping ~~he would buy it as a salute back~~it was even remotely appropriate.

"What can I do for you?"

Praying to ~~Pasha~~Yorira for aid in the deception, Katin lowered her voice. "The foreigners." She had been ~~think~~rehears~~ing of~~ this phrase the entire way here, so it would roll off her tongue as if she were a native Setish speaker. "The Apex Councilor says they aren't worthy to see the light. Supposed to take them to the caves."

"Now? The eternal moon will be full in less than half an hour. You won't get them there before prayer time."

She shrugged, as if she didn't care. "Orders."

His frown deepened. "And by yourself? For twenty men?"

Before the guard could finish enumerating the reasons that this made no senese, Katin had the end of the tube pressed against his forehead. He choked off his words, going cross-eyed looking at the weapon. His swallow was audible in the stillness of the night.

"Is this clearer? Take me to the foreigners."

He held very still, which was fortunate, as she had no idea what to do with the weapon ~~she held~~. Only the fact that one end was obviously a handle gave her even a hint of how to hold it. Reaching forward, she pulled his weapon from the sheath ~~on his belt~~ and tucked it into her ~~own~~ belt.

His voice was steadier than hers would have been. "I could yell."

"I could kill you."

"The gunshot would call the other guards."

"So the outcome for me is the same either way<u>, but very different for you</u>." She pressed the tube against his head more firmly. "Stand<s>.</s> <u>If you want a chance to live.</u>"

The guard wet his lips and let out a slow breath. He slowly rose and led her down the hall to where the <u>crew</u>members of ~~the~~ ship—no<s>,</s>—to where her fellow countrymen were being held. Katin followed behind, with the weapon trained upon his back.

When they reached the cell, she rested the tip on his spine. "Unlock the door."

The guard reached for his keys. They unclipped from his belt<s>,</s> and fell to the ground with a clatter. Katin scowled at him. That was clever. He had followed her instructions, but in such a way as it would force her to take the gun off his back to pick up the keys.

And this was where the ~~Seven~~<u>Five</u> Sisters<u>'</u> meditation exercises came in handy. Katin kept the weapon against his back as she reached forward with one foot. Sliding the keys toward her, she was able to scoop them off the floor with the toe of her boot as if she were practicing Dorot's stance. With her free hand, Katin<u> gave them back. "Unlock the door."</u>

The guard grimaced ~~and pulled the weapon out~~<u>but did so</u>, without attempting anything else.

~~He opened~~<u>When</u> the door ~~and~~<u>swung open,</u> Katin gave him a shove forward. In the cell, the crew of her ship sat up, blinking in their beds. Tempting as it was to look to the captain, Katin kept her gaze on the guard. She spoke in her native tongue. "Someone secure him. Quietly."

~~Porit~~<u>One sailor</u> stared at her in open disbelief for a moment, before yanking a rope made of torn sheets out of he~~r~~<u>is</u> cot's mattress. Where had the rope come from? In a matter of minutes, the guard was stripped of his uniform and trussed in <u>the </u>makeshift rope with a wad of cloth shoved in his mouth for a gag. The other crewmen scrambled into their clothes, pulling on boots and shirts in disciplined silence.

Now, Katin could take the time to look to Captain Stylian.

He stood by his bed, pulling on the guard's uniform. That morning he could barely sit and now<u>,</u> aside from a wince as he slipped the shirt on, it was as if his health had never been in question.

They had been planning an escape and had not told her. A knot of nausea twisted in her stomach. They had not trusted her because her people were from here. Clenching her jaw, Katin turned away from him and headed to the door.

A moment later, Stylian was by her side. He leaned down to breathe in her ear. "I give thanks to the ~~s~~<u>S</u>isters that you are safe."

Katin shook her head. "You've been pretending to be sicker than you are."

"I kept hoping that they would take me out of the cell to a doctor, or bring a doctor here <u>that</u> we could use as a hostage."

"You didn't tell me."

"It seemed safer to pretend to everyone than to chance our captors guessing."

She snorted, just letting the air huff out of her nose softly. "You were ready to leave without me."

"We were ready to come find you." He la~~y~~<u>id</u> two fingers on her wrist. "I wouldn't leave one of my crew behind."

<u>At his words, H</u>~~h~~er nausea eased ~~at his words~~. They were all fellow countrymen in this place. Katin handed the captain one of the weapons. "Thank you."

By the door, ~~the navigator~~<u>a sailor</u> waved he~~r~~<u>is</u> hand, signaling that the hall was empty<u>.</u> ~~and t~~<u>T</u>hey headed out into the moon's cold light.

#

With each turn, Katin expected them to be caught<u>,</u> but the shadows served them well. As the moon ~~rose~~<u>swelled</u> to ~~its~~ ~~full height~~, the cold silver light flooded the streets and houses. They were exposed when crossing the streets, but tucked under the eaves, in the shadows, they were nearly invisible.

The wind carried hints of salt air, and the captain straightened his head. Even without a nautical background, Katin's own stride quickened at the scent. The sea would carry her home. ~~All this time, seeking her people's homeland and she was fleeing it in the night.~~

~~In front of them, Porit~~<u>The captain</u> held up he~~r~~<u>is</u> hand, signaling a stop. ~~She beckoned Stylian and Katin closer. In a low murmer, the navigator said, "We should send one ahead. In case they are waiting for us."~~

~~"Likely they are." The captain~~<u>He</u> eyed the end of the street, where the harbor lay. He chewed ~~the inside of~~ his lip and straightened the guard's uniform. "I'~~ll~~<u>m</u> going to scout ahead in case they are waiting for us."

"~~Don't be silly,~~" Katin whispered<u>.</u>~~,~~ "~~You need to be aboard to get us home~~<u>I can go</u>."

"~~Mostly you need Porit for that." Captain Stylian eyed the end of the street, where the harbor was just visible. "Besides~~ I can tell the state of the ship<u>,</u> and you won't know what to look for."

It was sensible, though she still wished he would not go. "Both of us? As if we are patrolling?"

He shifted his weight, looking again to the end of the street. "Agreed. It will look more natural with a pair, I think."

~~Katin lead the way before Stylian could change his mind. He caught up with her a moment later and~~<u>As</u> they strode down the street toward the harbor<u>,</u>~~.~~

~~T~~<u>t</u>he captain rested his hand upon the hilt of the tube weapon. "Do you know how to work this?"

"No idea."

~~He inhaled sharply a moment later. "Thank the sisters. No one has noticed our absence yet."~~

Ahead of them lay their ship, tied to the same dock they had first arrived at. Only a single guard ~~stood~~waited at the foot of the gangplank.

The captain's breath eased out in relief. "Thank the Sisters. No one has noticed our absence yet."

-Better than ~~merely standing~~that, the guard lay on his back on a mat, with~~he had~~ his face tilted up to face the moon in an attitude of prayer. Their arrival coincided with the midnight moon reaching its full~~est~~ brightness. Though Katin and Stylian were exposed walking down the street, the guard would be night-_blind from staring at the bright orb overhead.

Stylian turned briefly to wave ~~Porit~~the crew forward.

The~~y crew~~ responded instantly and hurried as one down the street to their ship. Katin quickened her own pace. ~~The sound of their footfalls changed w~~When they hit the wood of the docks, ~~and~~their footsteps echoed ~~back~~ against the houses behind them. The guard looked down from the moon.

He blinked, staggering to his feet. "Alarm!"

As his voice rose into the night, Katin recognized him—not a guard at all, but Proctor Veleh. Behind them, metal clattered as a half dozen soldiers appeared on the dock, cutting off their retreat.

Katin sprang forward and shoved the tube against the Proctor's chest. Her bluff had worked once~~,~~; perhaps it would again. In Setish, she shouted, "Stop! Or the Proctor ~~is a dead man~~dies."

The soldiers slowed at the end of the pier, their weapons raised to point at the sailors. There were far more sailors than soldiers, but every single ~~one of the~~ guards had one of these cursed tubes.

The proctor looked past her to the sailors and appeared to be counting their number. "I confess surprise. I had not thought to check the prison after your escape from the caves."

"Tell your soldiers to leave."

"No. You may shoot me if you like, but you shall not escape judgment under the blessed light of the eternal moon." Proctor Veleh looked down his nose at Katin.

"As long as we escape here, I'm fine taking my chance on judgment."

"Even if I stepped aside and let you aboard, what then? You are advocating a heresy, and the Apex Council will find you no matter where ~~in the kingdom~~ you go."

"We're from across the sea." The image of the moon sinking below the horizon gave her an idea. "If your ship follows us, our ~~Seven~~Five Sisters will drown the moon."

The Proctor laughed. "You think we do not know that our world is round? The moon does not drown if one goes too far ~~we~~ast. She remains over the capital to provide her blessings upon our people. ~~No life exists outside of her divine sight.~~"

Katin ~~did not bother giving him an answer. She~~ looked to the captain and switched back to her native language. "Ideas on what to do?"

"This?" Stylian pointed his weapon at the guards.

A tremendous flash and clap rang out in the night. The guards scattered, ducking behind barrels and poles, but none of them fell. Th~~is~~e sound unleashed the sailors to fall upon the guards. More claps resounded through the night.

Yells, cries of pain, and a brimstone stench crowded against each other. Katin pushed the Proctor hard in the chest, and he stumbled back. His heel went out past the edge of the dock and he tumbled over.

"Move! Move!" Stylian bellowed, and like wharf rats, the sailors ~~obeyed their captain~~swarmed aboard the ship.

Scrambling and cursing, ~~Porit was the first past~~ Katin~~,~~ haul~~ing~~ed a wounded sailor up, throwing his arm over her shoulders. The others followed, leaving behind the bodies of the guards, but not their fellow shipmates.

As soon as the last one was aboard, Captain Stylian gave the order to cast off. Katin ~~retreated to the rail~~helped with the wounded, attempting to serve some purpose ~~by watching for pursuit~~ as they pulled away from the dock.

She glanced back once.

~~Her last image of the city was of~~ Proctor Veleh splash~~ing~~ed in the water at the base of the dock. The blessed light of the moon shone upon him.

#

They sailed due east under full sails for hours. ~~Porit told the captain to take the course that would put the most distance between them and the land and she would get them home from there.~~ Katin stood with her hands tucked ~~under~~beneath her arms. Between her fingers she rolled the barre~~ll~~ of the weapon as if it were a prayer bead, begging each of the ~~s~~Sisters for aid in their escape.

The prayer was automatic, but the ~~belief~~comfort did not follow. ~~Katin had been to her homeland and discovered that it was not the thing of legends.~~ There was no safe place for her people. Not at home, not here.

The captain came to join her at the rail, still in his borrowed uniform. He sank down on a coil of rope with a groan.

Katin tore her gaze away from the ~~thi~~wan~~ning~~ moon. "Are you all right?"

"I may have lied a little about faking my illness."

She snorted and went back to watching the path behind them.

"Thinking about your ~~s~~Sisters' birthplace?"

She rolled the barrel another turn. "The Apex Councill~~l~~or said that they would send ships after us."

"You mean the fellow at the dock? Even if they got a crew up and running as soon as he was out of the water, we've got a significant head start on them."

"No. His boss. And I don't mean just *us*, I mean Marth. I think they're going to invade." ~~She held up the gun. "I keep thinking that our country will need to work to catch up with their weapons~~The map of the Center Kingdom had no borders. Remember? They've conquered the entire continent. Bringing everyone under the light of the eternal moon."

He ~~gru~~pointed ~~and stared up~~ at the ~~sky~~weapon in her hand. "~~I guess~~With those... Maybe the ~~seven~~Five ~~s~~Sisters ~~may have~~ lead us here to give us warning."

Katin ~~turned to~~ stare__d__ at him. "That's the third time you've spoken of the ~~s~~__S__isters tonight. You don't have to act like you believe in them."

"To my surprise . . . I'm not. Not pretending, I mean." The captain pointed at the cluster of stars in the sky. "You told me that every story has some truth behind it. Finding the truth here . . . ? Makes me trust the parts I haven't seen the truth of yet. __Feel like they must have been watching over us, you know?__"

Katin followed his gaze up, to where the ~~s~~__S__isters traveled their path across the heavens. __The trail of stars behind them might even hold Lesid.__ Maybe the truth was that the ~~Seven~~__Five__ Sisters had fled their homeland, or maybe they had been blown off course, or ~~perhaps~~__maybe__ they were guardians who looked over her people. *And the light of M~~onde~~__us__a lay behind them, casting silver across the sea.*

   __Brightest light in the darkness, it consumes all who enter. . . . Not all. She had passed through the light of the moon and returned.__

The moon threw its silver light in a band across the sea ~~them~~, chasing her home.

The Making of I.E.Demon

WRITING EXCUSES 7.35

BRAINSTORMING WITH DAN

Dan: My friend George Scott who runs Peerless Books in Alpharetta, Georgia, has a very cool charity called Books for Heroes, where he sends books overseas to soldiers. They're doing a short story anthology connected to that, and he asked me to participate, which is awesome. It's specifically military thrillers, which I've never written before, and I don't really know what to do. I asked him if I could throw in some supernatural elements, and he said yes. I was telling Howard about this idea last week, and he gave me the coolest title ever, "I.E.Demon." Which I think is such a cool, Afghanistan—

Howard: IED is improvised explosive device.

Dan: I would like to use that title.

Brandon: Improvised Explosive Demons.

Howard: Just I.E.Demon, not Improvised Explosive—

Mary: It's Internet Explorer Demon, which is much more destructive.

Brandon: Okay. We're brainstorming I.E.Demon for you.

Dan: I have that title, and I have a couple of ideas, and I have nothing else. We need to turn this into a story in the next fifteen minutes.

Mary: What are the couple of ideas you have?

Dan: One, for example, is to just go right with the IED, the little bomb that is hidden in the road, that they can trigger and blow up a passing convoy of soldiers. If that is a demon, then let's say the Taliban has run out of resources. They don't have actual bombs anymore, so they've made a pact with horrible dark forces from beyond, and they've got a demon buried under this road, and when a tank drives over it, they chant and it explodes, and out comes a demon and starts eating people.

Howard: An alternative to that is the demon is being provided by Halliburton as armor. It's under the Humvee. There are demons riding under the Humvees whose job it is to absorb the killing blow of the explosive.

Brandon: So they've got good demons?

Howard: Not necessarily good demons—if the IED goes off in the wrong way, you end up with loose demons who are injured and angry.

Brandon: Right, okay. On one side, the Taliban is demonic consulting. On the other side, it is the US military who is using them as armor.

Howard: I'll be honest with you, the first idea was the first one I went to. At risk of kowtowing to political correctness, portraying terrorists as demon worshippers—

Mary: Yeah, that is problematic.

Howard: Portraying Halliburton as demon mongering is just funny.

Brandon: It is a charity to support soldiers, correct?

Dan: There's a definite element of fan service in the anthology.

Brandon: There is that. If you're considering where it's coming from, painting these soldiers as using demon technology—

Howard: The way I'd roll with this is—a common theme in military fiction is your equipment was built by the lowest bidder. The idea that somebody built armor and got the lowest bid—

Dan: They undercut Halliburton.

Howard: —so the soldiers don't know what's in here, so you have them fighting a runaway demon as a result of the IED going off.

Brandon: Now that's cool. I love that idea.

Mary: That is a great deal of fun. The lowest bidder—

Howard: Do you want me to write it for you now, Dan?

Dan: Yes, please. That's awesome.

Mary: I'm also going to point out that *Partials* has a fair bit of military—

Dan: That's true. There's a lot of military fiction stuff in *Partials*.

Brandon: Here's the question I want to ask you, Dan. Do you want this to be alternate history or alternate earth? Demons are common—or maybe not common, but known of—so if we go with Howard's concept, the lowest bidder, you're not sure what weird magic they use in this armor.

Dan: Yeah, I can see that. It could be a world in which the lowest bidder is the one who happens to have discovered demon summoning. Or like you're saying, it could be an alternate earth where the low bidder is the one who didn't use the right kind of chalk in the circle, and so the demons are a lot more likely to break out.

Brandon: You don't normally build armor out of demons, but it could be an alternate universe where—"Wait a minute, they built our armor out of demons," rather than—

Howard: How long is the story?

Mary: That's a good question.

Dan: At least 2,000 words, probably not more than 5,000 or 6,000.

Howard: Okay, so what you're talking about is a short story. The idea that we have thrown in, that your vehicle armor has occult properties that are problematic when it gets hit in a certain way, is a sufficient idea to carry a story of that length. It's not too big. I would move away from an alternate universe and put it in our universe, so that you can leverage as many of the things as you can that the soldiers who are reading the anthology are familiar with, so that when there's an element that's new they recognize it as new. They're your target audience. You still make them out to be the heroes because now they have to go kill the runaway—

Mary: Better than kill. The IE is improvised explosive, so what if they repurpose the demons?

Dan: Oh, that's clever.

Mary: They're trapped. They're behind enemy lines. Their armor has failed because the lowest bidder used—

Howard: The Humvee is upside down and the demon is loose.

Mary: One of them realizes they can use the demon as an improvised explosive device to defeat the enemy.

Brandon: They bind it to the rocket in their rocket launcher and say, "All right, let's just send that baby that way. We can't contain him."

Howard: If you want to lean toward humor, the TLA—the three-letter acronym—is huge. I.E.Demon, and you end with R.P.Gremlin, where rocket-propelled grenade is RPG.

Mary: I was only coming up with role-playing game.

Howard: Rocket-propelled gremlin, where they've trapped the demon, bound it to a grenade, and fired it into the enemy, where it bounces around and wreaks havoc, and they get away. I don't know how you want to wrap that up, but there you have a little bit of symmetry with the title. Yes, I went for the easy joke.

Dan: That's actually very clever.

Brandon: I like the gremlin thing also, potentially. It's a way you could go, with the demon as a makes-things-break demon rather than an I'm-going-to-slaughter-you-all. I think that might play into—for soldiers in the field, you're out here, and your stuff keeps breaking, and you think, "Can't we get anything to keep working? We can't."

Mary: Because gremlins have been part of the military for a long time.

Brandon: If they find out that indeed this gremlin was bound.

Howard: That's how the demon was supposed to work. We're playing with "demon" and "gremlin" interchangeably. You can, for purposes of your quick mythology primer for the soldiers, make gremlin a demon subtype. They bound a gremlin into the armor, because the whole point of the gremlin is that as it goes over the explosive device and the explosive device goes off, the gremlin in active self-preservation makes it fail.

Dan: Yeah, there we go.

Howard: But he doesn't make it fail well enough. It's damaged. The Humvee flips over, the gremlin-demon is now loose, and nothing works.

Dan: Can the demon's name be Snafubar?

Mary: It's your story.

Brandon: All right, Dan, I want to hand this back to you. Where do you want us to go with our brainstorming session from here? What is working for you? What is not working for you? Do you want us to start talking about a character?

Dan: I think character might be the next way to go, but let's look at the considerations of this. First of all, I love the idea. I really, really liked Howard's idea of using a gremlin specifically for its malfunctioning property. Let's make the IEDs malfunction as we drive over them, and therefore we're protected. That suggests to me that we might want this to be an alternate earth.

Brandon: You could just go with the idea of: We have this new device. We wanted the bidding to happen, and they came through and we've got this new thing, and they're working real well, the other armors, and we're going to get one and then put someone in the team—

Dan: We don't know how it works, but it does. What that means is that we have approximately 5,000 words to present the technology, to show the attack, the soldiers figure out what's going on, and then turn it to their own ends.

Howard: It's actually really easy to do the setup on this. You have a couple of soldiers who are in the Humvee, who are talking about the new armor. Basically one of the guys is saying, "Look, the new armor has never actually been field tested. An IED has not gone off under it yet. All we've had is fizzles and whatever else." And the other guy says, "Yeah, but that's exactly how it's supposed to work. I don't know, it's like magic." He can say those exact words. "It's like magic. It rolls over the top and the IEDs fail; that's what it's supposed to do."

Dan: That's what I'm wondering now. It seems like we need a character who's at least passingly familiar with the supernatural—

Brandon: —so he can identify a gremlin.

Mary: One of the things I was going to say is if this is an alternate history, but contemporary, it seems like you would have a branch of the military who specialize in this. You have your gremlin specialist.

Howard: I think that's too big for this story.

Mary: I don't. Please, I could do that in 500 words.

Dan: Whether it's real world or alternate world, either way we need a character who can identify it as a gremlin, and then figure out how to bind it to a grenade.

Brandon: Now I would suggest, if I were writing this story, that the main character who figures out how to bind it to a grenade is not the expert in the gremlins. There is someone else in the team who acts as a sidekick information repository, because if you give your main character too much expertise in what's going on, he or she won't feel like a fish out of water in the same way that I think we want the reader to feel.

Howard: Another military trope is reading the field manual while under fire. If I'm under fire, there's a problem. What the heck has gone wrong? This armor piece came open. There's smoke coming out of this hatch, and now suddenly everything is broken. Let me look at the field manual.

Brandon: There's a classified section.

Howard: What are these symbols here in the field manual?

Brandon: I would love that. "If this happens, break the seal on the back." You say, "What?" You open it and says, "Your gremlin has escaped." Then you say, "What!"

Dan: Please sit down to read Section 7.

Howard: "If you have a shoe leather MRE"—which is the chicken breast MRE, I think that's the one they refer to as shoe leather—"please open packet number 3. The gremlins will totally go for this."

Brandon: And they ask, "Who's got—"

Howard: "I gave all those away."

Brandon: That would be a wonderful way to go.

Dan: Okay, that could work well. The other direction which I'll throw out—I don't know if it's a better idea—is to actually have somebody there riding along with them, who's part of the field test.

Howard: Yeah, that's what I was going on about.

Brandon: The government spook, or the contractor, says, "Oh no."

Dan: The little weasel guy.

Mary: Yeah. The other option would be to really just completely pop-culture it and have one guy on the team who's a D&D guy. He says, "Dudes, this is a gremlin," and everyone else says, "No, it's not. What are you going to do? A saving throw?" And he says, "It's a gremlin."

Howard: Yeah, and he reaches into his pocket and pulls out a fistful of D6s and says, "Watch this," and throws them, and they all come up ones. "Now watch again." Ones.

Dan: It's a gremlin.

Mary: Since we're starting to move toward talking about cast, if your cap is 5,000 words, this has to be a tiny, tiny cast, which is one of the challenges with military fiction. You usually have a troop of people moving together, so you need to come up with a way to make sure that you only have probably no more than three characters.

Dan: A bomb going off could thin the ranks, but that's horrible to do to the soldiers.

Brandon: Mary's the expert here. I would say, can't you have three named characters, and then the rest of the squad that you don't name? There's like eight of them, but three are involved in this, and the others are taken care of with "You two watch perimeter. You two do this—"

Howard: The other thing that works—the Humvee is part of a convoy, and a radio call comes in for the spook. "We need him back at base right now. Turn around and come home." "How many do you want us to peel off?" "Just you guys." "This is against procedure, we're not supposed to do this." "Look, you just cleared this road. You're fine, come on home." And so then we have an isolated single vehicle, five or six people, only two or three of whom are going to be carrying the plotline. The other guys are holding down the perimeter with weapons.

Mary: I want to go back to what Brandon said, because what he's talking about with the unnamed characters is not keeping them in the scene, but giving them a reason to go someplace else, and that's an important distinction. Sorry, I know you know that, Dan—but for our readers.

Howard: And for Howard.

Dan: Don't assume that I know anything.

Brandon: I think this went really well.

Dan: I have a very cool story I can write now.

Writing I.E. Demon

Dan Wells

This story went through four main iterations, each one homing in closer to the story I wanted to tell, in the way I wanted to tell it. The differences between the first draft and the second are massive; the differences in the latter three drafts are more subtle, but pretty interesting, so I wanted to include them all.

When we talked about this story in our brainstorming episode, I came away with a very clear sense of the story I wanted to tell; you can think of these as the "load-bearing" elements of the story, the basic skeleton that holds it all together:

1. A team of soldiers stationed in Afghanistan is sent out to field test a new piece of anti-bomb equipment.
2. The equipment fails, releasing a gremlin.
3. The soldiers are shocked by the sudden appearance of the supernatural, and their lives are in danger, but . . .
4. . . . they can't get any help because an insurgent attack is keeping their backup busy.
5. The soldiers figure out how to contain the gremlin and use it against the insurgents, thus solving both problems and being heroes.

Starting with those points as a core to build around, there are a ton of different ways to go, so I sat down with my trusty Seven-Point Structure and outlined a story. I came up with something I liked, but as I was writing it the problems leapt out at me almost immediately.

FIRST DRAFT

As you can see, this draft was never finished, which is actually kind of fun to look at because it means I never went back to clean it up; it's got a few weird half-sentences, from edits I made on the fly while writing, and it's absolutely littered with all-caps placeholders like "four Humvees, a TRUCK, and a TANK." The plan was to get the story down on paper, then go back later and fill in all the appropriate military equipment and jargon. This was part of my plan to make the military aspects of the story as accurate as possible, though you'll see in the second draft that even this way I still made tons of mistakes. I use placeholders like this a lot when I write, though I've started putting them in brackets just to make them easier to search for. Placeholders help me write quickly, without getting bogged down in the details, and then I go back—usually within a day or two—and do the research and plug in the right pieces. I don't like to wait until the project is completely finished, because what if the piece of info I find for that placeholder turns out to be interesting and cool, and inspires another idea for the story?

The major problem with this draft is how slow it is—and I could tell that right from the beginning, which is why I only made it four pages in before I abandoned the story and took everything back to the drawing board. More than anything, this is because I still tend to think and outline like a novelist, so I filled the story with too much stuff. On page four of the final story we've already seen the gremlin, and the characters are scrambling for their lives; on page four of the first draft we're only halfway through the testing phase, and we've spent almost half that time in conversations about who should go back to base, who they should take with them, and so on. That's there to set up Load-Bearing Plot Element #4, but it's boring, and it's the slowest possible way to do that setup. I was also introducing a ton of characters, most of whom were not essential to the story (though I have to say that "Rank James" is a hilarious name that I want to use again sometime). So instead of throwing you into this cool story full of action and a fun magical puzzle to solve, I was wasting your time making you memorize names and laying the groundwork for way more story than I needed. It was a mess, and it was time to chuck it and start over.

SECOND DRAFT

I pared this draft back to the bare bones, cutting out a lot of the unnecessary business and characters in order to get straight into the actual plot. I took this so far, in fact, that I jettisoned the characters' names altogether, mostly as an experiment; some of my readers didn't like this, some of them did, but I thought it worked really well so I kept it all the way to the final.

Most of the changes I made for this new draft came from a close examination of the Load-Bearing Plot Elements, thinking long and hard about what I really needed to accomplish and what I didn't, and what would be the best way of going about it. For example, #4 required them to be alone, but it didn't demand that they get separated from a larger convoy; I had them in a large convoy in the first draft because it felt natural, but that's not the same thing as load-bearing, so out it went. They leave the base on their own, and boom we're done—no two pages of conversation required. That's not to say that the convoy was a bad idea, just not a good fit for this situation and length.

The characters changed a bit as well, most notably by turning the spook into an engineer. The spook was kind of a fun, smarmy weasel to write about, but making him a weasel meant that I was adding a conflict I didn't need: a personality clash between a military hero and a government villain withholding information. That kind of conflict would need an arc of its own, even a small one, and eventually a resolution; again, it was simply too much for such a short piece, so out it went. Making the government dude into a scared egghead allowed me to piggyback the "hero vs. outsider" conflict onto the core "holy crap how do we get out of this" conflict. It's worth noting that all of these personality changes could have been made without altering the character's profession—I could have had a weasel engineer or an egghead secret agent—but my research told me that equipment field tests are more typically overseen by engineers, so that decided it.

Making the government person less competent overall also helped my main character have more room to shine as a hero. Where the weaselly spook might have stepped up and tried to deal with the gremlin himself, the terrified engineer is completely out of his element, giving the main character a chance to make important decisions and come up with clever plans on his own. I also gave him a little boost by splitting the engineer into two guys and then killing one of them, so the team is left with some basic knowledge about how the gremlin works, but none of the expertise needed to deal with him; the main character gets to step into that gap and save the day. Last of all, I made the switch from third- to first-person specifically as a way of getting into that character's head and showing more of his thought process, his anger at being hung out to dry, and his determination to make it all work anyway. I probably could still have done all that in third-person, but the previous draft convinced me that first-person was the way to go.

As you can see, this draft is very close to final. I was happy with the flow, the voice, and so on. There was still a lot of polishing to do, but it's more subtle, which is why it's important to do multiple revisions: the first pass took care of all the big-ticket problems, but the second one drilled down to some very specific stuff. In this case, most of that stuff was military: I sent this draft to two friends of mine, Ethan Skarstedt and Mike Kupari, both Afghanistan veterans, and they gave me pages and pages of incredibly valuable notes covering everything from the specific gear choices (the AT4 grenade launcher I have them using in the second draft is a single-shot, disposable weapon, so they would not have different rounds for it) to the personnel (the vehicle they drive would have a three-man team of leader, driver, gunner, without the extra bomb squad guy I'd thrown in). Most importantly, they let me know that the circumstances of my story were implausible to the point of being ridiculous: the idea that a Taliban insurgency force would directly assault a US firebase is laughable, and even if they did they wouldn't have the kind of numbers, or present the kind of threat, that I described in this draft. Time to change it again.

THIRD AND FINAL DRAFTS

The major changes leading into the third draft were, as I said, mostly military in nature: I gave the characters different gear, adjusted the story to fit, and changed the ending so they used the gremlin to rescue a convoy instead of an entire firebase. The insurgent force presented in this version of the story is still huge, as Taliban forces go, but it's more believable, especially because the sheer volume of IEDs in the story has primed us to expect a higher-than-average Taliban presence. Luckily, my Load-Bearing Plot Elements did not demand that the firebase be attacked, only that the characters use the gremlin to save somebody, so I could make these changes without altering the core story.

At this point the plot works, the characters work, the military details work, and I'm really happy with it. Peter Ahlstrom, a good friend and an excellent editor, ran through it for a final editing pass, cleaning up some of the proofing and consistency errors, and while I agreed with almost all of the changes there were a handful I didn't like, so I said no. I want to make a point of this because I do it all the time, and I think most authors do. In this case, the only change I had any serious objection to was Peter's attempt to de-capitalize my jargon terms like Bound Supernatural Entity and Rocket-Propelled Gremlin. It is, I admit, "correct" to have these terms in lowercase, but I could not possibly care less about that. I wanted these words capitalized because I think they add to the story and the world, and I liked being able to call attention to them not just as phrases but as specifically military terms. Military jargon is overflowing with acronyms, and my story relies on them heavily—even the title is an acronym joke. Choosing to ignore the copyeditor's suggestions for meaningful stylistic reasons is an important part of the editing process. This is also good to remember the next time you find an error in a published book: don't blame the proofreaders, because for all you know they found it and the author changed it back. We're jerks like that sometimes.

I'm very pleased with this story. I think it's hands-down my best piece of short fiction—which is maybe not a very impressive claim because I don't write a lot of short fiction—but I'm working at it, and I think this one stands up proudly. I hope you like it as much as I do.

First Draft: I.E. Demon

DAN WELLS

"It's like magic," said the spook. The Humvee bumped wildly on the dirt road, jarring Private Harkness in the back seat, but the spook seemed unfazed. "We've tested this a thousand times back in the states, with every type of explosive you can think of—pressure mines, improvised mines, remotely triggered explosives, everything. The BSE stops them all."

They were deep in the Afghani desert, about an hour from base, performing a field test on the BSE—Harkness didn't know what the BSE was, only that it was installed on the undercarriage of their Humvee, and that it allegedly 'stopped' explosive attack. Not 'shielded against them,' not 'detected them,' but 'stopped' them. Harkness had no idea, and the rest of the team—four Humvees, a TRUCK, and a TANK—seemed to be just as clueless as he was. The spook seemed supremely confident, but then, didn't they all? Harkness couldn't decide if the man's sublime arrogance was heartening or obnoxious, but he was leaning toward the latter. It was one thing to have faith in your mysterious new mine-killer, but it was just plain stupid to be this far from a forward base without a helmet.

And I'm supposed to protect him, thought Harkness. *This guy's one ambush away from Taliban-assisted suicide, and I'm the one who's going to catch hell for it when he goes down.* He offered the spook a helmet, the seventeenth time now that he'd tried, but the spook waved him away.

RANK Gomez, their Truck Commander, pressed the spook for more information. "You keep saying it 'stops' the explosions, but how does it stop them? How does it work?"

The spook smiled. "Flawlessly."

"That's not an answer."

"That's the only answer you're cleared to receive," said the spook, and Harkness saw the man's unflappable calm fade, just for a moment, revealing a steel-eyed coldness lurking just underneath the surface. Harkness shifted his position in the back seat of the Humvee. A year ago, a look like that would have made him shift defensively, moving himself away from danger, but six months in Afghanistan had changed him. Without even thinking about it, he'd shifted to give himself greater access to his sidearm.

"Hold up," squawked the radio, "we found another one."

"Another?" asked Gomez, his voice dripping with disbelief. The spook smiled triumphantly, and the driver brought the Humvee to a stop. The field test was almost brutally simple: the spook's Humvee, equipped with the BSE, drove at the head of the column, followed by a TRUCK equipped with every bomb-detector and metal detector they could put in it, scanning the road for IEDs. In the past hour they'd turned up two, and now potentially a third. None had gone off. Harkness waited while the bomb disposal team got out and neutralized the device, and soon the bomb squad RANK approached their truck.

"It's an IED alright. Completely non-functional, same as the others."

The spook leaned forward. "What about the pattern you observed in the other explosives?"

"The pattern continues," said the RANK. "Each bomb is less non-functional than the one before it: the first bomb looked like they'd built in wrong, the second had a fuse out of place, and this one just . . . didn't go. It could have, but it didn't; we don't know why."

"Thank you," said the spook, and sat back in his seat.

"I assume you *do* know why it didn't work?" asked Gomez.

"That's why I'm here," said the spook. "The batteries are low, so to speak, and the BSE is losing its effectiveness. I recommend we head back immediately—on the road we've already cleared."

"I'll call it in," said Gomez, and thumbed the radio, nodding to the bomb squad RANK to tell him to spread the word. "Camp Alfred, this is Operation Shatter. Our mission is complete and we request permission to return home."

"Negative, Shatter, we just had a recon ping in your area and need you to check it out."

The spook started to protest immediately, but Gomez quieted him with a reassuring wave. "I have a civilian and a piece of experimental equipment, Alfred, I can't be doing recon right now."

"It's probably nothing, Shatter, just a glitchy drone. Just do a drive by and give us a visual confirmation and you can come straight home."

"How many regulations do you want me to break, Alfred? Get your boss on the phone so I can talk to someone who isn't an ASVAB waiver."

There was a slight pause, and then the voice spoke again—the same voice, Harkness noticed, not his superior officer. "Movement reqs in your area allow for two-truck groups. Bring the bomb squad and come home, but send the rest of your convoy else to LOCATION, under the command of . . . RANK James."

"Orders confirmed," said Gomez. He hung up the radio, and by now the bomb squad RANK had collected the other officers in the convoy. RANK James leaned on Gomez's open window.

"I'm taking the convoy?"

"Looks like it," said Gomez. "The moron on the radio said it was just a glitch, but he had his panties in a wad about something. Be careful."

"We'll be fine," said James, "you're the ones on your own in Taliban country."

"There's no way we should be traveling with only two trucks in this region," said the bomb squad RANK. "We've seen three IEDs in an hour—this place is crawling with insurgents."

"Then let's stop wasting time and get out of here," said Gomez.

#

The column started moving again, and They only traveled a few minutes, however, before another call came in over the radio.

"RANK Gomez, this is Camp Alfred; you are ordered to return to base immediately. RANK James will continue north with the rest of your column to investigate an insurgent sighting. Over."

Gomez frowned. "Message received, Alfred, but movement reqs in this area don't allow us to travel alone. We need to peel at least one other vehicle off the column. Over."

There was a pause, and then the voice came back. "Affirmative. Bring the bomb squad with you. Over and out."

Gomez grumbled as he stepped out of the Humvee, slamming the door behind him and stomping off for a final conversation with RANK James. Harkness looked at the spook, and was gratified to see that the man looked nervous for the first time since leaving the base. A potential live-fire situation could have that effect, especially on civilians. Harkness suppressed a smile and offered him the helmet for the eighteenth time. He took it.

Gomez returned a moment later, and soon the column was splitting in half. Harkness felt braver now, having seen a sign of weakness in the spook, and ventured a question. "What happens if it fails?"

"The BSE?"

"We keep asking how it works, and you won't tell us, so I figured I'd ask the opposite: what happens if it stops working? Will you know, or will the bomb squad behind us figure it out when we blow up?"

The spook gave him a strange look. "That's an interesting question."

"Seems like a pretty fair one to me," said Gomez. "How will you know if it fails, or am I not cleared for that either?"

Second Draft: I.E. Demon

Dan Wells

They called it the BSE-7, but they didn't tell us what it stood for. We were just the grunts, after all, and they were the engineers: they created the technology, and we had to test it. And that was fine; that's the way it had been since I'd been stationed in Afghanistan six months earlier, and that's the way it had been for years—for centuries—before that.

"What kind of test do you want?"

"The BSE-7 is an explosives nullification device," said the engineer. "We've installed it in an up-armored Humvee, and we need you take that Humvee through hostile territory and see if it works."

"'See if it works?'"

"If nothing blows up, it works," said the engineer. "We'll follow you with a bomb squad to see if we can find anything the BSE-7 nullifies."

"And how exactly does it 'nullify' IEDs?"

"I'm afraid you're not cleared for that information," said the engineer, so I kept a civil expression and got in the Humvee and headed out into the desert. I wasn't cleared to know what I was driving, but I was cleared to drive it through Taliban Central hoping somebody tried to blow us up. The glamorous life of a soldier.

The first IED turned up in a spot called The Brambles, about an hour north of our firebase and some of the worst terrain in Afghanistan. We didn't see anything, but the minesweeper behind us called an all-stop because their detectors had turned up a broken one—not so much broken, once we looked at it, as it was just built wrong from the beginning. I'd never seen an IED so poorly put together; it looked like a broken clock in a Bugs Bunny cartoon, with wires and bits hanging off it in all directions. I told the two engineers I was sorry we hadn't found a real IED to test their device on, but they seemed just as excited with the broken one as you could possibly imagine, like it was the most thrilling damn thing dug out of the desert since King Tut. I rolled my eyes and got back in the Humvee, and my crew drove on through the Brambles for about 20 more minutes before the engineers called another all-stop. I got out to look at the new find.

"Useless," said the bomb tech, examining the new mine we'd driven over. "Better than the last one, but still hopelessly broken. The fuse isn't connected to anything."

"This is wonderful!" said the lead engineer.

"Two IEDs inside half an hour," I said gravely. "There's active insurgents in the area, no question."

"Grossly incompetent insurgents," said my driver.

"They only have to get lucky once," I said, but the engineers insisted we keep going, and my orders were to follow them, so I did. The third IED was only 15 minutes down the road, and the bomb tech practically took the thing apart before he let any of us get close.

"This one was live," he said, showing us the disassembled pieces. "You drove right over it, and it could have gone off, and as far as I can tell it should have gone off, but it didn't. I can't explain it."

"The insurgents' bomb guy is getting better," said my driver.

"Or our bomb-nullifier is getting worse," I said, looking at the engineers. "The BSE-7 is what's doing this, right? Whatever your little device is, it breaks the IEDs before they go off."

"Correct," said the lead engineer.

"But it's not necessarily getting weaker," said the second engineer.

"He might be calibrating his power output to a sustainable level," said the lead engineer. "We don't need to destroy them, like he did with the first, just stop them, like he did with this one."

I narrowed my eyes. "He?"

"It," said the first engineer. "I misspoke." He smiled, and the other engineer smiled, and I looked at the bomb tech and then at my driver and I could tell they felt just as nervous as I did. I glanced at my gunner, perched in the turret and looking for trouble, and he gave me a thumbs up. No Taliban in sight. I looked back at the engineers.

"So what happens on the next one?" I asked. "Is it calibrating its energy, or running out of it?"

"We won't know until we get more data."

"Another IED," I said.

"Correct."

"Which will either break, like these did, or blow up my Humvee."

"Correct," he said again. "But it's up-armored, so you should be fine."

I had a lot less faith in the armor than they did, and a lot more faith in the armor than in the BSE-7, but orders were orders, and when I radioed back to the firebase they agreed with the engineers. This test, and this device, were too crucial to give up halfway. I hung up the radio, shrugged my shoulders, and shook my driver's hand. "Alpha Mike Foxtrot," I said. "It's been nice to know you."

The fourth IED exploded.

It wasn't a big explosion—it didn't tear the Humvee in half, the way I've seen them do in other attacks—but it flipped us upside down off the side of the road. My gunner manged to duck down into the turret before the roll crushed him, and we were rattled and bruised but alive, and thanks to endless days of crash drills we managed to get all three of us out of the Humvee in just a few seconds. We came up just in time to see a wrinkly green three-year-old beating the living hell out of the engineers' truck, and I want to be as clear as possible about this, so there's no misunderstanding: when I say the living hell, I mean the living, breathing, ever-loving hell. He was remarkably spry, that three-year-old, naked as can be and jumping around that truck like he was on springs, and every where he touched it the truck fell apart—not just fell apart, burst apart. Two quick leaps took him from the ground to the fender to the top of the grill, and the fender fell off before his toes even touched down on the hood. He reached out with one hand and grabbed the headlight, and somehow both headlights exploded—not just the one he touched, but both of them, simultaneously, like New Years Eve firecrackers packed with chrome and broken glass. The latch on the hood failed suddenly, spectacularly, launching the little green something in the air while below him the now-exposed engine erupted in a modern dance of bursting caps and hoses, each cylinder and compartment blowing off more steam than they could possibly have been holding, pop pop pop one after another like gunshots. The windshield cracked as the green thing sailed over it, and all I could see inside was the bomb tech fighting to get out of a seatbelt that whipped and coiled like a snake, and behind him the engineers scrambling in their packs like madmen, their faces white with fear.

My crew and I ran toward them, racing to help, and as I ran I raised my rifle to fire at the little green thing dancing madly on the roof. The trigger fell off in my hand, and then the stock, and then the entire gun seemed to field strip itself in a cascade of oily gunmetal. The bullets spit and jumped on the ground like popcorn, their charges exploding impossibly in the dry dirt of the Brambles. My driver reached the truck's door and yanked on the handle; I expected the handle to come off, but was surprised to see the entire door come flying off, knocking the driver flat on his back as the sudden shift in weight unbalanced him. My gunner reached for the jammed seatbelt with his knife in his hand, but the belt frayed before the knife even got close, evaporating like water, and the bomb tech fell out at a dead run. The little green man was dancing on the roof now, metal cracking and warping and rusting with each wrinkly footstep. I tried to open the back and pull the engineers to safety (the door didn't come off, just peeled away in long, corroded strips), but as scared as they were they refused to leave without their bags.

"Just get out!" I said. Springs were bursting out of the seats like twisted daggers, sending puffs of upholstery wafting through the chaos like fat foam snowflakes.

"We need MREs!"

"What?" Somehow, despite the crazy green weirdo destroying the truck—or maybe because of it—this was the last thing I'd ever expected them to say.

"We need the MREs," they continued, scouring madly through their bags, "it's the only way to stop it!"

"To stop the ... green guy?" He was chewing on the ceiling now, literally tearing into it with his teeth and ripping out chunks of metal, cackling like a madman.

"Just help us!"

"You can look for them outside," I said, and hauled the engineers out by anything I could reach, shoulders and necks and arms, throwing the men in the dirt and tossing their heavy packs on the ground beside them. My belt came apart as I worked, the buckle bending nearly in half like someone was crushing it with invisible pliers, and the truck bucked wildly as the tires exploded in a string of deafening bursts. I went for my sidearm, drawing on the wrinkly green man at close range, but the rack slid off like it wasn't even attached, and the bullets sprayed up out of the clip like a metal fountain.

"This one caught shrapnel in his neck," my driver shouted, but the other engineer drowned him out with cries of "MREs! Find the MREs, as many as you can!" he was already tearing open a plastic bag, dumping the interior pouches in the dirt and fumbling for one in particular. I ran to the wounded engineer and found a twisted chunk of truck frame lodged in his neck. He was already dead.

"We need to get out of here!" I shouted.

"I found one!" cried the lead engineer, and he tore open the smallest pouch from the MRE, the salt, and threw a fistful of the stuff at the wrinkly green thing still tearing the truck to pieces. When the salt hit him the green man screamed, leaped off the truck, and scampered behind a boulder.

I stared in surprise, my eyes wide. "We need more salt," I said, and turned to the group with a shout. "Find more MREs!" Soon all of us were tearing open pouches of food, searching for the little packets of salt, and the engineer led us back to the flipped Humvee and directed us to dump the salt in a circle around it. We had barely enough to complete a thin, scattered border before the wrinkly green thing charged us in a rage, howling and brandishing a jagged tailpipe. When he came within a few feet of the salt circle his howl turned to a scream of fear, and he retreated again behind the demolished truck.

My breath came in gasps. "What," I asked, "in the bright blue hell, is that thing?"

"It's a BSE-7," said the engineer, collapsing to the ground and leaning back against the Humvee. "Though it isn't really bound anymore, so it's just an SE. A supernatural entity: Lambda-class demon, minor manifestation."

"Minor?"

"It's a gremlin," he said. "They destroy technology. Made them a bitch to study in the lab."

I had no idea what to think, and my mouth seemed incapable of forming any words beyond the first aborted syllables of sentences: "To—A—I—." I shook my head. "What?"

"The BSE-7 is a Bound Supernatural Entity," said the engineer, "a gremlin maliciously eager to destroy anything technological it comes across."

"And you strapped it to my Humvee?"

"It was bound," he said quickly. "Its energies were directed, like a . . . like a shaped explosive. All the tech-breaking power is pointed out and down, so anything you drive over, like a landmine or an IED, gets broken before it can do anything to hurt you. It can't do anything to your own vehicle—unless, obviously, the binding breaks and it gets loose." He gestured feebly at the truck, which the gremlin was now gleefully disemboweling.

"That thing came after us," said the bomb tech. "Unless one of you's a robot and didn't tell me, I don't think it limits its destruction to technological devices."

"Case in point," said my gunner, "your dead friend over there."

"Now you understand why we needed to find the salt as quickly as possible," said the engineer. "The salt will hold it, though, as long as nothing breaks the circle."

"So we're safe here until it the next stiff breeze," I said, "or until we starve to death, whichever comes first."

"We could probably retrieve the MREs without any major problems," said the driver.

"I think I'd prefer to starve," said the gunner.

"There's got to be a way to kill it," I said. "Our guns fell apart, but the knife didn't—maybe that's too simple a machine to be affected?"

"You can't kill a demon," said the lead engineer. "Trust us on this one. You can only bind it."

"Exactly what kind of engineer are you?" I asked.

He didn't answer.

"We can't forget the Taliban," said my driver. "This is the fourth IED we've run across in the last hour. There's a group here, and they're active, and they're doing something they don't want anyone to see. And after all the noise our gremlin's been making, they're going to know we're here."

I turned to the engineers. "Can we use the radio with that thing's . . . antitechnology field ruining everything?"

"Anything inside the salt circle should work fine."

"Get it working," I told my driver. "Tell them where we are, and that we've been hit with an IED. Leave the . . . weirder details vague." He saluted and climbed through the window of the overturned vehicle. I looked at the engineer. "Now: tell me everything you know about this gremlin."

"It would be probably be easier to just read the manual."

"You have a manual for a gremlin?"

"The BSE-7 is intended for field use," he said. "We have a Dash-10 operator's manual already printed, though it's obviously just a prototype." He pulled a slim paper booklet from his backpack and handed it to me.

"'BSE-7 Vehicle-Mounted Anti-Explosive Device,'" I read. "'The BSE-7 is powered by a Lambda-class demon, commonly called a gremlin. It is designed to be mounted under. . . .'" I skipped ahead, leafing past the usage sections to the fifth chapter: Maintenance. "'If the device fails and the supernatural entity becomes unbound, it can be held at bay with salt.' which we've done. 'Salt can be found in every MRE, and should be easy to come by, even in the field. Your first action should be to contain the demon in a circle of salt, as an unbound gremlin inside of a base or camp can be surprisingly destructive.'" I threw the manual down. "Our first action should be to contain the demon, you idiot, not us."

"The manual makes that sound a lot easier than it is."

"They always do." I picked up the booklet, found the same page again, and continued reading. "'With the demon neutralized in a salt circle, report the malfunction immediately to your assigned demonologist.' We have an assigned demonologist?"

"They're still in training," said the engineer, "with plans to deploy just before the BSEs go into general use. We'd never send a demon into the field without a trained demonologist to wrangle it."

"And you wouldn't test it without one, either," I said. "Is that you?"

He looked sadly at the corpse of the other engineer, and I nodded. "Of course it's him. Awesome. I was worried this would be too easy."

"There should be a chapter on troubleshooting," said the engineer meekly.

I looked up at the gremlin, still loudly tearing the truck to pieces. "Does it just say to shoot it?"

"I don't recommend it."

"We have an AT4 in the trunk," said the gunner.

"I really don't recommend it," the engineer insisted. "Any weapon you use against it will fail as soon as it leaves the salt circle, and I don't think I have to tell you what happens when a rocket propelled grenade fails."

"It was just a suggestion," said the gunner.

"'Chapter 6,'" I read, "'Troubleshooting. If you have no access to a demonologist, your first priority is to reinforce the salt circle containing the demon and requisition a new demonologist immediately.' Thanks, that's very helpful. 'If you absolutely must attempt to control the demon without a trained expert, there are some tricks that may be be useful. One: Gremlins love sugar.' Seriously?"

"Absolutely love it," said the engineer.

"Huh. 'Two: the binding agent on the BSE-7, unless completely destroyed, can be used again, with the understanding that damaged binding agents are prone to unexpected catastrophic failure.'"

"Take a picture of him eating the truck," said the driver, crawling out of the Humvee. "You can put the photo in the manual as a perfect demonstration of 'unexpected catastrophic failure.'"

"Did the radio work?"

"Well enough. The good news is, the insurgents in this area won't be coming after us, because they're engaged in a firefight with a our base."

"And the bad news," I said, "is that they can't come get us because they're engaged in a firefight."

"Exact-a-mundo. And so far they're losing, so they might not come get us at all. This a very big group of insurgents."

I stood up and looked at the Humvee's blackened undercarriage. "So we're on our own, in enemy territory, under direct assault by a demon, and the only thing we can use to stop it is that thing." I pointed at the shattered BSE-7, a charred lump that looked like an upside-down pie plate. It had been torn open, and the inside was full of something dark and sticky.

"Smells sweet," said the bomb tech.

"They like sugar," said the engineer with a shrug.

I leaned in and smelled it. "Smells like . . . strawberry jam."

"That gremlin's almost three feet tall," said the gunner. "If he was crammed inside that tiny thing, it's no wonder he's pissed."

"That goop—which, yes, probably contains strawberry jam—is the binding agent," said the lead engineer. "Once he's bound into it, the physical space doesn't really matter; you could bind him into a teaspoon, and that's all the space you'd need. The majority of the BSE-7 is made up of the shaping agents that direct the gremlin's power away from the vehicle."

"How do we get it back in?"

"The manual explains it in detail," said engineer, "but the basic gist is fire and symbols and blood."

"That's horrible."

"It's a demon," he said, "what did you expect?"

I sat down again, a plan slowly forming in my head. "What kind of grenades to we have for the AT4?"

"Donkey Punchers," said the gunner.

"You really don't want to shoot him," said the lead engineer.

"Sure I do," I told him, skimming through the section on demon binding. It was far more gruesome than expected. "Just not in the way you think." I pointed at the gunner. "Get me a grenade. And you," I said, pointing at the bomb tech, "take it apart." I pointed at the driver, "you get a fire going," and last I pointed at the engineer. "One of those MREs we dumped out looking for salt was Spaghetti, which means that somewhere out there is a pouch full of cherry cobbler. Go get it."

"Out there?"

"Unless you brought it with you, yeah."

"That's. . . . On the other side of the salt line? There's a gremlin out there."

"There's *you're* gremlin out there," I said, "so anything it does to you you probably deserve. Don't be scared, though, I'm coming with you—I"ll grab the body, you get me the cobbler."

"Why do you need the body?"

"Have you read these demon binding notes?"

His face went pale. "Cobbler. Check."

I took a pinch of salt from the edge of the circle, careful not to break it completely, and on three we ran, me for the dead man and the engineer for the pile of scattered MRE pouches. The gremlin ignored us at first, too busy trashing the truck, but as I dragged the body back toward the Humvee he finally noticed us, and leaped forward with a cry of wicked joy. I threw the dead body into the circle and ran back toward the engineer, still scrambling on his hands and knees for the cherry cobbler. I threw the salt at it, buying us a few precious seconds, and together we found the pouch of cobbler and ran back to the Humvee. The engineer's shirt pocket was stained dark blue, and his pants and belt were singed.

"All my pens broke," he said sadly."

"And the burn marks?"

"My phone caught fire."

I tore open the cobbler pack, reached out past the salt, and placed it on the ground. The gremlin snarled at us, furious that we'd gotten away a second time, but soon he paused, sniffed the air, and crept closer. He looked at the cobbler, then at the salt, then at us. He sniffed again and took another step. A few moments later he was sitting by the open dessert pouch, his hands and face smeared with thick red syrup as he munched happily on the cherries.

"That's the weirdest damn thing I've ever seen," said the gunner.

"You got my grenade?"

"Here." The bomb tech handed me an HEDP 502, the 'High Explosive Donkey Punch,' basically a metal tube with a short, stubby point on the end. He'd removed the tapered endpiece, exposing a cone of explosives inside, and I set that part down far away from the fire. The empty endpiece I filled with binding agent from the BSE-7, and then I sat back, looking at the others.

"This is going to get gross."

They nodded, eyes grim. I took a deep breath, propped open the demon's Dash-10 manual with a rock, and proceeded to form unspeakably horrible acts on the body of the dead engineer. The lead engineer fainted twice before the ritual was done, and I admit that I was pretty woozy as well—from disgust rather than blood loss, since I only needed a couple of drops. With the bloody symbols drawn on the sides of the grenade, and the endpiece thoroughly smeared with horrifically-reinforced binding goop, I took a deep breath, said a quick a prayer (apologizing, as I did, for dabbling in demonology), and tossed the endpiece out past the salt and into the gremlin's half-finished cobbler. The Dash-10 included a handy pronunciation guide for the incantation, and the gremlin was sucked into the binding agent like a genie going back into a bottle.

"I take it back," said the gunner. "*That* is the wierdest damn thing I've ever seen."

"Fit it back on," I said, and handed the bomb tech the gently smoking endpiece. He looked at it, then at the exposed explosives of the grenade, and shook his head.

"You want me to attach a 'make things break' demon to a high explosive warhead? I'm not convinced that this is the smartest thing either of us have ever done."

"Just fit it on," I said. "It'll hold for a couple of hours at least."

The engineer was awake again. "What now?" he asked.

"Now we shoot him."

He frowned, confused, and I smiled.

"Now we shoot him *at the insurgents.*"

The Taliban were still attacking our base, and because we'd been driving so slowly, looking for mines, the hour we'd spent driving had only taken us about five klicks away from it; with the gremlin no longer wreaking havoc on the truck we could hear the occasional burst of gunfire. The bomb tech finished reassembling the grenade, and loaded as much gear as we could before running back through the desert. The Afghanistan hills were steep and rocky under any circumstances, and even more so here in the The Brambles; our travel was slow, but the engineer kept up more admirably than I expected. We made it to a low ridge after barely twenty minutes of running. We didn't have a perfect view of the battle, but we could tell the insurgents were winning—they had mortars, snipers, good cover, and higher ground than our guys, who were essentially pinned down behind the smoking wreckage of their vehicles. There was no backup in sight; well, none but us. I loaded the Rocket Propelled Gremlin in the AT4 and handed it to the gunner.

"Don't worry about a target," I said, "just land the little bastard in the middle of their forces and let him go to work."

The gunner judged the distance carefully, tested the wind, aimed high for extra distance. "Alpha Mike Foxtrot," he whispered, and pulled the trigger.

The grenade sailed over the valley, trailing smoke in a fierce, straight line, and exploded in a giant ball of fire against the back of a jeep. One by one we watched as the distant insurgents stopped firing forward and turned to look at their own battle, at the clouds of dust and oil that flew up first in one place and then another. We were too far away to see the gremlin himself, but we could track his progress easily, watching as a truck fell to pieces, as a mounted machine gun sloughed parts like a crumbling cookie, as a mortar misfired and exploded on the ground. Some of the Taliban tried to fight it, but others simply ran in terror, some toward us and some toward our base. No longer pinned down by fire, our friendly forces caught them easily. We ziptied their thumbs, frisked them for weapons, and started the slow walk around the frenzied gremlin.

"There's enough machinery in that insurgent battle line to keep him busy for a week," I said. "You'd better get another demonologist in by then, because if I have to do another binding ritual I'm using you for parts."

"I'll put in a call the instant we get back to base."

"Good," I said. "Now tell me something else: this gremlin was the BSE-7?"

"Correct."

"So there are at least six other Bound Supernatural Entities being developed for field use?"

"Eleven, actually." The engineer smiled. "How would you like to perform another test next week?"

EDITS: I.E. DEMON

DAN WELLS

They called it the BSE-7, but they didn't tell us what it stood for. We were just the ~~grunts~~EOD team, after all, and they were the engineers: they created the technology, and we had to test it. And that was fine; that~~'~~ was the way it had been since I'd been stationed in Afghanistan six months earlier, and that~~'~~ was the way it had been for years—for centuries—before that.

"What kind of test do you want?"

"The BSE-7 is an explosives nullification device," said the engineer. "We've installed it in a~~n up-armored Humvee~~JERRV, and we need you ~~take that Humvee~~to drive it through hostile territory and see if it works."

"'See if it works~~'?~~.'"

"If nothing blows up, it works," said the engineer. "We'll follow you with ~~a bomb squad~~the best detection equipment we have, to see if we can find anything the BSE-7 nullifies."

"And how exactly does it 'nullify' IEDs?"

"I'm afraid you're not cleared for that information," said the engineer, so I kept a civil expression ~~and~~, got in the ~~Humvee~~JERRV, and headed out into the desert with my driver and my gunner. ~~I was~~We weren't cleared to know what ~~I was~~we were driving, but ~~I was~~we were cleared to drive it through Taliban Central hoping somebody tried to blow us up. The glamorous life of a soldier.

We were stationed in a firebase in what we called the Brambles: not only some of the worst terrain in Afghanistan, but famous for having the most IEDs per square mile of any region in the field of operations. I figured I'd be proud of that fact someday, if I lived long enough to brag about it in a bar, but for now it was a dubious accolade at best. Especially when it attracted the attentions of contractors trying to field-test their latest brain fart. It was far too dangerous to go outside the wire alone, so we joined a convoy; well, "joined." Seven MRAPs loaded for bear were heading north on a recon mission, and we were following on a nearby road, shorter but more likely to have IEDs. My team drove the modified JERRV, and the engineers followed behind in an MRAP of their own. If we got into any serious trouble, the convoy could reach us—theoretically—in just a few minutes. I hate relying on "theoretically."

The first IED turned up ~~in a spot called The Brambles,~~ about an hour north of our firebase ~~and some of the worst terrain in Afghanistan.~~; ~~W~~we didn't ~~see~~notice anything, but the minesweeper behind us called an all-stop because their detectors had turned up a broken one—not so much broken, once we looked at it, as it was just built wrong from the beginning. ~~I'd never seen an IED so~~Most IEDs are simple: two planks of wood separated by foam, with contact plates made of scrap metal, and an old lamp cord leading to a big yellow bucket of explosive. This one was one of the most poorly put together I'd ever seen; it looked like a broken clock in a Bugs Bunny cartoon, with wires and bits hanging off it in all directions. I told the two engineers I was sorry we hadn't found a real IED to test their device on, but they seemed just as excited with the broken one as you could possibly imagine, like it was the most thrilling damn thing dug out of the desert since King Tut. I rolled my eyes and got back in the ~~Humvee~~JERRV, and my crew drove on through the Brambles for about ~~20~~twenty more minutes before the engineers called another all-stop. I got out to look at the new find.

"Useless," ~~said the bomb tech~~I told them, examining the new ~~mine~~IED we'd driven over. "Better than the last one, but still hopelessly broken. The ~~fuse~~cord isn't even connected to anything."

"This is wonderful!" said the lead engineer.

"Two IEDs inside half an hour," I said gravely. "There's active insurgents in the area, no question."

"Grossly incompetent insurgents," said my driver.

"They only have to get lucky once," I said, but the engineers insisted we keep going, and my orders were to follow the~~m~~ir orders, so I did. The third IED was only ~~15~~fifteen minutes down the road, and ~~the bomb tech practically took the thing apart before he let any of us get close~~when I got out to examine it I didn't like what I saw.

"This one was live," ~~he~~I said, showing ~~us~~them the disassembled pieces. "~~You~~We drove right over it, and it could have gone off, and as far as I can tell it should have gone off, but it didn't. I can't explain it."

"The insurgents' bomb guy is getting better," said my driver.

"Or our bomb-nullifier is getting worse," I said, looking at the engineers. "The BSE-7 is what's doing this, right? Whatever your little device is, it breaks the IEDs before they go off~~.~~?"

"Correct," said the lead engineer.

"But it's not necessarily getting weaker," said the second engineer.

"He might be calibrating his power output to a sustainable level," said the lead engineer. "~~W~~He do_e_sn't need to destroy them~~,~~ like he did with the first two, just stop them~~,~~ like he did with this one."

I narrowed my eyes. "He?"

"It," said the first engineer. "I misspoke_._" He smiled, and the other engineer smiled, and I looked at ~~the bomb tech and then at~~ my driver and I could tell ~~they~~ felt just as nervous as I did. I glanced at my gunner, perched in the turret and looking for trouble, and he gave me a thumbs-up. No Taliban in sight. I looked back at the engineers.

"So what happens on the next one?" I asked. "Is it calibrating its energy, or running out of it?"

"We won't know until we get more data."

"Another IED," I said.

"Correct."

"Which will either break, like these did, or blow up my ~~Humvee~~ JERRV."

"Correct," he said again. "But it's up-armored, so you should be fine. None of these bombs we've examined has been big enough to kill you."

I had a lot less faith in the armor than they did, and a lot more faith in the armor than in the BSE-7, but orders were orders, and when I radioed back to the firebase they agreed with the engineers. This test, and this device, were too crucial to give up halfway. I hung up the radio, shrugged my shoulders, and shook my driver's hand. "Alpha Mike Foxtrot," I said. "It's been nice to know you."

The fourth IED exploded.

It wasn't a big explosion—it didn't tear the ~~Humvee~~ JERRV in half, so the ~~way I've seen them do in other attacks~~ armor did its job—but it flipped us upside down off the side of the road. My gunner managed to duck down into the turret before the roll crushed him, and we were rattled and bruised but alive, and thanks to endless days of crash drills we managed to get all three of us out of the ~~Humvee~~ vehicle in just a few seconds. We came up just in time to see a wrinkly green three-year-old beating the living hell out of the engineers' truck, and I want to be as clear as possible about this~~,~~ so there's no misunderstanding: when I say the living hell, I mean the living, breathing, ever-loving hell. He was remarkably spry, that three-year-old, naked as can be and jumping around that truck like he was on springs, and every-where he touched it the truck fell apart—not just fell apart, *burst* apart. Two quick leaps took him from the ground to the fender to the top of the grill, and the fender fell off before his toes even touched down on the hood. He reached out with one hand and grabbed the headlight, and somehow both headlights exploded—not just the one he touched, but both of them~~,~~ simultaneously, like New Year's Eve firecrackers packed with chrome and broken glass. The latch on the hood failed suddenly, spectacularly, launching the little green something in the air while below him the now-exposed engine erupted in a modern dance exhibition of bursting caps and hoses, each cylinder and compartment blowing off more steam than they could possibly have been holding, *pop pop pop* one after another like gunshots. The windshield cracked as the green thing sailed over it, and all I could see inside were ~~was the bomb tech fighting to get out of a seatbelt that whipped and coiled like a snake, and behind him~~ the two engineers ~~scrambling in~~ digging through their packs like madmen, their faces white with fear.

My crew and I ran toward them, racing to help, and as I ran I raised my rifle to fire at the little green thing dancing madly on the roof. The trigger fell off in my hand, and then the stock, and then the entire gun seemed to field strip itself in a cascade of oily gunmetal. The bullets sp~~i~~at and jumped on the ground like popcorn, their charges exploding impossibly in the dry dirt of the Brambles. My driver reached the truck's door and yanked on the handle; I expected the handle to come off, but was surprised to see the entire door come flying off, knocking ~~the~~my driver flat on his back as the sudden shift in weight unbalanced him. My gunner ~~reached for~~tried the ~~jammed~~lead engineer's seatbelt ~~with his knife in his hand~~, but ~~the belt frayed before the knife even got close, evaporating like water, and the bomb tech fell out at a dead run~~it was jammed too tight to move. The little green man was dancing on the roof now, metal cracking and warping and rusting with each wrinkly footstep. I tried to open the ~~back~~other door and pull the engineers to safety (the door didn't come off, just peeled away in long, corroded strips), but as scared as they were they refused to leave without their bags.

"Just get out!" I said. Springs were bursting out of the seats like twisted daggers, sending puffs of upholstery wafting through the chaos like fat foam snowflakes.

"We need MREs!"

"What?" Somehow, despite the crazy green weirdo destroying the truck—or maybe because of it—this was the last thing I'd ever expected them to say.

"We need the MREs," they continued, scouring madly through their bags~~,~~. "~~i~~It's the only way to stop it!"

"To stop the . . . green guy?" He was chewing on the ceiling now, literally tearing into it with his teeth and ripping out chunks of metal, cackling like a madman.

"Just help us!"

"You can look for them outside," I said, and hauled the engineers out by anything I could reach, shoulders and necks and arms, throwing the men in the dirt and tossing their heavy packs on the ground beside them. My belt came apart as I worked, the buckle bending nearly in half like someone was crushing it with invisible pliers, and the ~~truck~~vehicle bucked wildly as the tires exploded in a string of deafening bursts. I went for my sidearm, drawing on the wrinkly green man at close range, but the rack slid off like it wasn't even attached, and the bullets sprayed up out of the ~~clip~~magazine like a bubbling metal fountain.

"This one caught shrapnel in his neck during that last burst," my driver shouted, looking at the second engineer, but the ~~other~~lead engineer drowned him out with cries of "MREs! Find the MREs, as many as you can!" ~~h~~He was already tearing open a plastic bag, dumping the interior pouches in the dirt and fumbling for one in particular. I ~~ran~~turned to the wounded engineer and found a twisted chunk of truck frame lodged in his neck. He was already dead.

"We need to get out of here!" I shouted.

"I found one!" cried the lead engineer, and he tore open the smallest pouch from the MRE, the salt, and threw a ~~fistful~~pinch of the stuff at the wrinkly green thing still tearing the truck to pieces. When the salt hit him the green man screamed, leaped off the truck, and scampered behind a boulder.

I stared in surprise, my eyes wide. I still didn't know what was going on, but I didn't need another demonstration to convince me. "We need more salt," I said, and turned to the group with a shout. "Find more MREs!" Soon all of us were tearing open pouches of food, searching for the little packets of salt, and the engineer led us back to the flipped ~~Humvee~~ JERRV and directed us to dump the salt in a circle around it. We had barely enough to complete a thin, scattered border before the wrinkly green thing charged us in a rage, howling and brandishing a jagged tailpipe. When he came within a few feet of the salt circle his howl turned to a scream of fear, and he retreated again ~~behind~~ to the demolished truck, smashing it with wicked glee.

My breath came in gasps. "What," I asked, "in the bright blue hell, is that thing?"

"It's a BSE-~~7~~," said the engineer, collapsing to the ground and leaning back against the ~~Humvee~~ JERRV. "Though it isn't really bound anymore, so it's just an SE. A supernatural entity: ~~L~~lambda-class demon, minor manifestation."

"Minor?"

"It's a gremlin," he said. "They destroy technology. Made them a bitch to study in the lab."

I had no idea what to think, and my mouth seemed incapable of forming any words beyond the first aborted syllables of sentences: "To— A—I—." I shook my head. "What?"

"Th~~at creature is the power source for the~~ BSE-7 ~~is a Bound Supernatural Entity~~," said the engineer. "A Bound Supernatural Entity. The 7 refers to a gremlin, maliciously eager to destroy anything technological it comes across."

"And you strapped it to my ~~Humvee~~ truck?"

"It was bound," he said quickly. "Its energies were directed, like a . . . like a shaped explosive. All the tech-breaking power is pointed out and down, so anything you drive over, like a landmine or an IED, gets broken before it can do anything to hurt you. It can't do anything to your own vehicle—unless, obviously, the binding breaks and it gets loose." He gestured feebly at the truck, which the gremlin was now gleefully disemboweling.

"That thing came after us," said the ~~bomb tech~~ driver. "Unless one of you's a robot and didn't tell me, I don't think it limits its destruction to technological devices."

"Case in point," said ~~my~~ the gunner, "your dead friend over there."

"Now you understand why we needed to find the salt as quickly as possible," said the engineer. "The salt will hold it, though, as long as nothing breaks the circle."

"So we're safe here until ~~it~~ the next stiff breeze," I said, "or until we starve to death, whichever comes first."

"We ~~could probably retrieve the~~'ve got plenty of MREs ~~without any major problems~~," said the driver.

"I think I'd prefer to starve," said the gunner.

"There's got to be a way to kill it," I said. "Our guns fell apart, but the knife didn't—maybe that's too simple a machine to be affected?"

"You can't kill a demon," said the ~~lead~~ engineer. "Trust us on this one. You can only bind it."

"Exactly what kind of engineer are you?" I asked.

He didn't answer.

"~~W~~And we can't forget the Taliban," said my driver. "This is the fourth IED we've run across in the last hour. There's a group here, and they're active, and they're doing something they don't want anyone to see. And after all the noise our gremlin's been making, they're going to know we're here."

I turned to the engineers. "Can we use the radio with that thing's . . . anti-technology field ruining everything?"

"Anything inside the salt circle should work fine."

"Get it working," I told my driver. "Tell them convoy where we are, and that we've been hit with an IED. Leave the . . . weirder details vague." He saluted and climbed in through the window of the overturned vehicle. I looked at the engineer. "Now: tell me everything you know about this gremlin."

"It would be probably be easier to just read the manual."

"You have a manual for a gremlin?"

"The BSE-7 is intended for field use," he said. "We have a Dash-10 operator's manual already printed, though it's obviously just a prototype." He pulled a slim paper booklet from his backpack and handed it to me.

"'BSE-7 Vehicle-Mounted Anti-Explosive Device,'" I read. "'The BSE-7 is powered by a Llambda-class demon, commonly called a gremlin. It is designed to be mounted under. . . .'" I skipped ahead, leafing past the usage sections to the fifth chapter: Maintenance. "'If the device fails and the supernatural entity becomes unbound, it can be held at bay with salt.' wWhich we've done. 'Salt can be found in every MRE, and should be easy to come by, even in the field. Your first action should be to contain the demon in a circle of salt, as an unbound gremlin inside of a base or camp can be surprisingly destructive.'" I threw the manual down. "OIt says our first action should be to contain the demon, you idiot, not us."

"The manual makes that sound a lot easier than it is."

"They always do." I picked up the booklet, found the same page again, and continued reading. "'With the demon neutralized in a salt circle, report the malfunction immediately to your assigned demonologist.' We have an assigned demonologist?"

"They're still in training," said the engineer, "with plans to deploy just before the BSEs go into general use. We'd never send a demon into the field without a trained demonologist to wrangle it."

"AndWhich means you wouldn't test it without one, either," I said. "Is that you?" He, and looked sadly at the corpse of the otherdead engineer, and I nodded. "Of course it's . "Is that him. Awesome. I was worried this would be too easy.?"

The living engineer shrugged helplessly. "There should be's a chapter on troubleshooting," he said the engineer meekly.

I looked up at the gremlin, still loudly tearing the truck to pieces. "DoesIf it just say tocauses trouble, we shoot it?"

"I don't recommend it."

"We have an AT4RPG-7 in the trunkJERRV," said the gunner. "Took it off some Taliban last week."

"I really don't recommend it," the engineer insisted. "Any weapon you use against it will fail as soon as it leaves the salt circle, and I don't think I have to tell you what happens when a rocket-propelled grenade fails."

"It was just a suggestion," said the gunner.

"'Chapter 6,'" I read, "'Troubleshooting. If you have no access to a demonologist, your first priority is to reinforce the salt circle containing the demon and requisition a new demonologist immediately.' Thanks, that's very helpful. 'If you absolutely must attempt to control the demon without a trained expert, there are some tricks that may be ~~be~~ useful. One: ~~G~~gremlins love sugar.' Seriously?"

"Absolutely love it," said the engineer.

"Huh. 'Two: the binding agent on the BSE-7, unless completely destroyed, can be used again, with the understanding that damaged binding agents are prone to unexpected catastrophic failure~~.~~'"

"Take a picture of him eating the truck," said the driver, crawling back out of the ~~Humvee~~JERRV. "You can put the photo in the manual as a ~~perfect~~ demonstration of 'unexpected catastrophic failure.'"

"Did the radio work?" I asked him.

"Well enough. The good news is, the insurgents in this area won't be coming after us, because they're engaged in a firefight with ~~a~~ our ~~base~~convoy."

"And the bad news," I said, "is that ~~they~~our convoy can't come get us because they're engaged in a firefight with insurgents."

"Exact-a-mundo. And so far they're losing, so they might not come get us at all. ~~This~~It's a very big group of insurgents."

I stood up and looked at the ~~Humvee~~JERRV's blackened undercarriage. "So we're on our own, in enemy territory, under direct assault by a demon, and the only thing we can use to stop it is that thing." I pointed at the shattered BSE-7, a charred lump that looked like ~~an upside-down~~a pie plate. It had been torn open, and the inside was full of something dark and sticky.

"Smells sweet," said the ~~bomb tech~~gunner.

"They like sugar," said the engineer with a shrug.

"So it *is* a pie plate." I leaned in and smelled it. "Smells like . . . strawberry jam."

"That gremlin's almost three feet tall," said the gunner. "If he was crammed inside that tiny thing, it's no wonder he's pissed."

"That goop—which, yes, probably contains strawberry jam—is ~~the~~ an arcane demon-binding agent," said the lead engineer. "Once he's bound into it, the physical space doesn't really matter; you could bind him into a teaspoon, and that's all the space you'd need. The majority of the BSE-7 is made up of the shaping agents that direct the gremlin's power away from the vehicle."

"How do we get it back in?"

"The manual explains it in detail," said the engineer, "but the basic gist is fire ~~and symbols~~ and blood."

"That's horrible."

"It's a demon," he said~~,~~. "~~w~~What did you expect?"

I sat down again, a plan slowly forming in my head. "What kind of grenades ~~t~~do we have for the ~~AT4~~captured RPG?"

"~~Donkey Punchers~~PG-2s," said the gunner. "Old Soviet stuff."

"You really don't want to shoot him," said the lead engineer.

"Sure I do," I told him, skimming through the section on demon binding. It was far more gruesome than expected. "Just not in the way you think." I ~~pointed at~~turned to the gunner. "Get me a grenade. ~~And you," I said, pointing at~~; take off the ~~bomb tech, "take it apart." I pointed at~~casing." I told the driver~~, "you~~ to get a fire going~~,~~; and last I pointed at the engineer. "One of those MREs we dumped out looking for salt was ~~S~~spaghetti, which means that somewhere out there is a pouch full of cherry cobbler. Go get it."

"Out ~~there~~side of the circle?"

"Unless you brought it with you, yeah."

"~~That's.~~But . . . ~~On the other side of the salt line? T~~there's a gremlin out there."

"There's *you're* gremlin out there," I said, "so anything it does to you, you probably deserve. Don't be scared, though, I'm coming with you—I~~'~~"ll ~~grab~~et the body, you get ~~me~~ the cobbler."

"Why do you need the body?"

"Have you read the~~se~~ demon binding ~~notes~~manual?"

His face went pale. "Cobbler. Check."

I took a pinch of salt from the edge of the circle, careful not to break it completely, and on three we ran, me for the dead man and the engineer for the pile of scattered MRE pouches. The gremlin ignored us at first, too busy trashing the truck, but as I dragged the body back toward the ~~Humvee~~JERRV he finally noticed us~~,~~ and leaped f~~t~~orward the engineer with a cry of ~~wicked~~malicious joy. I threw the dead body into the circle and ran back toward the engineer, still scrambling on his hands and knees for the cherry cobbler. I threw the salt at ~~i~~the gremlin, buying us a few precious seconds, and together we found the pouch of cobbler and ran back to the ~~Humvee~~JERRV. The engineer's shirt pocket was stained dark blue, and his pants and belt were singed.

"All my pens broke," he said sadly~~."~~, gesturing at the stains.

"And the burn marks?"

"My phone caught fire."

I tore open the cobbler pack, reached out past the salt, and placed it on the ground. The gremlin snarled at us, furious that we'd gotten away a second time, but soon he paused, sniffed the air, and crept closer. He looked at the cobbler, then at the salt, then at us. He sniffed again and took another step. A few moments later he was sitting by the open dessert pouch, his hands and face smeared with thick red syrup as he munched happily on the cherries.

"That's the weirdest damn thing I've ever seen," said the gunner.

"You got my grenade?"

"Here." ~~The bomb tech~~He handed me a~~n~~ ~~HEDP 50~~PG-2~~, the 'High Explosive Donkey Punch,'~~ basically a metal tube with a short, stubby ~~point~~metal cone on the end. He'd removed the tapered endpiece, exposing a cone of explosives inside, and I set that part down far away from the fire. The empty endpiece I filled with binding agent from the BSE-7, scooping it out with the flat of my knife, and then I sat back, looking at the others.

"This is going to get gross."

They nodded, eyes grim. I took a deep breath, propped open the demon's Dash-10 manual with a rock, and proceeded to perform unspeakably horrible acts on the body of the dead engineer. The lead engineer fainted twice before the ritual was done, and I admit that I was pretty woozy as well—from disgust rather than blood loss, since I only needed a couple of drops of my own. With the bloody symbols drawn on the sides of the grenade, and the endpiece thoroughly smeared with ~~horrifically~~ newly reinforced binding goop, I took a deep breath, said a quick ~~a~~ prayer (apologizing, as I did, for dabbling in demonology), and tossed the endpiece out past the salt and into the gremlin's half-finished cobbler. The Dash-10 included a handy pronunciation guide for the incantation, and as I recited the words the gremlin was sucked into the binding agent like a genie going ~~back~~ into a bottle.

"I take it back," said the gunner. "*That* is the w~~ei~~irdest damn thing I've ever seen."

"~~Fit it back on~~Reassemble the grenade," I said, and handed ~~the bomb tech~~him the gently smoking endpiece. He looked at it, then at the exposed explosives of the grenade, and shook his head.

"You want me to attach a 'make things break' demon to a high-explosive warhead? I'm not convinced that this is the smartest thing either of us ha~~ve~~s ever done."

"Just fit it on," I said. "~~I~~This fresh, it'll hold for a couple of hours ~~at least~~without any trouble."

The engineer was awake again. "What now?" he asked.

"Now we shoot him."

He frowned, confused, and I smiled.

"Now we shoot him *at the insurgents*."

The Taliban were still attacking our ~~base~~convoy, and ~~because we'd been driving so slowly, looking for mines, the hour we'd spent driving had~~we were only ~~taken us~~ about five klicks away ~~from it~~; with the gremlin no longer wreaking havoc on the truck we could hear the occasional burst of gunfire. The ~~bomb tech~~gunner finished reassembling the grenade, and ~~loaded~~we packed as much gear as we could before running back through the desert. The Afghanistan hills were steep and rocky under any circumstances, and even more so here in the ~~The~~ Brambles; our travel was slow, but the engineer kept up more admirably than I expected. We made it to a low ridge after barely twenty minutes of running. We didn't have a perfect view of the battle, but we could tell the insurgents were winning—they had mortars, snipers, good cover, and higher ground than our guys, who were essentially pinned down behind the smoking wreckage of their vehicles. ~~T~~It was the biggest group of insurgents I'd ever seen, and there was no backup in sight; well, none but us. I loaded the Rocket-Propelled Gremlin in the ~~AT4~~launch tube and handed it to the gunner.

"Don't worry about a target," I said, "just land the little bastard in the middle of their ~~forces~~gun line and let him go to work."

The gunner judged the distance carefully, tested the wind, aimed high for extra ~~distance~~range. "Alpha Mike Foxtrot," he whispered, and pulled the trigger.

The grenade sailed over the valley, trailing smoke in a fierce, straight line, and exploded in a giant ball of fire against the back of a Taliban jeep. One by one we watched as the distant insurgents stopped firing forward and turned to look at their own battle line, at the clouds of dust and oil that flew up first in one place and then another. We were too far away to see the gremlin himself, but we could track his progress easily, watching as a truck fell to pieces, as a mounted machine gun sloughed parts like a crumbling cookie, as a mortar misfired and exploded on the ground. ~~Some~~A few of the Taliban tried to fight it, but others simply ran in terror, some toward us and some toward our ~~base~~convoy. No longer pinned down by fire, our friendly forces caught them easily. We zip-tied their thumbs, frisked them for weapons, and started the slow walk around the frenzied gremlin toward our convoy.

"There's enough machinery in that insurgent battle line to keep him busy for a week," I said. "You'd better get another demonologist in by then, because if I have to do another binding ritual I'm using you for parts."

"I'll put in a call the instant we get back to base."

"Good," I said. "Now tell me something else: this gremlin was the BSE-7?"

"Correct."

"So there are at least six other Bound Supernatural Entities being developed for field use?"

"Eleven, actually." The engineer smiled. "How would you like to perform another test next week?"

The Making of An Honest Death

Writing Excuses 8.9

Brainstorming with Howard

Howard: Let me start with three pitches. You guys pick the one that interests you most. The first is a horrible, filthy story set in a—
Mary: Yes.
Brandon: Mary's sold.
Dan: You already got Mary.
Howard: Set in a near future that is in many ways very similar to ours. There has been a technological advance in which instead of carrying phones, we all have implants. And a serial stalker has multiple restraining orders against him. The way restraining orders are applied is via your implant. The people who you are or were stalking can always track you. Whoever has a restraining order against you knows where you are, and if you get within 300 meters of them, you feel pain. And my character gets off on pain. He's a masochist who has found a way to always get his fix. So that's pitch number one. And yes, it can be a horrible, filthy, terrible story.
Howard: Pitch number two: a pharmaceutical company, a big medical company, has for the last couple of years been researching how to make money off the fact that a treatment they're about to release will effectively make people immortal. They know that it will disrupt society. They know it will make a mess. But they're trying to do everything they can to minimize the impact, so that society will survive the change. The CEO is up in his office and Death appears to him. I'll say more about that if that interests you at all.

Howard: The third one is based on the principle of electronic voice phenomena, which ghost hunters like to hunt with microphones. They don't hear any voices or anything while they're at the site. Then they listen to the tapes after the fact, and they will often hear voices that none of them heard before, saying things that you can actually hear and understand. I've heard some of these on Tom Carr's tapes, from Wasatch Paranormal Investigators.
Dan: They can be surprisingly easy to understand, and it's pretty creepy.
Howard: Really creepy when nobody else on the tape reacts to it, and you realize, yeah, that was not somebody saying that, because somebody else would have responded. Basically, the story is we have a couple of ghost hunters, and one of them has decided to murder the other one. They're doing some listening on-site, and the EVPs are trying to warn the guy who is about to be a murder victim of the impending treachery.
Brandon: I like the second two better than the first, personally.
Howard: That's good, because I don't like writing about the first guy, which is why that story has been abandoned.
Dan: I like the middle one the best, I think. That's the one that has me the most intrigued right now.
Mary: I also lean toward the middle one.

Mostly because I feel like it's going to play to your strengths and be funny.

Brandon: Dark funny, but funny.

Mary: But there is more potential for comedy in there. Plus, I also really like the juxtaposition of the—

Brandon: It plays to Howard's strengths a lot. I will agree the middle one's probably the one we should do. Though personally I like the third story the best.

Howard: I am happy to play to what you guys *don't* think are my strengths. I would like an opportunity to write against type, and write something where there is maybe some character humor in it, but it's a horror story.

Brandon: I would love to have a horror story from you, which is also funny.

Dan: But if he wants to do something that's not a comedy, then let's do something that's not a comedy.

Howard: But I mean, you guys pick. What do you—

Mary: The other thing that appeals to me about number two is, I like the juxtaposition of high technology with mythic elements. I think that that can be fun.

Brandon: Okay. Let's go with it.

Dan: There's ways to do that that aren't really very funny at all.

Brandon: The CEO about to release an immortality drug gets a visit from Death, who's going to do what? Try to talk him out of it.

Howard: The scene that I have written that sort of talked me into this is Death explaining to him, "If you release this, everybody you know, the whole board of directors, everybody who is close to you, will die in the next seven days. I will personally guarantee that. So you have to not release this." The CEO says, "Well, you've got to make me a counteroffer, because right now all you're doing is threatening me, and I don't take kindly to threatening." That was my setup. My thought on this is that Death, the hooded figure that we see, is an extra-dimensional race—there's not just one Death—that feeds off the passing of our spirits from this life into the next one. And if that stops happening naturally, they will have to start harvesting. And that's something they don't want to do for some reason or another.

Dan: It could be—for example the nice, horrific way to go—that they can't. Part of his threat is, if you make everyone immortal, we're going to make you our harvester. You will personally be responsible for making sure people die.

Brandon: See, but how can they force that?

Mary: Because the reason that they don't want to do this is that they have experience with harvesting before, which was the Black Plague.

Brandon: Or something like that. Hey, a little bit of a secret history.

Howard: A secret history element would be fun.

Mary: That they very nearly overharvested the earth.

Brandon: His people are not good at restraining themselves. So he could say, "I've been around for a long time. I am more restrained. But if the floodgates open, the common people will just take it. If it stops coming, they'll get so hungry they will break through."

Howard: One of the horrific mythos elements I was thinking about: what is the nature of the human soul? The nice version is the energy state change when we die, the release of the spirit is what they are harvesting. The spirit itself escapes into whatever it needs to. The not nice one is that when they feed, the spirit is damaged, and it's actually painful and torturous. If you are one of those people who is unfortunate enough to see Death when you are dying, you don't have an afterlife to look forward to.

Brandon: Or you're going to be tortured for a while.

Howard: I know which one I like better, but then I prefer happy endings.

Brandon: Where do you want to go? Because the first one allows you to maintain the mystique of Death. "We're an extradimensional race. We don't know what happens to the spirit. Like an atom being split, there is energy released and we feed on that, then the spirit goes somewhere."

Howard: That appeals to me. Maintaining the mystique of the beyond, and that they are feeding off of—

Mary: The passage itself.

Howard: But there has to be a reason why them harvesting is problematic. I like the overfishing sort of—

Dan: It could be that it's a very druglike reaction for them, and that they have to restrain themselves constantly to avoid becoming addicted. If they have to actively start harvesting us, then the likelihood of addiction becomes much worse. You could even go further into secret history and say, "You know some of these people that your culture considers serial killers? Those are actually some of us who've gone rogue and are just complete drug addicts of death."

Brandon: More secret history that would be cool is if someone, during the Black Plague, discovered the secret of immortality. They created the philosopher's stone, or whatever it is they're trying.

Mary: I was looking to see where Ponce de León fell in. Unfortunately not someplace useful in the timeline.

Brandon: But you'd find something in that timeline, I think. Your character could be a scientist, whoever is alive at that time. There's going to be somebody. Alchemy's around.

Howard: Depending on the length of the story, I could still work Ponce de León in there. Our protagonist, our corporate guy, says, "Wait. You mean like Ponce de León and the fountain of youth?" "Oh, yes, that was a nice cover story. But it actually happened during the Black Plague with this dude you've never heard of."

Brandon: Or it could just be Ponce de León did, I mean, all this happened, they came to him and made the same deal, and he's like, "Oh, okay."

Dan: You could start before Death shows up with that piece and say, "In our research we found that scientist who was close to the secret of immortality, and didn't take the next step." And then Death shows up and says, "Actually he did. That's what caused the Black Plague."

Mary: So, the counteroffer—Death says, "I'll let you use it, and I'll introduce you to this secret cabal of immortal people."

Brandon: You can become one of the Illuminati, you and your family. I'll give immortality to you and fifteen people you choose. So it is tempting. Not only do you get immortality, but you get to join this group that is ruling your people.

Howard: Now, I want to have an upbeat ending. In fact, I want to play against the type of "Oh, the corporation discovers something super cool, and gets bought off because somebody makes them a better offer." I want human immortality to actually get released. I want there to be a win-lose scenario, where we win and Death loses.

Brandon: I like that. That's very much not where anyone expects this to go.

Dan: So the way that we presented this, we could have Death leave, and the guy at that point reveals the twist, that this secret cabal of immortal people, who have all been contacted by Death throughout history, had seen this coming and got to the CEO first—they're sick of being bullied around by the aliens, and so they gave him something that will end the rule.

Mary: They have, in fact, been working on this through their entire very long lifetime.

Dan: The whole thing could be a con job on the aliens.

Howard: Now, here is a thought. If Death and his people need to feed, and need to feed in order to survive, then they can die. This guy's got a team of scientists behind him. It occurred to me that maybe he makes that connection. "Oh, you need to eat to live. Well, if you need to eat to live, then there are things that can kill you. Starvation being one of them. What are the other things? I'm going to look for that, and then when you begin your horrible harvest, we will be armed with—I don't know—space syringes."

Mary: But if they eat energy, then all you have to do is come up with corrupting a waveform of some sort.

Dan: I love the idea that this was all pre-planned, and it may be that the whole point was to get Death to come and present this guy with the offer, and while he's there infect him, and he goes back and spreads this infection among the rest of his people.

Brandon: We're talking about two different stories here, and Howard has to make the call between them. The whole first story is a conversation with Death, and by the end we have the twist ending, and we've pulled a con on Death. The conversation has to give us all the foreshadowing with him acting ignorant, then ends with the con. The second story is, Death shows up. There is a short sequence between them. Guy says, "Okay, I'll think about it." And then immediately goes into "We've got to find a way around this," and the story is actually a problem story. "We are going to figure out how to defeat these things." And you write a story about that. One is about the conversation. One is about the problem.

Howard: If I am allowed to write a conversation, I will write and write and write, and you don't get jack for descriptions, because all I do with *Schlock Mercenary* is write dialogue anyway. So a story that forces me to block action sequences in prose would be more challenging. Now I'm not saying that the first story isn't interesting. I love the first story. But let's crawl out of my comfort zone a little bit.

Mary: But let me also just raise one other flag, which is that those two stories are very different lengths. The first story you can really—

Brandon: You can do that in 2,500 words easy.

Mary: I was going to say 1,500.

Brandon: You see the fantasy writer over here versus the more restrained fantasy writer. But the other one is 7,000.

Dan: The second one, you're looking at several scenes of research. Potentially very creepy research scenes. Because if you're trying to figure out what they feed on, then he needs to know what energy is released at the point of death, which means he has to do a lot of analysis of death.

Brandon: The cool direction to go here would be, what are they actually feeding on? What are souls? Is there such a thing?

Mary: He has to contact some ghost hunters.

Brandon: That could be useful.

Howard: Now I've got a whole novel, because I roll in the EVP storyline. And this, fair reader, is where novels come from. You have a good idea, and another good idea, and you realize that when they marry they have 400,000 pages' worth of babies.

Dan: I'm intrigued by this research into death, because there's a lot of folk science that's been done on that. People have calculated the weight of a human soul.

Howard: I would love to acknowledge the debunking of all of that in one swoop and say, "Yeah, all of that's garbage." I've got to reach past that. I've got to find something else. One of the things that occurred to me is that in order for Death to appear, he has to manifest himself in some way, which might make him vulnerable.

Brandon: Let me throw out what I've got here. So, the thing that they're feeding on, they say it's death. It could be the emotion at the moment of death. They call themselves Death. But that utter panic that only a human feels—they have to sometimes feed on people who come back from the brink, because otherwise we would never know about them. And that's why we have this whole folklore, because it will work for them if you *think* you're going to die at that moment, and then you actually don't, but they've still gotten their fix. The answer is he's going to release the immortality drug. You haven't said if everyone knows it's coming out. But they tweak the formula to make it that once you take this, you are just peaceful. He's drugging the whole population. Everybody's going to want this stuff. Death can come in. They will commit this genocide, but they will starve anyway, and that's his solution.

Howard: Yes. That's horrific.

Dan: The starving aliens are probably going to kill every last one of us in desperation.

Brandon: You could bring up the Black Plague. You say, "This is what we did because we got within an inch of death, and they came and did this." There's enough of them to depopulate a country. He's pulling a "To save the world I'm going to sacrifice this." But I don't know which country it's going to be. I'm not committing the ultimate crime. He is still a noble character, but—

Howard: Yeah, he's still going to feel like a monster to me.

Mary: What if it actually takes an enormous amount of energy for them to cross over into our world? But it's a happy accident that our souls release energy through their world. So he realizes that Death is, in fact, bluffing. There's no way for the entire population to come over and harvest everybody, which is getting rid of the Black Death scenario.

Brandon: I really like the Black Death thing, though. The secret history is great for this.

Mary: Maybe when they manifest over here, they all manifest at the size of fleas.

Dan: Or rats. What is the method of immortality? Is it a drug?

Howard: I hadn't really made up my mind. Because I'm a sci-fi guy, it's a mixture of—

Dan: If that itself is a form of energy, like an energy wave he can just disperse across the planet, that could be tweaked to mess up the aliens.

Howard: All right, yeah. I may have to actually sit down and write the story and let it—

Dan: See where it takes you.

Mary: I went and wrote an outline last night.

Dan: If she can do it, why can't you do it?

First Draft: An Honest Death

HOWARD TAYLER

When the guy dressed as Death showed up in my office I did what any sensible person would do. I punched the "security" button on my comm center and said "eviction, please." I hadn't seen how the costumed freak got in, but I was going to watch him leave.

"We must speak privately," Death-dude said. His voice was deep and musical, but not like Barry White. It was artificial, like somebody was auto-tuning Christopher Lee.

"No, we mustn't. You're leaving," I said. I heard my office's outer door open.

"Mister McDonald! Are you okay?" Blakely's voice came from my office foyer, and from the sound of footsteps he'd brought a couple of the heavies.

"I'm just fi—" I stopped mid-word as Death evaporated. I might have screamed at that point, because Blakely came through the door with his weapon out of its holster. His eyes met mine, and then he and his team did a quick left-right sweep of my office. It was reassuring to see them look so competent, but I guess my face didn't look reassured.

"Sir? Are you okay?" Blakely asked.

"I'm okay. He's gone."

"Who's gone, sir? And . . . um . . . gone where?" Blakely stepped to my window and placed a hand on it.

I considered the next words out of my mouth very, very carefully. My office has no cameras or other recording equipment in it, and it would not do for me to seem even a little bit crazy.

"Blakely, you've just earned a raise." I looked at my watch. "Twenty-six seconds, and the way you came in here you could star in an action movie. One of the good ones, where they get all the details right."

"This was a test, sir?"

"We're getting ready to change the world, Blakely. This was a drill." I'm accustomed to pinpoint prevarication. Though in this case I was going to need to support the fict after the fact. "I'll take care of things with HR. I'll also provide a little pad in your budget" I gestured at the two heavies covering my doorway "to additionally compensate your team."

"Thank you, sir." Blakely said. He looked me right in the eye the way the vast majority of my employees do not. "If you're sure you're all right, we'll leave you."

"I'm fine," I lied. "A little adrenaline is all, Mister Action Movie. You're good."

#

I wasn't lying about changing the world. Our gene-therapy team was ready for public trials of a plasmid that, if our private testing was to be believed, would put an end to old age. It went beyond revolutionary. Treatments would be expensive, at least at first, but human beings were about to start getting a lot older.

Two years ago we acquired a think-tank of sociologists, economists, and anthropologists. For the last twenty-two months they'd been running simulations, trying to figure out how we could make money on immortality without starting the last war humans would ever fight. I'm not a big fan of war. Folks paint us C-level executives as profiteering monsters who'll ruin a million lives for a few percentage points on their stock options, but that's not me. Especially not once our think-tank explained how long human memory was about to get. "Be generous now," they counseled. "Be very generous. We're not playing the short game anymore."

What they didn't say, but what I know, is that the long game is made of a bunch of short games, and you can't afford to lose too many of those outright, especially not early on.

#

I was musing upon a few of those short games—acquisitions, lobbying for legislation, and some key hires—when Death showed up again. This time I saw how he got in, or at least, I saw when and where he got in. I don't know the "how" behind his sudden appearance in the center of my office.

"Please do not call security this time, Mr. Macdonald."

"So . . . I'm either not crazy, or I'm extra-crazy."

"You are not crazy," said Death. "I have not shown myself to anyone in quite some time."

"This must be pretty important to you. What do you want?"

"I want you to sabotage your company's life extension technology."

"My stockholders will be very disappointed, and not just because the company won't survive if this project fails. Some of those folks sit on the board, and expect to live to see the next millennium."

"I promise you that they will not."

"Be disappointed?"

"Live to see the next millennium."

"That sounds a lot like a threat." I reached for my comm-center, finger hovering over the SECURITY button.

"If you push that button, you, your board, and everyone you know or care about will die in the next seven days."

"So it is a threat."

"If you fail to sabotage the life-extenders, then the same thing will happen."

I waggled my finger over the button. "You ran from security last time."

"You are supposed to ask me what is in this for you."
"Okay, I'll bite. What is in it for me?"

The general outline is to have Death be part of a race of people that feed on human souls when humans die. They're otherwise invisible and immaterial, but when they're feeding they're vulnerable and visible. There aren't many of them, and they can control some of the aspects of their appearance.

I don't have all the details of the mythos locked in. Souls might survive the feeding, but be in great pain. They might be destroyed. Death-folks' numbers may have bloomed in the last few centuries, and if life extension takes off they'll quickly starve.

This is supposed to end in a call to arms to whomever reads the letter. The life extension is going out, and we're fighting Death wherever they attempt to show up.

Second Draft: An Honest Death

HOWARD TAYLER

The chirp in my earbud means that Sinclair Wollreich has pushed the panic button in his office. I slide my sidearm clear of its shoulder-holster and point at the floor in front of me in less than a second. Barry and Mohammed have theirs out and down as well, and the three of us run for the office door. I nod at Barry, who grabs the door handle and pulls the door open, stepping clear as Mo and I sweep straight into the room.

In, and to the left. My side is clear.

"Clear" says Mo, and I reply "clear!"

I can hear Barry swing in behind and between us, a third set of eyes on a room that is empty except for our boss.

Mister Wollreich looks pale, like he's seen a ghost, or maybe just jumped back onto the curb after being missed by a bus. Other than that he looks fine— middle-aged, and a little soft, but dressed to the nines in a suit that costs more than my car.

"What is it, sir?" I ask.

"It's . . ." he glances around, still wearing that I-dodged-a-bullet-but-maybe-there's-another-one-coming look, and then he turns and looks me in the eye, and for only the third time in the eighteen months I've worked for him, he lies to me. "It's nothing, Cole. Just a drill."

Mo makes that noise that means he's barely stifling a stream of blasphemy.

"Yes sir," I say. "Let's finish like it's the real thing, then. Mo, take the corners. Barry, window. I'll check the desk."

"Cole," Wollreich addresses me again, "It's okay. I just wanted to see how quickly you guys could get here. I think you took four seconds."

Liar. Also, that was seven seconds, at least. I don't know what he's hiding, but my brain is already spinning scenarios. Something scared him, something he thought we could protect him from, but by the time we arrived it was gone. Or maybe it had never been here. Maybe Sinclair Wollreich hallucinated something frightening, and is now covering up for that hallucination. That . . . that makes a lot of sense. He doesn't strike me as the hallucinating type, but he is the head of a pharmaceutical company, so maybe he's on something.

Regardless, he pushed the panic button, and that means I don't get to stand down until I'm sure he's safe. He lied to me, very uncharacteristically, and that means his safety may be in question from an unusual angle.

"Sorry, sir. You're feigning duress pretty effectively. We have to finish the sweep, and put our eyes on everything."

Barry looks at me from behind Wollreich, and I nod. *Eyes on everything* is his cue for some impromptu misdirection. He holsters his weapon, pulls a chair over to the window and steps onto it as if to check the upper frame. He balances poorly—deliberately poorly—on the chair, and begins to fall.

"Oops, watch out!" he says as he corrects and jumps clear of the tipping chair.

Wollreich turns, and also steps clear.

Mo, in the far corner of the room, reaches up and sticks a cam-dot on the spot where the molding joins the ceiling, a position where it can see the entire room while remaining almost invisibly unobtrusive.

Wollreich's office has no cameras in it by design. I objected to this on general principle a year and a half ago, but backed down. Now it does have a camera in it.

"First day in the new shoes, Barry?" asks Mo.

"Actually, it's the fourth day, but I'm trying new inserts today and I don't think I like them."

"Secure the chatter, guys," I say, scolding them. Part of the act.

"It's okay, it's okay," says Wollreich. His face has returned to normal. "The way you came through that door, you startled me even though I knew you were coming. You guys looked like you were straight out of an action movie—one of the good ones where they get everything right."

"They never get everything right, sir," I say. "But thank you."

"No, thank you, Cole. It's apparent that I'm not paying you or your team enough. I think a fifteen-percent raise is in order. I'll send word to HR."

That wasn't a lie. That was him committing to the earlier lie with a bribe, which means, if I'm reading him correctly, that he knows I know he lied, and he wants to talk to me in private about why he really pushed the button.

"Thank you, sir," I respond.

"Very generous, sir. Sorry about the chair thing," says Barry.

"I'll make sure Barry spends his bonus on better inserts," says Mo.

"We'll leave you to your business, sir." And we do.

Out in the anteroom, which does have cameras, I screen Mo as he sits down at the edge of the camera's field of vision and reaches around and under the chair. The receiver he plants against the wall looks exactly like a wall-plate.

I check my phone's Bluetooth list, and "GENERIC HEADSET" appears on the list. I select it, punch in my phone number, and it vanishes from the list. Just like it's supposed to.

#

I've been in this business a long time. When I started I was twenty-five, and thought that after a tour of duty with the Marines, facing down the occasional rambunctious citizen would be a piece of cake. I wasn't sure what I wanted out of life, but being shot at less seemed like a good start.

Ten years later I'd figured out that private security guys do tend to get shot at less than combat zone marines, but they still get shot at, and it's even harder to tell where the shot is going to come from. I still didn't know what I wanted out of life, but I'd saved the lives of a few people who did know.

I'm forty-four now, and I guess the fact that I'm still doing this means I'm done looking for meaning in my own life, and have settled for protecting the meaning in others. And Wollreich is the best man I've ever worked for.

That afternoon Wollreich calls me into his office.

"Sir?" I ask.

"Take a seat, Cole," Wollreich says.

I sit, and wait for Wollreich to speak.

"You know that wasn't just a drill earlier?"

"Yes, sir. Something scared you. What was it?"

"Probably a hallucination. There was somebody in my office. I looked up, sensing movement I guess, and then hit the panic button when I didn't recognize the intruder. I think he was about to speak, but as soon as I hit the panic button he vanished."

"Vanished how, sir?"

"Like a screen-wipe." Wollreich is describing a Power Point transition. I know exactly what that looks like, having been a captive audience for more than a few of them. "Except," he continues after a moment, "there was some dissolve to it as well. As if, from top to bottom, the interloper was evaporating. Only faster than that."

He's not lying to me.

I'm not sure exactly how I know this, but it's something I've been able to do for my entire adult life. Kind of like how some people always know where there's a speed-trap. There are cues out there to be read, but I'm reading them unconsciously. It's not a hundred-percent accurate, but once I've spent enough time with somebody I'm never wrong.

"I believe you sir."

"You believe it happened, or you believe that I saw what I'm telling you I saw?"

"I believe your account of the event, sir. You're not making this up. I suspect you're also concerned. Concerned for your own sanity, and for your position here with the company."

He blows out the breath he'd been half-holding.

"There's more to it than that, Cole. I'm concerned that this may be a side-effect. How much have you been told about our upcoming product lines?"

"We're approaching the approval phase of a 'vaccination' against Alzheimer's, we're in late-stage testing on a Telomerase regulator that promises to prevent a large percentage of cancers, and we've just gotten approval for an HIV treatment."

"Very succinct."

"That's a summary of what I've been told, sir. I can tell there's something else going on, and that I'm not supposed to be in on the secret."

He sits back in his chair, steeples his fingers, and purses his lips.

"Are you? Have you figured it out?"

"No, sir. But if you're about to let me in on the secret, please keep in mind that if the information is valuable enough, a competitor may be willing to kill to get it. You're paying me and my team quite well, but if you're sitting on a billion dollars' worth of information, my threat assessment will change, we'll have to hire more people, and everybody will get paid more."

"So be it. Cole, the drug interaction between these three products is going to extend human lifespan by about an order of magnitude."

I think about that for a moment. If this is true . . .

"Sir, are you sure this works?"

"Quite sure. We've tested it extensively, in secret trials on in-house volunteers. Including me. We were ninety-five percent sure before we started those tests two years ago."

"Sir, I think this secret is worth way more than just a billion dollars."

"There's more. You know that inbound marketing team we created?"

"That happened two months before I was hired, sir. But yes. You acquired a brain-trust and brought all your market research in-house."

"They're not doing market research. They're trying to position the company for the long game. We already know what the short-term future looks like. When the news breaks that this three-drug interaction extends the human lifespan, the entire product line will be nationalized by overwhelming popular demand, probably in a special legislative session. But before the United States does that, half a dozen other countries will already have deployed it within their national health care systems. We won't own any of it."

I nod. As predictions go, this makes perfect sense. There might be some small variations, but the end result is the same.

"So" he continues, "the only way for us to make money is for us to be pre-positioned in other fields. That team is preparing us to capitalize on the disruptions introduced by an order-of-magnitude increase in human longevity."

"I get it. We're not going to get rich selling immortality. We're going to get rich helping the Human Race make the transition to immortality."

"How valuable do you think this secret is?"

"In numbers? I have no idea. But if a competitor got wind of this strategy, no, if anybody got wind of the existence of this strategy, the information in this building, in our cloud, and in our heads would be too valuable to allow to go free. Those with the most resources to spend on acquiring that information and destroying any competing copies would be forced to spend those resources."

"Exactly."

I shake my head sadly. "Sir, I should resign. My team is good, but if a sovereign state decides to pull a hostile takeover, the only thing we can do for you is shoot you before they have a chance to begin interrogating, and we'd hesitate."

"You can't resign now. You know too much."

"Oh, I know that. I'm already contemplating expanded perimeters, plainclothes agents, dead-man-switch alarms. And of course I'm even more concerned about why you pushed the panic button."

"Yes . . . about that. The intruder . . . I never described him to you."

"I figured you'd get around to it."

"It was Death."

#

Wollreich agrees to an extended physical the next day. I don't know how you go about testing to see if someone is prone to hallucinating, or if something's going wrong with their brain, but Tuesday morning's checkup runs into Wednesday with no breaks. And me, or one of my people has had eyes on Wollreich, or his bedroom door, ever since the event Monday morning, and it's proving to be a bit of a strain.

It's six AM on Wednesday. Mo and I are in the lobby having coffee with two other team members, Failalo and Jace.

"How long are we going to keep this up, Cole?" asks Failalo. She's a soft-spoken Samoan woman with a wide jawline and crooked nose. Nobody shortens her name to "Fail" more than once.

"The extra shifts? Until HR and I can clear some more team members."

Mo sips at his coffee. "What's the holdup?"

"Well, if the event in Wollreich's office was enemy action, probative or otherwise, then we're up against somebody connected and equipped."

I've told my team that our boss saw an intruder, all in black, who then vanished. The leading theory is that it was a hologram made with lasers, but none of us have the background to research that.

I didn't tell them about immortality drugs, or that our boss thinks he saw Death. And only Mo and Barry know about the camera we planted.

"Oh, I get it," says Failalo. "You think we're being played. Somebody's planted their own people amid our candidates. They shoot some lasers through the window to spook us, we beef up, and now they've got peeps on the inside."

"That's one scenario. They might also have our hiring pool bugged, tapped, and flagged on their end, so they can watch our background check process and find the holes in it. So yes, I'm concerned that somebody pushed our panic button, and now we're reacting instead of acting."

"Don't go Princess Bride paranoid, boss," says Mo. "Both cups might be poisoned." He tosses back his coffee, swallows, then smiles broadly at me. "And there aren't enough of us for a land war in Asia."

I've always loved that scene. I used to imagine how I would have handled things if I'd been in Vizzini's shoes, and it was fun until I realized that I wouldn't have taken that job in the first place.

My phone chirps. I'm out of range for the Bluetooth connection, so that phony wall-plate is texting me to let me know the feed is active after-hours. The message looks innocent enough. "SUP YO. GO 4 EATS?"

Mo's smile flattens. "Somebody miss breakfast?" He knows the codes.

"Upstairs, now. Mo, you're with me in the service elevator. Failalo, Jace, take a lobby elevator to 31, then take the west stairs to forty." I drop a ten on our table to take care of the barista who usually doesn't have to clean up after us.

On our way to the service elevator Mo places a call.

"Hey Sal. Mohammed here. Check electrical, and find out if the lights just went on in Wollreich's office."

Good thinking. Building security doesn't have cameras in there, but there is a motion-detector on his light-switch, and our electrical system monitors usage as part of some conservation plan.

"Got it. Thanks." He turns to me as we reach the elevator. "Lights just went on. Lights are still out in the anteroom and the west hallway. Whoever turned on the office lights didn't walk in the usual way. Also, the cameras haven't seen anybody since Wollreich went up with Barry to drop stuff in his office at 3am."

I key the elevator for an nonstop ride. The illuminated numbers count up quickly. Mo and I are silent, but we're both listening.

At 40 the elevator doors slide open. That motion sets off the detectors, and the hallway lights come up.

Mo moves to step out, but I stop him. Somebody got onto this floor, and into Wollreich's office, and we know nothing about them. They got here first, and might be expecting us. Maybe they spoofed the cameras and the motion detectors, but we can't do that. As the hall lights just demonstrated, anywhere we go the lights will come up, so we can't be stealthy.

Then again, whatever spooked Wollreich the first time vanished pretty quickly, perhaps because it was afraid of us. If we're slow, we'll miss it, and if it's afraid of us, that might mean we've got it outgunned.

Or maybe both cups are poisoned. Ah, Vizzini, how I hate being you. Just once I want to be the guy with the locaine immunity and the winning plan.

"We go fast. Straight to the office, then standard entry."

Mo and I both draw and begin to run, weapons held low in two-handed grips. We run through two hallway intersections without clearing them properly, and each time I worry that I'm being a reckless idiot. But nobody shoots at us, and those intersections light up to the north and south, so nobody else came that way recently.

Through the frosted glass the anteroom is dark. Not full-dark, because it's got big west-facing windows, but it's oh-six fifteen. I hear a soft "tick" as the lock-pad next to the door reads my badge and unlocks things for me.

I'm in first, pushing the door open and sweeping with it to the left as the lights come up.

"Clear" says Mo.

"Clear."

"TING" says my phone. Bluetooth connection, with data streaming in. We can look at that later.

I key in my code for the door to Wollreich's office. Tick. I grab the handle and pull the door open, for Mo, who goes to the left in the brightly-lit office. I go right.

"Clear," says Mo.

"And empty," I say. Not that I expected to find anybody here, not really.

Mo steps to the corner of the room where our cam dot should be.

"It's still there."

"I'm pretty sure there's no point sweeping the rest of the floor." I holster my weapon. "Let's see if the camera saw anything."

I pull out my phone. Swipe, code, and then a tap on the spy-app, whose icon looks like the one for a pizza place. I respond to the "ZIP CODE" prompt with an eleven-digit passphrase, and up comes the video file. I push play.

The video begins with the room dark, but it's not full-dark because of those west-facing windows. Then a human-sized shadow dissolve-wipes into existence in the middle of the room, backlit by the windows so I can't make out any details the moment it appears, but the lights come up very quickly.

"Holy shit," says Mo.

Hooded and all in black, the stereotypical, iconic representation of Death, complete with a scythe, stands in the middle of the office, and turns to face the camera.

#

We've got my phone configured to 'cast to the wall screen by the time Mister Wollreich arrives in his office with Barry on his heels. Wollreich is flushed, there are bags under his eyes, and he's angry. Barry has all the expression of a granite bust, which means Wollreich has been chewing him out on the way over here.

"Cole, how long have you been spying on me?"

"Since Monday morning, sir. I'm sorry, but it seemed prudent."

"Prudent? After the lecture you gave me about the value of secrets? Spying on me is a lot of things, but prudent is not one of them."

"With all due respect, sir, you called us in a panic, then lied to us. I made a snap decision in order to ensure that my team and I could keep you safe. I'm standing by it, and I think you should watch this before we continue to discuss the matter."

"Fine."

I push PLAY, and Death appears on screen.

Wollreich gasps.

"That's him. Hot damn, Cole, you got him!"

I push PAUSE.

"We did, sir, but he's about to start talking, and he talks fast. You really need to listen to this."

Wollreich nods, and I push PLAY.

Death is facing the camera, and begins to speak.

"Sinclair Wollreich and . . . friends," he begins. The voice is deep, male, and almost musically artificial, like somebody auto-tuned Christopher Lee. "You must immediately cancel your organization's life extension plans. Further, you must destroy the information related to it. Otherwise human beings will lose all access to the eternal realms."

Mo and I have already watched the whole thing. Then I had to explain to Mo that yes, the company was going to be extending human life. I watched it a second time while Mo called Barry and told him to get the boss in here. Right now I'm watching Wollreich, who is sneering and eyerolling, giving the screen his "this is bullshit" face.

"The human spirit, or soul, is a turbulent waveform. At death, this turbulence allows the waveform to imprint across the boundary wave, transducing the wave to an eternal state with minimal degradation. As humans grow older, however, the turbulence is reduced. Some very old humans fail to imprint. Their original waveforms cease. In your terms, this means they die forever. Should human lives be extended to more than a century, very few humans will imprint successfully, and eternal life will be denied to your race."

Wollreich's "this is bullshit" face gives way to deep concern.

"You have the ability, Sinclair Wollreich, to end this project and save humans eternally. Act swiftly."

Death vanishes. A moment later, Mo and I can be heard entering the anteroom, and then the video shows us bursting through the office door. Mo reaches up to check the camera, and the image freezes because I've pushed STOP.

Wollreich is leaning against his desk, arms folded, head down.

"Cole, could this have been faked?"

"Probably. I'm not a video expert. But the second time I watched it I looked out the window. There's a cloud that remained unchanged between the Death part and the part where Mo and I arrived. We could probably match that to other cameras in the building."

Wollreich straightens up.

"Is that the only copy of the video?" he asks as he points at my phone.

"There's a copy in the transmitter, too."

"And one in the cache on the wallscreen," says Mo. "That one's in dynamic allocation, though. Might already be gone."

"Bring me the transmitter, and then we're all waiting in here for the experts."

#

Wollreich's office is big, but with nine of us it's starting to feel crowded. Three members of that special "marketing team" have arrived, and one of them has video tools on hand. Two senior members of R&D are here as well, and they're both scientist-types, complete with the lab coats. Wollreich, Mo, Barry, and I are the only ones in suits.

We've all watched the video.

"This is spaghetti-monster stuff," says Kurtzman, one of the labcoat guys. "It's non-falsifiable. We can't test any of what he told us. Sure, it sounds convincing because he used words like waveform and transducing, but there's no science in here for us to help with."

"Sure there is," says Michel. He's the marketing guy with the black hardcase. "I need to see the camera, though."

Mo pulls it down from the corner of the room and passes it to Michel. It's about the size of a pencil eraser.

Michel turns it over in his hands and squints at it.

"Yup! We have science. This camera sees in broad-spectrum. The transmitted video is standard HD, but the raw file has some goodies in it." He takes the transmitter from the table, jacks a cable into it, and bends over his equipment. "This'll take a few minutes."

Wollreich turns to Kurtzman.

"The statements Death made are non-falsifiable, yes. We have no way to prove or disprove any of what we were told. Due diligence suggests that we at least consider the information, and that's why you're here."

"Can we not refer to him as Death, please?" says Kurtzman. "That costume he was wearing was part of the message, and if we accept it at face value, we're undermining our ability to evaluate any of this. Oh, and for the record, I think it's a crank, and what we should be doing is grilling the hired guns."

When the boss is in a meeting I only speak when spoken to. My job is to be invisible. Under the current circumstances, that's not going to work well.

"Grill away, Mister Kurtzman," I say.

"DOCTOR Kurtzman."

"My apologies, Doctor. But please, grill us. Ask us anything. From your perspective, my team and I are your prime suspects. From our perspective, we need to get cleared as quickly as possible so that we're free to continue doing our jobs."

"I've already got an independent agency running deep checks on you, Cole," says Wollreich. "Your whole team, in fact. They've been doing it since Monday, when I brought you into the fold."

"Outstanding, sir."

Kurtzman looks stymied.

"And Doctor Kurtzman," Wollreich continues, "I think you're absolutely right. We don't call our intruder Death anymore. He is The Intruder."

"I'm not quite sure how this video plays into any corporate espionage scenario," says Lee, a stout woman in khakis and a Hawaiian print shirt. "I haven't plugged any of this into our X-form, but I shouldn't have to. The payoffs and strategies, the incentive matrix . . . those don't change. This should align itself with existing player strategies, and it does not."

"Doctor Lee is a game theorist," says Wollreich. "Without the jargon now, Doctor?"

"The X-form assumes rational and informed agents in the access tier. An irrational, uninformed agent might adopt the dress-like-death tactic in hopes of a payoff, but . . ."

"I said without the jargon."

"She means," says Michel, "that we're either dealing with an irrational, uninformed person with a stupid agenda, but who has access to our plans, or there are payoffs missing from the matrix."

"There aren't any payoffs missing," says Lee.

"Let's come back to that," says Michel. "I have more video for you to watch."

He gestures at the screen. "This is the original image, with an overlay of neon-green representing UV frequencies all the way to the edge of the camera's range."

On the wall-screen the video begins again, muted. It looks exactly the same as before, except a green shimmer appears in the middle of the room. It brightens, and then flashes as The Intruder appears. It then fades to a low shimmer again, surrounding his form as he speaks. The flash occurs again when he vanishes.

"Michel, what does that mean?"

"It means that The Intruder's appearance and disappearance were accompanied by UV emissions."

"Michel," says Lee, "those speakers in your office, the ones that build the audible cone out of interference patterns? Could somebody make a hologram by doing that with light? Like, ultraviolet lasers bouncing off each other just right to make a picture?"

The hologram thing. That was Mo's theory.

"Maybe, but did you notice how there wasn't any green in the sky outside the window, or in the sunrise reflections on the buildings across the street? These windows filter UV. Any laser that tried to beam UV through them would have to cut the glass to do so."

"Then how did the UV get into the room?"

"Obviously it came with The Intruder," Michel answers. "But what you really want to see is the infrared. Watch this. No UV this time. I'm only going to play the infrared channel."

The picture returns, and now it's a monochromatic green.

Several of us gasp when the intruder appears. Including me.

I've seen infrared video of people before, and most folks have at least seen it simulated in movies. This is not that.

The form under the cloak is clearly outlined, and asymmetrical. The torso is short, and high. The legs are too long, and appear to bend the wrong way. If there's a left arm, it's not showing up. The right arm reaches all the way to the floor, then up to head-height, where it ends in the scythe blade.

But the cloak itself is the freakiest part. Lacy networks of veins are visible throughout it, and they all connect to the torso, the scythe-limb, and the legs. It's not clothing. It's a layer of skin, like bat-wing, wrapped around The Intruder and hooding his face.

His? I see no male genitalia, and this thing is alien enough that I'm not ready to suggest that means it's female.

Kurtzman speaks first.

"Michel, how hard would it be to fake that?"

"Not very hard. If the whole thing was computer animated and hacked into the camera feed, the infrared and ultraviolet elements would simply be another part of the model. It's the work of a real artist, though."

"Okay, good," says Kurtzman blowing out a sigh of relief. "I'm going to choose to believe that this was a brilliant computer animation modeled by someone with an outstanding attention to anatomical detail. Because I refuse to believe that an alien teleported into this office."

#

I tune out a little bit as Wollreich's brain trust begins working that angle. Michel seems to think that it's possible for the camera's tiny transmitter to have been hacked, so that the images arriving at the larger wall transceiver were different than what actually happened in this office.

It's interesting, but I'm doing a threat assessment, and it's distracting. I do threat assessments all the time, they're part of my job, but right now I'm assessing the threat to Mo, Barry, and I, and our jobs. I know that we didn't fake anything, or take part in any fakery, but I can't expect the scientists and game theorists in here to take our word for that. It's only going to be a few minutes before they determine that a hack on the camera's feed is only likely or manageable if the—

"Mister Cole," says Michel. "

Outline of what comes next

Grilling Mo's team. How was the camera hacked? Get a forensic computing expert in here to look at the file. Account for Mo and Cole's movements during the last two weeks. Mo, Barry, and Cole surrender their weapons. (How paranoid is paranoid enough?)

The alien plan— Once personal security is disarmed, the aliens are free to attack, and everybody is in the same room. If security is NOT disarmed it's probably because the message is being taken seriously. Win. Actually, the most likely scenario is that the message is disregarded. What would the aliens do then? Plan B is harvest humans directly.

BONEYARD

"Go on."

"Well, if it's a side-effect then the company is gambling several billion dollars on a bet that is suddenly a lot less sure. But more importantly, you know that if the technology exists somewhere, anywhere, to allow someone to materialize and dematerialize here in your office, then the information here in your office is exactly where it would be used. But that would only happen if the secret was out, and was far enough out that somebody with very, very advanced technology had gotten wind of it."

Wollreich's eyes widen as I speak. A mixture of fright and incredulity, like he's been told a very believable ghost story.

"Cole, that sounds like science-fiction."

"You're the one cooking up the immortality drugs, sir," I say with a forced smile.

"There's a big difference between identifying a series of exploits in organic chemistry, and defying the laws of physics."

"I'm not a physicist, sir. Maybe it was a hologram, or an induced hallucination. My point stands. If somebody out there can do it, and the existence of this secret is out, your office is where they'd use it."

"Well . . . how do we proceed?"

"Address the most likely issue first. Get tested. I assume the private meeting with R&D each Tuesday morning is a physical?"

"It is. What do we do if I'm fine?"

"If you're fine, then somebody materialized in this room, or created the illusion of materializing. They had unknown means and unknown intent, but we can surmise that they did not want to be discovered by me or my team. I'll need some time to chew on that. Also, my team should introduce an additional external perimeter, and someone should remain with you at all times from here on out. I hope that's okay with you."

"Perfectly okay, Cole."

"Outstanding." I pause for a moment. I should have asked this next question earlier in this interview. "Sir, did you get a look at the guy?"

Wollreich locks eyes with me, and looks deep. I look back.

"Yeah. It was Death."

Writing Excuses 9.31

WORKSHOPPING AN HONEST DEATH

Brandon: The part of Dan will be played by a rowdy group of European soccer hooligans watching American football for the first time. And we once again have Eric James Stone joining us. Thank you so much, Eric.

Eric: Thanks for inviting me.

Brandon: We've done this with the other people in the Writing Excuses crew, where we each wrote a story and have critiqued them. Last but not least is our friend Howard. We will include in the book the draft that Mary, Eric, and I just read so that you can read the final version, read our critique, and have in front of you the original draft so you can see what we went through. It makes us feel much better if you've read the final version first, because seeing it in its glory and beauty—

Howard: Because one of the things that we're going to talk about is the fact that what Brandon, Mary, and Eric have read really isn't the whole story. I'm stuck and need help getting the characters, plot, and everything to one of the possible endings I had in mind.

Mary: The reason we decided to go ahead and do this with a partial story is that we know this is something that happens to a lot of writers. We'll be talking about the tools that you can use to get yourself out of this spot.

Brandon: I'm just going to lead the discussion, as I normally do with these. Whenever I do a critique, I like to start with what's working, because I don't want the writer to "fix" what's already working. So, what did we like about this piece?

Eric: One of the things I really liked is the main character, the security guard. I like stories about people who are competent.

Brandon: He was very competent, and that was *shown* to me. There was very little *telling* of that, which was great.

Eric: With a competent character, if they run up against something that's outside their competency zone, that creates some good conflict. Now, this story has a really neat concept. With the impending immortality and then, is it Death? Is it aliens? What's interfering here? I really liked the concept there and really wanted to know how it was going to end.

Brandon: One thing I want to highlight that was working very well for me was the pacing. The way that you included your scene breaks really enhanced the sense of pacing. You had a little zing at the end of most of the scenes. I was really engaged by the story all the way through.

Howard: I remember you actually cursing me when you got to the part of the document that said "Boneyard" instead of—

Brandon: Yeah. "What?!" You had indicated you didn't finish, and I hoped that just meant you didn't know what to do with the epilogue, like with my story. But no, it just stops, and I said, "Aaaaaahhh, Tayler!"

Mary: One thing I liked was the dialogue, particularly because you're writing in first-person present tense. I like the immediacy that that gives, and I also like the character interactions.

Brandon: I feel you picked the right tense. It helps enhance the story.

Howard: That is very gratifying, because as I was first writing this I remember thinking, "I already used first-person present tense when I was writing the horror story for *Space Eldritch*. I should just go with straight third-person limited," but I could not find the voice for the character, so I changed characters. The original pitch for this was that our protagonist was the CEO. But in that version of the story, he was just telling people what to do. And I thought, "This is boring." Yes, he has to think a lot and do things, but all he's doing is telling people things. So I switched characters and it still didn't feel immediate enough, and then I switched tenses and that appears to be where my stride fit the pacing of the story. So I'm glad it's working.

Brandon: I remember having brainstormed part of this with you, but—

Mary: I was still surprised by stuff.

Brandon: So that was working real well. I still don't know what the ending is, even though we brainstormed the concept. I don't know if this is an alien, or if it's actually Death, or if it's industrial espionage, and I love that about it.

Brandon: Let's go ahead and look at what's not working for the part that's already here. Then after that we'll tackle this larger issue of "How do I end the story, can you guys help me brainstorm an ending?"

Mary: For me, his subordinates are too similar. I found that I was often confusing who else was there. I think it has to do with speech patterns, and also his assessment of where they fit in competency. Because everybody seemed to be of equal competency levels, doing the same kind of things.

Brandon: One thing that snapped for me was when I learned that "Mo" was short for Mohammed. That character suddenly became clearer in my head. It's the whole Orson Scott Card thing, right? Where it's not necessarily that he was an ethnicity, but the fact that he was now a longer name, different from the other ones and of a different— Orson Scott Card has said, "When you're naming characters, try to make each name distinctive from the others in an interesting way."

Howard: And that was exactly what I was doing. With regard to their extreme similarity—that is always a problem with me during first and second drafts. It's not until I have the story shaped the way it needs to be shaped that I can go back in and tweak the dialogue so that the characters' speech patterns identify them.

Brandon: Looking back at the start, you called him Mohammed the first time, but I wasn't into the story yet. He was Mo for a long time, and then when you called him Mohammed again that's the first time I grabbed onto Mohammed.

Mary: I completely missed it. It wasn't sticky for me.

Eric: Yeah, it didn't stick for me either. The one that did stick for me was the—

Howard: Failalo? The Polynesian name?

Eric: Yes.

Brandon: Talking about other things that didn't quite work, I'm going to start larger and go smaller. I've got some text-based things, but we'll get to those later. I felt there were a couple of places where the narrative got a little clunky for me. One was the maid-and-butlering in the scene with Wollreich and our protagonist. It was "As you know, we hired these people," and there was a lot of information in there that as a reader I felt like I didn't need.

Mary: I saw a lot of that too, and I went through and marked it in the text. For me, it was a lot of the stuff about how incredibly valuable this thing was. I just need somebody to tell me this is valuable, and I do not need them to justify it.

Brandon: In that same sequence we have the main character saying, "I'm thinking of stepping down," which didn't seem to work. I can understand him being shocked, but somebody needs to run security for this. It makes perfect sense that it would be him, but he says, "I've just realized my mission parameters are much larger than I thought. This is a big deal, and I'm overwhelmed." There is this discussion of "I may need to quit, sir." Is he going to hire someone better than you? I don't understand that interaction completely. And it was part of the "Do we need all of this?" I've been presented with a character who says, "Tell me what I need to do. I'm going to take the next few steps." And for him to then say, "Wow, you're doing this awesome thing, okay. I will have to deal with that." It felt like—

Howard: I'm going to have to figure out how to fix that. At least in the way I'm envisioning the further unfolding of the story, the corporate espionage angle here is pretty important. One of the principles behind protecting against corporate espionage is the value of the data and the value of the knowledge that the data exists.

Mary: But you don't need to spend as much time on the page getting to that.

Brandon: Yeah, that's what I feel. This is all good. In fact, I liked his conflict of "Am I capable of handling this?" It just felt there was way too much spinning of wheels in this scene for me. That's my reader response.

Howard: No, that's good. What I want to make sure of is that the thematic element isn't the problem. It's the way I'm overnarrating it.

Mary: Yes, it is.

Brandon: One thing I highlighted just to go back to is something like, "You know that inbound marketing team we created?" Why do we need to know about—what? They're doing market research? I think in just a couple lines you could get across the idea of "This is how we're going to profit on this." With less back and forth. I was bored there.

Mary: Likewise. It was because I got it really early on. So I think you need to figure out—

Howard: Part of this is the worldbuilder's trap of "I have figured out how the CEO and the board of directors are structuring this to protect the data as well as they can, and I want to share how clever I am with my readers."

Mary: Yeah. You don't actually need it for the story progression.

Howard: Dialing back the sharing of the clever.

Brandon: Though, on another tack, I'm not sure if it's this way for everyone else or not, but I kind of want to know—if you're going to mention, "We've discovered the secret to immortality," should they just say that, or do they need to go further and say what the extrapolation of that is. I don't know. Maybe this isn't the right time for it. But at the end all he says is, "We've introduced an order of magnitude increase in human longevity," and the guy says, "You're sure this'll work?" And the reader thinks, "What do you mean, you're sure this'll work? You only have two years." Does it mean "Our cells are no longer breaking down"? I want a little line of proof.

Eric: I had some plausibility problems with that as well. You can say, "It's working in mouse studies, and the original mouse who got it five years ago is still alive." I don't know how long mice live.

Brandon: I just need something. I don't need all the technobabble, but I need him to offer our guy some proof.

Mary: Yeah, if you said, "On a cellular level, aging is no longer happening."

Brandon: Yes, and that right there tells me what kind of immortality this is.

Mary: One of the places that I had a suspension of disbelief issue was that his team—granted, all hypercompetent and everything—would just happen to carry around bugging equipment on them when they're doing a panic call. Because he says, "It's about the size of a wall plate," when he's talking about the transceiver. Having the camera dot, maybe that's just in your bag all the time, but what budget item was your secret bugging equipment on?

Brandon: My problem with the bugging equipment was that I didn't have explained to me how it worked. You assumed I knew, and when they went in and said, "Let's download the feed," I said, "What?" I thought you were going to have someone watching a live feed on a screen all the time, because that's how security footage works for me. I was very confused.

Mary: I also thought there was going to be a "We want live footage of him." The problem with this is that it's one of the places where you demonstrate their work as a team, so it's important for the overall story structure. But in terms of getting us the next information we need? All you had to do was get rid of his prohibition against having the—

Brandon: I'm going to go a different direction on this. I'm going to disagree. I really like that scene. I think it's easily justified by simply having him say, "I've been looking for an excuse to convince myself to bug his room for a long time now, and my men knew that. I had not gone forward with it because bugging my employer is not something I do unless I have a good reason." There's your answer right there.

Howard: Yep, that solves it. One of the reasons that it's important to me is that on a story level the reader needs to be shown that the interloper, whatever he is—Death, an alien, whatever—the interloper already knows enough to know exactly where the camera is and to speak to the camera.

Brandon: Right, and the camera is not the corporation's. It is our individual security team's.

Howard: Now we're swiftly running up to the corner that I've written myself into.

Brandon: Let's address the big problem, which is that this story we were all really enjoying doesn't have an ending.

Howard: Let me start by telling you the intended structure of the story. The easy, logical answer for what's going on is that our protagonist and his team are for some reason spoofing everybody with their camera and their tricks, and now this team has been brought into the full corporate secret. The bodyguards are there in a room full of the company's brain trust, and the bodyguards are all armed. This is a situation the brain trust is probably very uncomfortable with, and their logical action would be to immediately demand that the bodyguards disarm themselves. Which makes perfect sense, it follows—

Brandon: If I were in this situation I wouldn't do that. If I suspected the bodyguard I would play along immediately, and would say, "Wow, we need to do more research and investigation into this. Let's set up a better surveillance and see if we can do this." And then once the bodyguards were gone, then I'd deal with it. I don't deal with it with them right there in the room.

Mary: When someone is in the room with you and they have weapons, you do not escalate. You defuse.

Howard: That works even better, because what they want to do is get the bodyguards out of the room. Which the interloper wants to have happen— And the interloper is playing everybody; that's something that needs to be made clear as the story unfolds—this is a story goal. That is what the interloper expects to happen, that the bodyguards will neutralized. And then the interloper and his interloper buddies will materialize in the room and murder everyone.

Brandon: Okay, so we're on our last act of this story. This is the climax right here.

Howard: Yes, we're heading straight into the last act.

Brandon: What do you want the interloper to be?

Howard: That's the other trick, revealing this information in some way. The interloper is some sort of extradimensional alien species that has found a way to feed off energies released when people die. They can materialize in our plane and kill us, but when they do that they're exposed to us killing them back, which is something they don't want to happen. If we just die naturally, that's awesome for them because then, "Hey, free food." If we stop dying, they all starve. What they're trying to do is set up a situation in which they can maintain the status quo, and for whatever reason this seems like the best strategy to them.

Mary: This is one of those scenarios where I feel like the bad guy's plan is too complicated. "I need to convince them to not do this"? Up to the point of "Let's stop this," that plan all makes perfect sense. The plan of "Let's kill all of these guys" is, forgive me, really really stupid. Because if you can materialize anywhere?

Brandon: You can just smash up all their computers and their equipment, for one thing.

Mary: Then you materialize in their bedrooms at night and kill them in their sleep. Smother them with pillows.

Brandon: Or you materialize in their bedroom while they're going to sleep and say, "I'm Death. Let's prove it. Go and lock yourself in any room you want, and I will appear there. I can prove to you I am Death, now stop what you're doing."

Howard: See, that's one of the problems I'm up against, because I was trying to define—for lack of a better term—a power set. Why don't they just materialize everywhere? What is the cost for them of materializing and dematerializing? It's got to be something beyond the risk of being seen. I also did some research into death imagery, and I wanted to play with the fact that they look like our classic representations of Death. That's cool. But those classic representations are in the last 800–900 years, so either they haven't always been around, or this isn't what they've always looked like. But once I start opening all these cans of worms, the story gets bigger and bigger, and that's not what I wanted.

Brandon: I think you're just fine saying they discovered our plane right about the time these depictions of Death started appearing. That solves a lot of your problems there. But the bigger problem is how do we end this? Eric, you've been quiet for a bit, and you're really good at this stuff. Do you have any advice?

Eric: Part of the problem is, how is the main character going to be involved in solving this problem?

Howard: I hadn't actually gotten around to describing that. The way I'd imagined it is that the main character, whether he is disarmed or sent from the room, realizes, "Oh, this is a scenario that someone has potentially planned for. Those people are now all in that room without protection, and I've identified a threat that can materialize anywhere. I need to be back in that room."

Brandon: I think Mary's argument that they can materialize in the bedrooms at night is really a big deal for this story.

Mary: This may be one of those places where you actually have to rejigger your middle a little bit. It might be that this big scene that we have happening in the office gets shifted to a bedroom.

Brandon: Right, or you can rejigger it so that their experiments with the immortality stuff involve the creatures' home plane. Because of the science that's going on in this lab, this causes the creatures to manifest here. They have broken open this plane, so it's not just chemical. This changes your story a lot, but it gives you a connection there. But that's me, I'm looking for a magic system explanation; this is what I do. Then fixing it is a matter of "If they can only manifest here, what do we do? Anywhere we're going to use this they manifest, so we come up with a solution that causes that they can't manifest where we're doing our research."

Howard: The original version of the ending, that leapt to mind as the story came to me while I was driving, is that there is a fight and we realize that we can kill them. We somehow realize what their plan is and that their numbers have bloated hugely as our numbers have gone up, because there is so much food. Now there are maybe millions of them who can appear at will, and will need to in order to eat. So we are going to give humanity immortality, and now we need to arm you because you're going to have to fight for it.

Brandon: That's a cool ending. I like that.

Howard: I just need to figure out how to get there.

Mary: You don't have to work so hard to get there. All you need for that ending is for your alien to appear, and for there to be a firefight, and for the alien to be killed. That's all you need. You already have everything in place, so you don't need to get your good guys out of the room, don't need to do—

Brandon: You need to do a "find out" on the alien. Have your good guy make the call, "I'm going to go to his house at night; one of these things is going to show up and I'm going to shoot it in the head" or something like Mary suggested earlier, which could be a valid way to go about this. The discovery that needs to be made is that these are aliens, and this is what they do.

Mary: If you want to do something with—have them look at the tape and notice, "This thing occurs right before he appears. This gives us a warning signal." Rather than have our guy push a panic button.

Howard: Was that UV scatter? I forget.

Mary: If UV scatter is happening, or look at the way he's looking at things. "We suspect that he's only seeing in this spectrum," or something.

Brandon: Right, and the other thing that you have going on here is that it looked right at the camera, so it saw them. What can it see and what can't it see? Can it see you because it was watching the room and it didn't get distracted by this thing? If you palm the thing and stick it somewhere less obvious? If there were two cameras and it only spotted one of them, it tells you something about the alien that you can use. You need some sort of information about the alien that can be exploited.

Mary: And something in our main character's area of competence, which would be about threat assessment. If all the scientists are looking at it and saying, "Well, it's alien," and he says, "Screw that, this thing doesn't have binocular vision," or something.

Howard: And that's exactly what I'm trying to set up. He approaches this from a threat assessment angle. They come close to threat assessment when they're talking about game theory and trying to understand what the motivation would possibly be for this sort of a scam.

Brandon: Using the theme of the story, I kind of like the ending being him rushing in someplace and shooting the thing, just because it matches the first scene so well.

Mary: It could be, "Clearly this thing wants to talk to you." The only time this thing appears is when this room is empty or when Wollreich is in it by himself. Let's set up a scenario where—

Brandon: You could have a "Let's interview the alien" scene where it says, "All right, we're going to talk."

Howard: I like that because part of what that can give me is a scene break in which a lot of the discussion among the brain trust—

Mary: Happens offstage.

Howard: Right. One of the problems I had is that I wanted all of this information to be revealed, and I wanted to show instead of telling. But I had too much information for one character to have it all, and too many characters for a short story to work. But if I can roll that offscreen and have somebody say, "Wollreich, we need you to be in the office by yourself, here's the list of questions, and let's see if this thing comes in." And our hero has not told anybody that his threat assessment is "When this thing appears, I'm going to let Wollreich start talking, and then I'm going to kick down the door and shoot it in the head."

Brandon: And see if it dies. We do have to wrap up; hopefully this was useful for you. You can see, this kind of story is really hard to give feedback on in a writing group, because it's not done. It's the same sort of problem we had with my story where my ending was not the right ending, and we kept searching for it and it was through the session that I got closer. But it's tough. We'll have to see how you do.

Howard: This discussion has shown me the corner I had painted myself into is shaped differently than I thought it was, and the part that I thought was a wall might be a door.

EDITS: AN HONEST DEATH

HOWARD TAYLER

The chirp in my earbud means that Sinclair Wollreich has pushed the panic button in his office. I slide my sidearm clear of its shoulder ~~-~~holster and point it at the floor in front of me in less than a second. Barry and Mohammed have theirs out and down as well, and the three of us run for the office door. I nod at Barry, who grabs the ~~door~~ handle and pulls the door open, stepping ~~clear~~back as Mo and I sweep straight into the room.

In~~,~~ and to the left. My side is clear.

"Clear," says Mo, and I reply~~,~~ "~~e~~Clear!"

~~I can hear~~ Barry swings in behind ~~and between~~ us, a third set of eyes on a room that is empty except for our boss.

~~Mister.~~ Wollreich looks pale, like he's seen a ghost, or maybe just jumped back onto the curb after being missed by a bus. Other than that he looks fine—middle-aged, and a little soft, but dressed to the nines in a suit that costs more than my car.

"What is it, sir?" I ask.

"It's . . ." ~~h~~He glances around, still wearing that I-dodged-a-bullet-but-maybe-there's-another-one-coming look~~. and t~~Then he turns and looks me in the eye, and for only the third time in the eighteen months I've worked for him, he lies to me. "It's nothing, Cole. Just a drill."

Mo ~~makes that noise that means he's barely~~mouths the word "inconceivable," quoting *The Princess Bride* in order to stifl~~ing~~e a stream of blasphemy.

"Yes~~,~~ sir," I say. "Let's finish like it's the real thing, then. Mo, take the corners. Barry, window. I'll check the desk."

"Cole," Wollreich addresses me again, "It's okay. I just wanted to see how quickly you guys could get here. I think you took four seconds."

Liar. Also, that was seven seconds~~,~~ at least. I don't know what he's hiding, but my brain is already spinning scenarios. Something scared him, something he thought we could protect him from, but by the time we arrived it was gone. Or maybe it had never been here. Maybe Sinclair Wollreich hallucinated something frightening, and is now covering up for that hallucination. That . . . that makes a lot of sense. He doesn't strike me as the hallucinating type, but he is the head of a pharmaceutical company, so maybe he's on something.

Regardless, he pushed the panic button, and that means I don't get to stand down until I'm sure he's safe. He lied to me, very uncharacteristically, and that ~~means his safety may be in question from an unusual angle~~worries me.

"Sorry, sir. You're feigning duress pretty effectively. We have to finish the sweep, and put our eyes on everything."

Barry looks at me from behind Wollreich, and I nod. *Eyes on everything* is his cue for some impromptu misdirection. He holsters his weapon, pulls a chair over to the window_,_ and steps onto it as if to check the upper frame. He balances poorly—deliberately poorly—~~on the chair,~~ and begins to fall.

"Oops, watch out!" he says as he corrects and jumps clear of the tipping chair.

Wollreich turns, and also steps clear.

Mo, in the far corner of the room, reaches up and sticks a cam-dot on the spot where the molding joins the ceiling, a position where it can see the entire room while remaining almost invisibl_e_~~y unobtrusive~~.

By design, Wollreich's office has no cameras in it ~~by design~~. I objected to this on general principle_s_ a year and a half ago, but backed down. Now it does have a camera in it_. Just because I backed down doesn't mean I didn't plan for contingencies._

"First day in the new shoes, Barry?" asks Mo.

"Actually_,_ it's the fourth day, but I'm trying new inserts today and I don't think I like them."

"Secure the chatter, guys," I say~~, scolding them~~. Part of the act.

"It's okay, it's okay," says Wollreich. His face has returned to normal. "The way you came through that door, you startled me even though I knew you were coming. You guys looked like you were straight out of an action movie—one of the good ones where they get everything right."

"They never get everything right, sir," I say. "But thank you."

"No, thank you, Cole. It's apparent that I'm not paying you or your team enough. I think a fifteen_-_percent raise is in order. I'll send word to HR."

That wasn't a lie. That was him committing to the earlier lie with a bribe, which means, if I'm reading him correctly, that he knows I know he lied, and he wants to talk to me in private about why he really pushed the button.

"Thank you, sir," I ~~respond~~say.

"Very generous, sir. Sorry about the chair thing," says Barry.

"I'll make sure Barry spends his bonus on better inserts," says Mo.

"We'll leave you to your business, sir." And we do.

Out in the anteroom, which does have cameras, I screen Mo as he sits down at the edge of the camera's field of vision and reaches around and under the chair. The receiver he plants against the wall looks exactly like a wall_-_plate.

I check my phone's Bluetooth list, and "GENERIC HEADSET" appears ~~on the list~~. I select it_,_ _and_ punch in my phone number, and it vanishes from the list. Just like it's supposed to.

#

~~I've been in this business a long time. When I started I was twenty-five, and~~

~~thought that after a tour of duty with the Marines, facing down the occasional rambunctious citizen would be a piece of cake. I wasn't sure what I wanted out of life, but being shot at less seemed like a good start.~~

~~Ten years later I'd figured out that private security guys do tend to get shot at less than combat zone marines, but they still get shot at, and it's even harder to tell where the shot is going to come from. I still didn't know what I wanted out of life, but I'd saved the lives of a few people who did know.~~

~~I'm forty-four now, and I guess the fact that I'm still doing this means I'm done looking for meaning in my own life, and have settled for protecting the meaning in others. And Wollreich is the best man I've ever worked for.~~

That afternoon, Wollreich calls me into his office.

"Sir?" I ask.

"Take a seat, Cole," Wollreich says.

I sit, and wait for Wollreich to speak.

"You know that wasn't just a drill earlier?"

"Yes, sir. Something scared you. What was it?"

"Probably a hallucination. There was somebody in my office. I looked up, sensing movement I guess, and then hit the panic button when I didn't recognize the intruder. I think he was about to speak, but as soon as I hit the panic button he vanished."

"Vanished how, sir?"

"Like a screen-wipe." Wollreich is describing a Power-Point transition. I know exactly what that looks like, having been a captive audience for more than a few of them. "Except," he continues after a moment, "there was some dissolve to it as well. As if, from top to bottom, the inter~~udl~~oper ~~was~~ evaporat~~ing~~ed. Only faster than that."

He's not lying ~~to me~~.

I'm not sure exactly how I know ~~this~~he's not lying, but I think it's ~~something I've been able to do for my entire adult life. K~~kind of like how some people always know where there's a speed-trap. There are cues out there to be read, but I'm reading them unconsciously. It's not a hundred-percent accurate at first, but once I've spent enough time with somebody I'm never wrong.

"I believe you, sir."

"You believe it happened, or you believe that I saw what I'm telling you I saw?"

"I believe your account of the event, sir. You're not making this up. I suspect you're also concerned. Concerned for your own sanity, and for your position here with the company."

He blows out the breath he'd been half-holding.

"There's more to it than that, Cole. I'm concerned that this may be a side-effect. How much have you been told about our upcoming product lines?"

"We're approaching the approval phase of a 'vaccination' against Alzheimer's, we're in late-stage testing on a ~~T~~telomerase regulator that promises to prevent a large percentage of cancers, and we've just gotten approval for an HIV treatment."

"Very succinct."

"That's a summary of what I've been told, sir. I can tell there's something else going on, and that I'm not supposed to be in on the secret."

He sits back in his chair, steeples his fingers, and purses his lips.

~~"Are you?~~So, what ~~H~~have you figured ~~it~~ out?"

"No~~thing~~, sir. ~~But~~And if you're about to let me in on the secret, please keep in mind that if the information is valuable enough, a competitor may be willing to kill to get it. You're paying me and my team quite well, but if you're sitting on a billion dollars' worth of information, my threat assessment will change, we'll have to hire more people, and everybody will get paid more."

"So be it. Cole, the drug interaction between these three products is going to extend human lifespan, maybe by ~~about an~~ full order of magnitude. Old-age deterioration is going to go away. You and I will live to see the twenty-second century, and I'm not betting against seeing the thirtieth."

I think about that for a moment. If this is true . . .

"Sir, are you sure this works?"

"Quite sure. We've ~~tested it extensively, in~~got a lab full of eight-year-old white mice, and we're three years into some secret trials on in-house volunteers. Including me. ~~We were ninety-five percent sure before we started those tests two years ago~~I've never felt better, and my eyesight has improved as the lenses in my eyes regained their youthful flexibility."

"~~Sir, I think~~Obviously this secret is worth way more than just a billion dollars."

"There's more. ~~You know that inbound marketing team we created?~~"

~~"That happened two months before I was hired, sir. But yes. You acquired~~We've got a brain -trust ~~and brought all your market research in-house."~~

~~"They're not doing market research. They're trying to~~ positioning the company for the long game. We already know what the short-term future looks like. When the news breaks that this three-drug interaction extends the human lifespan, the entire product line will be nationalized by overwhelming popular demand, probably in a special legislative session. But before the United States does that, half a dozen other countries will already have deployed it within their national health care systems. We won't own any of it."

I nod. As predictions go, this makes perfect sense. There might be some small variations, but the end result ~~is the same~~sounds spot on.

"So," he continues, "the only way for us to make money is for us to be pre-positioned in other fields. That team is preparing us to capitalize on the disruptions introduced by an order-of-magnitude increase in human longevity."

"Oh, I get it. ~~We~~You're not ~~go~~planning to get rich selling immortality. ~~We~~You're going to get rich helping the ~~H~~human ~~R~~race make the transition to immortality."

"How valuable do you think this secret is?"

"In numbers? I ~~have no idea~~can't count that high. ~~But if a~~You don't need to be protected from competitors. ~~got wind of this strategy, no, if anybody got wind of the existence of this strategy, the information in this building, in our cloud, and in our heads would be too valuable to allow to go free. Those with the most resources to~~

~~spend on acquiring that information and destroying any competing copies would be forced to spend those resources~~You need to secure yourself against governments. They'll break all their own laws and empty their treasuries to control this, if they think they can."

"Exactly."

I shake my head sadly. "Sir, ~~I should resign. M~~my team is good, but if a sovereign state decides to pull a hostile takeover, the only thing we can do for you is shoot you before they have a chance to begin interrogating, and ~~we'd hesitate~~they'll probably just take us down before we see them coming. You need an army, and a bunker."

"~~You can't resign now. You know too much~~Those aren't realistic options."

"Oh, I know that. I'm already contemplating expanded perimeters, plainclothes agents, dead-man-switch alarms. And of course I'm even more concerned about why you pushed the panic button."

"Yes . . . about that. The intruder . . . I never described him to you."

"I figured you'd get around to it."

~~BONEYARD~~

~~"Go on."~~

~~"Well, if it's a side-effect then the company is gambling several billion dollars on a bet that is suddenly a lot less sure. But more importantly, you know that if the technology exists somewhere, anywhere, to allow someone to materialize and dematerialize here in your office, then the information here in your office is exactly where it would be used. But that would only happen if the secret was out, and was far enough out that somebody with very, very advanced technology had gotten wind of it."~~

~~Wollreich's eyes widen as I speak. A mixture of fright and incredulity, like he's been told a very believable ghost story.~~

~~"Cole, that sounds like science-fiction."~~

~~"You're the one cooking up the immortality drugs, sir," I say with a forced smile.~~

~~"There's a big difference between identifying a series of exploits in organic chemistry, and defying the laws of physics."~~

~~"I'm not a physicist, sir. Maybe it was a hologram, or an induced hallucination. My point stands. If somebody out there can do it, and the existence of this secret is out, your office is where they'd use it."~~

~~"Well . . . how do we proceed?"~~

~~"Address the most likely issue first. Get tested. I assume the private meeting with R&D each Tuesday morning is a physical?"~~

~~"It is. What do we do if I'm fine?"~~

~~"If you're fine, then somebody materialized in this room, or created the illusion of materializing. They had unknown means and unknown intent, but we can surmise that they did not want to be discovered by me or my team. I'll need some time to chew on that. Also, my team should introduce an additional external perimeter, and someone should remain with you at all times from here on out. I hope that's okay with you."~~

~~"Perfectly okay, Cole."~~
~~"Outstanding." I pause for a moment. I should have asked this next question earlier in this interview. "Sir, did you get a look at the guy?"~~
~~Wollreich locks eyes with me, and looks deep. I look back.~~
"~~Yeah.~~ It was Death."

\#

<u>I went into the Marines when I was eighteen, bright-eyed, broad-shouldered, and ready to save the world. Most of that idealism got sanded flat in Afghanistan, but in the intervening twenty years I've determined that I don't need to save the world. I just need to save good people. I started my own firm so I could be picky about my clients, and Sinclair Wollreich is the best man I've ever worked for.</u>

<u>Which is why I'm aching inside. The bug in Wollreich's office is a betrayal of trust, and I know that. He came clean with me, and I didn't come clean with him. I could have told him about the bug, but I didn't.</u>

<u>I did, however, get him to</u> ~~Wollreich~~ agrees to ~~an extended~~<u>a</u> physical the next day.

\#

I don't know how you go about testing to see if someone is prone to hallucinating, or if something's going wrong with their brain, but Tuesday morning's checkup runs into Wednesday with no breaks. ~~And me, or one of my people has~~<u>We've</u> had eyes on Wollreich~~, or his bedroom door,~~ ever since ~~the event Monday morning~~<u>he briefed me</u>, and <u>that's meant double shifts. Triple for me. I</u>~~i~~t's proving to be a bit of a strain.

It's six ~~AM~~<u>a.m.</u> on Wednesday. <u>Barry has just checked in to let me know Wollreich is sleeping in today. Sleeping in sounds nice, but personal security for our CEO now means securing where he's going to be, not just where he is.</u>

Mo and I are in the <u>second-floor</u> lobby having coffee with two other team members, Failalo and Jace. <u>We've got a nice view of the buildings that stand between us and the sunrise. We're not really securing anything right now, to be honest. We're hoping the sunlight will perk us up a bit.</u>

"How long are we going to keep <u>doing</u> this ~~up~~, Cole?" asks Failalo. She's ~~a~~ soft-spoken ~~Samoan woman with a wide jawline and crooked nose.~~<u>,</u> but n~~N~~obody shortens her name to "Fail" more than once.

"The extra shifts? Until HR and I can clear some more team members."

Mo sips at his coffee. "What's the holdup?"

"Well, if the event in Wollreich's office was enemy action, probative or otherwise, then we're up against somebody connected and equipped."

I've told my team that our boss saw an intruder, all in black, who then vanished. ~~The leading~~<u>Mo's</u> theory is that it was a hologram made with lasers, but none of us have the background to research that. I didn't tell them about<u> the</u> immortality drugs, or that our boss thinks he saw Death. And only Mo and Barry know about the camera we planted.

"Oh, I get it," says Failalo. "You think we're being played. Somebody's planted their own people am~~id~~<u>ong</u> our candidates. They shoot some lasers through the window to spook us, we beef up, and now they've got peeps on the inside."

"That's one scenario. They might also have our hiring pool bugged, tapped, and flagged on their end, so they can watch our background check process and find the holes in it. So yes, I'm concerned that somebody ~~push~~yanked our ~~panic button~~chain, and now we're reacting instead of acting."

"Don't go *Princess Bride* paranoid, boss," says Mo. "Both cups might be poisoned." He tosses back his coffee, swallows, then smiles broadly at me. "And there aren't enough of us for a land war in Asia."

I've always loved that scene. I used to imagine how I would have handled things if I'd been in Vizzini's shoes, and it was fun until I ~~realized that I wouldn't have taken that job in the first place~~finally figured out that he'd been outplayed from the start. If Westley didn't kill him, Humperdinck certainly would have.

My phone chirps. ~~I'm out of range for~~It's a text message from the ~~Bluetooth connection, so that~~ phony wall-plate ~~is texting me~~, an alert to let me know the feed is active ~~after-hours~~. The camera has seen something. The message looks innocent enough~~.~~: "SUP YO. GO 4 EATSZ?"

Mo's smile flattens. "Somebody miss breakfast?" He knows the codes.

"Upstairs, now. Mo, you're with me in the service elevator. Failalo, Jace, take a lobby elevator to ~~31~~thirty-one, then take the west stairs to forty." I drop a ten on our table to take care of the barista who usually doesn't have to clean up after us.

On our way to the ~~service~~ elevator, Mo places a call. "Hey, Sal. Mohammed here. Check electrical~~,~~ and find out if the lights just went on in Wollreich's office."

Good thinking. Building security ~~doesn't~~may not have cameras in ~~there~~Wollreich's office, but there is a motion-detector on his light-switch, and ~~our electrical system~~the company monitors usage ~~as part of some~~for conservation ~~plan~~purposes.

"Got it. Thanks." He turns to me as we reach the elevator. "Lights just went on. ~~Lights are~~They're still out in the anteroom and the west hallway. Whoever turned on the office lights didn't walk in the usual way. Also, the cameras on the rest of the floor haven't seen anybody since Wollreich ~~went up~~left with Barry ~~to drop stuff in his office~~ at ~~3~~three a.m."

I key the elevator for ~~an~~ nonstop ride. The illuminated numbers count up quickly. Mo and I are silent, but we're both listening.

At ~~40~~forty the elevator doors slide open. That motion sets off the detectors, and the hallway lights come up.

Mo moves to step out, but I stop him. Somebody got onto this floor~~,~~ and into Wollreich's office, and we know nothing about them. They got here first, and might be expecting us. Maybe they spoofed the cameras and the motion detectors, but we can't ~~do that. As the hall lights just demonstrated, a~~nywhere we go the lights will come up, so we can't be stealthy.

Then again, what~~o~~ever spooked Wollreich the first time vanished pretty quickly, perhaps because ~~it was~~they were afraid of us. If we're slow~~,~~ we'll miss ~~it~~them, and if ~~it's~~they're afraid of us, that might mean we've got ~~it~~them outgunned.

Or maybe both cups are poisoned. Ah, Vizzini, how I hate being you. Just once I want to be the guy with the ~~l~~iocaine immunity and the winning plan.

"We go fast. Straight to the office, then standard entry."

Mo <u>nods,</u> and ~~I~~<u>we</u> both draw and begin to run, weapons held low in two-handed grips. We run through two hallway intersections without clearing them properly, and each time I worry that I'm being a reckless idiot. But nobody shoots at us, and those intersections light up to the north and south, so nobody else came that way recently.

<u>We reach the office.</u> Through the frosted glass the anteroom is dark. Not full-dark, ~~because it's got big~~ <u>thanks to</u> west-facing windows, but it's oh<u>-</u>six fifteen. I hear a soft <u>"</u>~~"~~tick<u>"</u>~~"~~ as the lock<u>-</u>pad ~~next to the door~~ reads my badge and unlocks ~~things for me~~<u>the anteroom door</u>.

I'm in first, pushing the door open and sweeping with it to the left as the lights come up.

"Clear," says Mo.

"Clear."

"~~TING~~<u>Ting</u>," says my phone. Bluetooth connection, with data streaming in. We can look at that later.

I key in my code for the door to Wollreich's office. <u>No frosted glass here, and the door is soundproofed. No way to know what's on the other side.</u>

<u>__</u>Tick. I grab the handle and pu~~ll~~<u>sh</u> the door open, ~~for~~<u>sweeping left while</u> Mo<u>,</u> ~~who~~ goes to the <u>right</u>~~left~~ in the brightly<u>-</u>lit office. ~~I go right.~~

"Clear," says Mo.

"And empty," I say. Not that I expected to find anybody here, not really.

Mo steps to the corner of the room where our cam dot should be. "It's still there."

"I'm pretty sure there's no point sweeping the rest of the floor." I holster my weapon. "Let's see if the camera saw anything."

I pull out my phone. Swipe, code, and then a tap on the spy<u>-</u>app, whose icon looks like the one for a pizza place. I respond to the "ZIP CODE" prompt with an eleven-digit pass~~phrase~~<u>code</u>, and up comes the video file. ~~I push play~~<u>PLAY</u>.

The video begins with the room ~~dark, but it's not full-dark because of those west-facing~~ <u>lit only by the brightening sky through the</u> windows. Then a human-sized shadow dissolve-wipes into existence in the middle of the room, backlit by th~~o~~<u>se</u> windows so I can't make out any details the moment it appears, but the lights come up very quickly.

"Holy shit," says Mo.

Hooded and all in black, the stereotypical, iconic representation of Death, complete with a scythe, stands in the middle of the office~~,~~ and turns to face the camera.

#

We've got my phone ~~configured to~~ <u>'</u>cast<u>ing</u> video to the wall screen by the time M~~ister~~<u>r.</u> Wollreich arrives in his office with Barry on his heels. Wollreich is flushed, there are bags under his eyes, and he's angry. Barry has all the expression of a granite bust, which means Wollreich has been chewing him out on the way over here.

"Cole, how long have you been spying on me?"

"Since Monday morning, sir. I'm sorry, but it seemed prudent."

"Prudent? After the lecture you gave me about the value of secrets? Spying on me is a lot of things, but prudent is not one of them."

"With all due respect, sir, you called us in a panic, then lied to us. I made a snap decision in order to ensure that my team and I could keep you safe. ~~I'm standing by it, and~~"

   "How come you didn't tell me about it later?"

   "Guilty conscience, sir. But I think you should watch this before we continue to discuss the matter."

"Fine."

I push PLAY, and Death appears on-screen.

Wollreich gasps. "That's him. Hot damn, Cole, you got him!"

I push PAUSE.

"We did, sir, but he's about to start talking, and he talks fast. You really need to listen to this."

Wollreich nods, and I push PLAY.

Death is facing the camera, and begins to speak.

"Sinclair Wollreich and . . . friends," he begins. The voice is deep, ~~male, and~~so it sounds masculine, but it's almost musically artificial, like somebody auto-tuned Christopher Lee. "You must immediately cancel your organization's life extension plans. Further, you must destroy the information related to it. Otherwise human beings will lose all access to the eternal realms."

Mo and I have already watched the whole thing. ~~Then~~ I had to explain to Mo that yes, the company was going to be extending human life. I watched it a second time while Mo called Barry and told him to get the boss in here. Right now I'm watching Wollreich, who is sneering and eyerolling, giving the screen his "this-is-bullshit" face.

"The human spirit, or soul, is a turbulent waveform. At death, this turbulence allows the waveform to imprint across the boundary wave, transducing the wave to an eternal state with minimal degradation. As humans grow older, however, the turbulence is reduced. Some very old humans fail to imprint. Their original waveforms cease. In your terms, this means they die forever. Should human lives be extended to more than a century, very few humans will imprint successfully, and eternal life will be denied to your race."

Wollreich's "this-is-bullshit" face gives way to deep concern.

"You have the ability, Sinclair Wollreich, to end this project and save humans eternally. Act swiftly."

Death vanishes. A moment later, ~~Mo and I can be heard entering the anteroom, and then~~ the video shows ~~us~~Mo and me bursting through the office door. Mo reaches up to check the camera, and the image freezes because I've pushed STOP.

Wollreich is leaning against his desk, arms folded, head down.

"Cole, could this have been faked?"

"Probably. I'm not a video expert. But the second time I watched it I looked out the window. There's a cloud that remained unchanged between the Death part and the part where Mo and I arrived. We could probably match that to other cameras in the building."

Wollreich straightens up.

"Is that the only copy of the video?" he asks as he points at my phone.

"There's a copy in the transmitter, too."

"And one in the cache on the wallscreen," says Mo. "That one's in dynamic allocation, though. Might already be gone."

"Bring me the transmitter, and then we're all waiting in here for the ~~experts~~brain trust."

#

Wollreich's office is big~~, but~~. Even with nine of us ~~it's starting to~~in here it doesn't really feel crowded. Tense, yes, but not crowded. Three members of ~~that special "marketing~~the genius team~~"~~ have arrived, and one of them has video tools ~~o~~in hand. Two senior members of R&D are here as well, and they're both scientist_-types, complete with the lab coats. Wollreich, Mo, Barry, and I are the only ones in suits.

We've all watched the video.

"This is spaghetti-monster stuff," says Kurtzman, one of the labcoat guys. "It's non-falsifiable. We can't test any of what he told us. Sure, it sounds convincing because he used words like waveform and transducing, but there's no science in here for us to ~~help with~~check."

"Sure there is," says Michel. He~~'s the marketing guy with the black hardcase~~ opens his case of video tools. "I need to see the camera, though."

Mo pulls it down from the corner of the room and passes it to Michel. It's about the size of a pencil eraser.

Michel turns it over in his hands and squints at it.

"Yup! We have science. This camera sees in broad-spectrum. The transmitted video is standard HD, but the raw file has some goodies in it." He takes the transmitter from the table, jacks a cable into it, and bends over his equipment. "This'll take a few minutes."

Wollreich turns to Kurtzman.

"The statements Death made are non-falsifiable, yes. We have no way to prove or disprove any of what we were told. Due diligence suggests that we at least consider the information, and that's why you're here."

"Can we ~~not refer to~~call him a~~something besides~~ Death, please?" says Kurtzman. "That costume he was wearing was part of the message, and if we accept it at face value, we're undermining our ability to evaluate any of this. Oh, and for the record, I think it's a crank, and what we should be doing is grilling the hired guns."

When the boss is in a meeting I only speak when spoken to. My job is to be invisible. Under the current circumstances, that's not going to work well.

"Grill away, ~~Mister~~. Kurtzman," I say.

"~~DOCTOR~~*Doctor* Kurtzman."

"My apologies, ~~D~~doctor. But please, grill us. Ask us anything. From your perspective, my team and I are your prime suspects. From our perspective, we need to get cleared as quickly as possible so that we're free to continue doing our jobs."

"I've already got an independent agency running deep checks on you, Cole," says Wollreich. "Your whole team, in fact. They've been doing it since Monday, when I brought you into the fold."

"Outstanding, sir."

Kurtzman looks stymied.

"And ~~Doctor~~ Kurtzman," Wollreich continues, "~~I think~~ you're absolutely right. We don't call our intruder 'Death' anymore. He is ~~T~~the Intruder."

"I'm not quite sure how this video plays into any corporate espionage scenario," says Lee, a stout woman in khakis and a Hawaiian print shirt. "I haven't plugged any of this into our X-form, but I shouldn't have to. The payoffs and strategies, the incentive matrix . . . those don't change. This event, this monologue, it should align itself with existing player strategies, and it does not."

"~~Doctor~~ Lee is a game theorist," says Wollreich. "Without the jargon now, ~~D~~doctor?"

"The X-form assumes rational and informed agents in the access tier. An irrational, uninformed agent might adopt the dress-like-death tactic in hopes of a payoff, but . . ."

"I said without the jargon."

"She means," says Michel, "that we're either dealing with an irrational, uninformed person with a stupid agenda, but who has access to our plans, or there are payoffs missing from the matrix."

"There aren't any payoffs missing," says Lee.

"Let's come back to that," says Michel. "I have more video for you to watch."

He gestures at the screen. "This is the original image, with an overlay of neon-green representing UV frequencies all the way to the edge of the camera's range."

On the wall-screen the video begins again, muted. It looks exactly the same as before, except a green shimmer appears in the middle of the room. It brightens, and then flashes as ~~T~~the Intruder appears. It then fades to a low shimmer again, surrounding his form as he speaks. The flash occurs again when he vanishes.

"Michel, what does that mean?"

"It means that ~~T~~the Intruder's appearance and disappearance were accompanied by UV emissions."

"Michel," says Lee, "those speakers in your office, the ones that build the audible cone out of interference patterns? Could somebody make a hologram by doing that with light? Like, ultraviolet lasers bouncing off each other just right to make a picture?"

The hologram thing. That was Mo's theory. I look at Mo, and he smirks.

"Maybe," says Michel, "but did you notice how there wasn't any green in the sky outside the window, or in the sunrise reflections on the buildings across the street? These windows filter UV. Any laser that tried to beam UV through them would have to cut the glass to do so."

"Then how did the UV get into the room?"

"Obviously it came with ~~T~~the Intruder," Michel answers. "But what you really want to see is the infrared. Watch this. No UV this time. I'm only going to play the infrared channel."

The picture returns, and now it's a monochromatic green.

Several of us gasp when the intruder appears. Including me.

I've seen infrared video of people before, and most folks have at least seen it simulated in movies. This is not that.

The form under the cloak is clearly outlined, and asymmetrical. The torso is short, and high. The legs are too long, and appear to bend the wrong way. If there's a left arm, it's not showing up. The right arm reaches all the way to the floor, then up to head-height, where it ends in the scythe blade.

But the cloak itself is the freakiest part. Lacy networks of veins are visible throughout it, and they all connect to the torso, the scythe-limb, and the legs. It's not clothing. It's a layer of skin, like a bat-wing, wrapped around the Intruder and hooding his face.

His? I see no male genitalia, but this thing is alien enough that I'm not ready to suggest that means it's female either.

Kurtzman speaks first.

"Michel, how hard would it be to fake that?"

"Not very hard. If the whole thing was computer animated and hacked into the camera feed, the infrared and ultraviolet elements would simply be another part of the model. It's the work of a real artist, though."

"Okay, good," says Kurtzman, blowing out a sigh of relief. "I'm going to choose to believe that this is a brilliant computer animation modeled by someone with an outstanding attention to anatomical detail."

"What would motivate that?" Lee asks. "Where is the payoff?"

"I'm going to let you figure that out, because I refuse to believe that an alien teleported into this office."

#

The brain trust begins yammering in jargon again.

It's esoteric jargon, but the gist of things is that somebody is looking at a different set of payoffs than we are, and without more information we have no way to deduce motivations. Lee has graphs that prove this. But even without this information nobody is seriously considering taking the Intruder's message about the afterlife at face value, and nobody seems willing to believe that the Intruder is an alien, or an angel, or anything other than a very complicated hoax.

Somebody needs to take the not-a-hoax angle. It's hard to think with all the noise, and technically I'm being paid to pay attention, not close my eyes and concentrate, but I close my eyes anyway.

If I were responsible for shepherding human souls into the afterlife, and I could teleport anywhere in the world, I'd go talk to the pope, or maybe the president. I'd offer evidence, and be as helpful as I could. Of course, appearing in those halls of power would be like begging to get shot. So I'd do what heads of state do, and find a way to make an appointment.

The Intruder is definitely not acting like I would. Maybe it can't teleport just anywhere. Maybe teleporting is difficult, dangerous, or expensive. Maybe the Intruder's brain is so different from mine that I can't figure out how it thinks. Except that line of thought is the same as giving up, so I'll throw that out, and keep assuming that if I knew more I could understand its motives.

I can spot a lie from somebody I know, but the Intruder is, frankly, alien. I can't tell if it's lying. Or at least I can't trust myself to spot the lie the easy way. But if I think this through, if I assume that the Intruder is a rational creature, then the way it delivered its message just reeks of subterfuge.

So if I assume that it's rational, I'm now assuming it's dishonest. If it's dishonest, what is it hiding? What does the lying accomplish?

If we believe the Intruder, then it will cost our company a lot of money, and it'll keep human lifespans from getting longer. From that perspective it's a lot like killing people. The Intruder is asking us to kill people. That's something I've got some experience with. Every day I remind myself that I might need to kill people who are trying to kill *my* people.

When I roll out of bed tomorrow morning and remind myself that I might have to kill someone, I should also consider where to aim if a one-armed, scythe-handed alien teleported into the room and tried to kill my boss.

That's actually something I can work on.

"Hey, Michel," I say, snapping out of my chair. "May I review the infrared again?"

"I'm busy trying to reverse-engineer the auto-tune effect on the voice, Mr. Cole."

"I'll do it," says Wollreich. "The play button is this one, right?"

Michel sighs in exasperation and fiddles with his kit. "There."

I look up at the screen, and there is the infrared image of the Intruder, the eerie vein pattern wrapped around it, with other green patches showing the limbs and the head. The intensity varies, steadily pulsing in some places, gradually shifting around in others. Human forms do the same thing in infrared, only without the vein-riddled cloak.

Like a human, the Intruder's head stays fairly bright. The distribution of heat is a little different, but it still looks like a head.

Then, just before the Intruder vanishes, a bulbous shape near its second elbow brightens and then fades quickly to black.

"That spot there!" I say, pointing. "What was that?"

Michel rewinds and pauses. "The cold patch?"

"Yeah. It was hot a few frames back."

Michel rewinds further. "Oh. So it is."

"I've never seen that happen before in infrared. Usually when something cools off you can see the heat migrating to surrounding tissues."

"Obviously," says Kurtzman, "the heat went into hyperspace where we can't see it. Now can you please go stand guard in your corner? Or maybe outside. You're making me nervous."

"Mo, I've got this," I say, stepping back into my corner. "Go put some coffee into Barry."

Mo nods, and he and Barry slip out.

Despite his sarcasm, Kurtzman made a good point. The elbow hot spot dumped heat someplace, and then the Intruder disappeared. "Hyperspace" is as good an answer as any. More importantly, I have the answer I was looking for. The Intruder's head emits steadily the same way a human head does. If I shoot the way I've practiced, a double-tap to the center of mass, and then a single shot to the head, that should work.

~~-~~Michel has begun lecturing Kurtzman and Lee on what can and cannot be hacked in the camera and the transmitter~~seems to think that it's possible for the camera's tiny transmitter to have been hacked, so that the images arriving at the larger wall transceiver were different than what actually happened in this office.~~, and what kind of supporting hardware would be required in the various scenarios.

—It's interesting, ~~but I'm~~ and I can actually follow most of it, but what I should be doing is a threat assessment~~, and it's distracting. I do threat assessments all the time, they're part of my job, but right now I'm assessing the threat to Mo, Barry, and I, and our jobs. I know that we didn't fake anything, or take part in any fakery, but I can't expect the scientists and game theorists~~ regarding a teleporting alien. Just in case.

Not that anyone else in here ~~to take our word for that. It's only going to be~~ is likely to think that's a good use of my time. The brain trust still thinks this is a hoax of some sort, and I suspect I've only got a few minutes before they ~~determine that a hack on the camera's feed is only likely or manageable if the~~ come back around to grilling—

"Mister~~.~~ Cole," says Michel. "Where did you acquire your spy gear?"

~~—Grilling Mo's team. How was the camera hacked? Get a forensic computing expert in here to look at the file. Account for Mo and Cole's movements during the last two weeks. Mo, Barry, and Cole surrender their weapons. (How paranoid is paranoid enough?)~~

~~—The alien plan— Once personal security is disarmed, the aliens are free to attack, and everybody is in the same room. If security is NOT disarmed it's probably because the message is being taken seriously. Win. Actually, the most likely scenario is that the message is disregarded. What would the aliens do then? Plan B is harvest humans directly.~~

Okay, then. Less time than I thought.

"Handbrains & Hi-Def, it's an electronics boutique uptown. Mostly they sell smartphones and surround-sound systems, but the owner is ex-CIA, and he's a friend of mine. He sells custom equipment like this out of his apartment upstairs."

"And you just happened to have this equipment on you on Monday?"

"No. I bought it thirteen months ago when I started feeling uneasy about the fact that this office was unmonitored. Then I felt guilty for buying it, so I told Mo to carry it. Then Mr. Wollreich lied to us about why he pushed the panic button, and I had Barry distract Mr. Wollreich while Mo planted the camera in the corner."

"Thirteen months? You've been planning to bug my office for over a year?" Wollreich is turning red.

Oh. If I had that bug for a year I can see how the hacking story would start to look good.

This is difficult to explain, but it's not the first time I've had this kind of conversation.

It's never pleasant.

"I plan a lot of things, sir. Every morning I get out of bed and I plan to shoot someone. I don't know who that someone is, but in my mind's eye they're trying to assault you, or perhaps shove you into a van. My life revolves around planning to do things I would really rather not have to do, but which I will do, without hesitation, to keep you safe. I carry a loaded weapon, as does every member of my team. I'm fifteen pounds lighter than I look because some of my upper-body bulk is a twelve-hundred-dollar undershirt that will allow me to intercept a bullet on your behalf and still come in to work the following week. So yes, I planned to bug your office, but I didn't plant the bug until it seemed important."

Wollreich stares at me, and I stare back.

Lee speaks first, and she sounds shaken. "You have a gun in here? In this office?"

I don't look away from Wollreich when I answer her. "I do, Dr. Lee. I'm sorry if that makes you uncomfortable."

And then it occurs to me that as a game theorist, she's been doing a threat assessment, same as me, only with math, and the numbers are telling her that the biggest threat in the room right now is me.

I look away from Wollreich, losing that staring contest on purpose. I slump my shoulders just a little bit, a trick a bouncer friend showed me for those times when you want to look less dangerous than you really are. I pull a chair away from the wall and sit down. Everybody is looking at me nervously.

"Yes, you can explain the video by pinning it on me and Mo, but there's no good reason for us to have done that, and that still doesn't account for what your CEO saw." I look up at Wollreich.

He's still red-faced. Angry about the bug, and probably angry at his colleagues for not believing he saw what he said he saw. He might have started doubting it himself.

"Cole," he says. "Humor them and wait outside, please."

I nod, and slip through the door. Wollreich clears his throat, a sure sign that he's about to start in on somebody, but the soundproof door shuts and I miss the show.

Wollreich knows my team and I didn't do this, doesn't he? I'm not out here because he doesn't trust me, though that trust did take a beating when I bugged the office. No, I'm out here because I look dangerous, even slouching, and Wollreich needs his geniuses to relax.

I understand. Armed people make everybody nervous. Hell, even the Intruder was careful not to be there when Mo and I arrived. It timed the whole speech perfectly. Smart.

How smart, though? Can it predict our behavior? Has it been observing us, and learning about us? If so, it must know that Wollreich's team won't just shut the project down. It might even know that they'd blame me and my team, and shoo us out of the office to the far side of the soundproof doors. . . .

Both cups are poisoned.
I draw my pistol and turn for the office door.
"Everybody, my position."
It doesn't matter what the brain trust decides. What matters is that they gather where they can be separated from their security. And if I'm wrong? I hope I am wrong, really.
I fumble the number on the keypad and get an angry beep. That's something I should have practiced more.
"Roger. All call to forty. Hang in there, boss." Right in my ear.
I fumble the number again, adding a forty right in the middle. I definitely should have practiced this more.
On my third attempt the door unlocks with a *click*. Weapon up, I throw the door open to the sound of screaming.
There is a shadow in the middle of the room, a shadow swinging a scythe.
The Intruder is ready for me, lunging. That scythe is swinging my way, and I have no doubts at all regarding its lethality. But unlike that damned keypad this is something I've trained myself to do. I focus on the center of mass, and squeeze off my first shot.
The Intruder staggers at the impact, lunge interrupted. My pistol returns to position, the recoil compensated for by rehearsed reflex.
I squeeze off the second shot just as the scythe swings into view, missing my face by inches. The round strikes the elbow joint, which explodes in light and sound, like a flash-bang grenade, but made out of purple and bells.
It's not blinding or deafening, but as I squeeze off my third shot, the headshot, I realize that my target is not where it was supposed to be. The Intruder has tucked and crumpled into a dark heap, and my third shot spalls into the bulletproof glass of the window.
I step into the room, sweeping for threats. Wollreich is crouched behind the end of his desk, the opposite end from where the panic button is concealed. Michel is under a chair in the corner. Kurtzman, Lee, and the two biologist types are all sprawled unmoving and bloody on the floor.
"Cole! What—"
Wollreich is cut off by a burst of static noise, and by more screaming as the room starts to fill with shadows.
I dive toward Wollreich and feel a tug at the collar of my suit. The shadows resolve into two more Intruders, scythes swinging.
My Glock 30 has a ten-round magazine. Seven of those rounds remain. I double-tap the nearest Intruder, and then put a third round through its pale face. It drops. I hip-check Wollreich to the ground as I spin toward the second, only to find a third much closer, the one whose scythe must have grazed my suit collar.
Double-tap, and one to the face. That one's down too.
Taking nothing but headshots is a trick for video game junkies. That's not what I've trained for, but the last Intruder's pale, dinner-plate-size face is an easier target than its shadow-shrouded center of mass, and I only have one round left.

I focus on that face as the Intruder rushes me, and then I fire. Its head rocks back, those weird arm and leg joints splay out almost spiderlike, and then it drops motionless.

I eject the empty magazine and reload. Reflex. I step around the table. Wollreich and Michel are fine, but the other four are slashed up and lie completely still. They look cold, like they've been dead for hours under the fresh blood. Those scythes must do more than just cut.

"My God, Cole . . . How did you know?"

"Strong hunch, but I didn't know anything. I was ready for you to fire me for barging in."

There is another burst of static. It's coming from the shuddering lump of darkness that is the original Intruder. That's right, I missed its head. But I did hit something important, because it hasn't teleported out of here.

I step over to it and put my foot on the scythe blade.

"Who are you and what do you want?"

There's more static, and then it clears and we're back to an auto-tuned Christopher Lee.

"We are the Angels of Death. We shepherd you to—"

"Oh, shut *up!*" says Wollreich. "You're no shepherd! You murdered four people!"

I still don't have a read on this thing, but I'm pretty sure it's lying.

"Talk," I say, gesturing with my pistol.

It hisses with static, and then speaks.

"We number in the millions. Your deaths sustain us. Our population has grown with yours, alongside yours. If you stop dying, we starve. If we cannot pick up fallen fruit, we will have to shake the tree."

It's telling the truth. I'm sure of it. Maybe there's more to my gift than the ability to read facial cues.

"You're done shaking trees. We know you're out there," Wollreich says.

"You know nothing. We can strike anywhere, at any time. We can see you, from our side. There will be a brief, bloody war, and then we will shepherd the rest of you more carefully. This will not be the first time we have culled in order to feed."

"Except this time you tried to negotiate," I say. "There are a lot of us, and we're smarter and tougher than we've ever been. You tried diplomacy and subterfuge because war is expensive."

I should know. I was in Afghanistan, fighting an actual land war in Asia. I smile.

Failalo shouts into my headset. "Cole! Intruders in the data center! They look like Death, sir."

I can hear gunshots in the background. Gunshots and screaming. "Grab your stuff and stay with me, gentlemen," I say to Wollreich and Michel. "We're not done."

This war is going to be more expensive than the one in Asia, but I think this time I may actually get to save the world.

Writing An Honest Death

HOWARD TAYLER

It started with an idea. What if something perched, like a predator, between human beings and the afterlife? What if it fed on us as we went toward the light? What if that trip was actually dangerous?

Then, of course, I began thinking about the ecology of such a system, and how these predators would die off if we made a leap forward in life extension.

We brainstormed that idea a bit during Writing Excuses Season 8 Episode 9, and my first draft of the story had the CEO as the viewpoint character. It was kind of tongue-in-cheek, and began as follows:

> When the guy dressed as Death showed up in my office I did what any sensible person would do. I punched the "security" button on my comm center and said "eviction, please." I hadn't seen how the costumed freak got in, but I was going to watch him leave.

But the farther in I got, the less compelling the protagonist was. CEOs are very interesting people, but a large portion of their work involves thinking and then talking to people, so this story was going to end up being all dialogue, and was feeling kind of expository. Kind of like "Hey, I had this clever idea, and my CEO character is here to tell you about it."

So I drafted it again with the bodyguard as the viewpoint character, and suddenly I had solutions to several problems. First, I no longer needed to be as smart as a CEO who is managing a brain trust of expert futurists. Second, I now had somebody onscreen who had a reason to have stuff explained to him. And third, I had guns.

This volume contains a draft of the story which did not yet have its ending in place. We critiqued that version during Writing Excuses Season 9 Episode 31 (for which you also have a transcript), and the upshot of all that stuff is that when I reached the end of that draft I still had a problem. Specifically, I had no reason for the Intruder to ever be honest. Nobody was in place who would explain my spooky Death-as-a-predator idea to the reader, and that had been the whole point of the story.

And that, ultimately, was what led to the fix. I began working backward. Why would the Intruder spill the beans? Possibly because it was injured and angry. But if it were injured, why wouldn't it teleport home? Probably because its teleporting widget got damaged.

So I wrote the Intruder's closing dialogue. From there I began reverse engineering the Intruder's actual plan, which I'd already figured had to do with getting all of the right people in one room, but which didn't seem to scan correctly until I began thinking about just how expensive a war is.

From there I had two more hurdles to clear. The first was our main character's motivation, and the second was the order of events that led to him leaving the room. I'll start with that second one: the solution was simple. I grabbed a couple of blocks of text and moved them earlier in the story, and then wordsmithed the seams. The motivation though, that was more difficult.

Then I remembered something a friend of mine told me about his decision to join the military, and his disillusionment upon leaving. That rang true, and the moment I wrote the words "save the world" in Cole's mini-biography I knew I had the payoff for my ending. All I had to do then was tie it to something in the middle, and oh! A land war in Asia was waiting right there for me.

The process I've described here seems like the sort of thing that should have taken about a week for 7,500 words. Thanks to the despair inherent in the realization that a story is broken forever and cannot be saved but my friends need it for the anthology and maybe I could write something else but that's cheating and this is so haaaaard... thanks to that, "An Honest Death" took about eighteen months to go from idea to finished product. The writing sessions where I broke through the blocks and fixed things? Those lasted about four hours each.

Making it look easy means never showing you this face.

The Making of Sixth of the Dusk

Writing Excuses 8.16

Brainstorming with Brandon

Brandon: I want to try brainstorming another story for me to write, using something from the writing prompt at the end of last week's episode: "psychic birds." The idea of a little bird that you keep on your shoulder—that gives you some sort of psychic or magical bonus because of how it evolved—is fascinating to me. We mentioned keeping away hunters. When the bird is on your shoulder, the hunters that sense for empathy, emotion, or mental thoughts can't find you; you're invisible to them. I also thought of all sorts of other birds, such as ones that give you ESP to let you see when your eyes are closed—different breeds of birds on a planet where humans have landed. Where can we go with that? We need a plot.

Mary: The way I approach things like this is to first do a little bit of worldbuilding. You've already got some of how they're used, but who's going to be most at jeopardy from this? I start tossing out things like: You're going to have bird trainers. You'll have bird breeders, users, brokers. You're going to have a restaurant owner who has to deal with people coming in with birds that will poop on the floor. I just start tossing this type of thing out there.

Brandon: So, I'm interested in an explorer who has a psychic bird. I like the idea that this is a frontier sort of thing.

Dan: When you talked about human settlers who have landed on a planet and have adopted these native birds, the first place my mind went was: Do the birds still work when you take them off the planet, and do they then become a galactic commodity that everybody wants?

Mary: Yes, or do they need group collective in order to work?

Howard: We've got a frontier planet where for the last fifteen years we've had an explosion in the proliferation and use of these birds. How do the birds feel about this? Part of our story is the discovery that there is a bird collective intelligence. I don't want to say hive mind, but maybe it's similar to that. Up until now the collective intelligence has felt, "Cooperating with humans and helping humans is good because our numbers are increasing. You're helping us keep predators away by adding to our senses. But now something that you're doing is not good for us."

Brandon: That's a very cool way to go. I want them to be animal intelligence—I'm just going to throw that out there. I really do like the idea of "Can they work off planet?" and maybe saying, "No, they can't right now," but there is a lot of interest in "Can we get these things to work?"

Mary: So then you've got a trader who would be very interested in getting them to work.

Brandon: Yes, that's definitely a possibility there.

Dan: If you have the ESP bird or a mind-reader

bird, then whatever galactic government you have, everybody is going to want one of those.

Mary: So we've got a couple of possible characters there. The next question to ask is, what are the implications of this?

Brandon: That's going to depend on the scope. For some reason I keep trying in my head to push this toward fantasy, even though we've talked the whole time as if it's science fiction.

Dan: Going back to fantasy, I love the idea that one person could have several birds, but they can only pick one at a time. So they would have a dovecote or something where they keep twenty different birds and have to choose, "Which one am I going to slot into this mixture?"

Howard: Another possibility is that for whatever reason, you can only have one bird at once, and yet there is somebody who has managed two birds. The second bird is psychically unlinked, but will psychically link to somebody who's standing close to you, and give you the ability through your bird to read minds. So we have somebody who has broken the rules and has become the worst sort of spy.

Brandon: He's hacking your bird and you.

Howard: The second bird is a little pocket bird—it's a baby of the bird on his shoulder, which is why he's able to do this.

Brandon: I'm liking that a lot. Let's push this more fantasy. What if it's a "new world" sort of thing? We've discovered these birds. We can't get them shipped; they die if they leave the continent for some reason. So we can have that whole interplay. We could have an explorer trying to figure out where this new bird came from.

Dan: It could be just that there's a new breed of bird. If they're explorers, there could be another tribe or a city where they have bred this new kind of bird that none of the other colonists are aware of yet.

Brandon: Okay, what's our ending?

Mary: Personally I think you're jumping way, way—

Brandon: I build my books around endings. When we did the other brainstorming episodes with you, I was always jumping to "What's the ending? Where are we going?" And I couldn't really see the story until I saw how it ends.

Mary: Right, but one of the things that I was asking when I was saying, "What are the implications?" is that knowing those allows you to ask, "How can it get worse?" That then becomes "How can we resolve this? What are the possible endings?" One of the other things in looking at possible endings is, what do your characters want? I feel like if it were me doing this, I wouldn't have enough groundwork laid before I could start jumping to endings. I could have the ending be the bird dies. Or the bird lays a double-yolked egg and for the first time people can have two birds at once. Or the avian flu comes and you can no longer carry the bird because it's going to kill everybody. There's so many different endings.

Howard: You mentioned avian flu. Maybe our protagonist is a doctor and the bird helps her be a better doctor through recognizing the pain of the people around her. She can more accurately gauge where it hurts, and as a result is a fantastic doctor. Then we have a plague that is sweeping through the city and she is trying to figure out why people are getting sick, what the problem is. Our ending is the discovery that there is a parasite living in the bird poop, and we have to kill all our birds.

Brandon: That just sparked me on something else. What if what's giving them the psychic power is not the birds but the parasite? So the twist is that we're using the birds like a parasite. We're symbiotic with the bird, but this has already happened. The birds figured it out first—it's the worms that the birds eat. The story can be that when we first catch these birds in the wild it's great. We get all these powers, but then the ones we raise—

Mary: Don't have the power.

Howard: The ones we raise don't work.

Brandon: The explorers all think, "Oh, it must be something about the bird society," and he's out trying to find that. And the ending is that it's the worms, and if we just give ourselves the worms we could actually—

Mary: We don't need those birds.

Brandon: But then he wonders, "Do I tell people, because the birds are cute and awesome!" I think that's a cool ending right there, because it plays up the theme of the symbiosis. We've created the symbiotic relationship that people love their birds, but—

Dan: It's really the worms the birds have.

Brandon: Let's explore this more now. In my mind we have a rudimentary plot. This is what's going to happen. Where that ending goes I still don't know, but that's fine. Whether it is that he or she discovers this and doesn't want to tell people. I want to work into it that it is a real moral quandary. Maybe we should talk about who the character is. What suggestions do we have? I like the explorer aspect. The question I end up with is that I don't know if I want a solitary person out there talking to the bird. Maybe I do.

Mary: The trapper that goes out by himself, that's a standard in pretty much every culture. Instead of just having him out by himself all the time, there is the outpost that he returns to. The trading post.

Howard: There is also a dynamic to consider, since you only have one bird. If you give him a human companion who has a bird that does something completely different, you get to explore the differences between the ways they interact with their psychic creatures.

Brandon: Or he meets a trapper from a rival company. They say, "Let's work on this together because it's for the good of the birds." Since we're following the process of brainstorming, at this point I am now kind of excited about the story. I'm saying, "Ooooh," but now I'm looking for extra coolness. So then I say, "Let's look at my setting." How can I make the setting interesting and cool? What can be distinctive about it? I don't want the setting to just be something generic. Even in a short story, I want it to be something that you read and say, "That's a different take on this setting." I want to be doing that with character also. The plot feels original to me, so where could we set this? What is this planet like? What can be interesting about it?

Dan: Lots of cool and interesting birds suggests jungle to me, at least in part. Jungle or Pacific Islands. Which could be really fun, as this is almost an archipelago type of situation.

Brandon: Ooooh, archipelago. That's cool!

Howard: Lots of little boats.

Mary: This also raises the question, if the worms are something that can infect people and give them the same ability, then they would be able to do that to other creatures. So perhaps this archipelago is filled with poisonous creatures.

Brandon: That comes back to the original concept that the bird keeps the predators from finding me, and that's why we started using them. I would probably shoot even for an age of industry in this. We started colonizing this continent, and we just kept getting eaten by these big monster things, but they never ate the birds. We figured out that if we tamed the birds the monster things couldn't find us.

Dan: Or you take the symbiotic idea and say the local chimpanzees always kept pet birds, which we thought was really weird until we figured out what was going on.

Brandon: Yeah, chimps with pet birds is awesome! I love the archipelago idea. Could I do bird/fish hybrid? Could they swim and fly?

Mary: Well you know there is that whole BBC documentary about the flying penguins on April Fools' Day, but I don't see any reason you can't. There are plenty of flying birds that are also divers.

Brandon: I'm thinking about a bird of paradise that is like an amphibian, in this fantasy or science fiction world. Could we do that, or is that just too weird?

Dan: No, you could do that. But why do you want to do that? What would you gain other than just "Hey, cool thing."

Brandon: I'm looking for neat.

Dan: Which is totally a good reason to do it.

Mary: If I were going to do that, I would probably look at doing a chameleon hybrid, because the psychic ability is all about camouflage.

Brandon: The feathers change colors? That gets into "This is cute," which is also good when you're doing an animal story.

Howard: The challenge with birds as also fish is that fish are effective as fish because of neutral buoyancy. If you're neutrally buoyant in the water you fly like a brick, but ducks have ballast bags. There's a way to do this.

Brandon: Okay, let's stop talking about that and think of other cool aspects for this story.

Dan: What about other symbiotic pairings of animals? If the powers come from a worm on these islands, maybe it's not just the birds. Maybe one species of deer always has psychic snakes living in its antlers or something. There are different pairings.

Mary: Actually, there is a good reason to do the birds as fish, if the worms come from seafood. So you've got psychic fish, which are clearly not going to be useful as pets.

Howard: Well, they don't have to be fish birds, but aquatic birds that eat a lot of seafood.

Dan: The problem there is that if the worms get into the ocean, it's easier to spread them around and they could potentially be all over the world. If they're land-based, they're stuck on this series of islands.

Brandon: Yeah, they're stuck on the archipelago. The question is why didn't humans figure out about the worms yet? The answer could be that the archipelago is really, really dangerous. So, we go in, we capture a bunch of birds and bring them back. They work, but the offspring don't. I'm liking that. The cool monsters are also something I want to explore.

Mary: If it's not just an archipelago, but a volcanic one, then you have hot mud baths. You have swampy things and earthquakes, and that can be one of the things the birds warn you of.

Howard: Birds warn you of earthquakes and volcanoes. You take the birds back to the mainland and the birds manage to predict the supercaldera volcano in time to save civilization— Sorry. The book has just gotten bigger.

Dan: If this is an island empire here, a bunch of islands that are so dangerous. They're full of earthquakes and volcanoes and predators. One of your cool elements could be that the civilization that has grown up around here is all water-based like the junk cities around Hong Kong. They all live on boats, and the cities can move around the weather. It's only the trappers that can venture onto the island looking for more birds.

Brandon: Okay, we've got a really cool story here. I'm very pleased with this.

First Draft: Sixth of the Dusk

Brandon Sanderson

Death hunted beneath the waves. Sixth saw it approach, though its details were hidden by the waters. A shadow wider than six narrowboats tied together, an enormous deep blackness within the deep blue. Sixth's hands tensed on his paddle, his heartbeat racing as he immediately sought out Kokerlii.

Fortunately, the bird sat in his customary place on the prow of the boat, idly biting at one clawed foot raised to his beak. The colorful bird lowered his foot and puffed out his feathers, as if completely unmindful of the enormous shadow that approached.

Sixth held his breath. He always did, even still, when unfortunate enough to run across one of these things in the open ocean. He did not know what they looked like beneath those waves. He hoped to never find out.

The shadow drew closer, almost to the boat now. A school of thinfish passing nearby, jumped into the air in a silvery wave, spooked by the shadow's approach. The terrified fish showered back to the water with a sound like rain. The shadow did not deviate. The thinfish were too small a meal to interest it.

A boat's occupants, however . . .

It passed directly underneath. Sak chirped quietly from Sixth's shoulder; the second bird seemed to have some sense of the danger. Creatures like the shadow did not hunt by smell or sight, but by sensing the minds of prey. Sixth glanced at Kokerlii again. There was a reason most sailors clipped their Aviar's wings, or at least tied them down. Sixth spurned such practices. But at times like this, with a shadow passing directly beneath—so large that it could have swallowed his boat whole—he wondered.

The boat rocked softly, the jumping slimfish stilled. Waves lapped against the sides of the vessel. Had the shadow stopped? Hesitated? Did it sense them? Kokerlii's protective aura had always been enough before, but . . .

The shadow slowly vanished beneath. It had turned to swim downward, Sixth realized. In moments, he could make out nothing through the waters. Just that endless deep. He hesitated, then forced himself to get out his mask. It was a new device he had acquired only two supply trips back: a glass faceplate with some kind of leather—perhaps a sheep's bladder or stomach—on the sides. He placed it on the water's top and leaned down, looking into the waters. They became as clear to him as the water of an undisturbed lagoon.

Nothing. Just the blue deep. *Fool man,* he though, tucking away the mask and getting out his paddle. *Didn't you just think to yourself that you never wanted to see one of those?*

Still, as he started paddling again, he knew that he'd spend the rest of this trip feeling as if the shadow were down there, following him. Lurking in those endless depths. That was the nature of the waters. You never knew what lurked there. You probably didn't want to.

He continued on his journey, paddling his outrigger canoe and reading the lapping of the waves to judge his position. Those waves were as good as a compass for any trained in wayfinding. Once, they would have been good enough for any of the Eelakin, his people. Anymore, just the trappers learned the old arts. Though, even he *did* carry one of the newest compasses, wrapped up in his pack with a set of sea maps from the latest surveys. You could not stop times from changing, his mother said, any more than you could stop the surf from rolling.

It was not long, after the accounting of tides, before he caught sight of the first island. Sori was a small island in the pantheon, and the most commonly visited. Its name meant child; Sixth remembered well training on her shores with his uncle.

It had been long since he'd burned an offering to Sori, despite how well she had treated him during his youth. Perhaps a small offering would not be out of line. Patji would not grow jealous. One could not be jealous of Sori, the least of the islands. Just as every trapper was welcome on Sori, every other island in the pantheon was said to be affectionate of her.

Be that as it may, Sori did not contain much in the way of valuable game. Sixth continued rowing, moving down the archipelago his people knew as the pantheon. From a distance, this archipelago was not so different from the home islands of the Eelakin, now a three week trip behind him.

From a distance. Up close, they were very, very different. Sixth rowed past Sori and then her three cousins, the first of the closed islands. He had never set foot on them. In fact, he had not landed on many of the forty-some islands in the pantheon. A trapper chose one island and worked there all his life. To do otherwise was foolhardy.

He saw no other shadows beneath the waves, but he kept watch. Not that he could do much to protect himself. Kokerlii did all of that work as he roosted happily at the prow of the ship, eyes half-closed. Sixth had fed him seed before the approach. Kokerlii did like it so much more than dried fruit.

Nobody knew why beasts like the shadows only lived here, in the waters near the pantheon. Why not travel across the seas to the Eelakin islands or the mainland, where food would be plentiful and Aviar like Kokerlii were far more rare? Once, these had not been questions men asked. The seas were what they were. Those days had passed. Now, men poked and prodded into everything. They asked, "Why?" They said, "we should explain it."

Sixth shook his head, dipping his paddle into the water. That sound—wood on water—had been his companion for most of his days. He understood it far better than he did the speech of men.

After the cousins, most trappers would have turned north or south, continuing along the wings of the pantheon until reaching their chosen island. Sixth continued forward, into the heart of the archipelago, until a large shape loomed before. Patji, largest of the islands. It towered taller than any of the others, like a wedge rising from the sea. A place of inhospitable peaks, sharp cliffs, and deep jungle.

Hello, old friend, he thought. *Hello, father.*

Sixth raised his paddle and placed it in the boat. He sat for a time, chewing on fish from last night's catch, feeding scraps to Sak. The black-plumed bird ate them with an air of solemnity. Kokerlii continued to sit on the prow, chirping occasionally, now that they had approached. He would be eager. Sak never seemed to grow eager about anything.

Approaching Patji was not a simple task, even for one who trapped his shores. The boat continued its dance with the waves as Sixth considered which landing to make. Eventually, he put the fish away, then dipped his paddle back into the waters. Those waters were still deep and blue, despite the proximity to the island. Some members of the pantheon had sheltered bays and gradual beaches that one could wade in. Patji had no patience for such foolishness. His beaches were rocky, and the drop-offs from them were so steep that deep water began only a few steps out.

You were never safe on his shores. In fact, the beaches were the most dangerous part of a very dangerous place. There, not only could the horrors of the land get to you, but you were still within reach of the deep's creatures. Sixth's uncle had cautioned him about this time and time again. Only a fool slept on the shores of Patji.

The tide was with him, and he avoided being caught in any of the swells that would crush him against those stern rock faces. Sixth approached what passed for a beach on Patji's shores, a partially-sheltered expanse of stone crags and outcroppings. Kokerlii immediately fluttered off, chirping and calling as he flew toward the trees.

Sixth immediately glanced at the waters beneath. No shadows. Still, he felt naked as he hopped out of the ship and pulled it up onto the rocks, warm water washing against his legs. Sak remained in her place on Sixth's shoulder.

Nearby in the surf, Sixth saw a corpse bobbing in the water. *Beginning your visions early, my friend?* he thought, glancing at Sak. The Aviar usually waited until they'd fully landed before bestowing her blessing.

The black-feathered bird just watched the waves.

Sixth continued his work. The body he saw in the surf was his own. It told him to avoid that section of water. Perhaps there was a spiny anemone that would have trapped him, or perhaps a deceptive undercurrent. Sax's visions did not always show such detail, they gave only warning.

Sixth got the boat out of the water, then detached the floats, tying them more securely onto the main part of the canoe. Following that, he worked the vessel carefully up the shore, mindful not to scrape the hull on sharp rocks. He would need to hide the canoe in the jungle. If another trapper discovered it, Sixth would be trapped on the island for several extra weeks preparing his spare. That would—

He stopped as his heel struck something soft as he backed up the shore. He glanced down, expecting a pile of seaweed. Instead he found a damp piece of cloth. A shirt? Sixth held it up, then noticed other, more subtle signs across the shore. Broken lengths of sanded wood. Bits of paper floating in an eddy.

Those fools, he thought.

He returned to moving his canoe. Rushing was never a good idea on a pantheon island. He did step more quickly, however.

As he reached the tree line, he caught sight of his corpse hanging from a tree nearby. Those were cutaway vines lurking in the fern-like tree top. Sak squawked softly on his shoulder as he hefted a large stone from the beach, then tossed it at the tree. It thumped against the wood, and sure enough, the vines dropped like a net, full of stinging barbs.

They would take a few hours to retract back up. Sixth pulled his canoe over and hid it in the underbrush near the tree. Hopefully, other trappers would be smart enough to stay away from the cutaway vines—and therefore wouldn't stumble over his boat.

Before placing the final camouflaging fronds, Sixth pulled out his pack. Though the centuries had changed a trapper's duties very little, the modern world did offer its benefits. Instead of sandals, Sixth tied on sturdy boots. Instead of a simple wrap that left his legs and chest exposed, he wore thick trousers with pockets on the legs and a buttoning shirt to protect his skin against sharp branches or leaves. And, instead of a shark-toothed club, he bore a machete of the finest steel. His pack contained luxuries like a steel-hooked rope, a lantern, and a firestarter that created sparks simply by pressing the two handles together.

He looked little like the trappers in the paintings back home. He didn't mind. He'd rather stay alive. He left the canoe, shouldering his pack, machete sheathed at his side. Sak moved to his other shoulder. Before leaving the beach, Sixth paused, looking at the image of his translucent corpse, still hanging from unseen vines at the tree.

Could he really have ever been foolish enough to be caught by cutaway vines? Near as he could tell, Sek only showed him plausible deaths. He liked to think that most were fairly unlikely—a vision of what could have happened if he'd been careless, or if his uncle's training hadn't been so extensive.

Once, Sixth had stayed away from any place where he saw his corpse. It wasn't bravery that drove him to do the opposite now. He just . . . needed to confront the possibilities. He needed to be able to walk away from this beach knowing that he could still deal with cutaway vines. If he avoided danger, he would soon lose his skills. He could not rely on Sek too much.

Sixth turned and trudged across the rocks along the coast. Doing so went against his instincts—he normally wanted to get inland as soon as possible. Unfortunately, he could not leave without investigating the origin of the debris he had seen earlier. He had a strong suspicion of where he would find their source.

He gave a whistle, and Kokerlii trilled above, flapping out of a tree nearby and winging over the beach. His protection would not be as strong as it would be if he were close, but that shouldn't matter. The beasts that hunted minds on the island were not as large as the shadows of the ocean, and so long as Kokerlii remained somewhat close, Sixth and Sak would be invisible.

About a half hour up the coast, he found the remnants of a large camp. Broken boxes, fraying ropes laying half submerged in tidal pools, ripped canvas, broken pieces of wood that might once have been walls. Kokerlii landed on a broken pole nearby.

There were no signs of his corpse nearby. That could mean that the area wasn't immediately dangerous. It could also mean that whatever might kill him here would swallow the corpse whole.

Sixth trod lightly on wet stones, listening to the water lapping over the edges of the broken campsite. No. Larger than a campsite. Sixth ran his fingers over a broken chunk of wood, stenciled with the words *Northern Interests Trading Company*. A powerful mercantile force from his homeland.

He had told them. He had *told* them. Do not come to Patji. Fools. And they had camped here on the beach itself! Was nobody in that company capable of listening?

Sixth picked his way through the remnants of the camp. How long had it been? He stopped beside a group of gouges in the rocks, as wide as his upper arm, running some ten paces long. They led toward the ocean.

Shadow, he thought. *One of the deep beasts.* His uncle had spoken of seeing one once, from a distance. An enormous . . . something that had exploded up from the depths. It had killed a dozen krell who had been chewing on oceanside weeds before retreating into the waters with its feast.

Sixth shivered, imagining this camp on the rocks, bustling with men unpacking boxes, preparing to build the fort they had described to him. But where was their ship? The great steam-powered vessel with an iron hull they claimed could rebuff the attacks of even the deepest of shadows? Did it now defend the ocean bottom, a home for slimfish and octopi?

There were no survivors—nor even any corpses—that Sixth could see. The beach was too dangerous. He pulled back to the slightly-safer local of the jungle's edge. Here, he scanned the foliage, looking for signs that people had passed this way. This attack was recent, within the last day or so. The company really *had* beat him to the islands, despite his head start.

He'd been certain they'd listen to reason. A dozen different trappers had spoken to them. Fools! He absently gave Sak a seed from his pocket as he located a series of broken fronds leading into the jungle. So there were survivors. At least one, maybe as many as a half dozen. They had each chosen to go in different directions, in a hurry. Running from the attack.

Running through the jungles was a good way to get dead. These company types . . . they thought themselves rugged, they thought themselves prepared. They were wrong. He'd spoken to a number of them, trying to persuade as many of their 'trappers' as possible to abandon the voyage.

Well, these survivors were likely dead now. He should leave them to their fates. Except . . .

The thought of it, outsiders on Patji . . . Well, it made him shiver in something that mixed disgust and anxiety. They were *here.* It was wrong. These islands were sacred, the trappers their priests.

The plants rustled nearby. Sixth whipped his machete about, leveling it, reaching into his pocket for his sling. It was not a refugee who left the bushes, or even a predator. Not a common one, at least. A group of small, mouse-like creatures crawled out, sniffing the air. Sak squawked. She had never liked meekers.

Food? the three meekers sent to Sixth. *Food?*

It was the most rudimentary of thoughts, projected directly into his mind. Though he did not want the distraction, he did not pass up the opportunity to fish out some dried meat for the meekers. As they huddled around it, sending him gratitude, he saw their sharp teeth and the single, pointed fang at the tips of their mouths. His uncle had told him that once, meekers had been dangerous to men. One bite was enough to kill. Over the centuries, the little creatures had grown accustomed to trappers. They had minds, thoughts beyond that of dull animals. Almost, he found them as intelligent as the Aviar.

If they were intelligent, they could be trained. Perhaps. *You remember?* he sent them, through thoughts. *You remember your task?*

Others, they sent back gleefully. *Bite others.*

Once, they had been dangerous to men. Trappers ignored them. Sixth figured that maybe, one of these little beasts could provide an unexpected surprise for one of his rivals. He had been cultivating small groups of them across the island. They'd have been frightened of the company and its many people. But perhaps . . .

Have you seen an other? Sixth sent them.

Bite others! came the reply.

Intelligent . . . but not *that* intelligent. Sixth turned back to the forest. After a moment's deliberation, he found himself striking inland, following one of the refugee trails. He chose the one that made him the most nervous, the one that looked as if it would pass uncomfortably close to one of his own safecamps, deep within the jungle.

Sixth passed out of the sun and beneath the jungle's canopy. It was hotter here, despite the shade. Comfortably sweltering. Kokerlii joined him, winging up ahead to a branch where a few lesser Aviar sat chirping. Kokerlii towered over them, but sang at them with enthusiasm. An Aviar raised around people never quite fit back in among their own kind. The same could be said of a man raised around Aviar.

Sixth followed the trail left by the refugee, expecting to stumble over the man's corpse at any moment. He did not, though his own dead body did occasionally appear along the path. He saw it laying half-eaten in the mud or tucked away in a fallen log with only the foot showing. He could never grow too comfortable with Sak on his shoulder. That was one primary reason he preferred her to other Aviar.

It did not matter if Sak's visions were truth or fiction. The constant reminder of how Patji treated the unwary was enough. It kept Sixth alert, and that kept him alive.

He fell into the familiar, but not comfortable, lope of a pantheon trapper. Alert, wary, careful not to brush leaves that could carry biting insects, cutting with the machete only when necessary, let he leave a trail another could follow. Listening, aware of his Aviar at all times, never outstripping Kokerlii or letting him drift too far ahead.

The man he tracked did not fall to the common dangers of the island—he cut across game trails, rather than following them. The surest way to run across predators was to fall in with their food. The refugee did not know how to mask his trail, but neither did he blunder into the nest of the firesnap lizards, or brush the deathweed bark, or step into the patch of hungry mud.

Was this another trapper, perhaps? A youthful one, not fully trained? That seemed something the company would try. Experienced trappers were beyond recruitment; none would be foolish enough to guide a group of clerks and merchants around the islands. But a youth, who had not yet chosen his island? A youth who, perhaps, resented being required to practice only on Sori until his mentor determined his apprenticeship complete? Sixth had felt that way ten years ago, when nearing the end of his uncle's training.

So the company had hired itself a trapper at last. That would explain why they had grown so bold as to come, despite the council of men like Sixth.

But Patji itself? he thought, kneeling beside the bank of a small stream. It had no name, at least not one that Sixth had given it, but it was familiar to him. *Why would they come here?*

The answer was simple. They were merchants. The biggest, to them, would be the best. Why waste time on lesser islands? Why not come for the Father himself?

The refugee had stopped by the river. Sixth had gained time on the man . . . or, rather, the youth. Yes, that footprint: judging by the depth it had sunk in the mud, Sixth could imagine the boy's weight and height. Sixteen, perhaps. Certainly not fully grown. Could he be younger? Trappers apprenticed at ten, but he could not imagine even the company trying to recruit one so ill trained.

Perhaps two hours gone, Sixth thought, turning a broken stem and smelling the sap.

The boy's path continued on toward Sixth's safecamp. How? He had never spoken of it to anyone else. Perhaps this youth was apprenticing under one of the other trappers who visited Patji. One of them could have found his safecamp and mentioned it.

Sixth crossed the stream and continued. Each member of the pantheon supported a variety of trappers. In ten years on Patji, he had only seen another trapper in person a handful of times. On each occasion, they had both turned and gone a different direction without saying a word. It was the way of such things. Trappers would not attack one another directly unless defending a camp.

Of course, they *would* try to kill one another. They just didn't do it in person. Better to let Patji claim rivals than to directly stain one's hands with their blood.

This one, though . . . this one was making directly for Sixth's safecamp. If he really was a youth, he might not know the proper way of things. Perhaps he had come seeking help, afraid to go to one of his master's safecamps for fear of punishment. Or . . .

No, best to avoid pondering it too much. Sixth already had a mind full of spurious conjectures. He would find what he would find.

He finally approached his safecamp as evening settled upon the island. Two of his tripwires were cut. That was not surprising; those were meant to be obvious. He crept forward, passing the deathant crack in the ground. It had been stoppered with a smoldering twig. The nightwind fungi that Sixth had spent years cultivating here had been smothered in water to keep the spores from escaping, and the next two tripwires—the ones not intended to be obvious—were *also* cut.

Nice work, kid, Sixth thought. Someone really needed to teach the boy how to move without being trackable, though. The youth had left more footprints, broken stems, and other signs than a mainlander might have if—

"Um, hello?"

Sixth froze, then looked up.

A woman hung from the tree branches above, trapped in a net made of jellywire vines—they left someone numb, unable to move.

A woman, Sixth thought, suddenly feeling stupid. *The smaller footprint, lighter step . . .*

"I want to make it perfectly clear," the woman said. "I have no intention of stealing your birds or infringing upon your territory."

Sixth squinted in the dimming light. He recognized this woman. She was one of the clerks who had been at his meetings with the company. "You cut my tripwires," Sixth said. Words felt odd in his, and they came out ragged, as if he'd swallowed handfuls of dust. The result of weeks without speaking.

"Er, yes, I did. I assumed you could replace them." She hesitated. "Sorry?"

Sixth settled back. The woman rotated slowly in her net, and he noticed an Aviar clinging to their outside. The bird had subdued white and green plumage; a Streamer, which was a breed that did not live on Patji. He did not know much about them.

The setting sun cast shadows, the sky darkening. Soon, he would need to hunker down for the night and await its passing. The jungle was even more deadly at night than it was at day, for that was when the most dangerous of predators came out.

"I promise," the woman said from within her bindings. What was her name? He believed it had been told to him, but he did not recall. Something untraditional. "I really don't want to steal from you. You remember me, don't you? We met back in the company halls?"

He gave no reply.

"Please," she asked. "I'd really rather not be hung by my ankles from a tree, slathered with blood to attract predators. If it's all the same to you."

"You are not a trapper."

"Well, no," she said. "You may have noticed my gender."

"There have been female trappers."

"One. One female trapper, Yaalani the Brave. I've heard her story a hundred times. You may find it odd to know that almost every society has its myth of the female role reversal. She goes to war dressed as a man, or leads her father's armies into battle, or lives alone on an island just like any man. I'm convinced that such stories exist so that parents can tell their daughters, 'You are not Yaalani.'"

This woman spoke. A lot. People did tha, back on the Eelakin islands. Her skin was dark, like his, and she had the sound of his people. The slight accent to her voice . . . he had heard it more and more when visiting the homeisles. It was the accent of one who was educated.

"Can I get down?" she asked, voice bearing a faint tremor. "I cannot feel my hands. It is . . . unsettling."

"What is your name?" Patji asked. "I have forgotten it." This was too much speaking. It hurt his ears. This place was supposed to be soft.

"Vathi."

That's right. It was an improper name. Not a reference to her birth order, but a name like the mainlanders used. That was not uncommon among his people now. It had something to do with the visits from the Ones Above.

He walked over and took the rope from the nearby tree, then lowered the net. The woman's Aviar flapped away, screeching in annoyance and frustration as she hit the ground, a bundle of dark curls and green linen skirts. She stumbled to her feet, shaking numb hands and shivering, an after-effect of the vines' skin poison.

"So . . . uh, no ankles and blood?" she asked, hopeful.

"That is a story mothers tell to children," Sixth said, walking away from her. "It is not something we actually do."

"Oh."

"If you had been another trapper, I would have killed you directly, rather than leaving you to revenge yourself upon me. Come. Step where I step."

She shook a small pack from the vines and straightened her skirts. She wore a tight vest over the top of them, and the pack had some kind of metal tube sticking out of it. A map case? As he led the way, she followed, and she did not attempt to attack him when his back was turned.

Darkness was coming upon them. Fortunately, his safecamp was ahead, and he knew by heart the steps to approach along this path. As they walked, Kokerlii fluttered down and landed on the woman's shoulder, then began chirping in an amiable way.

Sixth stopped, turning. The woman's own Aviar had moved down her dress away from Kokerlii to cling near her bodice. The bird hissed softly, but Kokerlii—oblivious, as usual—continued to chirp happily.

"Is this . . ." Vathi said, looking to him. "Yours? But of course. The one on your shoulder is not Aviar."

Sak settled back, puffing up her feathers. No, she was not Aviar. At least, her species was not. Sixth continued to lead the way.

"I have never seen a trapper carry a bird who was not from the islands," Vathi said from behind.

It was not a question. Sixth, therefore, felt no need to reply.

This safecamp—he had three total on the island, though this was the largest—lay atop a short hike following a twisting trail. Getting to it either required climbing this single path and exposing oneself to the traps or somehow coming down the cliff above. At the top of the trail lay a small stand of trees, the largest of which held aloft a single-room structure. Trees were one of the safer places to sleep on Patji. The treetops were the domain of the Aviar, and most of the big predators all walked.

Sixth lit his lantern, then held it up, letting the orange light bathe his home. "Up," he said to the woman.

She hesitated, then looked out into the darkening jungle. By the lanternlight, he saw that the whites of her eyes were red from lack of sleep. She looked exhausted, despite the unconcerned smile she gave him before climbing up the stakes he'd planted in the tree.

"How did you know?" he asked.

Vathi hesitated, near to the trap door leading into his home. "Know what?"

"Where my safecamp was. Who told you?"

"I followed the sound of water," she said, nodding toward the small spring that bubbled out of the mountainside here. "When I found traps, I knew I was coming the right way."

Sixth frowned. That was impossible. One could not hear this water, and the stream vanished only a few hundred yards away, resurfacing in an unexpected location. Following it here . . . that would be virtually impossible.

So was she lying, or was she just lucky?

"You wanted to find me," he said.

"I wanted to find *someone*," she said, pushing open the trap door, voice growing muffled as she climbed up into the building. "I figured that a trapper would be my only chance for survival." Above, she stepped up to one of the netted windows. "This is nice. Very roomy for a shack on a mountainside in the middle of a deadly jungle on an isolated island surrounded by monsters."

Sixth climbed up, holding the lantern in his teeth. The room at the top was perhaps four paces square, tall enough to stand in, but only barely. "Shake out those blankets," he said, nodding toward the stack and setting down the lantern. "Then lift every cup or bowl on the shelf and check inside of them."

Her eye widened. "What am I looking for?"

"Deathants, scorpions, spiders, bloodscratches..." He shrugged, putting Sak on her perch by the window. "Better to find them now than when sleeping. The room is built to be tight, but this is Patji. The Father likes surprises."

As she hesitantly set aside her pack and got to work, Sixth continued up a ladder to check the roof of his structure. There, a group of bird-sized boxes lay arranged in a double row. Kokerlii landed on top of one, trilling—but softly, now that night had fallen. Other coos and chirps came from the other boxes.

Sixth climbed out to check each bird for hurt wings or feet. These Aviar pairs were his life's work; the chicks each one hatched became his primary stock and trade. Yes, he would trap on the island, trying to find as many nests and wild chicks as he could get—but that was never as efficient as raising nests.

"Your name was Sixth, wasn't it," Vathi said from below, voice accompanied by the sound of a blanket being shaken.

"It is."

"Large family," Vathi noted.

An ordinary family. Or, so it had once been. His father had been a twelfth and his mother an eleventh.

"Sixth of what?" Vathi prompted below.

"Of the dusk."

"So you were born in the evening," Vathi said. "I've always found the traditional names so... uh... *descriptive*."

What a meaningless comment, Sixth thought. *Why do homeislers feel the need to speak all of the time, particularly when there is nothing to say?*

He moved on to the next nest, checking the two drowsy birds inside for wounds, then inspecting their droppings. They responded to his return with happiness. An Aviar raised around people—particularly one that had lent its talent to a person at an early age—would always see people as part of their flock. These birds were not his companions, like Sak and Kokerlii, but they were still special to him. He had raised each one, and had chosen to keep them for breeding rather than taking them back to the homeisles for sale.

"No insects in the blankets," Vathi said, sticking her head up out of the trap door behind him.

"The cups?"

"I'll get to those in a moment. So these are your breeding pairs, are they?"

Obviously they were, so he didn't need to reply.

She watched him check them. He felt her eyes on him. Finally, he spoke. "Why did your company ignore the advice we gave you? Coming here was obviously a disaster."

"Yes."

He turned to her.

"Yes," she continued, "this whole expedition will likely be a disaster. One that takes us a step closer to our goal."

He checked Sisisru next, working by the light of the now-rising moon. "Foolish."

Vathi folded her arms before her on the roof of the building, torso still disappearing into the lit square of a trapdoor below. "Do you think that our ancestors learned to wayfind on the oceans without experiencing a few disasters along the way? Ships lost, people vanishing on the waves? Or what of the first trappers? You have knowledge passed down for generations, knowledge earned through trial and error. If the first trappers had considered it too 'foolish' to come explore, where would you be?"

"They were single men, well-trained, not a ship full of clerks and dockworkers."

"The world is changing, Sixth of the Dusk," she said softly. "The Ones Above . . . the technology we have discovered . . . The people of the land grow hungry for Aviar companions; that things were once restricted to the very wealthy can be within the reach of ordinary people. We've learned so much, yet the Aviar are still an enigma. Why don't chicks raised on the homeisles bestow talents? Why—"

"Foolish arguments," Sixth said, putting Sisisru back into her nest. "I do not wish to hear them again. You may sleep in my safecamp tonight."

"And then what?" she asked. "You turn me out into the jungle to die?"

"You survived well on your way here," he said, grudgingly. She was not a trapper. A scholar should not have been able to do what she did. "You will probably survive."

"I got lucky. I should be dead. I walked a few hours upstream to find this place—I'd never make it across the entire island."

Sixth paused. "Across the island?"

"To the main company camp."

"There are *more* of you?"

"I . . . Of course. You didn't think . . ."

He turned on her. "What happened?" *Now who is the fool?* He thought to himself. *You should have asked this first.* Talking. He had never been good with it, even before becoming a trapper.

She shied away from him, eyes widening. Did he look dangerous? Perhaps he had barked that last question forcefully. No matter. She spoke, so he got what he needed.

"We set up camp on the far beach," she said. "We have two ironhulls armed with cannons watching the waters. Those can take on even a deepwalker, if they have to. Two hundred soldiers, half that number in scientists and merchants. We're determined to find out, once and for all, why the Aviar must be born on one of the Pantheon Islands to be able to bestow talents.

"One team came down this direction to scout sites to place other fortresses. The company is determined to hold Patji against other interests. I thought the smaller expedition a bad idea, but had my own reasons for wanting to circle the island. So I went along. And then, the deepwalker . . ." She looked sick.

Sixth had almost stopped listening. Two *hundred* soldiers? On his island? Crawling across Patji like ants on a fallen piece of fruit. Unbearable! He thought of the quiet jungle broken by the sounds of their racketous voices. The sound of humans yelling at each other, clanging on metal, stomping about. Like a city.

A flurry of dark feathers announced Sak coming up from below and landing on the lip of the trapdoor beside Vathi. The black-plumed bird limped across the roof toward Sixth, stretching her wings, showing off the scars on her left. Even flying a dozen feet was a chore for her.

Sixth reached down scratch her neck, feeling stunned. It was happening. An invasion. He had to find a way to stop it. Somehow . . .

"I'm sorry, Sixth," Vathi said. "The Trappers are one of my areas of scholarship. I've read of your ways, and I respect them. But this *was* going to happen someday. The Aviar are too valuable to leave in the hands of a couple hundred eccentric woodsmen. They are a resource that we must protect."

"The chiefs . . ."

"All twenty chiefs in council agreed to this plan," Vathi said. "I was there. If the Eelakin do not secure these islands and tame them, someone else will."

Sixth stared out into the night. "Go and make certain there are no insects in the cups below."

"But—"

"*Go*," he said, turning to the woman, "and make *certain* there are no insects in the cups below!"

The woman sighed softly, but retreated into the room, leaving him with his Aviar. He continued to scratch Sak on the neck, seeking comfort in the familiar motion and in her presence. Dared he hope that the shadows would prove too deadly for the company and its iron-hulled ships? Vathi seemed confident.

She did not tell me why she joined the scouting group. She had seen a shadow, witnessed it destroying her team, but had still managed the presence of mind to find his camp. She was a strong woman. He would need to remember that.

She was also a company type, as removed from his experience as a person could get. Soldiers, craftsmen, even kings he could understand. But these soft-spoken scribes who had quietly conquered the world with a sword of commerce, they baffled him.

"Father," he whispered. "What do I do?"

Patji gave no reply. Well, none beyond the normal sounds of night on the island. Things moving, hunting, rustling. At night, the Aviar slept, and that gave opportunity to the most dangerous of the island's predators. In the distance, he heard a nightmaw roar, its horrid voice echoing through the trees. In his hands, Sak spread her wings, leaning down, head darting back and forth. The sound always made her tremble.

In truth, it did the same to Sixth.

He sighed, and started to rise, placing Sak on his shoulder. He turned, and almost stumbled as he saw his corpse at his feet. He came alert immediately; there wasn't supposed to be anything in his safecamp that could kill him. What was it? Vines in the tree branches? A spider, dropping quietly from above? Something larger? On Patji, any one of a hundred different animals could kill a man in a heartbeat.

Sak cried out.

It was a screech; he had not heard her screech in years. Nearby, his other Aviar cried out as well, a cacophony of squawks, screeches, chirps. No, it wasn't just them. All around... echoing in the distance, from both near and far, wild Aviar squawked. They rustled in their branches, a sound like a powerful wind blowing through the trees.

Sixth spun about, holding his hands to his ears, eyes wide as corpses appeared around him. His own body, eyes staring dead, appearing and vanishing. They piled high, one atop another, some bloated, some bloody, some skeletal. Haunting him. Dozens upon *dozens*.

He dropped to his knees, yelling. That put him eye-to-eye with one of the corpses. Only this one... this one was not quite dead... Blood dripped from its lips as it tried to speak, mouthing words that Sixth did not understand.

It vanished.

They all vanished. All of the corpses, every last one. He turned about, wild, but saw none of them. The sounds of the Aviar quieted, and his flock settled back into their nests. Sixth breathed in and out deeply, heart racing. He felt tense, as if at any moment, a shadow would explode from the blackness around his camp and consume him. He anticipated it, felt it coming. He wanted to run, run *somewhere*.

What had that been? In all of his years with Sak, he had never seen anything like it. What could have upset all of the Aviar at once in that way? What had they felt? Was it something about the nightmaw he had heard?

Don't be foolish, he thought at himself. *This was different, different from anything you've seen. Different from anything that has been seen on Patji.* But what? What had changed...

Sak had not settled down like the others. She stared northward. Toward where Vathi had said the main camp of invaders was setting up.

Sixth stood up, then clamored down into the room below, Sak on his shoulder. "What are your people doing?"

Vathi spun at his harsh tone. She had been looking out of the window, northward. "I don't—"

He took her by the front of her vest, pulling her toward him in a two-fisted grip, meeting her eyes from only a few inches away. "*What are your people doing?*"

Her eyes widened, and he could feel her tremble in his grip, though she set her jaw and held his gaze. Scribes were not supposed to have grit like this. He had seen them scribbling away in their windowless rooms. Sixth tightened his grip on her vest, pulling the fabric so it dug into her skin, and found himself growling softly.

"Release me," she said, "and we will speak."

"Bah," he said, letting go. She dropped down a few inches, hitting the floor with a thump. He hadn't realized he'd lifted her off the ground.

She backed away, putting as much space between them as the room would allow. He stalked to the window, looking through the mesh screen at the night. His corpse dropped from the roof above, and he stepped back, worried that it was happening again.

It didn't, not the same way as before. However, when he turned back into the room, his corpse lay in the corner, bloody lips parted, eyes staring sightlessly. The danger, whatever it was, had not passed.

Vathi had sat down on the floor, holding her head, trembling. Had he frightened her that soundly? She did look tired, exhausted. She wrapped her arms around herself, and when she looked at him, there was a cast to her eyes that hadn't been there before. As if she were regarding a wild animal, let off of its chain.

That seemed fitting.

"What do you know of the Ones Above?" she asked him.

"They live in the stars," Sixth said. "They claim that we once did too."

"We at the company have been meeting with them. We don't understand them, at least not their ways. They look like us, at times they talk like us. But they have... rules, laws that they won't explain. They refuse to sell us their marvels, but in like manner, they seem forbidden from taking things from us, even in trade."

"That is fine," Sixth said. "They are not of us, no matter what they look like. If they leave us alone, we will be better for it."

"You haven't seen the things they can do," she said softly, getting a distant look in her eyes. "We have barely worked out how to create ships that can sail on their own, against the wind. I thought that development to be amazing until the Ones Above arrived. They can sail the skies . . . sail the stars themselves. They know so much, and they won't *tell* us any of it."

She shook her head, reaching into the pocket of her skirt. "They are after something, Sixth. Their laws forbade them from contacting us until we were able to harness steam on our own. Now they can speak to us, but their laws won't let them teach us. If that is the case, what interest do we hold for them? From what I've heard them say, there are many worlds like ours, with cultures that cannot sail the stars. We are not unique, yet the Ones Above come back time and time again. They *do* want something. You can see it in their eyes . . ."

"What is that?" Sixth asked, nodding to the thing she took from her pocket. It rested in her palm like the shell of a clam, but had a mirror-like face on the top.

"It is a machine," she said. "Like a clock, only it never needs to be wound, and it . . . shows things."

"What things?"

"The location of Aviar."

"*What?*"

"It's like a map," she said. "It points the way to Aviar."

"That's how you found my camp," Sixth said, stepping toward her.

"Yes." She rubbed her thumb across the machine's surface. "We aren't supposed to have this. It was the possession of an emissary sent to work with us, but he died. The death was natural; he choked while eating. They *can* die, it appears, even of mundane things. That . . . changed how I view them.

"The others have asked after his machines, and we will have to return them soon. But this, this tells us what they are after: the Aviar. The Ones Above are always fascinated with them. I think they want to find a way to trade for the birds, a way their laws will allow. They hint that we might not be safe, that not everyone Above follows their laws."

"But why did the Aviar react like they did, just now?" Sixth said, turning back to the window. "Why did . . ." *Why did I see what I saw? What I'm still seeing, to an extent?* His corpse was there, wherever he looked. Slumped by a tree outside, in the corner of the room, hanging out of the trapdoor in the roof. Sloppy. He should have closed that.

Sak had pulled into his hair like she did when a predator was near.

"There . . . is a second machine," Vathi said.

That's right. She had said machines, earlier. More than one.

"Where?" he demanded.

"On our ship."

The direction the Avair had looked.

"It's much larger," Vathi said. "This one in my hand is limited in what it can do. The larger one . . . it can create an enormous map, one of an entire island, then *write* out a paper with a copy of that map. That map will include a dot marking every Aviar."

"And?"

"And we were going to turn on the machine tonight," she said. "It takes hours to get ready—like an oven, growing hot—before it's ready to draw its map for us. The schedule was to turn it on tonight just after sunset so we could use it in the morning."

"The others," Sixth demanded, "they'd use it without you?"

She grimaced. "Happily. Captain Eusto probably did a dance when I didn't return from scouting. He's been worried I would take too much of the credit for this expedition. But the machine isn't harmful; it merely locates Aviar. You don't need to worry so much."

"Did it do *that* before," he demanded, waving toward the night. "When you last used it, did it draw the attention of all the Aviar? Discomfort them?"

"Well, no," she said. "But the moment of discomfort has passed, hasn't it? I'm sure it's nothing."

Nothing. Sak quivered on his shoulder. Sixth saw death all around him. The moment they had used that machine, the corpses had piled up.

If they used it again, the results would be horrible. Sixth knew it. He could *feel* it.

"We're going to stop them," he said.

"What?" Vathi asked. "*Tonight?*"

"Yes," Sixth said, walking to a small hidden cabinet in the wall. He pulled it open, and began to pick through the supplies inside. A second lantern. Extra oil. He would need those.

"That's insane," Vathi said. "Nobody travels the islands at night."

"I've done it once before. With my uncle."

His uncle had died on that trip.

"You can't be serious, Sixth. The Nightmaws are out. I've heard them."

"Traveling quickly," Sixth said, stuffing supplies into his pack, "and cutting across the center of the island, we can be to your camp by morning. We can stop them from using the Above machine again."

"But why would we *want* to?"

He shouldered the pack. "Because if we don't, it will destroy the island."

She frowned at him, cocking her head. "You can't know that. Why do you think you know that?"

"Come on." He walked to the hatc down and pulled it open.

Vathi rose, but pressed back against the wall. "I'm staying here."

"They won't believe me," he said. "You will have to tell them to stop. You are coming."

Vathi licked her lips in what seemed to be a nervous habit. She glanced to the sides, looking for escape, then back at him. Right then, Sixth noticed his corpse hanging from the pegs in the tree beneath him. He jumped.

"What was that?" she demanded.

"Nothing."

"You keep glancing to the sides," Vathi said. "What do you think you see, Sixth?"

"We're going. Now."

"You've been alone on the island for a long time," she said, obviously trying to make her voice soothing. "You're upset because something unexpected has happened in our arrival. You aren't thinking clearly. I understand."

Sixth drew in a deep breath. "Sak, show her."

The bird launched from his shoulder, flapping across the room, landing on Vathi. She turned to the bird, frowning.

Then she gasped, falling to her knees. Vathi pulled back against the wall, eyes darting from side to side, mouth working but no words coming out. Sixth left her to it for a short time, then raised his arm. Sak returned to him on black wings, dropping a single, dark feather to the ground. She settled in again on his shoulder. That much flying was difficult for her.

"What was *that*?" Vathi demanded.

"Come on," Sixth said, taking his pack and climbing down out of the room.

Vathi scrambled to the open hatch. "No. Tell me. What *was* that?"

"You saw your corpse."

"All about me. Everywhere I looked."

"Sak grants that Talent."

"There is no such Talent."

Sixth looked up at her, halfway down the pegs. "You have seen your death. That is what will happen if your friends use that machine. Death. All of us. The Aviar, everyone living here. I do not know why it will happen, but I know that it will."

"You've discovered a new Aviar," Vathi said. "How . . . When . . ."

"Hand me the lantern," Sixth said, raising a hand.

Looking numb, she obeyed, handing it down. He put it into his teeth and climbed down the pegs to the ground. Then he raised the lantern high, looking down the slope toward the jungle below. The inky jungle at night. Like the depths of the ocean.

He shivered, then whistled. Kokerlii fluttered down from above, landing on his other shoulder. He would hide them. Hide their minds, at least. With that, they had a chance.

Vathi scrambled down the pegs behind him, her pack with the strange tube in it over her shoulder. "You have two Aviar," she said. "You use them both at once?"

"My uncle had three."

"How is that even possible?"

"They like trappers." So many questions. So much talking. Could she not think about what the answers might be before asking?

"We're actually going to do this," she said, whispering, as if to herself. "The jungle at night. I should stay. I should refuse . . ."

"You've seen your death if you do."

"I've seen what you claim is my death. I don't know anything. A new Aviar . . . It has been centuries." Though her voice still sounded reluctant, she walked after him as he strode down the slope and passed his traps, entering the jungle again.

His corpse sat at the base of a tree. That made him immediately look for what could kill him here, but Sak's senses seemed to be off. Impending death was upon them all, and it was so overpowering, it seemed to be smothering smaller dangers. He might not be able to rely upon her visions until the machine was destroyed.

That worried him. If he was going to cross the island at night, her aid would have been invaluable. The thick jungle canopy seemed to swallow them. It was hot here, even at night; the ocean breezes didn't reach this far inland. That left the air feeling stagnant, and it dripped with the scents of the jungle. Fungus, rotting leaves, the perfumes of flowers.

The accompaniment to those scents were the sounds of an island that did not sleep. When the Aviar slumbered, much of the rest of the island came alive. The deeper Sixth went, the more omnipresent the sounds became. A constant crinkling in the underbrush, like the sound of maggots writhing in a pile of dry leaves.

The lantern's light did not seem to extend as far as it should, and Vathi pulled up close to him behind. "Why did you do this before?" she asked. "The other time you went out at night?"

More questions.

"I was wounded," Sixth said. "We had to get from one safecamp to the other to recover my uncle's store of antivenom." Because Sixth, hands trembling, had dropped the other flask.

"You survived it? Well, obviously you did, I mean. I'm surprised is all."

She seemed to be talking to fill the air. Homeislers did that.

"They could be watching us," she said, looking into the darkness. "Nightmaws."

"They are not."

"How can you know?" she asked, voice hushed. "Anything could be out there, in that darkness."

"If the nightmaws had seen us, we'd be dead. That is how I know." Obviously. He shook his head, sliding out his machete and cutting away a few branches before them. Any could hold deathants skittering across their leaves. In the dark, it would be difficult to spot them, and so brushing against foliage seemed a poor decision.

We won't be able to avoid it, he thought, leading the way down through a gully thick with mud. He had to step on stones to keep from sinking in. Vathi followed with remarkable dexterity, for a scribe. *We have to go quickly. I can't cut down every branch in our way.*

He hopped off of a stone and onto the bank of the gully, passing his body sinking into the mud. Nearby, however, he spotted a second corpse, so translucent it was nearly invisible. He raised his lantern, hoping it wasn't happening again.

Others did not appear. Just these too. And the very faint image . . . yes, that was a sinkhole there. Sak chirped softly, and he fished in his pocket for a seed to give her. She had figured out how to send him help anyway. The fainter images—he would have to watch for those.

"Thank you," he whispered to her.

"That bird of yours," Vathi said, speaking softly in the gloom of night, "are there others?"

They climbed out of the gully, continuing on, crossing a krell trail in the night. He stopped them just before the wandered into a patch of deathants. Vathi looked at the trail of tiny insects, moving along their path. They were practically blind, but stumble into them . . .

Well, they weren't the greatest of Patji's dangers.

"Sixth?" she asked as they rounded the ants. "Are there others? Why haven't you brought any chicks to market?"

"I do not have any chicks."

"So you found only the one?" she asked.

Questions, questions. Buzzing around him like flies.

Don't be foolish, he told himself, shoving down his annoyance. *You would ask the same, if you saw someone with a new Aviar.* He had tried to keep Sek a secret; for years, he hadn't even brought her with him when he left the island. But with her hurt wing, he hadn't wanted to abandon her.

Deep down, he'd known he couldn't keep his secret forever. "There are many like her," he finally said, in answer to those buzzing questions. "But only she has a talent to bestow."

Vathi stopped in place as he continued to cut them a path. He turned back, looking at her alone on the new trail. He had given her the lantern to hold.

"That's a mainlander bird," she said. She held up the light. "That's what I knew it was when I first saw it, but when you said it had a talent, I assumed I had been wrong. I wasn't. It *is* a mainlander bird."

Sixth turned back and continued cutting.

"You brought a mainlander chick to the pantheon," Vathi whispered behind. "And it *gained a talent.*"

With a hack he brought down a branch, then continued on. Again, she had not asked a question, so he needed not answer.

Vathi hurried to keep up, the glow of the lantern tossing his shadow before him as she stepped up behind. "Surely someone else has tried it before. Surely . . ."

He did not know. He had not heard it spoken of, however.

"But why would they?" She continued, quietly, as if to herself. "The Aviar are special. Everyone knows the breeds and what they do. Why assume that a fish would lean to breathe air, if raised on land? Why assume a non-Aviar would become one if raised on Patji . . ."

They continued through the night. Sixth led them around many dangers, though he found that he needed to rely upon Sak's help even more than he would have during day. *Do not follow that stream, which has you corpse bobbing in its waters. Do not touch that tree; the bark is poisonous with rot. Turn from that path. Your corpse shows a deathant bite.*

Sak did not speak to him, but each message was clear. They seemed more clear than normal, actually—though these images were faint, almost invisible. When he stopped to let Vathi drink from her canteen, he held Sak and found her trembling. She did not peck at him as normal when he enclosed her in his hands.

They stood in a small clearing, pure dark all around them, the sky shrouded in clouds. He heard distant rainfall on the trees. Not uncommon, here.

Nightmaws roared, one then another, in the night air. They only did that when they had already made a kill, or when they were seeking to frighten prey. Often, Krell herds slept near Aviar roosts. Frighten away the birds, and you could sense the Krell.

Vathi had taken out her tube. Not a scroll case—and not something scholarly at all, considering the way she held it as she poured something into its end. She held it like one would hold a weapon. Beneath her feet, Sixth's body lay mangled. Not one of the visions Sak was trying to send him, but one of the ones from the danger.

He did not ask after Vathi's weapon, not even as she took some kind of short, slender spear and fit it into the top end. No weapon could penetrate the thick skin of a Nightmaw. You either avoided them, or you died.

Kokerlii fluttered down to his shoulder, chirping away. He seemed confused by the darkness. Why were they out like this, at night, when birds normally made no noise?

"We must keep moving," Sixth said, placing Sak on his shoulder again and taking out his machete.

"You realize that your bird changes everything," Vathi said, joining him, shouldering her pack and carrying her tube in the other hand.

"There will be a new kind of Aviar," Sixth said, stepping over his corpse.

"That's the *least* of it. Sixth, our entire understanding of them is wrong. We assumed that chicks raised off of these islands did not develop their abilities because they were not around others to train them. We assumed that their abilities were part of them, like men have the ability to speak—innate, but requiring help from others to develop properly."

"So, that can still be the way," Sixth said. "Other species can merely be trained to speak."

"And your bird? Was it trained by others?"

"Perhaps." He did not know everything Sak had done in her life.

Of course, he suspected something else. He did not say it. It was a thing of trappers. Beyond that, he was stopped by something. A body on the ground before them.

It was not his.

He held up a hand immediately, stilling Vathi as she continued on to ask another question. What was *this*? That body was relatively fresh—though the meat had been picked off of much of the skeleton, the clothing still lay strewn about, ripped open by those that feasted upon it. Small, fungus-like plants had sprouted around the ground near it, tiny red tendrils reaching up out of the ground to enclose parts of the skeleton.

He looked up at the great tree, at the foot of which rested the corpse. The flowers were not in bloom. Sixth released his breath.

"What is it?" Vathi whispered. "Deathants?"

"No. Patji's Finger."

She frowned. "Is that . . . some kind of curse?"

"It is a name," Sixth said, stepping forward carefully, inspecting the corpse. Machete. Boots. Rugged gear. One of his colleagues had fallen. He *thought* he recognized the man from the clothing. An older trapper named First of the Sky. Sixth's uncle had known him.

"Of the person?" Vathi asked, peeking over his shoulder.

"Of the tree," Sixth said, poking at the clothing of the man, careful of insects that might be lurking inside. "Raise the lamp."

"I've never heard of that tree," she said skeptically.

"They are only on Patji."

"I have read a lot about the flora on these islands . . ."

"And you know little, still. Here you are a child. Light."

She sighed, raising it for him. He prodded at pockets on the ripped clothing with a stick. He had been killed by a tuskrun pack, larger predators—almost as large as a man—that prowled mostly at day. Their movement patterns were normally predictable. Unless one happened across one of Patji's Fingers in bloom.

There. He found a small book in the man's pocket. Sixth raised it, then backed away. Perhaps he could have stopped Vathi from peering over his shoulder, but he was too interested in the book at the moment. Still, homeislers stood so *close* to each other sometimes. They had a whole island, mostly to themselves. Did she need to stand right by his elbow.

He checked the first pages, finding a list of dates. Yes, this death was fresh, only a few days old, judging by the last date written down. The pages after that detailed the locations of First's safecamps, along with explanations of the traps guarding each one. The last page contained the farewell.

I am First of the Sky, taken by Patji at last. I have a brother on Suluko. Care for them, rival.

Few words. Few words were good. Sixth carried a book like this himself, and he had said even less on his last page.

"He wants you to care for his family?" Vathi asked.

"Don't be stupid," Sixth said, tucking the book away. "In this, 'them' means his birds."

"That's actually kind of sweet," Vathi said. "I had always heard that trappers were incredibly territorial."

"We are," he said, noting how she said it. Again, her tone made it seem as if she considered trappers to be like animals. "But our birds might die without care—they are accustomed to humans, and are no longer part of their flocks. Better to give them to a rival than to let them die."

"Even if that rival is the one who killed you?" Vathi asked. "The traps you set, the ways you try to interfere with one another . . ."

"It is our way."

"That is an awful excuse," she said, looking up at the tree. It was massive, with drooping fronds. At the end of each one was a large closed blossom, as long as two hands put together. "You don't seem worried, though the plant seems to have killed that man."

"These are only dangerous when they bloom."

"Spores?" she asked.

"No." He picked up the fallen machete, but left the rest of First's things alone.

Let Patji claim him. Sixth scanned the area, ignoring his corpse draped over a log. Sak gave him no direction, so he started out northward, continuing the trek toward the other side of the island.

"Sixth?" Vathi asked, raising the lantern and hurrying to him. "If not spores, then how does the tree kill?"

"So many questions."

"My life is about questions," she replied. "And about answers. If my people are to work on this island—"

She cut off as he spun on her, then she stepped back.

"It's going to happen," she said, more softly. "You can't stop it, Sixth. I'm sorry. Perhaps we will be defeated, but others will come."

"Because of the Ones Above," he said, turning away and continuing to lead through the dark underbrush.

"Well, they may spur it," Vathi said. "But it will happen without them. The world is changing. One man cannot slow it, no matter how determined."

He stopped in the path.

You cannot change it, Sixth. No matter how determined you are. His mother's words. Some of the last he remembered from her.

Sixth continued on his way. The woman followed. He would need her, though a treacherous piece of him whispered that she would be easy to end. With her would go her questions, and more importantly, her answers. The ones he suspected she was very close to discovering.

You cannot change it . . .

He could not. He hated that he could not, but he could not. Killing this woman would accomplish nothing. Besides, had he sunk so low that he would take a helpless scribe and murder her in cold blood? He would not even do that to another trapper, unless they approached his camp and did not retreat.

"The blossoms can think," he found himself saying as he turned them away from a mound that showed the tuskrun pack had been rooting here. "The Fingers of Patji. They attract predators like a wounded animal, which has thoughts full of pain and worry. The predators fight one another, sometimes, and the tree feeds off of the corpses. That is what you saw growing beneath the man's body."

Vathi gasped. "A *plant*," she said, "that broadcasts a mental signature? Are you certain?"

"Yes."

"I need one of those blossoms." The light shook as she turned to go back.

Sixth spun and caught her by the arm. "No. We are not here to collect samples. We must keep moving."

"But—"

"You will have another chance." He took a deep breath. "Your people will soon infest this island like maggots on carrion. You will see other trees. Tonight, we must go. Dawn is approaching."

He let go of her and turned back to his work. He had judged her wise, for a mainisler. Perhaps she would listen.

She did. She followed behind, walking quietly for a time.

"I'm sorry," she finally said.

"It was not dusk when I was born," Sixth said, hacking down a swampvine, then holding his breath against the noxious fumes that it released toward him a moment later. They were only dangerous for a few moments.

"Excuse me?" Vathi asked, keeping her distance from the swampvine. "You were born..."

He looked over, meeting her eyes in the frail lanternlight. "My mother did not name me for the time of day. It was not dusk, not in the day of my birth. I was named because my mother saw the dusk of our people. The sun will soon set, she often told me." He turned, looking up toward the dark canopy. "I guess it has finally done just that."

He looked back to Vathi. Oddly, she smiled at him. Perhaps she realized he had shared something personal. He had not spoken those words to his uncle; only his parents had known. He was not certain why he'd told this scribe from an evil company.

A nightmaw broke through between two trees behind Vathi.

The enormous beast would have been as tall as a tree if it had stood upright on two legs. Instead, it leaned forward in a prowling posture, two clawed forelegs ripping up the ground as it reached forward its long neck, open beak on the end razor sharp and deadly. This was the closest he had ever seen one. It looked kind of like a bird, in the same way that a wolf looked like a lapdog.

He threw his machete. An instinctive reaction, for he did not have time for thought. He did not have time for fear. That snapping beak—as tall as a door—would have the two of them dead in moments.

His machete glanced off of the beak, actually cutting it on the side of the head. Sixth leaped for Vathi, to pull her away, to—

The explosion deafened him. Smoke burst into the air from Vathi, who stood—wide eyed—having dropped the lantern, oil spilling from the ground. The sudden sound stunned him, and he almost collided with her as the Nightmaw slumped and fell, skidding, the ground *thumping* from the impact.

Sixth found himself on the ground. He had tripped. He scrambled to his feet, backing away from the twitching Nightmaw mere feet in front of him. The light was already dying. He couldn't look toward the fallen lantern, though. He stared at the beast in front of him, all leathery skin that was prickled and bumpy, like that beneath a bird that had lost its feathers.

It was dead. She had killed it.

Vathi said something.

She had *killed* a nightmaw.

"Sixth!" her voice seemed distant.

He raised a hand to his forehead, which had belatedly begun to prickle with sweat. His body tense, he felt as if he should be running. He had never wanted to be so close to one of these. *Never.*

She'd actually killed it.

He turned toward her, his eyes wide. Vathi was trembling, but she covered it well. "Well, that worked," she said. "We weren't certain it would, even though we'd prepared these specifically for the nightmaws."

"It's like a cannon," Sixth said. "Like from one of the ships, only in your *hands*."

"Yes."

He turned back toward the beast. He had been wrong, earlier. It wasn't dead, not completely. It twitched, and let out a plaintive screech. That was soft, though. He could make out the large hole in its breast as he walked around it; the weapon had fired a spear of some sort that had gone right into it chest. It quaked and thrashed a weak leg. It wasn't dead yet, but it soon would be.

"We could kill them all," Sixth said, still feeling stunned. He turned, then rushed over to Vathi, taking her by the arm. "With those weapons, we could kill them *all*. Every nightmaw. Maybe the shadows too!"

"Well, yes, it has been discussed. However, they are important parts of the ecosystem on these islands. Removing the apex predators could have undesirable results."

"Undesirable results?" Sixth ran his hand through his hair. "They'd be gone. All of them! I don't care what other problems you think it would cause. They would all be *dead*."

Vathi snorted, picking up the lantern and stamping out the fires it had started. "I thought trappers were connected to nature."

"We are. That's how I know we would all be better off without any of these things." No more nightmaws. What a different world it would be.

"You are disabusing me of many romantic notions about your kind, Sixth," she said, circling the dying beast. "I wish we had time . . . Nobody has ever been able to study one of these up close."

"With those weapons, you should have plenty of chances." Sixth whistled, holding up his arm. Kokerlii fluttered down from high branches; in the chaos and explosion,

Sixth had not seen the bird fly away. Sak still clung to his shoulder with a death grip, her claws digging into his skin through the cloth. He hadn't noticed.

Kokerlii landed on his arm and gave an apologetic chirp.

"It wasn't your fault," Sixth said soothingly. "They prowl the night. Even if they cannot sense our minds, they can hear us, smell us." Nightmaws did not have good vision, nor was their hearing excellent. Their sense of smell, however, was said to be incredible. This one had come up the trail behind them; it must have crossed their past and followed it.

Dangerous. His uncle always claimed the Nightmaws were growing smarter, that they knew they could not hunt men only by their minds. *I should have taken us across more streams,* Sixth thought, reaching up and rubbing Sak's neck to sooth her. *There just isn't time . . .*

His body lay wherever he looked. Draped across a rock, hanging from the vines of trees, slumped beneath the dying Nightmaw's claw . . .

The beast trembled once more in what seemed a final way, then amazingly it lifted its gruesome head and let out a screech. Not as loud as those that normally sounded in the night, but bone-chilling and horrid. Sixth stepped back despite himself, and Sak chirped nervously.

In the night, distant, other Nightmaw screeches rose.

Sixth twisted his head to the side, stumbling backward, looking out into that deep blackness. At least five other beats sounded in the night. That sound . . . he had been trained to recognize that sound as the sound of death.

"We're going," he said, stalking across the ground and pulling Vathi away from the dying beast, which had lowered its head and fallen silent. It might *be* dead. It no longer moved.

"Sixth?" She did not resist a he pulled her away, though she did look over her shoulder at the monster.

One of the other nightmaws sounded again in the night. Was it closer? *Oh, Patji,* Sixth thought. *No. Not this.*

"Come!" he said, pulling her faster and reaching for his machete. He had thrown it. He did not go back for it; he took out the one he had gathered from his fallen rival and began to hack at leaves, only when necessary. He could no longer worry about brushing against deathants.

A greater danger was coming.

The calls of death came again. "Are those getting *closer*?" Vathi asked.

Sixth did not answer. It was a question, but one he did not know the answer to. He released her head, moving more quickly, almost at a trot—faster than he ever wanted to go through the jungle, day or night.

"Sixth!" Vathi hissed. "Will they come? To the call of the dying one? Is that something they do?"

"How should I know?" he snapped, turning back on her. "I have never known one of them to be killed before." He saw the tube, again carried over her shoulder, lit by the light of the lantern she carried.

That gave him pause. Though his instincts screamed at him to keep moving, he paused. The weapon. He felt a fool. They had a weapon that could kill nightmaws! That such a thing existed still amazed him.

"Your weapon," he said. "You can use it again?"

"Yes," she said. "Once more."

"*Once* more?"

A half dozen screeches sounded in the night.

"Yes," she replied. "I only brought three of spears this thing fires, and enough powder for three shots. I tried firing one at the shadow. It didn't do much."

One more attack. So his instincts were right. He spoke no further, towing her into the jungle as those calls came again and again. Agitated.

How did one escape Nightmaws? His Aviar clung to him, one on each shoulder. He had to leap over his corpse periodically as they traversed a gulch and came up the other side.

How do you escape them? He thought, remembering his uncle's training. *You don't draw their attention in the first place!*

They were fast. Kokerlii would hid his mind from them, but if they picked up his trail at the dead one . . .

Water. He stopped in the night, turning right, then left. Where would he find a stream? Patji was an island. Fresh water came from rainfall, mostly. The largest lake . . . the only one, really . . . was up the wedge. Toward the peak.

Patji was shaped something like a wedge. Along the eastern side, the island rose to some heights with cliffs on all sides. It was not terribly tall, but was elevated further than the rest of the island. Rainfall collected there, in Patji's Eye, and could not escape except slowly. The river, his tears.

It was a dangerous place to go, with Vathi in tow. Their path had skirted the slope up the heights, heading across the island toward the northern beach. It would only be a small diversion . . .

Those screeches behind spurred him on. *Patji forgive me,* he thought, seizing Vathi's hand an towing her a slightly different direction. She did not complain, though she did keep looking over her shoulder.

The screeches grew closer.

He ran. He ran as he had never expected to do on Patji, wild and reckless. Leaping over troughs, around fallen logs coated in moss. Through the dark underbrush, scarring away meekers and startling Aviar slumbering in the branches above. It was foolish. It was crazy.

He did not fear death to insect bites or falling vines. Somehow, he knew. The kings of Patji hunted him; lesser dangers would not dare steal from their betters.

Vathi followed with difficulty. Those skirts were trouble, but Sixth had to occasionally stop and cut their way through underbrush. Urgent, frantic, he did so. He expected her to keep up, and she did. A piece of him—buried deep beneath the terror—was impressed. This woman would have made a fantastic tracker.

Instead she would probably destroy them.

He froze as screeches sounded behind, so close. Vathi gasped, and Sixth turned back to his work. They were close. He hacked through a dense patch of undergrowth and ran on, sweat streaming down the sides of his face. Jostling light came from the lantern behind, clutched by Vathi, and the scene before him as he ran was one of horrific shadows dancing on the jungle's bows, leaves, ferns, and rocks.

This is your fault, Patji, he thought with an unexpected fury. *Why must you try to kill us, those who protect you?*

The screeches seemed almost on top of him. Was that breaking brush he could hear behind?

We are our priests, and yet you hate us! You hate all.

Sixth's uncle had explained that Patji needed to be deadly to keep away the unwelcome, the unworthy. And yet, Vathi was nearly as good as any trapper, though she had not set foot on Patji until recently. Did that make her worthy? Did that make her welcome?

Sixth broke from the jungle and out onto the banks of the river. Small, by mainland standards—he had once seen a river there so wide, no man could have jumped it. Still, this would do. He led Vathi right into it, splashing into the cold waters.

He turned upstream. What else could he do? Downstream was to lead closer to those sounds, the calls of death.

Of the Dusk, he thought. *Of the Dusk.*

He led Vathi upriver. The waters came only to their calves, bitter cold. The coldest water on the island, though he did not know why. They slipped and scrambled as they ran, best they could, upriver. This passed them through some narrows, with lichen-covered rock walls on either side twice as tall as a man.

They burst out into the basin, halfway up the heights. A place men did not go. A place he had visited only once. A cool, emerald lake rested here, sequestered.

Sixth towed Vathi to the side, out of the river, toward some brush. Perhaps she would not see. He huddled down with her, raising a finger to his lips, then turning down the light of the lantern she still held. Nightmaws could not see well, but perhaps the dim light would help. In more ways than one.

They waited there, on the shore of the small lake, hoping that the water had washed away their scent—hoping the Nightmaws would grow confused and be unable to track them. For one thing about this place was that the basin had steep walls, hidden as it was in Patji's depths. There was no way out other than the river, and if the Nightmaws came up it, Sixth and Vathi would be trapped.

The screeches sounded behind. The creatures had reached the river. Sixth waited in almost near darkness, and so squeezed his eyes shut. He prayed to Patji, whom he loved, whom he hated.

Vathi gasped softly. "What . . . ?"

So she had seen. Of course she had. She was a seeker, a learner. A questioner.

Why must men ask so many questions?

"Sixth! There are Aviar here! Hundreds of them." She spoke in a hushed, frightened tone. Even as they awaited death itself, however, she saw and could not help speaking. "Have you seen them? What is this place?" She hesitated. "So many juveniles. Barely able to fly . . ."

"They come here," he whispered. "Every bird from every island. "In their youth, they must come here."

He opened his eyes, looking up at the rim of the basin. He had turned down the lantern, but it was still bright enough to see them roosting there. Some stirred at the light and the sound. They stirred more as the nightmaws screeched below. They had not left the banks of the river. They were searching.

Sak chirped on his shoulder, terrified. Kokerlii, for once, had nothing to say.

"Every bird from every island . . ." Vathi said, putting it together. "They all come here, to this place. Are you certain?"

"Yes." It was a thing that trappers knew. You could not capture a bird before it had visited Patji.

Otherwise it would be able to bestow no talent.

"They come here," she said. "We knew they migrated between islands . . . Why do they come here? What is the point."

Was there any point in holding back now? She would figure it out. Huddled here in the night though they were, she would figure it out.

Still, he did not speak. Let her do so.

"They gain their talents here, don't they?" she asked, looking to him. "How? Is it where they are trained? Is this how you made a bird who was not an Aviar into one? You brought a hatchling here, and then . . ." She frowned, raising her lantern. "I recognize those trees. They are the ones you called Patji's fingers."

A dozen of them grew here, the largest concentration on the island. And beneath them, their fruit littered the ground. Much of it eaten, some of it only halfway so, bites taken out by birds of all stripes. Vathi saw him looking, and frowned.

"The fruit?" she asked.

"Worms," he whispered in reply.

A light seemed to go on in her eyes. "It's not the birds. It never has been . . . it's a parasite. They carry a parasite that bestows talents! That's why those raised off of the islands cannot gin the abilities, and why a mainland bird you brought here could."

"Yes."

"This changes everything, Sixth. Everything."

"Yes."

Of the Dusk. Born during that dusk, or bringer of it? What had he done?

Downriver, the nightmaws screeched. Then, those yells drew closer. They had decided to search upriver. They were clever, more clever than men off of the islands thought them to be. Vathi gasped, turning toward the small river canyon.

I am trying to protect you! Sixth thought in anger, looking toward Patji's fingers. *I need to stop the men and their device. I know it! Why? Why do you hunt me?*

But he knew so much. Too much. More than any man had known. For he had asked questions.

Men. And their questions.

"They're coming for us, aren't they?" she asked.

The answer seemed obvious. He did not answer.

"No," she said, standing. "I won't die with this knowledge, Sixth. I *won't*. There must be a way."

"There is," he said, standing beside her. He took a deep breath. *So I finally pay for it.* He took Sak carefully in his hand, and placed her on Vathi's shoulder. He pried Kokierlii free too.

"What are you doing?" Vathi asked.

"I will go as far as I can," Sixth said, handing Kokerlii toward her. The bird bit with annoyance at his hands, never strong enough to draw blood. "You will need to hold him. He will try to follow me."

"No, wait. We can hide in the lake, they—"

"They will find us!" Sixth said. "It isn't deep enough by far to hide us."

"But you can't—-"

"They are nearly here, woman!" he said, forcing Kokerlii into her hands. "The men of the company will not listen to me if I tell them to turn off the device. You are smart, you can make them stop. You can reach them. With Kokerlii you can reach them. Be ready to go."

She looked at him, stunned, but she seemed to realize that there was no other way. She stood, holding Kolerlii in two hands as he stepped back into the river. He could hear rushing downstream. He would have to go quickly to reach the end of the canyon before they arrived. If he could draw them out into the jungle even a short ways to the south, Vathi could slip out.

As he entered the stream, his visions of death finally vanished. No more corpses bobbing in the water, laying on the banks. Sak had realized what was happening.

She gave a final chirp. He started to run.

One of Patji's Fingers, growing right next to the mouth of the canyon, was blooming.

"Wait!"

He should not have stopped as Vathi yelled at him. He should have continued on, for time was so slim. However, the sight of that flower—along with her yell—made him hesitate.

The Flower ...

Vathi ran up, letting go of Kokerlii, who immediately flew to his shoulder and started chirping at him in annoyed chastisement. Vathi pulled the flower off—it was as large as a man's head, with a large bulging part at the center.

"A flower that can think," Vathi said, breathing quickly. "A flower that can draw the attention of predators."

Both of their heads turned toward the tube, her weapon, which lay sticking from her pack on the bank of the river. Sixth pulled out his rope as she ran for it, then he ripped the flower from its branch.

He tried the rope to it as Vathi ran up with her weapon, the spear sticking out slightly from the end. Sixth tied the other end of his rope to it as the Nightmaw yells echoed up the cavern. He could see their shadows, hear them splashing.

He stumbled back from Vathi as she crouched down, setting the weapon's butt against the ground, and pulled a lever at the base.

The explosion, once again, nearly deafened him.

Aviar all around the rim of the basin screeched and called in fright, many taking wing. A storm of feathers and flapping ensued, and through the middle of it, Vathi's spear shot into the air towing the rope and with it the flower. That arced out over the canyon into the night.

Sixth grabbed her by the shoulder and pulled her back along the river, into the lake itself. They slipped into the shallow water, Kokerlii on his shoulder, Sak on hers. They left the lantern burning, giving a quiet light to the suddenly-empty basin.

The lake was not deep. Two or three feet. Even crouching, it didn't cover them completely.

Nightmaws stopped in the canyon. His lanternlight showed a couple of them in the shadows, large as huts, turning and watching the sky. They were smart, but like the meekers, not as smart as men.

Patji . . . Sixth thought. *Patji, please. She is right. The secrets cannot remain secret forever. Not with the way the world changes. They will get out.*

I will carry them, and do what I can with them.

The Nightmaws turned back down the canyon, following the mental signature broadcast by the flowering plant.

Sixth counted to a hundred, then slipped from the waters. Vathi, sodden in her skirts, did not speak as she grabbed the lantern. They left the weapon, its shots expended.

The calls from the Nigtmaws grew further and further away as Sixth led the way out of the canyon, then directly north, slightly downslope. He kept expecting yells to turn and follow.

They did not.

#

The company fortress was a horridly impressive sight. A work of logs and cannons right at the edge of the water, guarded by an enormous iron-hulled ship. Smoke rose from it, the burning of morning cook fires.

Sixth sat on a rock a short distance from what appeared to be a dead shadow, its mountainous corpse draped half in the water, half out. He did not enter the fortress. Better to stay out here, near the dead shadow, even though his skin prickled as he looked at it.

His own corpse lay in the shallows beside it. Sak rested on his shoulder, dozing, and Kokerlii trilled from a branch closer to the forest. He seemed in good spirits.

As Sixth waited, his corpse slowly vanished from the shadows, fading like a shadow blending with darkness at the fall of night.

Vathi finally left the fortress. Alone, thankfully, though two more men joined the guards at the gate. All bore weapons similar to the one she had used to kill the nightmaw.

She had not changed. Her muddied skirts were stuck with twigs, her hair a mess. Her eyes were alight. She stepped up to him.

The surf washed against Patji's rocks. He could not decide if he found it a violent sound or a peaceful one.

"It is done," she said.

But he already knew that it was. The vision had ended. The danger had passed.

"Eusto was not pleased at my survival," Vathi noted, "though he could not say so. He was reluctant to stop the device, but my authority supersedes his own."

Sixth nodded. His eyes fell again on the dead shadow.

"Come into our fortress," Vathi said, glancing at it. "Get some rest, some food."

"I must return and check on my Aviar."

"They will survive another day without you. They live on this island for weeks at a time without your presence."

He did not reply.

"Sixth... we could use your knowledge. Your wisdom."

"I know," he said. "You could." He turned back toward Patji. He could not interpret events of the night. Had the nightmaws been Patji, seeking to cover his secrets? Or had the flower been redemption, sent by his father? Which was Sixth? Condemned or rescued? Neither? Both?

"What happened to the One Above," Sixth said. "The one who died while eating, the one to whom these devices of yours belonged?"

"His body was reclaimed by the others," Vathi said, frowning. "Why do you ask?"

"I do not think he is really dead," Sixth said. "They have tricked you."

Vathi raised an eyebrow at him.

"The machine is a trap," Sixth said. "They expected you to use it, and they knew the damage it would cause."

"That's an interesting theory," Vathi said, studying him in the morning light. She looked exhausted. The things she had been through... It had been less than a day since his arrival back on Patji, and yet, so much had happened.

"It is true," Sixth said. "You were to use it, and in so doing endanger the Aviar."

"That makes no sense."

"It does. They Ones Above seek an excuse to come down and take control of these islands. Just as you have sought an excuse to do the same. If they could prove—to themselves, perhaps to those who watch them—that you are dangerous to the Aviar, they would come and rescue them. To protect a resource. Is that not the argument you used? They will use the same."

"You don't know them, Sixth," Vathi said, shaking her head. "They're strange. Though they look like us, they're as different from you and me as... well, as we are from the Aviar."

"Yes, so different," Sixth said. "The Aviar use the worms. We use the Aviar. And now the Ones Above seek to use us... It is the way of things. I am right. This was a trap. I can see traps. It is what I do."

"Perhaps," Vathi said.

He climbed off of his rock. "I have brought you back to safety," he said. "Farewell."

"Sixth..."

She seemed to search for words. That seemed odd for a homeisler. They always seemed to have plenty of words, piled atop one another, ready to spew out.

Of course, those were the wrong words. Right words were far more difficult. He understood her silence, then, as he walked away from her back into the jungle.

His trip back to his safecamp was accomplished with far less difficulty—and far less speed—than had been required by frantic crossing during the night. He tried to get into the rhythm of trapping, the familiar motions that had been his companions for many years.

However, the jungle looked different to him now. It had been conquered. Oh, the outpost was new, but the secrets were out and the peak had been crossed.

By the time he reached his safecamp, dusk was again approaching. He did only a cursory check of things here before finding himself striking out toward the beach. He arrived as night settled, and despite Kokerlii's complaints, he shoved his canoe back out into the waters and climbed aboard.

He rowed all the way out into the waters, where he could look upon Patji as a whole. He sat there, dark waves undulating beneath his ship, as the moons rose and the stars came out.

Patji. Father. Killer and provider. A dark wedge in the night, crammed with life—so much that it seemed to spill out sometimes. The waves rolled and shook.

Sixth slept on his canoe that night. In the morning, while the sun rose behind him, he paddled around the island and came back to the fortress. He landed and went to its gates, demanding to speak to Vathi.

She came to the gates, changed, refreshed. She smiled as she saw him.

"I will come in," he said, "and I will help you. But you will do something for me."

"What?"

"Eventually, the Ones Above will take some of the Aviar with them," Sixth said. "They will find a way around their laws; they will get what they want. It is inevitable."

"You are probably right," she said, cautious.

"When those birds go," Sixth said, "I go with them. Into the Above. I don't care what it takes. You will find a way. If you send Aviar, you send me."

She frowned. "There has been talk of sending an ambassador with them, to their worlds in the Above. It was thought a politician or scientist should be chosen."

It was not a question. So Sixth did not reply.

"A trapper, though," Vathi said. "That makes a kind of sense, in and of itself. Who better to explore where none of us have yet gone." She chewed on the idea. "I will try. I cannot promise anything, Sixth, but you have my word to try."

She held out her hand to him.

He considered it as he would a cutaway vine hanging from a tree ahead. His corpse appeared at her feet, and Sak chirped warningly. Danger.

He took Vathi's anyway and stepped into the fortress.

WRITING EXCUSES 9.28 and 9.29

WORKSHOPPING SIXTH OF THE DUSK

Brandon: This week we're doing a critique of my story "Sixth of the Dusk," and we're going to run this like I run my writing group. A lot of people ask us questions such as "How do you guys workshop? What's your process?" This critique will cover the way my process works with my writing group. When we do Mary's story, we will use her writing group's process. This way, you're learning two things. You're seeing how our critique groups work, and you're also seeing how we go about revision.

Brandon: In my writing group, we start off talking briefly about what's working in the story, so the author doesn't accidentally take that out, doesn't screw it up. We talk about what's good, what's fun, what we enjoy. Then we go on to large-scale problems with the story. And from there, if we have time left over, we talk about medium-level issues. So, let's start off with "Sixth of the Dusk." What did you guys like?

Mary: I thought the worldbuilding was a lot of fun. It was compelling. The journey across the island was tense, and you managed the geography quite well. The characters were consistent. The prose was serviceable. Which I wouldn't say to anyone normally, but . . .

Brandon: My first drafts have a weakness: the prose.

Mary: Actually, the way you described the prose, I was expecting it to be awful. And it's not.

Brandon: No, it's just wordy, and each sentence could be a little tighter.

Dan: I liked the details in it. In particular, you don't just tell us the main character is a trapper. You show us the animals and the plants and the tricks that he uses and the culture that he's from. It's very well developed and really pulled me into the story.

Howard: First of all, I enjoyed the whole story. Beginning, middle, end, I thought the plot structure worked. The emotional arc of things was shaped right. The reveals felt like they were, for the most part, in the right places. The thing that struck me the most, that I think I liked the most, was the subverting of the "noble savage" trope. Your trapper recognizes that metal tools and pants are superior to what his people have been using for a long time. So, he's just fine with metal tools and trousers and boots and those things. I liked that.

Brandon: Listening to what Mary, Dan, and Howard just said, I wrote all of this down with the name of the person who said it. Usually, before I do a revision, I'll set this aside for a while and then I'll come back. So when I look at my notes, I want to know the context, who said what. This is because I know my writing group, and I know sometimes to pay more attention to someone I know is specialized in a certain area they do a really good job with. For example, when Howard says, "This is where your humor was working," I think, "Okay. I need to look at that and see what I was doing that actually made Howard laugh." Now, we'll move on to the large-scale problems.

Dan: I have one more thing I want to say before we move on. This is a minor note, and I know this was your intention the whole time, but it's worth pointing out that you successfully wrote a very unique world. Fantasies set in jungles are few and far between. This stands out just because of that.

Mary: Yeah. You did manage to make psychic birds make sense. So, kudos for that.

Brandon: All right. Big issues. In my writing group, it's not one person taking a turn. Just throw it out there, and then I encourage everyone to have a conversation about what they felt about that.

Dan: Does the dude's name count as a big issue? This was not by any means the biggest problem in the story, but "Sixth"—that is very hard to say. It was really getting on my nerves by the end. I was wishing he had an older brother so he could be Seventh.

Mary: No, because then he's Seventh of Nine, which was the thing that triggered me in the beginning.

Howard: The problem I had is: Statistically speaking, every other child is going to be named either First or Second. Which just seems weird.

Dan: That was cool. I'm willing to accept a weird naming convention. How many Jasons do we have?

Mary: It's not even that. That's not unusual. That's the way they were doing things in Rome. That's the way they do things in China, people going by their birth order.

Howard: That's a fair cop. If the first name is more like a surname. They don't have surnames. So many of you are going to be First, Second, or Third that it seems to be what would actually be differentiating you is what comes later. Which for him is Dusk. Which turns out not to be time of day.

Mary: It's the combination.

Dan: I apologize for starting this rant about a relatively minor thing. But a triple consonant cluster, or when it gets possessive a quadruple consonant cluster, was just hard for me say every time.

Brandon: Got it.

Mary: So, your ending.

Brandon: I will say, this is unfair to the readers. I did warn you that my ending had issues.

Mary: Yes, but I would flag that anyway. What I feel like is that you've got, basically, a triple ending going on. The reason I think that's happening is you've got the thing where they defeat the monster, which is not really the ending because that's an internal event. The bigger event that they have to solve is the stopping of the . . .

Dan: Machine. The mapping machine.

Mary: Which they do, and then he leaves and goes off to sea. And then he comes back, and then they go away. Leaving and going off to sea was a second ending, and going out into space is your third ending. I think there's a couple things going on besides that. One suggestion is to combine all of those so that you only end once. Because he needs to wrap up all of the problems. But I think the going away and coming back is currently not working.

Brandon: So you're saying not the "defeat the monster." But the other ending.

Mary: Right. No, the "defeat the monster" I don't count as an ending.

Brandon: The ones you're talking about are the "stop the machine" and the "go away and come back."

Dan: Going away works, in a sense. It's obviously in there because you knew you needed to separate those two endings in some way. One solution would be giving him a reason to come back that is actually good with this story. I liked having the breather to go out, look at the island—look at his Father—and then come back. But there wasn't anything bringing him back.

Mary: Yeah, I agree with that. But this is where I was going to head—the very end with his decision to come back and then go into space. At the beginning of the story, he is not dissatisfied with his life. He has a life that he likes. He feels like he's good at his job. Yes, the job is changing, but there's nothing about his life that indicates that he's lonely or wants to leave. You end with him taking her hand, which symbolizes a connection with someone else. There's nothing about the way his life is structured that indicates that the fact that he is not connecting with other people is a problem. None of that seems to be an issue for him. I think that if you want to keep that part of it, you have to go back to the beginning and insert something so that he is somewhat dissatisfied. If we're using the classic MICE structure [milieu, idea, character, event], right now you have a milieu story, and then you have an event. Then you wrap up the event and you wrap up the milieu. Then you suddenly have this character ending. And hello, where did this come from? And then he goes away, which resolves "I am not satisfied with my position in life." Also, there are two disruptions to the status quo. One is what is happening to the birds, which represents the larger disruption. There's also that we have space aliens coming down to visit us. Those are both related things. Right now, with the way the ending is structured, you have them as two separate things. I think that you would have a stronger emotional punch if you could find a way to have him come to that decision at the end. I also like him going back out to sea, but I don't think it's working.

Dan: It's not. So, he either needs to go out to sea and then have a compelling reason, something that drives him back—or we need to remove the need for him to go out to sea.

Mary: If we're looking at the process, you know your structures. The story starts with a character and ends with a place. Or leaving a place. We could count the entrance into the fortress as the exit from the island. He arrives on the island on his boat, but he is leaving via another door. That could count if you go back to the beginning and add in some character stuff.

Dan: Or just have him get onto their other boat—the iron boat. Coming in on a little canoe and leaving on a big iron boat solves that very subtle problem. We keep interrupting Howard.

Brandon: This is Mary's expertise. So I'm willing to just let Mary talk.

Mary: I just wanted to second what Dan said, in particular. Putting him on the iron boat allows you to have that look back at the island. And that is a really strong image.

Howard: I had a process question. I'll be blunt: Dan and Mary are fixing your story. Is that the sort of critique you're accustomed to getting?

Brandon: That's a good question. In my writing group, I always want Dan in particular to fix my story. Here's the thing. This may be a bad example for the readers because I'm sitting with two of the authors I respect most in the world, and with Howard. (That's for the thing you did between sessions, by the way.)

Howard: That's just fine.

Brandon: Dan and I know each other really well. We have been workshopping together forever. We know each other's stories. In some cases, this can be a bad thing in that since we know what the other is trying for, sometimes that gets us into trouble. Since Dan knows my writing so well, he'll miss things that are wrong because he assumes he knows what I was trying for.

And he's right. But a really good critiquer can dig into "This is the problem, and here are ways to fix it." Now, you as the writer may not take those suggestions. I'm experienced at getting critiqued. I know when to take advice and when not to take it. So, allowing two really good writers to go back and forth on what is wrong with my writing and what can fix it—I'm perfectly willing to let happen and be excited by it. But for a lot of new workshoppers, I suggest not to do this. I suggest they describe their emotions and not give fixes to the writer.

Mary: I'm going to second you on that. If I were critiquing someone else, I would not be offering the prescription.

Brandon: This is one of the reasons I wanted readers to know that I said to you, "I think my ending's broken. Do you guys have any suggestions?" Because I'm actively soliciting help, which is different from my usual goal in a critique session. And now, I'm going to open the floor to any other major issues the story has that you noticed.

Howard: Now, the readers may be familiar with the episode we did with Lou Anders, on the Hollywood Formula. One of the ways in which I think this ending failed is that, while I could feel the presence of the various emotional threads, they didn't all hit close enough together. I think that's a good way to sum up what Mary said. All of these things kind of needed to happen, but they needed to happen closer together. Aside from the Hollywood Formula, the two biggest problems I had involve me wanting clues. First, I wanted some foreshadowing with regard to "Dusk" a little bit earlier. That was a neat reveal; I liked that. But when by the end of the story we realized that he's mulling over his name as a foretelling, I thought maybe he should have been mulling over his name as a foretelling earlier. That could be the discontent that he's feeling, that Mary suggested. The second issue is that I think we were almost halfway through the story before it mentioned that they had made contact with people from the stars, and that needed to drop a little bit sooner.

Dan: That needed to at least be hinted at earlier. I don't mind the revelation coming where it does.

Howard: Oh, the revelation was awesome.

Dan: But I was not prepared for it.

Brandon: There is a mention on page two.

Dan: Well, obviously none of us saw it. If you feel the need to defend your story, that means it's wrong. Okay, here's my thing. Even more so than the ending, this is my biggest problem with the story.

Mary: Where is that on page two? That is so not on page two.

Brandon: Search for "the Ones Above."

Mary: Oh, please.

Dan: Sixth gives away so much information for no reason that I could discern. He focuses so heavily on the fact that he doesn't like talking, that this woman talks too much. And then he just cannot stop himself from spilling every secret he knows, and he doesn't get anything out of it. He's not trying to get anything from her. It felt very weird to me, like the plot engine would take over—"We need to know another secret now, so he's just going to tell us."

Mary: I had some issues with that. I felt like a lot of his motivation for why he was telling her was that people already know this and it's going to come out. I felt like usually there was motivation behind that and I could accept it, but there were a couple of places where I thought, "Why are you telling her this?"

Dan: See, if that's his motivation, I think it would need to be accompanied by his reaction. Not just an acceptance, but some form of guilt or betrayal or whatever. That was there a little bit, but not enough to sell it.

Mary: Yeah. Also I think that if he was doing some of that in the beginning, when I was talking about needing some form of him being dissatisfied with life, before he even meets her. If they've got steam they've got probably newspapers or something, and maybe some article had been published and he thinks, "People are starting to talk about stuff that has traditionally been kept between us." And also, "Ones Above" is not until page twenty-two. So there.

Dan: The seeds are there to have this "letting go of the past" aspect. You plant early on that he's wearing more modern clothes. He has a compass. He has the scuba mask that he talks about. But he completely accepts that, whereas . . . Brandon knows what I mean at this point.

Howard: Brandon, what does Dan mean?

Brandon: I try to avoid talking too much when my submission is being critiqued, but Dan is talking about that Sixth is accepting all of these things, but is there any regret? Is there any sense of loss? I mean, he's just moving along with it, and is that a wasted opportunity there or not?

Mary: I completely agree with that. I think that if you can give us hints of that in the beginning, that will inform a lot of the decisions that he makes later.

Dan: The other thing that I wanted say, the other seed that is being sown there is that he, by bringing in mainland birds, has already started to corrupt the island. That was never brought up, and never addressed. If that's a direction you decide to go, he could solve some of this problem, that he's already party to the corruption of the island.

Mary: I thought that you dealt with that a little when he said, "Let's kill all of the nightmaws." I thought that the bird he had, Sak, was a mainland bird that had been blown off course, and he just got lucky with that one. But you're right, he is bringing chicks in now, because he's saying there will be more of these. That may be one of those things where he's not aware of the ecosystem issues that he's going to cause by doing that. That's something Vathi could bring up, and have him make those connections.

Howard: That is a neat piece of symmetry. The groundwork is already laid for that, where he is worried about change. He recognizes himself as an agent of change. His name means he is an agent of change. But he does not recognize the extent of the change that would occur if he does what he wants. Whereas Vathi is definitely an agent of change. She's there as part of changing things. But her mission is to change things while at the same time protecting them, in a way that hasn't occurred to him. There's a neat symmetry there. That's the sort of thing which, Brandon, you do a great job with in your other works that I've read where you've had a chance to tighten up the prose. Those are the things that just naturally flow out. As you're tightening up these words, you realize, "Oh, I need to use this word here, and then this word again here," and the reader grabs that symmetry without you having to throw down a whole paragraph that says, "This is what he believed." That's one of the reasons why I spend so much time drilling down on my prose so early in a project, because my editor is an idiot.

Brandon: Well, let's continue to thrash my story, everyone. What are your medium-level problems? Just things that occurred to you that may not require a big revision, but that bothered you.

Mary: This is a tiny thing. It's actually just an order of information flow issue. On page seven when you introduce Sak, it says, "The Aviar usually waited until they'd landed before bestowing her blessing." It made me think, the corpse is a vision? Because

I wasn't completely clear. Why is that a blessing? Why is the vision of the corpse a blessing? You answer it two sentences later. But because the two sentences are "The black-feathered bird just watched the waves, and Sixth continued—" You're right, Dan, that is hard to say. "Sixth continued his work."

Howard: We have an audiobook problem here.

Mary: I thought you were done, and I thought that I wasn't going to get the answer, so I was confused. I really think that just moving the body he saw, moving that little section somewhere, just so there's not quite that tiny buffer between, would have fixed that for me. It's a small thing.

Howard: A medium-level thing for me—I guess it's a mixture of things—was the mechanic of the foretelling. We never get, at any point, a vision from Sak that tells us something that then comes true. So yes, he's been very careful and he's survived all of this time as a result of stuff from Sak, but I've never seen Sak foretell something, and then see that thing actually happen. Which I know wouldn't work, because we're only getting his corpse.

Mary: Yeah, but what we do see is Sak give the warning and Sixth looks closer, and says—

Howard: Oh yes, there's a thing there.

Dan: Like with the vines coming out of the trees.

Howard: See, that's why I'm saying it's a medium-level problem. If I could see one of those prophecies come true, I would be much more satisfied with the bird's ability. The other thing that was a little weird is the concatenation of his corpse everywhere, which—

Dan: Was awesome.

Mary: Intense.

Howard: No, I liked it. It was powerful. It was awesome. But to my mind, it was never explained. I didn't understand why.

Dan: I was bothered as well by the fact that we never find out what this mapping machine is, or what it's going to do to the island. But I was not super bothered by it. I don't know if I would have even brought it up, had Howard not mentioned it. It's a hole in the story, but it feels like it's an excusable hole because that's not what the story is focusing on.

Mary: See, I was okay with that. I thought, "Well, why would mapping machinery do that? That doesn't make any sense." But then Sixth says, "Hey, I think it's because this is a trap and it's not actually mapping machinery. It's designed to cause this disruption."

Howard: I liked that reveal a lot. That was cool.

Mary: I did too. But where my problem lay was that I didn't see his logical steps to get to that. We're in his POV, but we didn't see him putting those pieces together. We just saw him say, "And here, let me give you this piece of exposition."

Dan: Yes. That exposition came out of nowhere. If he arrives there by the same process you just did, that would solve two whole different problems for me at the same time. Now, here's another problem that maybe didn't bug anybody else. The gun that she has, I couldn't figure out why it was a harpoon gun. That was weird enough to me that I thought, "Oh, it's going to be important later that it's a harpoon gun." And it is, because you can't tie a flower onto a bullet, so therefore it had to be a harpoon. That, as far as I could see, was the only reason for it to be a harpoon. I'm cool with other cultures having other kinds of guns. But this was never used in a way that would make a harpoon more valuable than a bullet.

Howard: They had the "shadow" sea creatures that they were up against sometimes. If you're going to shoot something like that, you do need a heavier projectile than a bullet, because a bullet won't go very far in the water. But she tried shooting at one, and it didn't work.

Dan: But I never got the sense that this was an underwater weapon.

Mary: She does say that it was specifically something that they had for the shadow, and that she grabbed it when she was fleeing. But that maybe needs to be brought out a little more. Along these lines, since we're talking about shadow and nightmaw and all of these things, oddly, when it mentioned a shark-toothed club I thought, "They have sharks on this world?" I don't know why that bothered me. Because birds didn't bother me; horses wouldn't have bothered me. But when we have all of these other cool flora and fauna that are clearly indigenous to the world, for some reason I thought, "Why would anyone import sharks?" I can understand importing birds. But why would anyone import sharks?

Dan: On a related note—this is actually a good thing that I thought was a neat little minor touch—is how you described the shadows, the big monsters. You never actually say that they look like krakens, or cthulhus, or whatever. But that's what I imagined in my head. But he had literally no idea how to describe it, or maybe it was the girl. Then in the next sentence, they talk about octopuses. I'm like, well if they know what an octopus is, and they still don't know how to describe what I assumed was a kraken, it must be even weirder than I thought it was. I thought that was a really neat moment.

Howard: I assumed it was a really big shark.

Mary: I just thought it was something bad.

Dan: You guys don't like to imagine tentacles as much as I do.

Mary: All right. This is again in that medium level. This is one of the places where I felt like there was an inconsistency. "If you had been another trapper, I would have killed you directly, rather than leaving you to revenge yourself upon me." But I thought that they didn't kill each other directly. Then I wondered, "Well, is that because she's at the safecamp?" Because there was an allusion to the only time that they fought was at the safecamp.

Dan: Not an allusion, but a direct reference. "We don't hurt each other. We let the island kill each other. We just help it."

Mary: Yeah. It was very close to this, so I was confused. Either cut or clarify. Let's see. What else did I have?

Dan: The little meekers were awesome.

Mary: Loved the meekers.

Dan: But I was sad that they didn't show up later. Essentially, I imagined him assaulting this enemy fortress, and I thought he was going to rouse his little band of nasty little bitey mice. Instead, he just scared some panthers in the woods, and then we jump-cut.

Mary: There were a lot of things in here that were really cool, that I love, but that I think you could cut to make this a tighter story. The meekers represent one of those, because you're not using them. So use it or lose it. I have no idea where you would insert them. But since you write long, this is something that you could cut and shorten it.

Brandon: Originally, they actually were going to kill Vathi. Offhandedly, because his paranoia was too—

Mary: I'm glad you didn't go there.

Brandon: I decided when I got there that it was the wrong emotional beat for this, but that's why they were there originally.

Mary: You can cut them now, and use them in a different story, because they're great. Except I will say that one thing they do—if you are emphasizing this theme of him disrupting island ecology—it is an example of him interfering with the way things naturally work on the island.

Howard: The other thing they do is that they help reinforce this idea that there is telepathy happening in nature everywhere. It's a broader sort of effect.

Mary: Yes. One of the ways you could use them is that maybe she was not the only person who escaped, and she had a companion who was killed by the meekers. Now, getting back to something that Dan had said earlier about how Sixth just seemed to be spouting information. There was a point where he says, "Coming here was obviously a disaster." But in the rest of the story, he is so annoyed with her saying all of these obvious things. So, the fact that he is actually using the word "obviously"—

Dan: That was a minor thing, but it stood out to me as well.

Mary: Yeah. I guess it's minor, but I'm just—

Dan: Not just the word choice, but just how verbose he became in those two sentences. Very wordy.

Mary: Yeah. Ooh, this is actually something I should have mentioned in the cool stuff. There is a point where he has been using her name for a while, and he gets angry at her, and for two paragraphs he only refers to her as "the woman," which was a really nice way of showing that he was thinking, "She is not a person to me."

Brandon: We are out of time, so I'm just going to let you send me the rest of your notes. Because the whole point of this was so that the readers can see what a writing group is like for us. Hopefully, the whole process of this, with us brainstorming it, writing it, and then polishing it, will help you as writers to see how this is going.

Edits: Sixth of the Dusk

Brandon Sanderson

Death hunted beneath the waves. ~~Sixth~~Dusk saw it approach, ~~though its details were hidden by the waters. A shadow wider than six narrowboats tied together,~~ an enormous ~~deep~~ blackness within the deep blue, a shadowed form as wide as six narrowboats tied together. ~~Sixth~~Dusk's hands tensed on his paddle, his heartbeat racing as he immediately sought out Kokerlii.

Fortunately, the colorful bird sat in his customary place on the prow of the boat, idly biting at one clawed foot raised to his beak. ~~The colorful bird~~Kokerlii lowered his foot and puffed out his feathers, as if completely unmindful of the ~~enormous shadow that approached~~danger beneath.

~~Sixth~~Dusk held his breath. He always did~~, even still~~, when unfortunate enough to run across one of these things in the open ocean. He did not know what they looked like beneath those waves. He hoped to never find out.

The shadow drew closer, almost to the boat now. A school of ~~th~~slin~~m~~fish passing nearby~~,~~ jumped into the air in a silvery wave, spooked by the shadow's approach. The terrified fish showered back to the water with a sound like rain. The shadow did not deviate. The ~~th~~slin~~m~~fish were too small a meal to interest it.

A boat's occupants, however . . .

It passed directly underneath. Sak chirped quietly from ~~Sixth~~Dusk's shoulder; the second bird seemed to have some sense of the danger. Creatures like the shadow did not hunt by smell or sight, but by sensing the minds of prey. ~~Sixth~~Dusk glanced at Kokerlii again, his only protection against a danger that could swallow his ship whole. ~~There was a reason most sailors~~He had never clipped ~~their Aviar~~Kokerlii's wings, ~~or at least tied them down. Sixth spurned such practices. B~~but at times like this~~, with a shadow passing directly beneath—so large that it could have swallowed his boat whole—he wondered~~ he understood why many sailors preferred Aviar that could not fly away.

The boat rocked softly~~,~~; the jumping slimfish stilled. Waves lapped against the sides of the vessel. Had the shadow stopped? Hesitated? Did it sense them? Kokerlii's protective aura had always been enough before, but . . .

The shadow slowly vanished ~~beneath~~. It had turned to swim downward, ~~Sixth~~Dusk realized. In moments, he could make out nothing through the waters. ~~Just that~~

~~endless deep.~~ He hesitated, then forced himself to get out his new mask. It was a ~~new~~modern device he had acquired only two supply trips back: a glass faceplate with ~~some kind of~~ leather ~~—perhaps a sheep's bladder or stomach—on~~ at the sides. He placed it on the water's ~~top~~surface and leaned down, looking into the ~~water~~ depths. They became as clear to him as ~~the water of~~ an undisturbed lagoon.

Nothing. Just ~~the blue~~that endless deep. *Fool man,* he thought, tucking away the mask and getting out his paddle. *Didn't you just think to yourself that you never wanted to see one of those?*

Still, as he started paddling again, he knew that he'd spend the rest of this trip feeling as if the shadow were down there, following him. ~~Lurking in those endless depths.~~ That was the nature of the waters. You never knew what lurked ~~there. You probably didn't want to~~below.

He continued on his journey, paddling his outrigger canoe and reading the lapping of the waves to judge his position. Those waves were as good as a compass for ~~any trained in wayfinding.~~ him—~~o~~Once, they would have been good enough for any of the Eelakin, his people. ~~Anymore~~These days, just the trappers learned the old arts. ~~T~~Admittedly, though, even *he* ~~did~~ carr~~y~~ied one of the newest compasses, wrapped up in his pack with a set of the new sea charts—maps ~~from~~given as gifts by the Ones Above during their visit earlier in the year. They were said to be more accurate than even the latest surveys, so he'd purchased a set just in case. You could not stop times from changing, his mother said, ~~any~~no more than you could stop the surf from rolling.

It was not long, after the accounting of tides, before he caught sight of the first island. Sori was a small island in the ~~p~~Pantheon, and the most commonly visited. ~~Its~~Her name meant child; ~~Sixth~~Dusk vividly remembered ~~well~~ training on her shores with his uncle.

It had been long since he'd burned an offering to Sori, despite how well she had treated him during his youth. Perhaps a small offering would not be out of line. Patji would not grow jealous. One could not be jealous of Sori, the least of the islands. Just as every trapper was welcome on Sori, every other island in the ~~p~~Pantheon was said to be affectionate of her.

Be that as it may, Sori did not contain much ~~in the way of~~ valuable game. ~~Sixth Dusk~~ continued rowing, moving down one leg of the archipelago his people knew as the ~~p~~Pantheon. From a distance, this archipelago was not so different from the home-isl~~and~~es of the Eelakin, now a three~~-~~-week trip behind him.

From a distance. Up close, they were very, very different. ~~Sixth~~Over the next five hours, Dusk rowed past Sori ~~and~~, then her three cousins~~, the first of the closed islands~~. He had never set foot on ~~them~~any of those three. In fact, he had not landed on many of the forty-some islands in the ~~p~~Pantheon. At the end of his apprenticeship, a trapper chose one island and worked there all his life. He had chosen Patji—an event some ten years past now. Seemed like far less.

~~He~~Dusk saw no other shadows beneath the waves, but he kept watch. Not that he could do much to protect himself. Kokerlii did all of that work as he roosted happily at the prow of the ship, eyes half-closed. ~~Sixth~~Dusk had fed him seed ~~before the approach.~~; Kokerlii did like it so much more than dried fruit.

Nobody knew why beasts like the shadows only lived here, in the waters near the ~~p~~Pantheon. Why not travel across the seas to the Eelakin ~~i~~Islands or the mainland, where food would be plentiful and Aviar like Kokerlii were far more rare? Once, these questions had not been ~~questions men~~ asked. The seas were what they were. ~~Those days had passed.~~ Now, however, men poked and prodded into everything. They asked, "Why?" They said, "~~w~~We should explain it."

~~Sixth~~Dusk shook his head, dipping his paddle into the water. That sound—wood on water—had been his companion for most of his days. He understood it far better than he did the speech of men.

Even if sometimes their questions got inside of him and refused to go free.

After the cousins, most trappers would have turned north or south, ~~continu~~moving along ~~the wing~~branches of the ~~pantheon~~archipelago until reaching their chosen island. ~~Sixth~~Dusk continued forward, into the heart of the ~~archipelago~~islands, until a ~~large~~ shape loomed before him. Patji, largest island of the ~~islands~~Pantheon. It towered ~~taller than any of the others,~~ like a wedge rising from the sea. A place of inhospitable peaks, sharp cliffs, and deep jungle.

Hello, old ~~friend~~destroyer, he thought. *Hello, ~~f~~Father.*

~~Sixth~~Dusk raised his paddle and placed it in the boat. He sat for a time, chewing on fish from last night's catch, feeding scraps to Sak. The black-plumed bird ate them with an air of solemnity. Kokerlii continued to sit on the prow, chirping occasionally~~, now that they had approached~~. He would be eager to land. Sak ~~never~~ seemed never to grow eager about anything.

Approaching Patji was not a simple task, even for one who trapped his shores. The boat continued its dance with the waves as ~~Sixth~~Dusk considered which landing to make. Eventually, he put the fish away, then dipped his paddle back into the waters. Those waters ~~were still~~remained deep and blue, despite the proximity to the island. Some members of the ~~p~~Pantheon had sheltered bays and gradual beaches ~~that one could wade in~~. Patji had no patience for such foolishness. His beaches were rocky~~,~~ and ~~the~~had steep drop-offs ~~from them were so steep that deep water began only a few steps out~~.

You were never safe on his shores. In fact, the beaches were the most dangerous part ~~of a very dangerous place. There~~—upon them, not only could the horrors of the land get to you, but you were still within reach of the deep's ~~creature~~monsters. ~~Sixth~~Dusk's uncle had cautioned him about this time and time again. Only a fool slept on ~~the~~Patji's shores ~~of Patji~~.

The tide was with him, and he avoided being caught in any of the swells that would crush him against those stern rock faces. ~~Sixth~~Dusk approached ~~what passed for a beach on Patji's shores,~~ a partially -sheltered expanse of stone crags and outcroppings, Patji's version of a beach. Kokerlii ~~immediately~~ fluttered off, chirping and calling as he flew toward the trees.

~~Sixth~~Dusk immediately glanced at the waters ~~beneath~~. No shadows. Still, he felt naked as he hopped out of the ~~ship~~ canoe and pulled it up onto the rocks, warm water washing against his legs. Sak remained in her place on ~~Sixth~~Dusk's shoulder.

Nearby in the surf, ~~Sixth~~Dusk saw a corpse bobbing in the water.

Beginning your visions early, my friend? he thought, glancing at Sak. The Aviar usually waited until they'd fully landed before bestowing her blessing.

The black-feathered bird just watched the waves.

~~Sixth~~Dusk continued his work. The body he saw in the surf was his own. It told him to avoid that section of water. Perhaps there was a spiny anemone that would have ~~trapp~~pricked him, or perhaps a deceptive undercurrent lay in wait. Sa~~x~~k's visions did not ~~always~~ show such detail~~,~~; they gave only warning.

~~Sixth~~Dusk got the boat out of the water, then detached the floats, tying them more securely onto the main part of the canoe. Following that, he worked the vessel carefully up the shore, mindful not to scrape the hull on sharp rocks. He would need to hide the canoe in the jungle. If another trapper discovered it, ~~Sixth~~Dusk would be strap~~pn~~ded on the island for several extra weeks preparing his spare. That would—

He stopped as his heel struck something soft as he backed up the shore. He glanced down, expecting a pile of seaweed. Instead he found a damp piece of cloth. A shirt? ~~Sixth~~Dusk held it up, then noticed other, more subtle signs across the shore. Broken lengths of sanded wood. Bits of paper floating in an eddy.

Those fools, he thought.

He returned to moving his canoe. Rushing was never a good idea on a ~~p~~Pantheon island. He did step more quickly, however.

As he reached the tree line, he caught sight of his corpse hanging from a tree nearby. Those were cutaway vines lurking in the fern-like tree-top. Sak squawked softly on his shoulder as ~~he~~Dusk hefted a large stone from the beach, then tossed it at the tree. It thumped against the wood, and sure enough, the vines dropped like a net, full of stinging barbs.

They would take a few hours to retract ~~back up~~. ~~Sixth~~Dusk pulled his canoe over and hid it in the underbrush near the tree. Hopefully, other trappers would be smart enough to stay away from the cutaway vines—and therefore wouldn't stumble over his boat.

Before placing the final camouflaging fronds, ~~Sixth~~Dusk pulled out his pack. Though the centuries had changed a trapper's duties very little, the modern world did offer its benefits. ~~Instead of sandals, Sixth tied on sturdy boots.~~ Instead of a simple wrap that left his legs and chest exposed, he ~~wore~~put on thick trousers with pockets on the legs and a buttoning shirt to protect his skin against sharp branches ~~or~~and leaves. Instead of sandals, Dusk tied on sturdy boots. And~~,~~ instead of a ~~shark~~-tooth-~~lined~~ club, he bore a machete of the finest steel. His pack contained luxuries like a steel-hooked rope, a lantern, and a firestarter that created sparks simply by pressing the two handles together.

He looked very little like the trappers in the paintings back home. He didn't mind. He'd rather stay alive. ~~He~~

Dusk left the canoe, shouldering his pack, machete sheathed at his side. Sak moved to his other shoulder. Before leaving the beach, ~~Sixth~~Dusk paused, looking at the image of his translucent corpse, still hanging from unseen vines ~~at~~by the tree.

Could he really have ever been foolish enough to be caught by cutaway vines? Near as he could tell, Se͟ak only showed him plausible deaths. He liked to think that most were fairly unlikely—a vision of what could have happened if he'd been careless, or if his uncle's training hadn't been so extensive.

Once, ~~Sixth~~Dusk had stayed away from any place where he saw his corpse. It wasn't bravery that drove him to do the opposite now. He just ... needed to confront the possibilities. He needed to be able to walk away from this beach knowing that he could still deal with cutaway vines. If he avoided danger, he would soon lose his skills. He could not rely on Se͟ak too much.

<u>For Patji would try on every possible occasion to kill him.</u>

Dusk~~Sixth~~ turned and trudged across the rocks along the coast. Doing so went against his instincts—he normally wanted to get inland as soon as possible. Unfortunately, he could not leave without investigating the origin of the debris he had seen earlier. He had a strong suspicion of where he would find their source.

He gave a whistle, and Kokerlii trilled above, flapping out of a tree nearby and winging over the beach. ~~His~~The protection <u>he offered</u> would not be as strong as it would be if he were close, but ~~that shouldn't matter. T~~the beasts that hunted minds on the island were not as large <u>or as strong of psyche</u> as the shadows of the ocean~~, and so long as Kokerlii remained somewhat close, Sixth~~. Dusk and Sak would be invisible <u>to them</u>.

About a half hour up the coast, ~~he~~Dusk found the remnants of a large camp. Broken boxes, fraying ropes l~~a~~ying half submerged in tidal pools, ripped canvas, ~~broken~~shattered pieces of wood that might once have been walls. Kokerlii landed on a broken pole ~~nearby~~.

There were no signs of his corpse nearby. That could mean that the area wasn't immediately dangerous. It could also mean that whatever might kill him here would swallow the corpse whole.

~~Sixth~~Dusk trod lightly on wet stones~~, listening to~~ <u>at</u> the ~~water lapping over the edges~~ of the broken campsite. No. Larger than a campsite. ~~Sixth~~Dusk ran his fingers over a broken chunk of wood, stenciled with the words *Northern Interests Trading Company*. A powerful mercantile force from his homeland.

He had told them. He had *told* them. Do not come to Patji. Fools. And they had camped here on the beach itself! Was nobody in that company capable of listening? ~~Sixth picked his way through the remnants of the camp. How long had it been?~~ He stopped beside a group of gouges in the rocks, as wide as his upper arm, running some ten paces long. They led toward the ocean.

Shadow, he thought. *One of the deep beasts.* His uncle had spoken of seeing one once~~, from a distance~~. An enormous ... *something* that had exploded up from the depths. It had killed a dozen krell ~~who~~<u>that</u> had been chewing on oceanside weeds before retreating into the waters with its feast.

~~Sixth~~Dusk shivered, imagining this camp on the rocks, bustling with men unpacking boxes, preparing to build the fort they had described to him. But where was their ship? The great steam-powered vessel with an iron hull they claimed could rebuff the attacks of even the deepest of shadows? Did it now defend the ocean bottom, a home for slimfish and octop~~ius~~?

There were no survivors—nor even any corpses—that ~~Sixth~~Dusk could see. The ~~beach was too dangerous~~shadow must have consumed them. He pulled back to the slightly ~-~safer local~e~ of the jungle's edge. ~~Here, he,~~ then scanned the foliage, looking for signs that people had passed this way. Th~~is~~e attack was recent, within the last day or so. ~~The company really had beat him to the islands, despite his head start.~~

~~He'd been certain they'd listen to reason. A dozen different trappers had spoken to them. Fools!~~ He absently gave Sak a seed from his pocket as he located a series of broken fronds leading into the jungle. So there were survivors. ~~At least one, m~~Maybe as many as a half dozen. They had each chosen to go in different directions, in a hurry. Running from the attack.

Running through the jungle~~s~~ was a good way to get dead. These company types~~ ... they~~ thought themselves rugged~~, they thought themselves~~ and prepared. They were wrong. He'd spoken to a number of them, trying to persuade as many of their ~-~"trappers~-~" as possible to abandon the voyage.

It had done no good. He wanted to blame the visits of the Ones Above for causing this foolish striving for progress, but the truth was the companies had been talking of outposts on the Pantheon for years. Dusk sighed. Well, these survivors were likely dead now. He should leave them to their fates.

Except ... The thought of it, outsiders on Patji~~ ... Well~~, it made him shiver ~~in~~with something that mixed disgust and anxiety. They were *here*. It was wrong. These islands were sacred, the trappers their priests.

The plants rustled nearby. ~~Sixth~~Dusk whipped his machete about, leveling it, reaching into his pocket for his sling. It was not a refugee who left the bushes, or even a predator. ~~Not a common one, at least.~~ A group of small, mouse-like creatures crawled out, sniffing the air. Sak squawked. She had never liked meekers.

Food? the three meekers sent to ~~Sixth~~Dusk. *Food?*

It was the most rudimentary of thoughts, projected directly into his mind. Though he did not want the distraction, he did not pass up the opportunity to fish out some dried meat for the meekers. As they huddled around it, sending him gratitude, he saw their sharp teeth and the single~,~ pointed fang at the tips of their mouths. His uncle had told him that once, meekers had been dangerous to men. One bite was enough to kill. Over the centuries, the little creatures had grown accustomed to trappers. They had minds~, thoughts~ beyond ~~that~~those of dull animals. Almost~,~ he found them as intelligent as the Aviar.

~~If they were intelligent, they could be trained. Perhaps.~~ *You remember?* he sent them~,~ through thoughts. *You remember your task?*

Others, they sent back gleefully. *Bite others~.~!*

~~Once, they had been dangerous to men.~~ Trappers ignored ~~them. Sixth~~these little beasts; Dusk figured that maybe~, one of these little beasts~ with some training,

~~the meekers~~ could provide an unexpected surprise for one of his rivals. He ~~had been cultivating small groups of them across the island. They'd have been frightened of the company and its many people. But perhaps . . .~~ fished in his pocket, fingers brushing an old stiff piece of feather. Then, not wanting to pass up the opportunity, he got a few long, bright green and red feathers from his pack. They were mating plumes, which he'd taken from Kokerlii during the Aviar's most recent molting.

He moved into the jungle, meekers following with excitement. Once he neared their den, he stuck the mating plumes into some branches, as if they had fallen there naturally. A passing trapper might see the plumes and assume that Aviar had a nest nearby, fresh with eggs for the plunder. That would draw them.

Bite others, Dusk instructed again.

Bite others! they replied.

He hesitated, thoughtful. Had they perhaps seen something from the company wreck? Point him in the right direction. *Have you seen any others?* ~~Sixth~~Dusk sent them. *Recently? In the jungle?*

Bite others! came the reply.

~~t~~They were ~~i~~ntelligent . . . but not *that* intelligent. ~~Sixth~~Dusk bade the animals farewell ~~and~~ turned ~~back~~ toward the forest. After a moment's deliberation, he found himself striking inland, crossing—then following—one of the refugee trails. He chose ~~the one that made him the most nervous,~~ the one that looked as if it would pass uncomfortably close to one of his own safecamps, deep within the jungle.

~~Sixth passed out of the sun and~~ It was hotter here beneath the jungle's canopy~~. It was hotter here~~, despite the shade. Comfortably sweltering. Kokerlii joined him, winging up ahead to a branch where a few lesser Aviar sat chirping. Kokerlii towered over them, but sang at them with enthusiasm. An Aviar raised around ~~people~~humans never quite fit back in among their own kind. The same could be said of a man raised around Aviar.

~~Sixth~~Dusk followed the trail left by the refugee, expecting to stumble over the man's corpse at any moment. He did not, though his own dead body did occasionally appear along the path. He saw it laying half-eaten in the mud or tucked away in a fallen log with only the foot showing. He could never grow too ~~comfortable~~placent, with Sak on his shoulder. ~~That was one primary reason he preferred her to other Aviar.~~

—It did not matter if Sak's visions were truth or fiction.~~ The~~; he needed the constant reminder of how Patji treated the unwary ~~was enough. It kept Sixth alert, and that kept him alive.~~

He fell into the familiar, but not comfortable, lope of a ~~p~~Pantheon trapper. Alert, wary, careful not to brush leaves that could carry biting insects~~,~~. ~~c~~Cutting with the machete only when necessary, lest he leave a trail another could follow. Listening, aware of his Aviar at all times, never outstripping Kokerlii or letting him drift too far ahead.

The ~~man he tracked~~refugee did not fall to the common dangers of the island—he cut across game trails, rather than following them. The surest way to ~~run~~

~~across~~encounter predators was to fall in with their food. The refugee did not know how to mask his trail, but neither did he blunder into the nest of ~~the~~ firesnap lizards, or brush the deathweed bark, or step into the patch of hungry mud.

Was this another trapper, perhaps? A youthful one, not fully trained? That seemed something the company would try. Experienced trappers were beyond recruitment; none would be foolish enough to guide a group of clerks and merchants around the islands. But a youth, who had not yet chosen his island? A youth who, perhaps, resented being required to practice only on Sori until his mentor determined his apprenticeship complete? ~~Sixth~~Dusk had felt that way ten years ago~~, when nearing the end of his uncle's training~~.

So the company had hired itself a trapper at last. That would explain why they had grown so bold as to ~~come, despite the council of men like Sixth.~~ —finally organize their expedition. *But Patji hi*~~t~~*mself?* he thought, kneeling beside the bank of a small stream. It had no name~~, at least not one that Sixth had given it~~, but it was familiar to him. *Why would they come here?*

The answer was simple. They were merchants. The biggest, to them, would be the best. Why waste time on lesser islands? Why not come for the Father himself?

Above, Kokerlii landed on a branch and began pecking at a fruit. The refugee had stopped by th~~e~~is river. ~~Sixth~~Dusk had gained time on the ~~man . . . or, rather, the~~ youth. ~~Yes, that footprint: j~~Judging by the depth ~~it~~the boy's footprints had sunk in the mud, ~~Sixth~~Dusk could imagine ~~the boy's~~his weight and height. Sixteen~~, perhaps. Certainly not fully grown. Could he be~~? Maybe younger? Trappers apprenticed at ten, but ~~he~~Dusk could not imagine even the company trying to recruit one so ill trained.

~~Perhaps t~~Two hours gone, ~~Sixth~~Dusk thought, turning a broken stem and smelling the sap. The boy's path continued on toward ~~Sixth~~Dusk's safecamp. How? ~~He~~Dusk had never spoken of it to anyone ~~else~~. Perhaps this youth was apprenticing under one of the other trappers who visited Patji. One of them could have found his safecamp and mentioned it.

~~Sixth crossed the stream and continued. Each member of the pantheon supported a variety of trappers.~~ Dusk frowned, considering. In ten years on Patji, he had ~~only~~ seen another trapper in person only a handful of times. On each occasion, they had both turned and gone a different direction without saying a word. It was the way of such things. ~~Trappers would not attack one another directly unless defending a camp.~~

—~~Of course, t~~They would try to kill one another~~. They just~~, but they didn't do it in person. Better to let Patji claim rivals than to directly stain one's hands ~~with their blood~~. At least, so his uncle had taught him.

~~This one, though . . .~~ Sometimes, Dusk found himself frustrated by that. Patji would get them all eventually. Why help the Father out? Still, it was the way of things, so he went through the motions. Regardless, this ~~one~~refugee was making directly for ~~Sixth~~Dusk's safecamp. ~~If he really was a~~The youth~~, he~~ might not know the proper way of things. Perhaps he had come seeking help, afraid to go to one of his master's safecamps for fear of punishment. Or . . .

No, best to avoid pondering it ~~too much~~. ~~Sixth~~Dusk already had a mind full of spurious conjectures. He would find what he would find. <ins>He had to focus on the jungle and its dangers. He started away from the stream, and as he did so, he saw his corpse appear suddenly before him.</ins>

<ins>He hopped forward, then spun backward, hearing a faint hiss. The distinctive sound was made by air escaping from a small break in the ground, followed by a flood of tiny yellow insects, each as small as a pinhead. A new deathant pod? If he'd stood there a little longer, disturbing their hidden nest, they would have flooded up around his boot. One bite, and he'd be dead.</ins>

<ins>He stared at that pool of scrambling insects longer than he should have. They pulled back into their nest, finding no prey. Sometimes a small bulge announced their location, but today he had seen nothing. Only Sak's vision had saved him.</ins>

<ins>Such was life on Patji. Even the most careful trapper could make a mistake—and even if they didn't, death could still find them. Patji was a domineering, vengeful parent who sought the blood of all who landed on his shores.</ins>

<ins>Sak chirped on his shoulder. Dusk rubbed her neck in thanks, though her chirp sounded apologetic. The warning had come almost too late. Without her, Patji would have claimed him this day. Dusk shoved down those itching questions he should not be thinking, and continued on his way.</ins>

He finally approached his safecamp as evening settled upon the island. Two of his tripwires ~~were~~<ins>had been</ins> cut<ins>, disarming them</ins>. That was not surprising; those were meant to be obvious. ~~He~~<ins>Dusk</ins> crept ~~forward, passing~~<ins>t</ins> <ins>another</ins>~~the~~ deathant nest in the ground—<ins>this larger one had a permanent</ins> crack ~~in the ground. It~~<ins>as an opening they could flood out of, but the rift</ins> had been stoppered with a smoldering twig. <ins>Beyond it,</ins> ~~T~~<ins>t</ins>he nightwind fungi that ~~Sixth~~<ins>Dusk</ins> had spent years cultivating here had been smothered in water to keep the spores from escaping~~;~~<ins>.</ins> ~~and t~~<ins>T</ins>he next two tripwires—the ones not intended to be obvious—~~were~~<ins>had</ins> *also* <ins>been</ins> cut.

Nice work, kid, ~~Sixth~~<ins>Dusk</ins> thought. ~~Someone~~<ins>He hadn't just avoided the traps, but disarmed them, in case he needed to flee quickly back this direction. However, someone</ins> really needed to teach the boy how to move without being trackable~~,~~<ins>.</ins> ~~though.~~ <ins>Of course, those tracks could be a trap unto themselves—an attempt to make Dusk himself careless. And so, he was extra careful as he edged forward. Yes, here t</ins>~~T~~he youth had left more footprints, broken stems, and other signs ~~than a mainlander might have if—~~<ins>....</ins>

~~"Um, hello?"~~

~~Sixth froze, then looked up.~~

<ins>Something moved up above in the canopy. Dusk hesitated, squinting.</ins> A *woman* hung from the tree branches above, trapped in a net made of jellywire vines—they left someone numb, unable to move. <ins>So, one of his traps had finally worked.</ins>

"Um, hello?" she said.

A woman, ~~Sixth~~<ins>Dusk</ins> thought, suddenly feeling stupid. *The smaller footprint, lighter step . . .*

"I want to make it perfectly clear," the woman said. "I have no intention of stealing your birds or infringing upon your territory."

~~Sixth squinted~~Dusk stepped closer in the dimming light. He recognized this woman. She was one of the clerks who had been at his meetings with the company. "You cut my tripwires," ~~Sixth~~Dusk said. Words felt odd in his mouth, and they came out ragged, as if he'd swallowed handfuls of dust. The result of weeks without speaking.

"Er, yes, I did. I assumed you could replace them." She hesitated. "Sorry?"

~~Sixth~~Dusk settled back. The woman rotated slowly in her net, and he noticed an Aviar clinging to the~~ir~~ outside. ~~The~~—like his own birds, it was about as tall as three fists atop one another, though this one had subdued white and green plumage~~;~~. ~~a~~A streamer, which was a breed that did not live on Patji. He did not know much about them, other than that like Kokerlii, they protected the mind from predators.

The setting sun cast shadows, the sky darkening. Soon, he would need to hunker down for the night ~~and await its passing. The jungle was even more deadly at night than it was at day~~, for ~~that was when~~darkness brought out the island's most dangerous of predators ~~came out~~.

"I promise," the woman said from within her bindings. What was her name? He believed it had been told to him, but he did not recall. Something untraditional. "I really don't want to steal from you. You remember me, don't you? We met back in the company halls?"

He gave no reply.

"Please," she ~~asked~~said. "I'd really rather not be hung by my ankles from a tree, slathered with blood to attract predators. If it's all the same to you."

"You are not a trapper."

"Well, no," she said. "You may have noticed my gender."

"There have been female trappers."

"One. One female trapper, Yaalani the Brave. I've heard her story a hundred times. You may find it ~~odd~~curious to know that almost every society has its myth of the female role reversal. She goes to war dressed as a man, or leads her father's armies into battle, or ~~lives alone~~traps on an island ~~just like any man~~. I'm convinced that such stories exist so that parents can tell their daughters, 'You are not Yaalani.'"

This woman spoke. A lot. People did that~~,~~ back on the Eelakin ~~i~~Islands. Her skin was dark, like his, and she had the sound of his people. The slight accent to her voice . . . he had heard it more and more when visiting the homeisles. It was the accent of one who was educated.

"Can I get down?" she asked, voice bearing a faint tremor. "I cannot feel my hands. It is . . . unsettling."

"What is your name?" ~~Patji~~Dusk asked. "I have forgotten it." This was too much speaking. It hurt his ears. This place was supposed to be soft.

"Vathi."

That's right. It was an improper name. Not a reference to her birth order and day of birth, but a name like the mainlanders used. That was not uncommon among his people now. ~~It had something to do with the visits from the Ones Above.~~

He walked over and took the rope from the nearby tree, then lowered the net. The woman's Aviar flapped ~~away~~down, screeching in annoyance ~~and frustration as she~~, favoring one wing, obviously wounded. Vathi hit the ground, a bundle of dark curls and green linen skirts. She stumbled to her feet, ~~shaking~~but fell back down again. Her skin would be numb ~~hands and shivering, an after-effect~~for some fifteen minutes from the touch of the vines~~' skin poison~~.

She sat there and wagged her hands, as if to shake out the numbness. "So . . . uh, no ankles and blood?" she asked, hopeful.

"That is a story ~~mother~~parents tell to children," ~~Sixth~~Dusk said~~, walking away from her~~. "It is not something we actually do."

"Oh."

"If you had been another trapper, I would have killed you directly, rather than leaving you to a~~re~~venge yourself upon me." He walked over to her Aviar, which opened its beak in a hissing posture, raising both wings as if to be bigger than it was. Sak chirped from his shoulder, but the bird didn't seem to care.

Yes, one wing was bloody. Vathi knew enough to care for the bird, however, which was pleasing. Some homeislers were completely ignorant to their Aviar's needs, treating them like accessories rather than intelligent creatures.

Vathi had pulled out the feathers near the wound, including a blood feather. She'd wrapped the wound with gauze. That wing didn't look good, however. Might be a fracture involved. He'd want to wrap both wings, prevent the creature from flying.

"Oh, Mirris," Vathi said, finally finding her feet. "I tried to help her. We fell, you see, when the monster—"

"Pick her up," Dusk said, checking the sky. "Follow~~Come~~. Step where I step."

Vathi nodded, not complaining, though her numbness would not have passed yet. She ~~shook~~collected a small pack from the vines and straightened her skirts. She wore a tight vest ~~over the top of~~above them, and the pack had some kind of metal tube sticking out of it. A map case? She fetched her Aviar, who huddled happily on her shoulder.

As ~~he~~Dusk led the way, she followed, and she did not attempt to attack him when his back was turned. Good. Darkness was coming upon them~~. Fortunately~~, but his safecamp was just ahead, and he knew by heart the steps to approach along this path. As they walked, Kokerlii fluttered down and landed on the woman's other shoulder, then began chirping in an amiable way.

~~Sixth~~Dusk stopped, turning. The woman's own Aviar ~~had~~ moved down her dress away from Kokerlii to cling near her bodice. The bird hissed softly, but Kokerlii—oblivious, as usual—continued to chirp happily. It was fortunate his breed was so mind-invisible, even deathants would consider him no more edible than a piece of bark.

"Is this . . ." Vathi said, looking to ~~him~~Dusk. "Yours? But of course. The one on your shoulder is not Aviar."

Sak settled back, puffing up her feathers. No, ~~she was not Aviar. At least,~~ her species was not Aviar. ~~Sixth~~Dusk continued to lead the way.

"I have never seen a trapper carry a bird who was not from the islands," Vathi said from behind.

It was not a question. ~~Sixth~~Dusk, therefore, felt no need to reply.

This safecamp—he had three total on the island~~, though this was the largest~~—lay atop a short hi~~ke~~ll following a twisting trail. ~~Getting to it either required climbing this single path and exposing oneself to the traps or somehow coming down the cliff above. At the top of the trail lay~~Here, a ~~small stand of trees, the largest of which~~stout gurratree held aloft a single-room structure. Trees were one of the safer places to sleep on Patji. The treetops were the domain of the Aviar, and most of the ~~big~~large predators ~~all~~ walked.

~~Sixth~~Dusk lit his lantern, then held it ~~up~~aloft, letting the orange light bathe his home. "Up," he said to the woman.

She ~~hesitated, then looked out~~glanced over her shoulder into the darkening jungle. By the lanternlight, he saw that the whites of her eyes were red from lack of sleep~~. She looked exhausted~~, despite the unconcerned smile she gave him before climbing up the stakes he'd planted in the tree. Her numbness should have worn off by now.

"How did you know?" he asked.

Vathi hesitated, near to the trap-door leading into his home. "Know what?"

"Where my safecamp was. Who told you?"

"I followed the sound of water," she said, nodding toward the small spring that bubbled out of the mountainside here. "When I found traps, I knew I was coming the right way."

~~Sixth~~Dusk frowned. ~~That was impossible.~~ One could not hear this water, ~~and~~s the stream vanished only a few hundred yards away, resurfacing in an unexpected location. Following it here . . . that would be virtually impossible.

So was she lying, or was she just lucky?

"You wanted to find me," he said.

"I wanted to find *someone*," she said, pushing open the trap-door, voice growing muffled as she climbed up into the building. "I figured that a trapper would be my only chance for survival." Above, she stepped up to one of the netted windows, Kokerlii still on her shoulder. "This is nice. Very roomy for a shack on a mountainside in the middle of a deadly jungle on an isolated island surrounded by monsters."

~~Sixth~~Dusk climbed up, holding the lantern in his teeth. The room at the top was perhaps four paces square, tall enough to stand in, but only barely. "Shake out those blankets," he said, nodding toward the stack and setting down the lantern. "Then lift every cup ~~or~~and bowl on the shelf and check inside of them."

Her eyes widened. "What am I looking for?"

"Deathants, scorpions, spiders, bloodscratches . . ." He shrugged, putting Sak on her perch by the window. "~~Better to find them now than when sleeping.~~ The room is built to be tight, but this is Patji. The Father likes surprises."

As she hesitantly set aside her pack and got to work, ~~Sixth~~Dusk continued up another ladder to check the roof ~~of his structure~~. There, a group of bird-sized boxes, with nests inside and holes to allow the birds to come and go freely, lay arranged in a double row. The animals would not stray far, except on special occasions, now that they had been raised with him handling them.

Kokerlii landed on top of one of the homes, trilling—but softly, now that night had fallen. More~~Other~~ coos and chirps came from the other boxes.

~~Sixth~~Dusk climbed out to check each bird for hurt wings or feet. These Aviar pairs were his life's work; the chicks each one hatched became his primary stock ~~and~~in trade. Yes, he would trap on the island, trying to find ~~as many~~ nests and wild chicks ~~as he could get~~—but that was never as efficient as raising nests.

"Your name was Sixth, wasn't it~~,~~?" Vathi said from below, voice accompanied by the sound of a blanket being shaken.

"It is."

"Large family," Vathi noted.

An ordinary family. Or, so it had once been. His father had been a twelfth and his mother an eleventh.

"Sixth of what?" Vathi prompted below.

"Of the ~~d~~Dusk."

"So you were born in the evening," Vathi said. "I've always found the traditional names so . . . uh . . . *descriptive*."

What a meaningless comment, ~~Sixth~~Dusk thought. *Why do homeislers feel the need to speak ~~all of the time, particularly~~ when there is nothing to say?*

He moved on to the next nest, checking the two drowsy birds inside ~~for wounds~~, then inspecting their droppings. They responded to his ~~return~~presence with happiness. An Aviar raised around ~~people~~humans—particularly one that had lent its talent to a person at an early age—would always see people as part of their flock. These birds were not his companions, like Sak and Kokerlii, but they were still special to him. ~~He had raised each one, and had chosen to keep them for breeding rather than taking them back to the homeisles for sale.~~

"No insects in the blankets," Vathi said, sticking her head up out of the trap-door behind him, her own Aviar on her shoulder.

"The cups?"

"I'll get to those in a moment. So these are your breeding pairs, are they?"

Obviously they were, so he didn't need to reply.

She watched him check them. He felt her eyes on him. Finally, he spoke. "Why did your company ignore the advice we gave you? Coming here was ~~obviously~~ a disaster."

"Yes."

He turned to her.

"Yes," she continued, "this whole expedition will likely be a disaster~~.~~ ~~One~~—a disaster that takes us a step closer to our goal."

He checked Sisisru next, working by the light of the now-rising moon. "Foolish."

Vathi folded her arms before her on the roof of the building, torso still disappearing into the lit square of ~~a~~the trapdoor below. "Do you think that our ancestors learned to wayfind on the oceans without experiencing a few disasters along the way? ~~Ships lost, people vanishing on the waves?~~ Or what of the first trappers? You have knowledge passed down for generations, knowledge earned through trial and error. If the first trappers had considered it too 'foolish' to ~~come~~ explore, where would you be?"

"They were single men, well-trained, not a ship full of clerks and dockworkers."

"The world is changing, Sixth of the Dusk," she said softly. "The ~~Ones Above . . . the technology we have discovered . . . The~~ people of the <u>main</u>land grow hungry for Aviar companions; ~~that~~ things ~~were~~ once restricted to the very wealthy ~~can be~~<u>are</u> within the reach of ordinary people. We've learned so much, yet the Aviar are still an enigma. Why don't chicks raised on the homeisles bestow talents? Why—"

"Foolish arguments," ~~Sixth~~<u>Dusk</u> said, putting Sisisru back into her nest. "I do not wish to hear them again<u>."</u>~~.~~

<u>"And the Ones Above?" she asked. "What of their technology, the wonders they produce?"</u>

<u>He hesitated, then he took out a pair of thick gloves and gestured toward her Aviar. Vathi looked at the white and green Aviar, then made a comforting clicking sound and took her in two hands. The bird suffered it with a few annoyed half bites at Vathi's fingers.</u>

<u>Dusk carefully took the bird in his gloved hands—for him, those bites would not be as timid—and undid Vathi's bandage. Then he cleaned the wound—much to the bird's protests—and carefully placed a new bandage. From there, he wrapped the bird's wings around its body with another bandage, not too tight, lest the creature be unable to breathe.</u>

<u>She didn't like it, obviously. But flying would hurt that wing more, with the fracture. She'd eventually be able to bite off the bandage, but for now, she'd get a chance to heal. Once done, he placed her with his other Aviar, who made quiet, friendly chirps, calming the flustered bird.</u>

<u>Vathi seemed content to let her bird remain there for the time, though she watched the entire process with interest.</u>

"You may sleep in my safecamp tonight~~.~~<u>,"</u> <u>Dusk said, turning back to her.</u>

"And then what?" she asked. "You turn me out into the jungle to die?"

"You ~~survived~~<u>did</u> well on your way here," he said, grudgingly. She was not a trapper. A scholar should not have been able to do what she did. "You will probably survive."

"I got lucky. ~~I should be dead. I walked a few hours upstream to find this place~~—I'd never make it across the entire island."

~~Sixth~~<u>Dusk</u> paused. "Across the island?"

"To the main company camp."

"There are *more* of you?"

"I . . . Of course. You didn't think . . ."

~~He turned on her.~~ "What happened?" *Now who is the fool?* ~~H~~he thought to himself. *You should have asked this first.* Talking. He had never been good with it~~, even before becoming a trapper~~.

She shied away from him, eyes widening. Did he look dangerous? Perhaps he had barked that last question forcefully. No matter. She spoke, so he got what he needed.

"We set up camp on the far beach," she said. "We have two ironhulls armed with cannons watching the waters. Those can take on even a deepwalker, if they have to. Two hundred soldiers, half that number in scientists and merchants. We're determined to find out, once and for all, why the Aviar must be born on one of the Pantheon Islands to be able to bestow talents.

"One team came down this direction to scout sites to place a<u>n</u>other fortress~~es~~. The company is determined to hold Patji against other interests. I thought the smaller expedition a bad idea, but had my own reasons for wanting to circle the island. So I went along. And then, the deepwalker . . ." She looked sick.

~~Sixth~~<u>Dusk</u> had almost stopped listening. Two *hundred* soldiers? ~~On his island?~~ Crawling across Patji like ants on a fallen piece of fruit. Unbearable! He thought of the quiet jungle broken by the sounds of their racketous voices. The sound of humans yelling at each other, clanging on metal, stomping about. Like a city.

A flurry of dark feathers announced Sak coming up from below and landing on the lip of the trapdoor beside Vathi. The black-plumed bird limped across the roof toward ~~Sixth~~<u>Dusk</u>, stretching her wings, showing off the scars on her left. ~~Even f~~<u>F</u>lying <u>even</u> a dozen feet was a chore for her.

~~Sixth~~<u>Dusk</u> reached down <u>to</u> scratch her neck~~, feeling stunned~~. It was happening. An invasion. He had to find a way to stop it. Somehow . . .

"I'm sorry, ~~Sixth~~<u>Dusk</u>," Vathi said. "The ~~T~~<u>t</u>rappers are ~~one of my areas of scholarship.~~<u>fascinating to me;</u> I've read of your ways, and I respect them. But this was *going* to happen someday<u>; it's inevitable. The islands *will* be tamed</u>. The Aviar are too valuable to leave in the hands of a couple hundred eccentric woodsmen. ~~They are a resource that we must protect.~~"

"The chiefs . . ."

"All twenty chiefs in council agreed to this plan," Vathi said. "I was there. If the Eelakin do not secure these islands and ~~tame them~~ <u>Aviar</u>, someone else will."

~~Sixth~~<u>Dusk</u> stared out into the night. "Go and make certain there are no insects in the cups below."

"But—"

"*Go*," he said~~, turning to the woman~~, "and make *certain* there are no insects in the cups below!"

The woman sighed softly, but retreated into the room, leaving him with his Aviar. He continued to scratch Sak on the neck, seeking comfort in the familiar motion and in her presence. Dared he hope that the shadows would prove too deadly for the company and its iron-hulled ships? Vathi seemed confident.

She did not tell me why she joined the scouting group. She had seen a shadow, witnessed it destroying her team, but had still managed the presence of mind to find his camp. She was a strong woman. He would need to remember that.

She was also a company type, as removed from his experience as a person could get. Soldiers, craftsmen, even ~~king~~chiefs he could understand. But these soft-spoken scribes who had quietly conquered the world with a sword of commerce, they baffled him.

"Father," he whispered. "What do I do?"

Patji gave no reply. ~~Well, none~~ beyond the normal sounds of night ~~on the island~~. ~~Thing~~Creatures moving, hunting, rustling. At night, the Aviar slept, and that gave opportunity to the most dangerous of the island's predators. In the distance, ~~he heard~~ a nightmaw ~~roar~~called, its horrid ~~voice~~screech echoing through the trees.

~~In his hands,~~ Sak spread her wings, leaning down, head darting back and forth. The sound always made her tremble.

~~In truth,~~ it did the same to ~~Sixth~~Dusk.

He sighed, and ~~started to~~ r~~i~~ose, placing Sak on his shoulder. He turned, and almost stumbled as he saw his corpse at his feet. He came alert immediately; ~~there wasn't supposed to be anything in his safecamp that could kill him~~. What was it? Vines in the tree branches? A spider, dropping quietly from above? ~~Something larger? On Patji, any one of a hundred different animals could kill a man in a heartbeat~~There wasn't supposed to be anything in his safecamp that could kill him.

Sak ~~cried out~~screeched as if in pain.

~~It was a screech; he had not heard her screech in years.~~ Nearby, his other Aviar cried out as well, a cacophony of squawks, screeches, chirps. No, it wasn't just them~~.~~! All around . . . echoing in the distance, from both near and far, wild Aviar squawked. They rustled in their branches, a sound like a powerful wind blowing through the trees.

~~Sixth~~Dusk spun about, holding his hands to his ears, eyes wide as corpses appeared around him. ~~His own body, eyes staring dead, appearing and vanishing.~~ They piled high, one atop another, some bloated, some bloody, some skeletal. Haunting him. Dozens upon *dozens*.

He dropped to his knees, yelling. That put him eye-to-eye with one of ~~the~~his corpses. Only this one . . . this one was not quite dead~~ . . ~~. Blood dripped from its lips as it tried to speak, mouthing words that ~~Sixth~~Dusk did not understand.

It vanished.

They all ~~vanished. All of the corpses~~did, every last one. He ~~turned~~spun about, wild, but saw no~~ne of them~~bodies. The sounds of the Aviar quieted, and his flock settled back into their nests. ~~Sixth~~Dusk breathed in and out deeply, heart racing. He felt tense, as if at any moment~~,~~ a shadow would explode from the blackness around his camp and consume him. He anticipated it, felt it coming. He wanted to run, run *somewhere*.

What had that been? In all of his years with Sak, he had never seen anything like it. What could have upset all of the Aviar at once ~~in that way~~? ~~What had they felt?~~ Was it ~~something about~~ the nightmaw he had heard?

Don't be foolish, he thought ~~at himself~~. *This was different, different from anything you've seen. Different from anything that has been seen on Patji. But what? What had changed . . .*

Sak had not settled down like the others. She stared northward~~.~~, ~~T~~toward where Vathi had said the main camp of invaders was setting up.

~~Sixth~~Dusk stood ~~up~~, then clam~~o~~bered down into the room below, Sak on his shoulder. "What are your people doing?"

Vathi spun at his harsh tone. She had been looking out of the window, northward. "I don't—"

He took her by the front of her vest, pulling her toward him in a two-fisted grip, meeting her eyes from only a few inches away. "*What are your people doing?*"

Her eyes widened, and he could feel her tremble in his grip, though she set her jaw and held his gaze. Scribes were not supposed to have grit like this. He had seen them scribbling away in their windowless rooms. ~~Sixth~~Dusk tightened his grip on her vest, pulling the fabric so it dug into her skin, and found himself growling softly.

"Release me," she said, "and we will speak."

"Bah," he said, letting go. She dropped ~~down~~ a few inches, hitting the floor with a thump. He hadn't realized he'd lifted her off the ground.

She backed away, putting as much space between them as the room would allow. He stalked to the window, looking through the mesh screen at the night. His corpse dropped from the roof above, ~~and he step~~hitting the ground below. He jumped back, worried that it was happening again.

It didn't, not the same way as before. However, when he turned back into the room, his corpse lay in the corner, bloody lips parted, eyes staring sightlessly. The danger, whatever it was, had not passed.

Vathi had sat down on the floor, holding her head, trembling. Had he frightened her that soundly? She did look tired, exhausted. She wrapped her arms around herself, and when she looked at him, there was a cast to her eyes that hadn't been there before~~.~~ ~~A~~as if she were regarding a wild animal~~,~~ let off ~~of~~ its chain.

That seemed fitting.

"What do you know of the Ones Above?" she asked him.

"They live in the stars," ~~Sixth~~Dusk said. ~~"They claim that we once did too."~~

"We at the company have been meeting with them. We don't understand ~~them, at least not~~ their ways. They look like us~~,~~; at times they talk like us. But they have . . . rules, laws that they won't explain. They refuse to sell us their marvels, but in like manner, they seem forbidden from taking things from us, even in trade. They promise it, someday when we are more advanced. It's like they think we are children."

~~"That is fine," Sixth said. "They are not of us, no matter what they look like.~~ Why should we care?" Dusk said. "If they leave us alone, we will be better for it."

"You haven't seen the things they can do," she said softly, getting a distant look in her eyes. "We have barely worked out how to create ships that can sail on their own, against the wind. ~~I thought that development to be amazing until~~But the Ones Above ~~arrived~~ . . . ~~T~~they can sail the skies~~ . . .~~, sail the *stars themselves*. They know so much, and they won't *tell* us any of it."

She shook her head, reaching into the pocket of her skirt. "They are after something, ~~Sixth~~Dusk. ~~Their laws forbade them from contacting us until we were able to harness steam on our own. Now they can speak to us, but their laws won't let them teach us. If that is the case, w~~What interest do we hold for them? From what I've heard them say, there are many_ other_ worlds like ours, with cultures that cannot sail the stars. We are not unique, yet the Ones Above come back _here_ time and time again. They *do* want something. You can see it in their eyes_._..."

"What is that?" ~~Sixth~~Dusk asked, nodding to the thing she took from her pocket. It rested in her palm like the shell of a clam, but had a mirror-like face on the top.

"It is a machine," she said. "Like a clock, only it never needs to be wound, and it ... shows things."

"What things?"

"Well, it translates languages. Ours into that of the Ones Above. It also ... shows ~~T~~_t_he locations of Aviar."

"*What?*"

"It's like a map," she said. "It points the way to Aviar."

"That's how you found my camp," ~~Sixth~~Dusk said, stepping toward her.

"Yes." She rubbed her thumb across the machine's surface. "We aren't supposed to have this. It was the possession of an emissary sent to work with us~~, but he died. The death was natural; h~~He choked while eating_ a few months back_. They *can* die, it appears, even of mundane ~~thing~~_causes_. That ... changed how I view them.

"~~The others~~_His kind_ have asked after his machines, and we will have to return them soon. But this~~, this~~ _one_ tells us what they are after: the Aviar. The Ones Above are always fascinated with them. I think they want to find a way to trade for the birds, a way their laws will allow. They hint that we might not be safe, that not everyone Above follows their laws."

"But why did the Aviar react like they did, just now?" ~~Sixth~~Dusk said, turning back to the window. "Why did ..." *Why did I see what I saw? What I'm still seeing, to an extent?* His corpse was there, wherever he looked. Slumped by a tree outside, in the corner of the room, hanging out of the trapdoor in the roof. Sloppy. He should have closed that.

Sak had pulled into his hair like she did when a predator was near.

"There ... is a second machine," Vathi said.

~~That's right. She had said machines, earlier. More than one.~~

"Where?" he demanded.

"On our ship."

The direction the Av~~ai~~_i_ar had looked.

"~~It~~_The second machine_ is much larger," Vathi said. "This one in my hand ~~i~~_has_ limited ~~in what it can do~~_range_. The larger one~~...it~~ can create an enormous map, one of an entire island, then *write* out a paper with a copy of that map. That map will include a dot marking every Aviar."

"And?"

"And we were going to ~~turn on~~_engage_ the machine tonight," she said. "It takes hours to ~~get ready~~prepare—like an oven, growing hot—before it's ready ~~to draw its map for us~~. The schedule was to turn it on tonight just after sunset so we could use it in the morning."

"The others," ~~Sixth~~Dusk demanded, "they'd use it without you?"

She grimaced. "Happily. Captain Eusto probably did a dance when I didn't return from scouting. He's been worried I would take ~~too much~~control of ~~the credit for~~ this expedition. But the machine isn't harmful; it merely locates Aviar. ~~You don't need to worry so much~~."

"Did it do *that* before~~,~~?" he demanded, waving toward the night. "When you last used it, did it draw the attention of all the Aviar? Discomfort them?"

"Well, no," she said. "But the moment of discomfort has passed, hasn't it? I'm sure it's nothing."

Nothing. Sak quivered on his shoulder. ~~Sixth~~Dusk saw death all around him. The moment they had ~~us~~engaged that machine, the corpses had piled up. If they used it again, the results would be horrible. ~~Sixth~~Dusk knew it. He could *feel* it.

"We're going to stop them," he said.

"What?" Vathi asked. "*Tonight?*"

"Yes," ~~Sixth~~Dusk said, walking to a small hidden cabinet in the wall. He pulled it open~~,~~ and began to pick through the supplies inside. A second lantern. Extra oil. ~~He would need those.~~

"That's insane," Vathi said. "Nobody travels the islands at night."

"I've done it once before. With my uncle."

His uncle had died on that trip.

"You can't be serious, ~~Sixth~~Dusk. The ~~N~~nightmaws are out. I've heard them."

"~~Traveling quickly~~Nightmaws track minds," ~~Sixth~~Dusk said, stuffing supplies into his pack~~,~~. "<u>They are almost completely deaf, and</u> ~~cutting~~<u>close to blind. If we move quickly and cut</u> across the center of the island, we can be to your camp by morning. We can stop them from using the ~~Above~~ machine again."

"But why would we *want* to?"

He shouldered the pack. "Because if we don't, it will destroy the island."

She frowned at him, cocking her head. "You can't know that. Why do you think you know that?"

"<u>Your Aviar will have to remain here, with that wound," he said, ignoring the question. "She would not be able to fly away if something happened to us." The same argument could be made for Sak, but he would not be without the bird. "I will return her to you after we have stopped the machine.</u> Come ~~on~~." He walked to the <u>floor</u> hatc~~h~~ ~~down~~ and pulled it open.

Vathi rose, but pressed back against the wall. "I'm staying here."

"Th~~ey~~<u> people of your company</u> won't believe me," he said. "You will have to tell them to stop. You are coming."

Vathi licked her lips in what seemed to be a nervous habit. She glanced to the sides, looking for escape, then back at him. Right then, ~~Sixth~~Dusk noticed his corpse hanging from the pegs in the tree beneath him. He jumped.

"What was that?" she demanded.

"Nothing."

"You keep glancing to the sides," Vathi said. "What do you think you see, ~~Sixth~~ Dusk?"

"We're going. Now."

"You've been alone on the island for a long time," she said, obviously trying to make her voice soothing. "You're upset ~~because something unexpected has happened in~~about our arrival. You aren't thinking clearly. I understand."

~~Sixth~~Dusk drew in a deep breath. "Sak, show her."

The bird launched from his shoulder, flapping across the room, landing on Vathi. She turned to the bird, frowning.

Then she gasped, falling to her knees. Vathi ~~phuddl~~ed back against the wall, eyes darting from side to side, mouth working but no words coming out. ~~Sixth~~Dusk left her to it for a short time, then raised his arm. Sak returned to him on black wings, dropping a single~~,~~ dark feather to the ~~ground~~floor. She settled in again on his shoulder. That much flying was difficult for her.

"What was *that*?" Vathi demanded.

"Come ~~on~~," ~~Sixth~~Dusk said, taking his pack and climbing down out of the room.

Vathi scrambled to the open hatch. "No. Tell me. What *was* that?"

"You saw your corpse."

"All about me. Everywhere I looked."

"Sak grants that ~~T~~talent."

"There is no such ~~T~~talent."

~~Sixth~~Dusk looked up at her, halfway down the pegs. "You have seen your death. That is what will happen if your friends use ~~that~~their machine. Death. All of us. The Aviar, everyone living here. I do not know why ~~it will happen~~, but I know that it *will* come."

"You've discovered a new Aviar," Vathi said. "How . . . When . . . ?"

"Hand me the lantern," ~~Sixth~~Dusk said~~, raising a hand~~.

Looking numb, she obeyed, handing it down. He put it into his teeth and ~~climbed down~~descended the pegs to the ground. Then he raised the lantern high, looking down the slope ~~toward the jungle below.~~

The inky jungle at night. Like the depths of the ocean.

He shivered, then whistled. Kokerlii fluttered down from above, landing on his other shoulder. He would hide ~~them. Hide~~ their minds, ~~at least. With~~and with that, they had a chance. It would still not be easy. The things of the jungle relied upon mind sense, but many could still hunt by scent or other senses.

Vathi scrambled down the pegs behind him, her pack ~~with~~over her shoulder, the strange tube ~~in it over her shoulder~~peeking out. "You have two Aviar," she said. "You use them both at once?"

"My uncle had three."

"How is that even possible?"

"They like trappers." So many questions. ~~So much talking.~~ Could she not think about what the answers might be before asking?

"We're actually going to do this," she said, whispering, as if to herself. "The jungle at night. I should stay. I should refuse . . ."

"You've seen your death if you do."

"I've seen what you claim is my death. ~~I don't know anything.~~ A new Aviar . . . It has been centuries." Though her voice still sounded reluctant, she walked after him as he strode down the slope and passed his traps, entering the jungle again.

His corpse sat at the base of a tree. That made him immediately look for what could kill him here, but Sak's senses seemed to be off. <u>The island's i</u>~~I~~mpending death ~~was upon them all, and it~~ was so overpowering, it seemed to be smothering smaller dangers. He might not be able to rely upon her visions until the machine was destroyed.

~~That worried him. If he was going to cross the island at night, her aid would have been invaluable.~~ The thick jungle canopy ~~seemed to~~ swallow<u>ed</u> them. ~~It was~~<u>,</u> hot ~~here~~, even at night; the ocean breezes didn't reach this far inland. That left the air feeling stagnant, and it dripped with the scents of the jungle. Fungus, rotting leaves, the perfumes of flowers. The accompaniment to those scents ~~were~~<u>was</u> the sounds of an island ~~that did not sleep. When the Aviar slumbered, much of the rest of the island came~~<u>coming</u> alive. ~~The deeper Sixth went, the more omnipresent the sounds became.~~ A constant crinkling in the underbrush, like the sound of maggots writhing in a pile of dry leaves.

~~—~~ <u></u>The lantern's light did not seem to extend as far as it should<u>.</u>~~-~~

<u></u>~~, and~~ Vathi pulled up close ~~to him~~ behind <u>him</u>. "Why did you do this before?" she ~~ask~~<u>whisper</u>ed. "The other time you went out at night?"

More questions. <u>But sounds, fortunately, were not too dangerous.</u>

"I was wounded," ~~Sixth~~<u>Dusk</u> ~~said~~<u>whispered</u>. "We had to get from one safecamp to the other to recover my uncle's store of antivenom." Because ~~Sixth~~<u>Dusk</u>, hands trembling, had dropped the other flask.

"You survived it? Well, obviously you did, I mean. I'm surprised<u>,</u> is all."

She seemed to be talking to fill the air. ~~Homeislers did that.~~

"They could be watching us," she said, looking into the darkness. "Nightmaws."

"They are not."

"How can you know?" she asked, voice hushed. "Anything could be out there, in that darkness."

"If the nightmaws had seen us, we'd be dead. That is how I know." ~~Obviously.~~ He shook his head, sliding out his machete and cutting away a few branches before them. Any could hold deathants skittering across their leaves. In the dark, it would be difficult to spot them, and so brushing against foliage seemed a poor decision.

We won't be able to avoid it, he thought, leading the way down through a gully thick with mud. He had to step on stones to keep from sinking in. Vathi followed with remarkable dexterity~~, for a scribe~~. *We have to go quickly. I can't cut down every branch in our way.*

He hopped off ~~of~~ a stone and onto the bank of the gully<u>, and there</u> pass~~ing~~<u>ed</u> his ~~body~~<u>corpse</u> sinking into the mud. Nearby~~, however~~, he spotted a second corpse, so translucent it was nearly invisible. He raised his lantern, hoping it wasn't happening again.

Others did not appear. Just these tw~~o~~o. And the very faint image . . . yes, that was a sinkhole there. Sak chirped softly, and he fished in his pocket for a seed to give her. She had figured out how to send him help ~~anyway~~. The fainter images <ins>were immediate dangers</ins>—he would have to watch for those.

"Thank you," he whispered to her.

"That bird of yours," Vathi said, speaking softly in the gloom of night, "are there others?"

They climbed out of the gully, continuing on, crossing a krell trail in the night. He stopped them just before the<ins>y</ins> wandered into a patch of deathants. Vathi looked at the trail of tiny <ins>yellow</ins> insects, moving ~~along their path. They were practically blind, but stumble into them . . .~~ <ins>in a straight line.</ins>

~~Well, they weren't the greatest of Patji's dangers.~~

"~~Sixth~~<ins>Dusk</ins>?" she asked as they rounded the ants. "Are there others? Why haven't you brought any chicks to market?"

"I do not have any chicks."

"So you found only the one?" she asked.

Questions, questions. Buzzing around him like flies.

Don't be foolish, he told himself, shoving down his annoyance. *You would ask the same, if you saw someone with a new Aviar.* He had tried to keep Se<ins>a</ins>k a secret; for years, he hadn't even brought her with him when he left the island. But with her hurt wing, he hadn't wanted to abandon her.

Deep down, he'd known he couldn't keep his secret forever. "There are many like her," he ~~finally~~ said~~, in answer to those buzzing questions~~. "But only she has a talent to bestow."

Vathi stopped in place as he continued to cut them a path. He turned back, looking at her alone on the new trail. He had given her the lantern to hold.

"That's a mainlander bird," she said. She held up the light. "~~That's what~~ I knew it was when I first saw it, ~~but when you said it had a talent,~~<ins>and</ins> I assumed ~~I had been wrong.~~ <ins>␣</ins>it wasn't. ~~It is~~ <ins>It is</ins> an Aviar, because mainlander bird<ins>s can't bestow talents</ins>."

~~Sixth~~<ins>Dusk</ins> turned back and continued cutting.

"You brought a mainlander chick to the ~~p~~<ins>P</ins>antheon," Vathi whispered behind. "And it *gained a talent*."

With a hack he brought down a branch, then continued on. Again, she had not asked a question, so he needed not answer.

Vathi hurried to keep up, the glow of the lantern tossing his shadow before him as she stepped up behind. "Surely someone else has tried it before. Surely . . ."

He did not know. ~~He had not heard it spoken of, however.~~

"But why would they?" ~~S~~<ins>s</ins>he continued, quietly, as if to herself. "The Aviar are special. Everyone knows the <ins>separate</ins> breeds and what they do. Why assume that a fish would lea<ins>r</ins>n to breathe air, if raised on land? Why assume a non-Aviar would become one if raised on Patji<ins>.</ins> . . ."

They continued through the night. ~~Sixth~~Dusk led them around many dangers, though he found that he needed to rely <u>greatly</u> upon Sak's help ~~even more than he would have during day~~. *Do not follow that stream, which has your corpse bobbing in its waters. Do not touch that tree; the bark is poisonous with rot. Turn from that path. Your corpse shows a deathant bite.*

Sak did not speak to him, but each message was clear. ~~They seemed more clear than normal, actually—though these images were faint, almost invisible.~~ When he stopped to let Vathi drink from her canteen, he held Sak and found her trembling. She did not peck at him as ~~norm~~<u>was usu</u>al when he enclosed her in his hands.

They stood in a small clearing, pure dark all around them, the sky shrouded in clouds. He heard distant rainfall on the trees. Not uncommon, here.

Nightmaws ~~roar~~<u>screech</u>ed, one then another~~, in the night air~~. They only did that when they had ~~already~~ made a kill~~,~~ or when they were seeking to frighten prey. Often, ~~K~~<u>k</u>rell herds slept near Aviar roosts. Frighten away the birds, and you could sense the ~~K~~<u>k</u>rell.

Vathi had taken out her tube. Not a scroll case—and not something scholarly at all, considering the way she held it as she poured something into its end. ~~She held~~<u>Once done, she raised</u> it like one would ~~hold~~ a weapon. Beneath her feet, Sixth-Dusk's body lay mangled. ~~Not one of the visions Sak was trying to send him, but one of the ones from the danger.~~

He did not ask after Vathi's weapon, not even as she took some kind of short, slender spear and fit<u>ted</u> it into the top end. No weapon could penetrate the thick skin of a ~~N~~<u>n</u>ightmaw. You either avoided them~~,~~ or you died.

Kokerlii fluttered down to his shoulder, chirping away. He seemed confused by the darkness. Why were they out like this, at night, when birds normally made no noise?

"We must keep moving," ~~Sixth~~<u>Dusk</u> said, placing Sak on his <u>other</u> shoulder ~~again~~ and taking out his machete.

"You realize that your bird changes everything," Vathi said<u> quietly</u>, joining him, shouldering her pack and carrying her tube in the other hand.

"There will be a new kind of Aviar," ~~Sixth said~~<u>Dusk whispered</u>, stepping over his corpse.

"That's the *least* of it. ~~Sixth, our entire understanding of them is wrong. We~~<u>Dusk, we</u> assumed that chicks raised ~~off of~~<u>away from</u> these islands did not develop their abilities because they were not around others to train them. We assumed that their abilities were ~~part of them~~<u>innate</u>, like ~~men have the~~<u>our</u> ability to speak—~~innate~~<u>it's inborn</u>, but <u>we requir</u>~~ing~~e help from others to develop ~~properly~~<u>it</u>."

"~~So, t~~<u>T</u>hat can still be ~~the way~~<u>true</u>," ~~Sixth~~<u>Dusk</u> said. "Other species<u>, such as Sak</u>, can merely be trained to speak."

"And your bird? Was it trained by others?"

"Perhaps." ~~He did not know everything Sak had done in her life.~~

~~Of course, he suspected something else.~~ He did not say ~~it~~<u>what he really thought</u>. It was a thing of trappers. ~~Beyond that, he was stopped by something. A body~~<u>He noted a corpse</u> on the ground before them.

It was not his.

He held up a hand immediately, stilling Vathi as she continued on to ask another question. What was *this*? T~~hat body was relatively fresh—though~~ he meat had been picked off ~~of~~ much of the skeleton, and the clothing ~~still~~ lay strewn about, ripped open by ~~those~~ animals that feasted ~~upon it~~. Small, fungus-like plants had sprouted around the ground near it, tiny red tendrils reaching up ~~out of the ground~~ to enclose parts of the skeleton.

He looked up at the great tree, at the foot of which rested the corpse. The flowers were not in bloom. ~~Sixth~~Dusk released his breath.

"What is it?" Vathi whispered. "Deathants?"

"No. Patji's Finger."

She frowned. "Is that . . . some kind of curse?"

"It is a name," ~~Sixth~~Dusk said, stepping forward carefully~~,~~ to inspect~~ing~~ the corpse. Machete. Boots. Rugged gear. One of his colleagues had fallen. He *thought* he recognized the man from the clothing. An older trapper named First of the Sky. ~~Sixth's uncle had known him.~~

"~~Of t~~The name of a person?" Vathi asked, peeking over his shoulder.

"~~Of t~~The name of a tree," ~~Sixth~~Dusk said, poking at the corpse's clothing ~~of the man~~, careful of insects that might be lurking inside. "Raise the lamp."

"I've never heard of that tree," she said skeptically.

"They are only on Patji."

"I have read a lot about the flora on these islands. . . ."

"~~And you know little, still.~~ Here you are a child. Light."

She sighed, raising it for him. He used a stick to prod~~ded~~ at pockets on the ripped clothing ~~with a stick~~. ~~He~~This man had been killed by a tuskrun pack, larger predators—almost as large as a man—that prowled mostly ~~at~~by day. Their movement patterns were ~~normally~~ predictable~~.~~ ~~U~~unless one happened across one of Patji's Fingers in bloom.

There. He found a small book in the man's pocket. ~~Sixth~~Dusk raised it, then backed away. ~~Perhaps he could have stopped~~ Vathi ~~from~~ peer~~ing~~ed over his shoulder~~, but he was too interested in the book at the moment~~. ~~Still, h~~Homeislers stood so *close* to each other ~~sometimes~~. ~~They had a whole island, mostly to themselves~~. Did she need to stand right by his elbow~~.~~?

He checked the first pages, finding a list of dates. Yes, ~~this death was fresh, only a few days old,~~ judging by the last date written down, this man was only a few days dead. The pages after that detailed the locations of ~~First~~Sky's safecamps, along with explanations of the traps guarding each one. The last page contained the farewell.

I am First of the Sky, taken by Patji at last. I have a brother on Suluko. Care for them, rival.

Few words. Few words were good. ~~Sixth~~Dusk carried a book like this himself, and he had said even less on his last page.

"He wants you to care for his family?" Vathi asked.

"Don't be stupid," ~~Sixth~~Dusk said, tucking the book away. "~~In this, 'them' means h~~His birds."

"That's ~~actually kind of~~ sweet," Vathi said. "I had always heard that trappers were incredibly territorial."

"We are," he said, noting how she said it. Again, her tone made it seem as if she considered trappers to be like animals. "But our birds might die without care—they are accustomed to humans~~, and are no longer part of their flocks~~. Better to give them to a rival than to let them die."

"Even if that rival is the one who killed you?" Vathi asked. "The traps you set, the ways you try to interfere with one another..."

"It is our way."

"That is an awful excuse," she said, looking up at the tree. ~~It~~
<u>She was right.</u>

<u>The tree</u> was massive, with drooping fronds. At the end of each one was a large closed blossom, as long as two hands put together. "You don't seem worried<u>,</u>" she noted<u>, "</u>though the plant seems to have killed that man."

"These are only dangerous when they bloom."

"Spores?" she asked.

"No." He picked up the fallen machete, but left the rest of ~~First~~Sky's things alone. Let Patji claim him. ~~Sixth scanned the area~~<u>Father did so like to murder his children. Dusk continued onward, leading Vathi,</u> ignoring his corpse draped ~~over~~<u>across</u> a log. ~~Sak gave him no direction, so he started out northward, continuing the trek toward the other side of the island.~~

"~~Sixth~~Dusk?" Vathi asked, raising the lantern and hurrying to him. "If not spores, then how does the tree kill?"

"So many questions."

"My life is about questions," she replied. "And about answers. If my people are going to work on this island—<u>...</u>"

~~She cut off as he spun on her, then she stepped back.~~
<u>He hacked at some plants with the machete.</u>

"It<u>′ is</u> going to happen," she said, more softly. "<u>I'm sorry, Dusk.</u> You can't stop ~~it, Sixth. I'm sorry~~<u>the world from changing</u>. Perhaps ~~we~~<u>my expedition</u> will be defeated, but others will come."

"Because of the Ones Above," he ~~said, turning away and continuing to lead through the dark underbrush~~<u>snapped</u>.

"~~Well, they~~<u>They</u> may spur it," Vathi said. "<u>Truly, when we finally convince them we are developed enough to be traded with, we will sail the stars as they do.</u> But ~~it~~<u>change</u> will happen <u>even</u> without them. The world is ~~chang~~<u>progress</u>ing. One man cannot slow it, no matter how determined <u>he is</u>."

He stopped in the path.

You cannot <u>stop the tides from</u> chang<u>ing</u> ~~it~~, ~~Sixth~~<u>Dusk</u>. No matter how determined you are. His mother's words. Some of the last he remembered from her.

~~Sixth~~<u>Dusk</u> continued on his way. ~~The woman~~<u>Vathi</u> followed. He would need her, though a treacherous piece of him whispered that she would be easy to end. With her would go her questions, and more importantly, her answers. The ones he suspected she was very close to discovering.

You cannot change it. . . .

He could not. He hated that it was so. He wanted so badly to protect this island, as his kind had done for centuries. He worked this jungle, he loved its birds, was fond of its scents and sounds—despite all else. How he wished he could prove to Patji that he and the others were worthy of these shores.

Perhaps. Perhaps then . . .

Bah. Well, killing this woman would not provide any real protection for the island. Besides, had he sunk so low that he would murder a helpless scribe in cold blood? He would not even do that to another trapper, unless they approached his camp and did not retreat.

"The blossoms can think," he found himself saying as he turned them away from a mound that showed the tuskrun pack had been rooting here. "The Fingers of Patji. They trees themselves are not dangerous, even when blooming—but they attract predators, imitating the thoughts of a wounded animal, that is full of pain and worry."

Vathi gasped. "A *plant*," she said, "that broadcasts a mental signature? Are you certain?"

"Yes."

"I need one of those blossoms." The light shook as she turned to go back.

Dusk spun and caught her by the arm. "We must keep moving."

"But—"

"You will have another chance." He took a deep breath. "Your people will soon infest this island like maggots on carrion. You will see other trees. Tonight, we must go. Dawn approaches."

He let go of her and turned back to his work. He had judged her wise, for a homas. Perhaps she would listen.

She did. She followed behind.

Patji's Fingers. First of the Sky, the dead trapper, should not have died in that place. Truly, the trees were not that dangerous. They lived by opening many blossoms and attracting predators to come feast. The predators would then fight one another, and the tree would feed off the corpses. Sky must have stumbled across a tree as it was beginning to flower, and got caught in what came.

His Aviar had not been enough to shield so many open blossoms. Who would have expected a death like that? After years on the island, surviving much more terrible dangers, to be caught by those simple flowers. It almost seemed a mockery, on Patji's part, of the poor man.

Dusk and Vathi's path continued, and soon grew steeper. They'd need to go uphill for a while before crossing to the downward slope that would lead to the other side of the island. Their trail, fortunately, would avoid Patji's main peak—the point of the wedge that jutted up the easternmost side of the island. His camp had been near the south, and Vathi's would be to the northeast, letting them skirt around the base of the wedge before arriving on the other beach.

They fell into a rhythm, and she was quiet for a time. Eventually, atop a particularly steep incline, he nodded for a break and squatted down to drink from his canteen. On Patji one did not simply sit, without care, upon a stump or log to rest.

Consumed by worry, and not a little frustration, he didn't notice what Vathi was doing until it was too late. She'd found something tucked into a branch—a long colorful feather. A mating plume.

Dusk leaped to his feet.

Vathi reached up toward the lower branches of the tree.

A set of spikes on ropes dropped from a nearby tree as Vathi pulled the branch. They swung down as Dusk reached her, one arm thrown in the way. A spike hit, the long, thin nail ripping into his skin and jutting out the other side, bloodied, and stopping a hair from Vathi's cheek.

She screamed.

Many predators on Patji were hard of hearing, but still that wasn't wise. Dusk didn't care. He yanked the spike from his skin, unconcerned with the bleeding for now, and checked the other spikes on the drop-rope trap.

No poison. Blessedly, they had not been poisoned.

"Your arm!" Vathi said.

He grunted. It didn't hurt. Yet. She began fishing in her pack for a bandage, and he accepted her ministrations without complaint or groan, even as the pain came upon him.

"I'm so sorry!" Vathi sputtered. "I found a mating plume! That meant an Aviar nest, so I thought to look in the tree. Have we stumbled across another trapper's safecamp?"

She was babbling out words as she worked. Seemed appropriate. When he grew nervous, he grew even more quiet. She would do the opposite.

She was good with a bandage, again surprising him. The wound had not hit any major arteries. He would be fine, though using his left hand would not be easy. This would be an annoyance. When she was done, looking sheepish and guilty, he reached down and picked up the mating plume she had dropped.

"This," he said with a harsh whisper, holding it up before her, "is the symbol of your ignorance. On the Pantheon Islands, nothing is easy, nothing is simple. That plume was placed by another trapper to catch someone who does not deserve to be here, someone who thought to find an easy prize. You cannot be that person. Never move without asking yourself, is this too easy?"

She paled. Then she took the feather in her fingers.

"Come."

He turned and walked on their way. That was the speech for an apprentice, he realized. Upon their first major mistake. A ritual among trappers. What had possessed him to give it to her?

She followed behind, head bowed, appropriately shamed. She didn't realize the honor he had just paid her, if unconsciously. They walked onward, an hour or more passing.

By the time she spoke, for some reason, he almost welcomed the words breaking upon the sounds of the jungle. "I'm sorry." ~~she finally said.~~

"You need not be sorry," he said. "Only careful."

"I understand." She took a deep breath, following behind him on the path. "And I *am* sorry. Not just about your arm. About this island. About what is coming. I think it inevitable, but I do wish that it did not mean the end of such a grand tradition."

"I . . ."

Words. He hated trying to find words.

"It . . . was not dusk when I was born," ~~Sixth~~he finally said, then hacked~~ing~~ down a swampvine~~, then holding~~ and held his breath against the noxious fumes that it released toward him ~~a moment later~~. They were only dangerous for a few moments.

"Excuse me?" Vathi asked, keeping her distance from the swampvine. "You were born . . ."

~~He looked over, meeting her eyes in the frail lanternlight.~~ "My mother did not name me for the time of day. ~~It was not dusk, not in the day of my birth.~~ I was named because my mother saw the dusk of our people. The sun will soon set on us, she often told me." ~~He turned, looking up toward the dark canopy. "I guess it has finally done just that."~~

—He looked back to Vathi~~,~~, letting her pass him and enter a small clearing.

Oddly, she smiled at him. ~~Perhaps she realized he~~ Why had ~~shared something personal.~~ he found those words to speak? He followed into the clearing, concerned at himself. He had not ~~spok~~given those words to his uncle; only his parents ~~had~~ kn~~e~~ew~~n~~ the source of his name.~~-~~

He was not certain why he'd told this scribe from an evil company. But . . . it did feel good to have said them.

A nightmaw broke through between two trees behind Vathi.

The enormous beast would have been as tall as a tree if it had stood upright ~~on two legs~~. Instead~~,~~ it leaned forward in a prowling posture, powerful legs behind bearing most of its weight, its two clawed forelegs ripping up the ground ~~as~~. It reached forward its long neck, ~~open~~ beak ~~on the end~~open, razor-sharp and deadly. ~~This was the closest he had ever seen one.~~ It looked ~~kind of~~ like a bird~~,~~—in the same way that a wolf looked like a lapdog.

He threw his machete. An instinctive reaction, for he did not have time for thought. He did not have time for fear. That snapping beak—as tall as a door—would have the two of them dead in moments.

His machete glanced off ~~of~~ the beak~~,~~ and actually cut~~ting it~~ the creature on the side of the head. That drew its attention, making it hesitate for just a moment. ~~Sixth~~Dusk leaped for Vathi~~,~~. She stepped back from him, setting the butt of her tube against the ground. He needed to pull her away, to—

The explosion deafened him.

Smoke ~~burst into the air from~~bloomed around Vathi, who stood—wide eyed—having dropped the lantern, oil spilling ~~from the ground~~. The sudden sound stunned ~~him~~Dusk, and he almost collided with her as the ~~N~~nightmaw ~~slump~~lurched and fell, skidding, the ground *thumping* from the impact.

~~Sixth~~Dusk found himself on the ground. ~~He had tripped.~~ He scrambled to his feet, backing away from the twitching ~~N~~nightmaw mere ~~feet in front of~~inches from him. ~~The~~ Lit by flickering lanternlight, it was ~~already dying. He couldn't look toward the fallen lantern, though. He stared at the beast in front of him,~~ all leathery skin that was ~~prickled and~~ bumpy, like that ~~beneath~~of a bird ~~that~~who had lost ~~its~~her feathers.

It was dead. ~~She~~Vathi had killed it.

~~Vathi~~She said something.

~~She~~Vathi had *killed* a nightmaw.

"~~Sixth~~Dusk!" ~~H~~her voice seemed distant.

He raised a hand to his forehead, which had belatedly begun to prickle with sweat. His ~~body~~wounded arm throbbed, but he was otherwise tense~~,~~. ~~h~~He felt as if he should be running. He had never wanted to be so close to one of these. *Never.*

She'd actually killed it.

He turned toward her, his eyes wide. Vathi was trembling, but she covered it well. "~~Well~~So, that worked," she said. "We weren't certain it would, even though we'd prepared these specifically for the nightmaws."

"It's like a cannon," ~~Sixth~~Dusk said. "Like from one of the ships, only in your hands."

"Yes."

He turned back toward the beast. ~~He had been wrong, earlier. It~~Actually, it *wasn't* dead, not completely. It twitched, and let out a plaintive screech~~. That was soft, though. He could make out the large hole in its breast as he walked around it;~~ the that shocked him, even with his hearing muffled. The weapon had fired a~~t~~hat spear ~~of some sort that had gone~~ right into ~~it~~the beast's chest. ~~It~~

The nightmaw quaked and thrashed a weak leg. ~~It wasn't dead yet, but it soon would be.~~

"We could kill them all," ~~Sixth~~Dusk said~~, still feeling stunned~~. He turned, then rushed over to Vathi, taking her ~~by~~with his right hand, the arm that wasn't wounded. "With those weapons, we could kill them *all*. Every nightmaw. Maybe the shadows too!"

"Well, yes, it has been discussed. However, they are important parts of the ecosystem on these islands. Removing the apex predators could have undesirable results."

"Undesirable results?" ~~Sixth~~Dusk ran his left hand through his hair. "They'd be gone. All of them! I don't care what other problems you think it would cause. They would all be *dead*."

Vathi snorted, picking up the lantern and stamping out the fires it had started. "I thought trappers were connected to nature."

"We are. That's how I know we would all be better off without any of these things. ~~No more nightmaws. What a different world it would be.~~

"You are disabusing me of many romantic notions about your kind, ~~Sixth~~Dusk," she said, circling the dying beast. ~~"I wish we had time . . . Nobody has ever been able to study one of these up close."~~

~~"With those weapons, you should have plenty of chances."~~ ~~Sixth~~Dusk whistled, holding up his arm. Kokerlii fluttered down from high branches; in the chaos and explosion, ~~Sixth~~Dusk had not seen the bird fly away. Sak still clung to his shoulder with a death grip, her claws digging into his skin through the cloth. He hadn't noticed.

—Kokerlii landed on his arm and gave an apologetic chirp.

-"It wasn't your fault," ~~Sixth~~Dusk said soothingly. "They prowl the night. Even ~~if~~when they cannot sense our minds, they can ~~hear us,~~ smell us." ~~Nightmaws did not have good vision, nor was their hearing excellent.~~ Their sense of smell~~, however,~~ was said to be incredible. This one had come up the trail behind them; it must have crossed their pa~~s~~th and followed it.

Dangerous. His uncle always claimed the ~~N~~nightmaws were growing smarter, that they knew they could not hunt men only by their minds. *I should have taken us across more streams,* ~~Sixth~~Dusk thought, reaching up and rubbing Sak's neck to soothe her. *There just isn't time. . . .*

His ~~body~~corpse lay wherever he looked. Draped across a rock, hanging from the vines of trees, slumped beneath the dying ~~N~~nightmaw's claw . . .

The beast trembled once more ~~in what seemed a final way~~, then amazingly it lifted its gruesome head and let out a last screech. Not as loud as those that normally sounded in the night, but bone-chilling and horrid. ~~Sixth~~Dusk stepped back despite himself, and Sak chirped nervously.

~~In the night, distant, o~~Other ~~N~~nightmaw screeches rose in the night, distant.

~~Sixth twisted his head to the side, stumbling backward, looking out into that deep blackness. At least five other beats sounded in the night.~~ That sound . . . he had been trained to recognize that sound as the sound of death.

"We're going," he said, stalking across the ground and pulling Vathi away from the dying beast, which had lowered its head and fallen silent. ~~It might be dead. It no longer moved.~~

"~~Sixth~~Dusk?" She did not resist as he pulled her away~~, though she did look over her shoulder at the monster~~.

One of the other nightmaws sounded again in the night. Was it closer? *Oh, Patji, ~~Sixth~~please, Dusk* thought. *No. Not this.*

~~"Come!" he said, pulling~~He pulled her faster ~~and~~, reaching for his machete at his side, but it was not there. He had thrown it. ~~He did not go back for it; h~~He took out the one he had gathered from his fallen rival ~~and began to hack at leaves, only when necessary~~, then dragged her out of the clearing, back into the jungle, moving quickly. He could no longer worry about brushing against deathants.

A greater danger was coming.

The calls of death came again.

"Are those getting *closer*?" Vathi asked.

~~Sixth~~Dusk did not answer. It was a question, but ~~one~~ he did not know the answer ~~to~~. At least his hearing was recovering. He released her hea~~n~~d, moving more quickly, almost at a trot—faster than he ever wanted to go through the jungle, day or night.

"~~Sixth~~Dusk!" Vathi hissed. "Will they come? To the call of the dying one? Is that something they do?"

"How should I know?~~" he snapped, turning back on her.~~ "I have never known one of them to be killed before." He saw the tube, again carried over her shoulder, lit by the light of the lantern she carried.

That gave him pause~~.~~, ~~T~~though his instincts screamed at him to keep moving~~,~~ and he ~~paused. The weapon. He~~ felt a fool. ~~They had a weapon that could kill nightmaws! That such a thing existed still amazed him.~~

—"Your weapon," he said. "You can use it again?"

"Yes," she said. "Once more."

"*Once* more?"

A half dozen screeches sounded in the night.

"Yes," she replied. "I only brought three ~~of~~ spears ~~this thing fires,~~ and enough powder for three shots. I tried firing one at the shadow. It didn't do much."

~~One more attack. So his instincts were right.~~ He spoke no further, ignoring his wounded arm—the bandage was in need of changing—and towing her ~~into~~through the jungle ~~as those~~. The calls came again and again. Agitated. How did one escape ~~N~~nightmaws? His Aviar clung to him, ~~one~~ a bird on each shoulder. He had to leap over his corpse ~~periodically~~ as they traversed a gulch and came up the other side.

How do you escape them? ~~H~~he thought, remembering his uncle's training. *You don't draw their attention in the first place!*

They were fast. Kokerlii would hide his mind ~~from them~~, but if they picked up his trail at the dead one . . .

Water. He stopped in the night, turning right, then left. Where would he find a stream? Patji was an island. Fresh water came from rainfall, mostly. The largest lake . . . the only one~~, really~~ . . . was up the wedge. Toward the peak.

—~~Patji was shaped something like a wedge.~~ Along the eastern side, the island rose to some heights with cliffs on all sides. ~~It was not terribly tall, but was elevated further than the rest of the island.~~ Rainfall collected there, in Patji's Eye~~, and could not escape except slowly~~. The river~~,~~ was his tears.

It was a dangerous place to go~~,~~ with Vathi in tow. Their path had skirted the slope up the heights, heading across the island toward the northern beach. ~~It would only be a small diversion~~They were close. . . .

Those screeches behind spurred him on. Patji would just have to forgive ~~me, he thought,~~ him for what came next. Dusk seiz~~ing~~ed Vathi's hand and tow~~ing~~ed her in a ~~slightly different~~more eastern direction. She did not complain, though she did keep looking over her shoulder.

The screeches grew closer.

He ran. He ran as he had never expected to do on Patji, wild and reckless. Leaping over troughs, around fallen logs coated in moss. Through the dark underbrush, scarring away meekers and startling Aviar slumbering in the branches above. It was foolish. It was crazy.

—He But did not fear death to insect bites or falling vines, it matter? Somehow, he knew those other things would not claim him. The kings of Patji hunted him; lesser dangers would not dare steal from their betters.

Vathi followed with difficulty. Those skirts were trouble, but she caught up to him each time DuskSixth had to occasionally stop and cut their way through underbrush. Urgent, frantic, he did so. He expected her to keep up, and she did. A piece of him—buried deep beneath the terror—was impressed. This woman would have made a fantastic trackpper.

—Instead she would probably destroy themall trappers.

He froze as screeches sounded behind, so close. Vathi gasped, and SixthDusk turned back to his work. They were closeNot far to go. He hacked through a dense patch of undergrowth and ran on, sweat streaming down the sides of his face. Jostling light came from theVathi's lantern behind, clutched by Vathi, and; the scene before him as he ran was one of horrific shadows dancing on the jungle's bowughs, leaves, ferns, and rocks.

This is your fault, Patji, he thought with an unexpected fury. *Why must you try to kill us, those who protect you?*

—The screeches seemed almost on top of him. Was that breaking brush he could hear behind? *We are your priests, and yet you hate us! You hate all.*

—Sixth's uncle had explained that Patji needed to be deadly to keep away the unwelcome, the unworthy. And yet, Vathi was nearly as good as any trapper, though she had not set foot on Patji until recently. Did that make her worthy? Did that make her welcome?

SixthDusk broke from the jungle and out onto the banks of the river. Small, by mainland standards—he had once seen a river there so wide, no man could have jumped it. Still, but ithis would do. He led Vathi right into it, splashing into the cold waters.

He turned upstream. What else could he do? Downstream was towould lead closer to those sounds, the calls of death.

Of the Dusk, he thought. *Of the Dusk.*

He led Vathi upriver. The waters came only to their calves, bitter cold. The coldest water on the island, though he did not know why. They slipped and scrambled as they ran, best they could, upriver. Thisey passed them through some narrows, with lichen-covered rock walls on either side twice as tall as a man.;

—Ttheny burst out into the basin, halfway up the heights.

— A place men did not go. A place he had visited only once. A cool, emerald lake rested here, sequestered.

SixthDusk towed Vathi to the side, out of the river, toward some brush. Perhaps she would not see. He huddled down with her, raising a finger to his lips, then turninged down the light of the lantern she still held. Nightmaws could not see well, but perhaps the dim light would help. In more ways than one.

They waited there, on the shore of the small lake, hoping that the water had washed away their scent—hoping the ~~N~~nightmaws would grow confused ~~and be unable to track them~~ or distracted. For one thing about this place was that the basin had steep walls, ~~hidden as it was in Patji's depths.~~ and ~~T~~there was no way out other than the river~~, and~~. ~~i~~If the ~~N~~nightmaws came up it, ~~Sixth~~Dusk and Vathi would be trapped.

~~The s~~Screeches sounded ~~behind~~. The creatures had reached the river. ~~Sixth~~Dusk waited in ~~almost~~ near darkness, and so squeezed his eyes shut. He prayed to Patji, whom he loved, whom he hated.

Vathi gasped softly. "What . . . ?"

So she had seen. Of course she had. She was a seeker, a learner. A questioner. Why must men ask so many questions?

"~~Sixth~~Dusk! There are Aviar here, in these branches! Hundreds of them." She spoke in a hushed, frightened tone. Even as they awaited death itself~~, however~~, she saw and could not help speaking. "Have you seen them? What is this place?" She hesitated. "So many juveniles. Barely able to fly . . ."

"They come here," he whispered. "Every bird from every island. ~~"~~In their youth, they must come here."

He opened his eyes, looking up ~~at the rim of the basin~~. He had turned down the lantern, but it was still bright enough to see them roosting there. Some stirred at the light and the sound. They stirred more as the nightmaws screeched below. ~~They had not left the banks of the river. They were searching.~~

Sak chirped on his shoulder, terrified. Kokerlii, for once, had nothing to say.

"Every bird from every island . . ." Vathi said, putting it together. "They all come here, to this place. Are you certain?"

"Yes." It was a thing that trappers knew. You could not capture a bird before it had visited Patji.

Otherwise it would be able to bestow no talent.

"They come here," she said. "We knew they migrated between islands. . . . Why do they come here? ~~What is the point.~~"

Was there any point in holding back now? She would figure it out. ~~Huddled here in the night though they were, she would figure it out.~~

—Still, he did not speak. Let her do so.

"They gain their talents here, don't they?" she asked~~, looking to him~~. "How? Is it where they are trained? Is this how you made a bird who was not an Aviar into one? You brought a hatchling here, and then . . ." She frowned, raising her lantern. "I recognize those trees. They are the ones you called Patji's ~~f~~Fingers."

A dozen of them grew here, the largest concentration on the island. And beneath them, their fruit littered the ground. Much of it eaten, some of it only halfway so, bites taken out by birds of all stripes.

Vathi saw him looking, and frowned.

—"The fruit?" she asked.

"Worms," he whispered in reply.

A light seemed to go on in her eyes. "It's not the birds. It never has been . . . it's a parasite. They carry a parasite that bestows talents! That's why those raised ~~of~~ ~~of~~away from the islands cannot gain the abilities, and why a mainland bird you brought here could."

"Yes."

"This changes everything, ~~Sixth~~Dusk. Everything."

"Yes."

Of the Dusk. Born during that dusk, or bringer of it? What had he done?

Downriver, the nightmaws screeche~~d. Then, those yells~~s drew closer. They had decided to search upriver. They were clever, more clever than men off ~~of~~ the islands thought them to be. Vathi gasped, turning toward the small river canyon.

"Isn't this dangerous?" she whispered. "The trees are blooming. The nightmaws will come! But no. So many Aviar. They can hide those blossoms, like they do a man's mind?"

"No," he said. "All minds in this place are invisible, always, regardless of Aviar."

"But . . . how? Why? The worms?"

Dusk didn't know, and for now didn't care. *I am trying to protect you, Patji!* Sixth Dusk ~~thought in anger,~~ look~~ing~~ed toward Patji's ~~f~~Fingers. *I need to stop the men and their device. I know it! Why? Why do you hunt me?*

~~But~~Perhaps it was because he knew so much. Too much. More than any man had known. For he had asked questions.

Men. And their questions.

"They're coming ~~for us~~up the river, aren't they?" she asked.

The answer seemed obvious. He did not ~~answer~~reply.

"No," she said, standing. "I won't die with this knowledge, ~~Sixth~~Dusk. *I won't.* There must be a way."

"There is," he said, standing beside her. He took a deep breath. *So I finally pay for it.* He took Sak carefully in his hand, and placed her on Vathi's shoulder. He pried Kok~~i~~erlii free too.

"What are you doing?" Vathi asked.

"I will go as far as I can," ~~Sixth~~Dusk said, handing Kokerlii toward her. The bird bit with annoyance at his hands, although never strong enough to draw blood. "You will need to hold him. He will try to follow me."

"No, wait. We can hide in the lake, they—"

"They will find us!" ~~Sixth~~Dusk said. "It isn't deep enough by far to hide us."

"But you can't—-"

"They are nearly here, woman!" he said, forcing Kokerlii into her hands. "The men of the company will not listen to me if I tell them to turn off the device. You are smart, you can make them stop. You can reach them. With Kokerlii you can reach them. Be ready to go."

She looked at him, stunned, but she seemed to realize that there was no other way. She stood, holding Kok~~l~~erlii in two hands as he pulled out the journal of First of the Sky, then his own book that listed where his Aviar were, and tucked them into her pack. Finally, he stepped back into the river. He could hear a rushing sound downstream. He would have to go quickly to reach the end of the canyon before they arrived. If he could draw them out into the jungle even a short ways to the south, Vathi could slip ~~out~~away.

As he entered the stream, his visions of death finally vanished. No more corpses bobbing in the water, ~~lay~~ing on the banks. Sak had realized what was happening.

She gave a final chirp.

He started to run.

One of Patji's Fingers, growing right next to the mouth of the canyon, was blooming.

"Wait!"

He should not have stopped as Vathi yelled at him. He should have continued on, for time was so slim. However, the sight of that flower—along with her yell—made him hesitate.

The ~~F~~flower...

It struck him as it must have struck Vathi. An idea. Vathi ran ~~up~~for her pack, letting go of Kokerlii, who immediately flew to his shoulder and started chirping at him in annoyed chastisement. ~~Vathi pulled~~Dusk didn't listen. He yanked the flower off—it was as large as a man's head, with a large bulging part at the center.

It was invisible in this basin, like they all were.

"A flower that can think," Vathi said, breathing quickly, fishing in her pack. "A flower that can draw the attention of predators."

~~Both of their heads turned toward the tube, her weapon, which lay sticking from her pack on the bank of the river. Sixth~~Dusk pulled out his rope as she ~~ran for~~ brought out her weapon and prepared it~~, then he ripped~~. He lashed the flower ~~from its branch.~~

~~He tried the rope~~ to ~~it as Vathi ran up with her weapon,~~ the end of the spear sticking out slightly from the tube~~end. Sixth tied the other end of his rope to it as the~~

Nightmaw ~~yell~~screeches echoed up the ca~~vern~~yon. He could see their shadows, hear them splashing.

He stumbled back from Vathi as she crouched down, ~~setting~~ the weapon's butt against the ground, and pulled a lever at the base.

The explosion, once again, nearly deafened him.

Aviar all around the rim of the basin screeched and called in fright, ~~many~~ taking wing. A storm of feathers and flapping ensued, and through the middle of it, Vathi's spear shot into the air ~~towing the rope and with it the~~, flower on the end. ~~Tha~~It arced out over the canyon into the night.

~~Sixth~~Dusk grabbed her by the shoulder and pulled her back along the river, into the lake itself. They slipped into the shallow water, Kokerlii on his shoulder, Sak on hers. They left the lantern burning, giving a quiet light to the suddenly -empty basin.

The lake was not deep. Two or three feet. Even crouching, it didn't cover them completely.

The ~~N~~nightmaws stopped in the canyon. His lanternlight showed a couple of them in the shadows, large as huts, turning and watching the sky. They were smart, but like the meekers, not as smart as men.

Patji~~...~~, ~~Sixth~~Dusk thought. Patji, please. ~~She is right.~~ ...

~~The secrets cannot remain secret forever. Not with the way the world changes. They will get out.~~

~~I will carry them, and do what I can with them.~~

The ~~N~~nightmaws turned back down the canyon, following the mental signature broadcast by the flowering plant. And, as Dusk watched, his corpse bobbing in the water nearby grew increasingly translucent.

Then faded away entirely.

~~Sixth~~Dusk counted to a hundred, then slipped from the waters. Vathi, sodden in her skirts, did not speak as she grabbed the lantern. They left the weapon, its shots expended.

The calls from the ~~N~~nightmaws grew f~~u~~arther and f~~u~~arther away as ~~Sixth~~Dusk led the way out of the canyon, then directly north, slightly downslope. He kept expecting ~~yell~~the screeche~~s~~ to turn and follow.

They did not.

#

The company fortress was a horridly impressive sight. A work of logs and cannons right at the edge of the water, guarded by an enormous iron-hulled ship. Smoke rose from it, the burning of morning cook fires.

~~Sixth sat on a rock a~~A short distance ~~from~~away, what ~~appeared to be~~must have been a dead shadow rotted in the sun, its mountainous ~~corpse~~carcass draped half in the water, half out. ~~He did not enter the fortress. Better to stay out here, near the dead shadow, even though his skin prickled as he looked at it.~~

He didn't see his own corpse ~~lay in the shallows beside it~~anywhere, though on the final leg of their trip to the fortress he had seen it several times. Always in a place of immediate danger. Sak ~~rested on his shoulder, dozing, and Kokerlii trilled from a branch closer to the forest. He seemed in good spirits~~'s visions had returned to normal.

~~As Sixth waited, his corpse slowly vanished from the shadows, fading like a shadow blending with darkness at the fall of night.~~

~~Vathi finally left the fortress. Alone, thankfully, though two more men joined the guards at the gate. All bore weapons similar to the one she had used to kill the nightmaw.~~

~~She had not changed. Her muddied skirts were stuck with twigs, her hair a mess. Her eyes were alight. She stepped up to him.~~

~~The surf washed against Patji's rocks. He could not decide if he found it a violent sound or a peaceful one.~~

~~"It is done," she said.~~

~~But he already knew that it was. The vision had ended. The danger had passed.~~

~~"Eusto was not pleased at my survival," Vathi noted, "though he could not say so. He was reluctant to stop the device, but my authority supersedes his own."~~

~~Sixth nodded. His eyes fell again on the dead shadow.~~

~~"Come into our fortress," Vathi said, glancing at it. "Get some rest, some food."~~

~~"I must return and check on my Aviar."~~

~~"They will survive another day without you. They live on this island for weeks at a time without your presence."~~

~~He did not reply.~~

~~"Sixth... we could use your knowledge. Your wisdom."~~

~~"I know," he said. "You could." He turned back toward Patji. He could not interpret events of the night. Had the nightmaws been Patji, seeking to cover his secrets? Or had the flower been redemption, sent by his father? Which was Sixth? Condemned or rescued? Neither? Both?~~

~~"What happened to the One Above," Sixth said. "The one who died while eating, the one to whom these devices of yours belonged?"~~

~~"His body was reclaimed by the others," Vathi said, frowning. "Why do you ask?"~~

~~"I do not think he is really dead," Sixth said. "They have tricked you."~~

~~Vathi raised an eyebrow at him.~~

~~"The machine is a trap," Sixth said. "They expected you to use it, and they knew the damage it would cause."~~

~~"That's an interesting theory," Vathi said, studying him in the morning light. She looked exhausted. The things she had been through... It had been less than a day since his arrival back on Patji, and yet, so much had happened.~~

~~"It is true," Sixth said. "You were to use it, and in so doing endanger the Aviar."~~

Dusk turned back to the fortress, which he did not enter. He preferred to remain on the rocky, familiar shore—perhaps twenty feet from the entrance—his wounded arm aching as the company people rushed out through the gate to meet Vathi. Their scouts on the upper walls kept careful watch on Dusk. A trapper was not to be trusted.

Even standing here, some twenty feet from the wide wooden gates into the fort, he could smell how wrong the place was. It was stuffed with the scents of men—sweaty bodies, the smell of oil, and other, newer scents that he recognized from his recent trips to the homeisles. Scents that made him feel like an outsider among his own people.

The company men wore sturdy clothing, trousers like Dusk's but far better tailored, shirts and rugged jackets. Jackets? In Patji's heat? These people bowed to Vathi, showing her more deference than Dusk would have expected. They drew hands from shoulder to shoulder as they started speaking—a symbol of respect. Foolishness. Anyone could make a gesture like that; it didn't mean anything. True respect included far more than a hand waved in the air.

But they did treat her like more than a simple scribe. She was better placed in the company than he'd assumed. Not his problem anymore, regardless.

Vathi looked at him, then back at her people. "We must hurry to the machine," she said to them. "The one from Above. We must turn it off."

Good. She would do her part. Dusk turned to walk away. Should he give words at parting? He'd never felt the need before. But today, it felt . . . wrong not to say something.

He started walking. Words. He had never been good with words.

"Turn it off?" one of the men said from behind. "What do you mean, Lady Vathi?"

"You don't need to feign innocence, Winds," Vathi said. "I know you turned it on in my absence."

"But we didn't."

Dusk paused. What? The man sounded sincere. But then, Dusk was no expert on human emotions. From what he'd seen of people from the homeisles, they could fake emotion as easily as they faked a gesture of respect.

"What *did* you do, then?" Vathi asked them.

"We . . . opened it."

Oh no . . .

"Why would you do that?" Vathi asked.

Dusk turned to regard them, but he didn't need to hear the answer. The answer was before him, in the vision of a dead island he'd misinterpreted.

"We figured," the man said, "that we should see if we could puzzle out how the machine worked. Vathi, the insides . . . they're complex beyond what we could have imagined. But there are seeds there. Things we could—"

"No!" Dusk said, rushing toward them.

One of the sentries above planted an arrow at his feet. He lurched to a stop, looking wildly from Vathi up toward the walls. Couldn't they see? The bulge in mud that announced a deathant den. The game trail. The distinctive curl of a cutaway vine. Wasn't it *obvious*?

"It will destroy us," Dusk said. "Don't seek . . . Don't you see . . . ?"

For a moment, they all just stared at him. He had a chance. Words. He needed *words*.

"That machine is deathants!" he said. "A den, a . . . Bah!" How could he explain?

He couldn't. In his anxiety, words fled him, like Aviar fluttering away into the night.

The others finally started moving, pulling Vathi toward the safety of their treasonous fortress.

"You said the corpses are gone," Vathi said as she was ushered through the gates. "We've succeeded. I will see that the machine is not engaged on this trip! I promise you this, Dusk!"

"But," he cried back, "it was never *meant* to be engaged!"

The enormous wooden gates of the fortress creaked closed, and he lost sight of her. Dusk cursed. Why hadn't he been able to explain?

Because he didn't know how to talk. For once in his life, that seemed to matter.

Furious, frustrated, he stalked away from that place and its awful smells. Halfway to the tree line, however, he stopped, then turned. Sak fluttered down, landing on his shoulder and cooing softly.

Questions. Those questions wanted into his brain.

Instead he yelled at the guards. He demanded they return Vathi to him. He even pled.

Nothing happened. They wouldn't speak to him. Finally, he started to feel foolish.

He turned back toward the trees, and continued on his way. His assumptions were probably wrong. After all, the corpses *were* gone. Everything could go back to normal.

... Normal. Could anything *ever* be normal with that fortress looming behind him? He shook his head, entering the canopy. The dense humidity of Patji's jungle should have calmed him.

Instead it annoyed him. As he started the trek toward another of his safecamps, he was so distracted that he could have been a youth, his first time on Sori. He almost stumbled straight onto a gaping deathant den; he didn't even notice the vision Sak sent. This time, dumb luck saved him as he stubbed his toe on something, looked down, and only then spotted both corpse and crack crawling with motes of yellow.

He growled, then sneered. "Still you try to kill me?" he shouted, looking up at the canopy. "Patji!"

Silence.

"The ones who protect you are the ones you try hardest to kill," Dusk shouted. "Why!"

The words were lost in the jungle. It consumed them.

"You deserve this, Patji," he said. "What is coming to you. You *deserve to be destroyed!*"

He breathed out in gasps, sweating, satisfied at having finally said those things. Perhaps there was a purpose for words. Part of him, as traitorous as Vathi and her company, was *glad* that Patji would fall to their machines.

Of course, then the company itself would fall. To the Ones Above. His entire people. The world itself.

He bowed his head in the shadows of the canopy, sweat dripping down the sides of his face. Then he fell to his knees, heedless of the nest just three strides away.

Sak nuzzled into his hair. Above, in the branches, Kokerlii chirped uncertainly.

"It's a trap, you see," he whispered. "The Ones Above have rules. They can't trade with us until we're advanced enough. Just like a man can't, in good conscience, bargain with a child until they are grown. And so, they have left their machines for us to discover, to prod at and poke. The dead man was a ruse. Vathi was *meant* to have those machines.

"There will be explanations, left as if carelessly, for us to dig into and learn. And at some point in the near future, we will build something like one of their machines. We will have grown more quickly than we should have. We will be childlike still, ignorant, but the laws from Above will let these visitors trade with us. And then, they will take this land for themselves."

That was what he should have said. Protecting Patji was impossible. Protecting the Aviar was impossible. Protecting their entire *world* was impossible. Why hadn't he explained it?

Perhaps because it wouldn't have done any good. As Vathi had said ... progress would come. If you wanted to call it that.

Dusk had arrived.

Sak left his shoulder, winging away. Dusk looked after her, then cursed. She did not land nearby. Though flying was difficult for her, she fluttered on, disappearing from his sight.

"Sak?" he asked, rising and stumbling after the Aviar. He fought back the way he had come, following Sak's squawks. A few moments later, he lurched out of the jungle.

Vathi stood on the rocks before her fortress.

Dusk hesitated at the brim of the jungle. Vathi was alone, and even the sentries had retreated. Had they cast her out? No. He could see that the gate was cracked, and some people watched from inside.

Sak had landed on Vathi's shoulder down below. Dusk frowned, reaching his hand to the side and letting Kokerlii land on his arm. Then he strode forward, calmly making his way down the rocky shore, until he was standing just before Vathi.

She'd changed into a new dress, though there were still snarls in her hair. She smelled of flowers.

And her eyes were terrified.

He'd traveled the darkness with her. Had faced nightmaws. Had seen her near to death, and she had not looked this worried.

"What?" he asked, finding his voice hoarse.

"We found instructions in the machine," Vathi whispered. "A manual on its workings, left there as if accidentally by someone who worked on it before. The manual is in their language, but the smaller machine I have . . ."

"It translates."

"The manual details how the machine was constructed," Vathi says. "It's so complex I can barely comprehend it, but it seems to explain concepts and ideas, not just give the workings of the machine."

"And are you not happy?" he asked. "You will have your flying machines soon, Vathi. Sooner than anyone could have imagined."

Wordless, she held something up. A single feather—a mating plume. She had kept it.

"Never move without asking yourself, is this too easy?" she whispered. "You said it was a trap as I was pulled away. When we found the manual, I . . . Oh, Dusk. They are planning to do to us what . . . what we are doing to Patji, aren't they?"

Dusk nodded.

"We'll lose it all. We can't fight them. They'll find an excuse, they'll *seize* the Aviar. ~~Tha~~It makes ~~no~~perfect sense.~~:~~"

~~"It does. They Ones Above seek an excuse to come down and take control of these islands. Just as you have sought an excuse to do the same. If they could prove—to themselves, perhaps to those who watch them—that you are dangerous to the Aviar, they would come and rescue them. To protect a resource. Is that not the argument you used? They will use the same."~~

~~"You don't know them, Sixth," Vathi said, shaking her head. "They're strange. Though they look like us, they're as different from you and me as . . . well, as we are from the Aviar."~~

~~"Yes, so different," Sixth said. "~~ "The Aviar use the worms. We use the Aviar. ~~And~~

The Ones Above use us. It's inevitable, isn't it?"

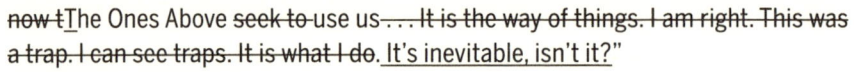

Yes, he thought. He opened his mouth to say it, and Sak chirped. He frowned and turned back toward the island. Jutting from the ocean, arrogant. Destructive.

Patji. Father.
And finally, at long last, Dusk understood.
"No," he whispered.
"But—"
He undid his pants pocket, then reached deeply into it, digging around. Finally, he pulled something out. The remnants of a feather, just the shaft now. A mating plume that his uncle had given him, so many years ago, when he'd first fallen into a trap on Sori. He held it up, remembering the speech he'd been given. Like every trapper.

This is the symbol of your ignorance. Nothing is easy, nothing is simple.

Vathi held hers. Old and new.

"No, they will not have us," Dusk said. "We will see through their traps, and we will not fall for their tricks. For we have been trained by the Father himself for this very day."

She stared at his feather, then up at him.

"Do you really think that?" she asked. "They are cunning."

"They may be cunning," he said. "But they have not lived on Patji. We will gather the other trappers. We will not let ourselves be taken in."

She nodded hesitantly, and some of the fear seemed to leave her. She turned and waved for those behind her to open the gates to the building. Again, the scents of mankind washed over him.

Vathi looked back, then ~~She~~ held out her hand to him. "You will help, then?"

~~He considered it as he would a cutaway vine hanging from a tree ahead.~~ His corpse appeared at her feet, and Sak chirped warningly. Danger. Yes, the path ahead would include much danger.

~~He~~Dusk took Vathi's hand ~~anyway~~ and stepped into the fortress anyway.

WHEN YOUR STORY'S CLIMAX ISN'T AN ENDING
FIXING SIXTH OF THE DUSK

BRANDON SANDERSON

INTRODUCTION

I'm very excited by how my story for the anthology turned out. The prose flowed very well, and I felt an excitement for the idea from the get-go. Polynesian culture fascinates me (something you can probably see hints of in my other works), and the idea of building a fantasy culture on that framework was exciting. A lot of things worked right from the start for me, including Dusk's personality, his relationship with the island, and his clash with his own people.

As I said in my brainstorming episode of Writing Excuses, I like to have an ending in mind when I begin writing a story. Usually when I say ending, I mean climax—that powerful moment when things come together, different threads intertwine, and the character and plot click together. Those are the moments I'm shooting for, and those are the kinds of things I need to be there to pull me through a story.

For this story, my outline was very simple. I knew I wanted to make it a cross-island trip, so we could experience the dangers of Patji. I also knew that I wanted to have Dusk interact with someone else, more of an outsider, to both contrast his character and give more depth to the setting. As I worked on the story, the clash between the old and the new became a theme, represented by the two characters. Dusk's resistance to change, along with having him already know the secret to making birds gain talents, came as a natural development.

My climax, then, became the information reveal about the nature of the birds both to Vathi and to the reader. I found quickly that I could align this reveal with a tense chase through the jungle, allowing the external conflict to come to a head at the same time that I reached the intellectual climax.

Perfect. Except it wasn't.

THE LESSER PROBLEM

As I wrote, I ran into two major hang-ups. The first was the question *why*. Why a tense chase across the jungle? What would drive the plot, make the protagonists move? My original intention—that of Dusk needing to return Vathi safely to her people—felt lukewarm to me. I wanted a more powerful motivator. I needed to up the stakes.

The solution came in the bird that showed Dusk's corpse. I'd put Sak in because I felt her power would be an evocative, cool thing to do with the magic—a visible manifestation, rather than just all happening in their heads, as I worried the psychic powers would feel. It wasn't part of the original brainstorming session, but played well with the other parts of the narrative.

However, as I approached the end of the first third of the story and realized I needed to up the stakes, Sak offered the perfect opportunity. She could show Dusk his corpse. Could she show the corpse of the island too? Could I devise an event so dangerous, it *drove* Dusk to cross the island at night, towing a half-trained home-isler? Could I put the entire island at risk?

Cracking this problem gave me the bulk of my story. The Ones Above, which were something I first intended to simply be a reference to set this story in the Cosmere, became more central to the plot. Vathi's devices from the Ones Above turned into the means by which I generated my big inciting incident. I liked this, as it allowed for another layer of new-meets-old, further entrenching the themes of the story. (Indeed, Dusk's own themes as a character.)

I wrote without major difficulty until the climax. It came together perfectly. And then . . . the story had no ending. It had a great climax, but that wasn't the ending. Something huge was missing.

A BIGGER PROBLEM

My climax wasn't my ending. This is rare for me, and is difficult to spot in an outline. Looking at this story structurally, I'd built it with several "bracketing" story layers. Each idea listed below is a plot cycle in the story that needed addressing.

{Relationship: Dusk and the island
    {Relationship: Dusk and Vathi
        {Objective: Cross the island}
    Relationship: Dusk and Vathi}
Relationship: Dusk and the island}

I introduced Dusk and his relationship to his island first, then introduced Vathi and the theme of modernity vs. tradition, then finally I introduced the objective of crossing the island. These were our three main plots or themes of the story, but my climax only covered two of them. I was able to close the bracket on crossing the island, and able to give a climax to the theme of old and new (by having the island's secret get out). But at the end, I had no closing bracket to Dusk himself. Beyond that, I felt the theme of modernity vs. tradition was only weakly explored. As explosively as the center bracket was executed, the story felt weak because of the other two brackets.

I came up with something to tie off the story and end it, but it gave only the lamest placeholder for closing that bracket. (You can read the placeholder ending in the first draft.) This problem hung me up for months. What was the *right* ending to this story? What would give emotional closure to my protagonist?

I ran the story through my writing group, then chatted with the Writing Excuses crew. I did that whole workshop session on the story, but never came to an understanding of the ending. It was problematic for me because often my ending and climax align quite well. Not so in this case.

THE RIGHT QUESTIONS

Before I made any headway on the story, I had to start asking myself questions. What promises was I making in the text? What nagging emotions did I have at the end, making me feel like the story didn't give me what I wanted? Also, in turn, what did the alpha and beta readers like about the story? What was its soul, and what was working? I had to make sure I didn't ruin any of that—and, in addition, perhaps what they were enjoying would give me a hint on what to emphasize in the next draft. (I've posted all of my notes from my writing group session at the end of this essay, if you want to take a look.)

These questions really helped me identify the problems with the story. I started to feel that the weakness of my ending was due to me not actually understanding Dusk's relationship with the island. What were his emotions? (The writing group's comments helped me start thinking along these lines as well.) I needed a more complex relationship between Dusk and Patji before I could develop a satisfying ending.

The second issue is that I felt like I'd cheated the ending. I realized that one thing I wanted as a reader was to know more about the device and the Ones Above. I felt that glossing over that aspect of the ending had created a major part of the weakness. I wanted to either see the device or at least have some kind of resolution involving it. More than just "Yeah, this worked. We're good."

I toyed with several different emotional connections between Patji and Dusk until I hit upon the idea that made it all start to work. Dusk being angry at Patji, then discovering that there was a reason for all of this danger. (At least, a reason in Dusk's mind.) I was able to tie this to the Ones Above more deeply, then turn the island and its traps into a greater metaphor for the future at large.

One thing the writing group loved was the idea that the Ones Above were trying to get around a "prime directive"-style set of laws preventing them from taking advantage of a less advanced culture. I had this as a fun little revelation, but I realized that I'd tossed this one in too freely, and that it really should be the climax. This is the unusual occurrence of an instance where something minor I'd added to the story (the Ones Above) along with a tiny subplot revelation (they're trying to find a way to trade for the birds) became the hook that I expanded to become the climax of the entire story.

At long last, after almost a year of trying, I had the ending of my story.

APPLICATION AND CONCLUSION

One of the things that fascinates me about the writing process is the way craft and art work together. Knowing the bones of how to create a sympathetic character is craft, like knowing which brush to choose when approaching the painting of a specific landscape feature. Yet the craftsmanship is overseen by the artistic sense, which is not nearly so easy to define. The tools are defined by the craft, but the art is defined by what "feels" right. One has to do with which nut to use with which bolt, and the other with the awe of a beautiful automobile.

I've said before that when I'm writing, I work on instinct, letting the artist dominate. During outlining and revision, however, the craftsman is more in charge. My experience with "Sixth of the Dusk" illustrates this. The artist knew something was wrong with the story, and so I stepped back and let the craftsman suggest tools and solutions, which the artist could then try out one after another until I hit on something that worked.

My process might not be your process, but it's likely that this alliance between craftsperson and artist is going to be part of it. In working with students, I've come to believe that relying too much on tools, schema, or archetypes when writing can easily lead to wooden stories. However, not understanding your process—and the tools you're using—can leave you in a very difficult position when something isn't working and you can't explain why. Writer's block as a whole seems to have some roots in this conflict.

I can also envision this specific problem—having a climax that is not an ending—popping up in your own writing. If you run into it, try asking yourself what promises you've made in the first half of the story, and examine if your climax—albeit dramatic—is fulfilling the wrong promises. Your solution may not be to change the ending, but instead to change the promises. In this story I did both, first by adding Dusk's frustration with Patji as a foreshadowing of a later resolution, then by moving the revelation regarding the true plans of the Ones Above to overlap Dusk's coming understanding.

It took well over eighteen months to get this one story right, but I'm supremely satisfied at having stuck to it and wiggled out the answers. Not just because I now have an awesome story to share with others, but because I feel I've learned another tidbit about my process and the writing experience as a whole.

Brandon Sanderson
April 18, 2014

WRITING GROUP NOTES FOR SIXTH OF THE DUSK

My writing group at this time included Ben and Danielle Olsen, Alan Layton, Kaylynn ZoBell, Kathleen Sanderson, Peter and Karen Ahlstrom, Isaac and Kara Stewart, and Emily Sanderson. We did the writing group session for this story in four chunks, and I've left a note by each part saying how much of the story that session included.

In writing group, we first mention things we like about the story. You can see from my revisions and essay that this can sometimes be as important as the critiques of what isn't working, as in revision I took one idea (the "prime directive" idea) that readers liked and moved it to become more central to the story. This was a big part of my path to fixing the ending.

You will see that I took many critiques, but not all. That's common. I also sometimes make notes of who said something just in case I need to ask for future clarification. But also I know these people really well, and sometimes noting who said what can help me understand the context of the comment when I'm doing revisions months later, as I can match the words to the person.

One final thing to note is that at the end of the fourth session (we meet once a week, so we went over this story for about a month, one quarter each week) we brainstormed to fix the ending. None of these ideas ended up being ones that I used, but the experience was still helpful in driving me to think about what kinds of promises I had made in the story.

Part One: Beginning until Dusk finds Vathi

GOOD THINGS
- Like the psychic link to the animals. World is fascinating. Shadow under boat. Islands being gods is very cool.

CRITIQUES
- **Karen:** I got confused about how it was an archipelago. It's a line, but there's a middle? Are his cargo pants wet, from being in surf? Or did he put them on after? (They think he should put them on after sailing in his loincloth.)
- **Isaac:** How big are the islands? How long does it take to pass them? Are they Hawaii-type islands?
- **Peter:** Beginning too slow? (Kathy mentions she also gets bored when people aren't talking.)
- **Isaac:** The trapper chooses his island. It sounds like he's out to choose his island for the first time. Should I establish earlier that he's chosen his island? Isaac also thought they stayed, and never left.
- What age is Dusk? Didn't discover it until later. Most thought he was older.
- Should he think, while tracking in the jungle, "Does this person want me to follow them? Is this a trap?"

Part Two: Up until he decides to leave into the forest

GOOD THINGS
- Creepy scene where the birds all go nuts and he sees his body everywhere was great. They ask me not to kill Dusk. Like his inner characterization.
- They say I'm getting really good at these shorter fantasies, feels very fleshed out.

CRITIQUES
- Isaac really wants a good payoff for this awesome scene where the birds freak out.

- **Kaylynn:** Am I supposed to like Vathi? Because I don't.
- **Karen:** He's got two Aviar who do two different things. Do all of them show people how they can die, or does every bird have its own trick?
- They have questions about what happened to her bird.
- The net was to numb her, but she didn't seem numbed. Ben was a little confused. Did she remain numb? She did things with no impediment.

Part Three: Up until the nightmaw is killed

GOOD THINGS
- Liked when he brought the bird over to show her so she'd go with him.
- **Peter:** Like how little he tells her. Like that he thinks to himself what to not tell her. Also liked him wanting to kill all of the nightmaws.

CRITIQUES
- **Kaylynn:** She keeps talking and there's never any thought of "predators may hear us" if she keeps talking. Would it at least annoy him, or give him anxiety?
- **Isaac:** Should he think about it more, having the bird give her visions? It runs a risk of showing her something that will lead to secrets being figured out.
- Some felt it was too abrupt when the nightmaw showed up. Others liked that abruptness.
- No mention of how she was holding her blunderbuss. Unclear how it looked. Did she set it? Was she holding it correctly? (Also a ton of smoke.)

Part Four: Until the ending

GOOD THINGS
- Liked the "They're trying to get us to break the prime directive so they can break the prime directive." Liked both of the characters for their intelligence, and the reveals. Liked talking to the island in his head.

CRITIQUES
- The tree with the flowers didn't try to kill them? The other one with the flowers did, right? Why didn't it attract predators?
- Why not hide in the lake? Ben lost where they were; a lot of the group had blocking issues here. Also, it's dark, how much can they see? Is there a moon?
- When they're hiding, she talks and talks and talks and talks. Not worried about being heard? (Maybe nightmaws can't hear well?)
- Kaylynn wanted him to notice the flower solution, not Vathi.
- If he was going to die, should he have given her the book and the other guy's book to protect the birds?

BRAINSTORMS WITH GROUP TO FIX ENDING
- So, should there be more of a sense that the island is forcing him to give up its secrets? It wants the secrets out. So how do I interpret that?
- Could he gain something, on the island, that stops them from being able to find the Aviar?
- Could she become his protégé?
- What happens if *he* ingests the worms?
- Sail away, think about how the island is forcing him to give up secrets, and sail back toward the fortress?
- Bird should have something to do with it, right?

ACKNOWLEDGMENTS

Many thanks to my writing group: First of the Olsens, Danielle Olsen, Alan Layton, Kaylynn ZoBell, Kathleen Sanderson, The Inserted Peter Ahlstrom, Karen Ahlstrom, Isaac Stewart, Kara Stewart, and Emily Sanderson. I'd also like to give a special thank you to Kekai Kotaki. I've always loved his *Magic: The Gathering* art, and I asked Isaac to contact him first on my list of potential artists for this illustration. Having a Polynesian illustrator for this story is distinctly cool.

Brandon

I would like to thank George Scott for inspiring my story.

Dan

Thanks to my writing group: Dave & Liz Brady, Bob Defendi, Sandra Tayler, Randy Tayler, and Dan Willis.

Especially, though, Sandra. She didn't just make it possible for me to run down the dreams I was chasing. She actively chased them with me and clubbed them into submission so we could drag them back to the cave and feast on them. And she still carries that club.

Howard

Thanks go to this volume's community proofreaders: Aaron Ford, Alice Arneson, Aubree Pham, Bao Pham, Bob Kluttz, Brian T. Hill, Gary Singer, Jakob Remick, Lyndsey Luther, Maren Menke, Mike Barker, Steve Godecke, and Trae Cooper.

Peter

Each of the artists deserves a special shout out for working with us on such a tight deadline and for providing top-notch illustrations. Many thanks to Julie Dillon, Rhiannon Rasmussen-Silverstein, Kathryn Layno, Ben McSweeney, Kekai Kotaki, and Howard Tayler.

Isaac